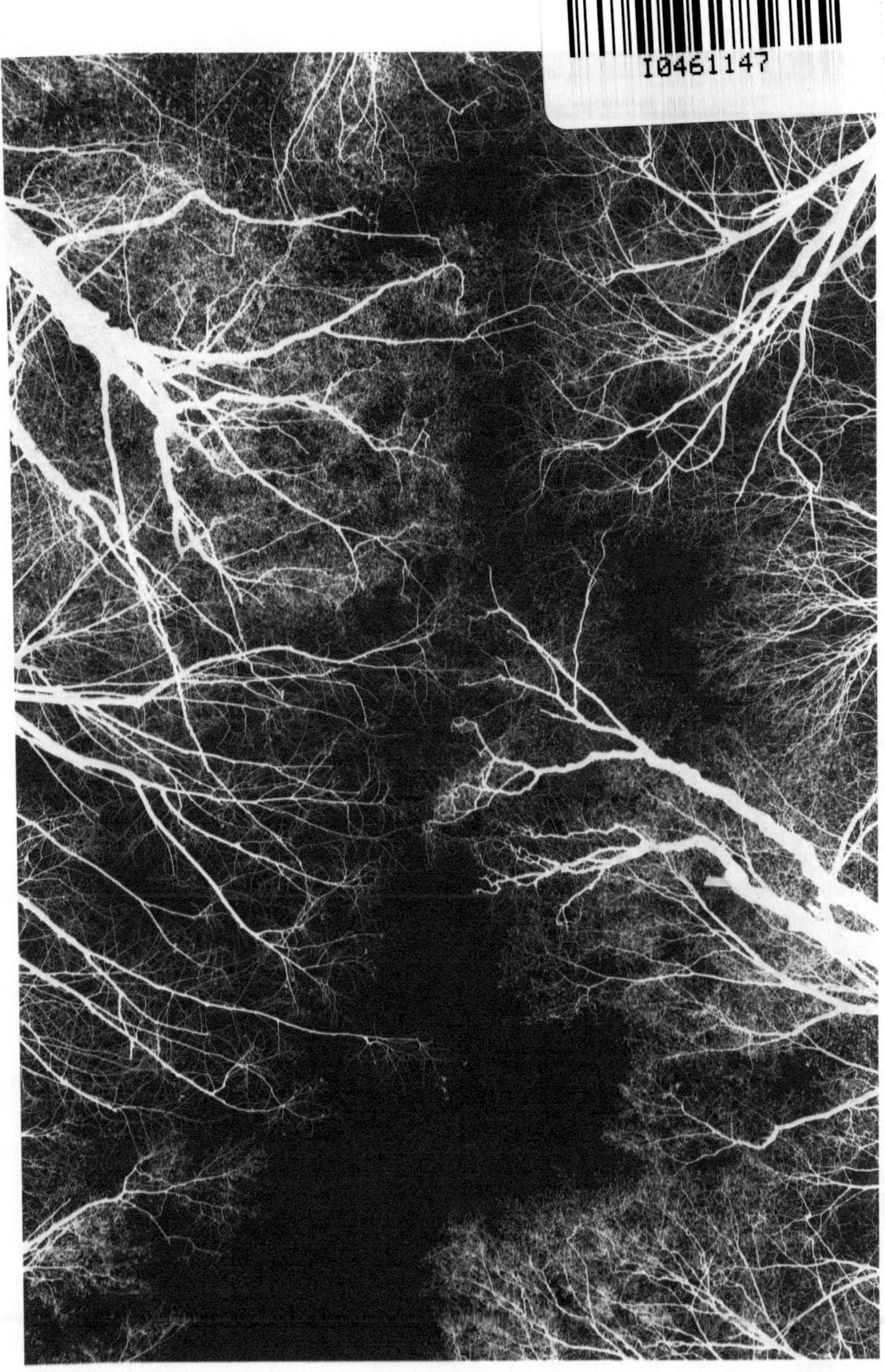

The Leaves in Winter

ALSO BY M.C. MILLER

PW2 2012: The End of the Beginning

Islands of Instability

Uberwoot!

M9D9 Enterprises

Published by M9D9 Enterprises, LLC
http://www.mcmillerbooks.com

ISBN: 0982930526 EAN-13: 978-0-9829305-2-6

Printed in the United States of America
10 9 8 7 6 5 4 3 2 1

First Edition

TO ALL THE CHILDREN YET TO BE

WHO WAIT FOR US, THE LIVING,

TO FIND A PATH TO HUMAN SURVIVAL

The Leaves in Winter

The seasons have all kinds of leaves,
yet unforgiving winter has only three.
There are leaves that have fallen,
leaves of hope for when warmth returns,
and a third kind.

Some leaves, caught by a sudden early freeze
long before they have a chance to turn color and fall,
stay green when nature would rather take its course.
They don't know they are dead.
They linger on the tree long into winter,
out of place for their time,
and only nature's blustery insistence
finally brings them down.

Equally unaware,
the living are too close to life
to realize that life itself has a season.
The callous winds of winter,
impersonal, capricious, and unrelenting as they are,
not only clear the way for the leaves in Spring,
they routinely, dispassionately,
if less often,
fell the ancient tree.

Prologue

"André, are you ready?" The field of view blurred.

Off camera, a shout carried back on the wind. "I've been ready for months. Start the second camera; let's be sure we get this."

The establishing shot came into focus. The horizon line dipped and yawed. The video frame filled with the restless motion of white-capped swells churning towards a vanishing point. Across the expanse of ocean, light blazed and faded as patches of clouds and sunbreaks rushed before a backdrop of blue sky.

The camera's viewfinder zoomed back to reveal the windswept deck of the environmental research ship PaxTerra. The captain cut the engines. Reacting to the signal, a man rocked into view wearing a black windbreaker. A ski mask hid his face. Its bright green color stretched in stark contrast with the surroundings. He raised a handmade sign and shoved it at the camera with outstretched arms.

Les Déchirures de la Sirène d'Opération (Operation Mermaid's Tears)
Mer Des Sargasses (Sargasso Sea)

Another man stepped in front of the sign. Leader of *Les Amis de L'océan (LALO), Friends of the Ocean*, André Bolard was stocky and powerful from working the docks of Marseille. He steadied himself and took aim at the camera with his eyes. The collar of his windbreaker flapped. He too hid his face behind the iconic green mask. The videographer adjusted the shot and captured André's impassioned shouts in French.

"A famous fairy tale says mermaids have no tears. Other tall tales claim the tears of mermaids turn into pearls. We've all been distracted by institutional fairy tales for far too long. If mermaids exist, they're crying for what's happening to our oceans. We've gotten very good at believing the lies we tell ourselves. Somehow we think we can go on living without proper regard for the oceans or the earth and get away with it. The governments and moneymen of the world are derelict in their duty to rescue the planet. The time for half-measures is over. The crisis is now. We are the *Friends of the Ocean*. Today in protest, we are staging *Operation Mermaid's Tears*."

The man raised his hand before the camera and displayed a pearl-like object between thumb and forefinger. "This is what a real mermaid's tear looks like today – it's plastic. Before this contagion finds its way into the ocean, this tiny pellet is called a nurdle. Each year more than 250 billion pounds of nurdles get shipped around the world to plastic processing factories. They become our toys, our packaging, everything from disposable forks to lawn furniture. Why do they start like this? Because these little resin pellets are a cheap way to ship large amounts of the raw plastic material used in all kinds of consumer goods. Ten percent of all the plastic trash in the ocean are nurdles; the rest comes from our garbage or from accidental spillage. Incredibly, container ships lose more than 10,000 of their large, seagoing containers overboard each year."

André measured his steps across deck as video coverage followed his movements. At the ship's fantail, he swept his arm towards the waves then turned back to the camera to face the onrushing wind. Staring into the lens from behind the militant green mask, his eyes burned with purpose.

"We've come to the edge of the Sargasso Sea. It is here where ocean currents swirl and concentrate much of the Atlantic Ocean trash into a gigantic gyre. Every ocean now has some kind of trash gyre like this accumulating on its surface. At last count, in five seas there are now eleven gyres. The one in the Pacific Ocean is twice the size of Texas. Much of this trash consists of consumer plastics that don't biodegrade. It will take hundreds of years for all of this to break down. Meanwhile, toxins and organic pollutants are easily absorbed by the nurdles. Birds and fish mistake the pellets for fish eggs or plankton and eat the plastic. If the nurdles collecting in their bellies don't kill them, the toxins they hold accumulate and filter up the food chain."

André reached into his windbreaker and pulled out a narrow silver flask. He held it in front of him as a trophy, then brandished it as a sword. Emblazoned on its side was a single warning symbol.

"Inside this container is something called a GAMA – a Genetically-engineered Anti-Material Agent. The living microbes inside this bottle were patented by the United States Naval Research Lab. The United States military genetically engineered this life form for a specific purpose – to eat plastic. These microbes eat plastic and reproduce until they can no longer find any plastic to eat. Without plastic, these little bugs have been designed to commit suicide."

André held the flask to his chest in a firm grip. "The time has come to put this GAMA to good use. Today we demonstrate our resolve to do whatever it takes to get the governments of the world actively involved in saving the earth. If they won't, then the people need to act independently on behalf of all life on this planet. We want everyone to see what we've done. Some will call it an act of desperation in defense of Mother Earth. We see it as a call to action for all people. It's time to wake up and do whatever is necessary to save the planet – before it's too late."

With a flourish of resolve, André turned from the camera and unscrewed the top of the silver flask. In one defiant motion, his arm swept overboard and emptied the slime green contents into the sea. The wind caught the falling liquid and whipped it out over the waves. The microbe-infected mist caught the whitecaps just as quickly and was gone.

Zooming in, the camera captured the moment when the experimental GAMA was turned loose. Only a week before, the microbes had been guarded within the security of a government research lab. Now the GAMA was free to reproduce and interact in the wild. In an act that many in the world would call eco-terrorism, LALO, by releasing the stolen GAMA, had finally made good on its threat and honored its promise.

André turned back to the camera. A fire of satisfaction danced in his eyes. "I challenge everyone who watches this to do something to make a difference – either that or suffer the consequences of a planet in peril."

"You have to admit; André has a point."

Eugene Mass stared into the flat screen TV and watched the gyrating decks of the PaxTerra rise and dip before a watery horizon. His voice was slight yet everyone in The Group had heard him. More importantly, they knew what he was insinuating.

Cloistered in a conference room with eight other men of high finance and global position, Mass suffered those around him with rising irritation. An imposing figure, even in his mid-60s, Mass could command attention merely by clearing his throat. His distinctive accent was still intact despite leaving his Bulgarian birthplace as a teenager and never looking back.

On his way to becoming rich, Eugene Mass had always been a global citizen. His only allegiance was to a consuming vision of the way the world could be. Always well-suited but never one to wear a tie, he was the billionaire with a signature tussle of white hair topping his lanky frame. As was his habit, he rubbed his right temple to feed energy to his thoughts.

Curtis Labon was not one to be bullied. A decade younger than Mass and physically less striking, Labon resented the way Mass assumed the role of elder statesman at Group meetings. Labon squinted behind wire-framed glasses, anticipating the confrontation that was coming. He was too familiar with the shifting dynamics within The Group to be outmaneuvered now.

For over twenty years, the private collaboration of influence and money had steered The Group's shared altruism into practical, global applications, legislation, even social movements – with mixed results. A few strident causes had been carefully financed and nurtured until they were successfully finessed into the popular zeitgeist. Frustratingly, their most important goal was yet to be achieved. Only recently had The Group agreed to compromise and try a limited approach using more aggressive measures – the kind favored by Mass.

Labon punched a button on his conference table and the recorded news footage froze to a still frame. "André Bolard is a loose cannon; a small fish. Now that the world has seen what he's done, he's served his purpose."

Pushing away from the table, Labon stood to face a wall of windows. Beyond the glass a pristine Canadian lake, the jewel of his expansive estate, stretched to a misty tree line. "Our alibi is established. If GAMA material is now discovered in the wild, it will be assumed it came from LALO's publicity stunt."

"So we proceed with the 1st Protocol." Mass' slight, accented voice delivered a statement, but to Labon it sounded more like an order.

Labon was reluctant to show agreement with Mass too readily in front of the others. The power plays between the two of them over the years were legend even if contained privately within The Group. An upper hand now meant so much more than ever before. Group direction was changing. Labon was acutely aware how their future course would impact the world.

In principle, the goal of what they were planning was sound. Labon had only questioned the methods to achieve their lofty ends. Mass was eager for results. He was convinced that the escalating world crisis of climate change, limited resources, and burgeoning population demanded methods of social engineering more determined than anything tried before. Labon believed there still was time to use less invasive methods. The 1st Protocol was their compromise – seen as radical to Labon but indicted as incomplete by Mass. As such, the concession oddly satisfied no one but the other seven members – and only because they weren't prepared to take sides.

The rest of The Group had agreed with Mass' plan for implementing what he called staged protocols – one they had decided on with others to be determined later. They had been convinced only after being fed a constant diet of dire planetary warnings over time by Mass. Labon worried that The Group's sudden new willingness to listen to Mass might be the slippery slope into everything they'd once told themselves they abhorred. All Labon needed was an inroad, an issue, something to swing The Group back to his side – and to reason.

A stable, appropriately-sized human population, sustainable and in harmony with planetary systems would come about – the only question was how. Would humanity respond to persuasion and education or would its recklessness precipitate a horrific collapse of civilization? The Group was in agreement – this was the primary issue facing the world in the 21st century. What were the alternatives? What would it take to nudge a natural balance back into the human equation? It seemed they had tried everything – within reason.

Labon tensed at the thought of what other options were left.

It was now clear; as different as they were, Eugene Mass and André Bolard had much in common. Both were impatient with the slow tides of progress on the world stage. Depending on how much of a world crisis one saw coming, a different devil was in the details. Depending on which devil of an idea drove them, there would be a custom hell to pay for someone.

Was it better to keep Mass close or at arm's length? Labon feared his own need to assert himself might make that choice before better instincts had figured it out.

Curtis Labon exhaled a fateful breath and turned back to the table.

"I see no reason why final lab work can't begin."

Hasuru Tamasu was the overly cautious one. He rarely attended Group meetings in person, preferring videoconference from his office in Tokyo. His presence at Labon's estate was testament to the security precautions demanded by today's topic. "Are we sure nobody's going to study LALO's bio-container? Harmless pond scum is not an alibi."

"You aren't suggesting we should have shared the real thing with those rabble-rousers are you?" Mass had a way of laughing without parting his teeth.

Labon answered the question. "LALO made their point; that's all they wanted. From what I heard, André deep-sixed the Navy's container on his way back to port."

Another voice spoke up. Heinrich was a stickler for detail. He also resented that primary genetics work on their project wasn't being done in Germany. "Are we sure the GAMA's suicide gene will work in our configuration? I'm not convinced we have an adequate way to test it under real-life conditions."

"The lab is working on that. We simply have to take our time and do it right."

"How long?"

"Whatever it takes."

Mass flicked one fingernail against another. "I thought we agreed to take action. Why endlessly test something that scientists in the United States have already proven? Our pathogen and payload are ready. Demonstrating that the suicide gene triggers apoptosis after delivery should be the easy part."

"Apoptosis?"

Mass flashed annoyance at the one Group member who dared to question basic terminology this far into the game.

Another member explained, "…programmed cell death."

Heinrich was only half-convinced. "I can't help but wonder – the way we're using the suicide gene is so different. The GAMA is a microbe – it's nothing like the virus within a virus we'll be using. These aren't interchangeable parts we're dealing with. We can't take chances with the interaction."

Mass was unruffled. He lectured the German. "Perhaps the reason you're so worried is because you know so little about this. Did you read the whitepaper that Kevin prepared?"

"Of course I did."

"Then refresh my memory – who engineered the microbe?"

"The U.S. Navy."

"But who engineered the suicide gene inside the microbe?"

Heinrich bristled. "I don't need to be quizzed."

"The U.S. Army." Mass tapped open the whitepaper in question on the display tablet before him and navigated the touchscreen.

Labon relished the opportunity to take Mass down a notch. "Actually, it was Boston University – under contract from the U.S. Army. The work was done at Natick Laboratories near Boston. Natick is a division of the U.S. Army Soldier & Biological Chemical Command."

Mass didn't look up from his tablet. "Quite right. And oddly enough, the U.S. Army was granted a patent for their lethal gene 'terminator system' on 9/11/2001." Mass looked up with a wry smile. "What a coincidence. I imagine news that the patent had been awarded didn't hit anybody's radar *that* day."

Heinrich leaned back. "What's your point?"

Mass donned reading glasses. "You have concerns; we need to deal with them." Mass scanned the text. "It says here the Army specifically tailored their suicide gene systems to work in biodegradative microbes, especially the anti-material Pseudomonas species engineered by the Navy."

"But we're not using a microbe."

Mass raised his hand. "Wait – let's read from the official document. The Army's patent claims 'new killing genes and improved strategies to control their expression' for the purpose of 'controlling genetically engineered organisms in the open environment, and in particular, the containment of microorganisms that degrade...' The system is adaptable and the patent asserts that 'a variety of bacterial and non-bacterial recombinant organisms can be controlled in this manner.'" Mass glared up over the rim of his reading glasses at Heinrich. "Did you get that? Non-bacterial recombinant organisms can be controlled by this suicide gene. Sounds like a virus to me. As a matter of fact, that sounds like what we're using. That's clever of them. They left the door open to many things besides microbes. They said it themselves – it's adaptable."

"That doesn't mean we can forgo testing."

"Testing, yes – but it would be overkill to conduct an exhaustive exercise to prove what the U.S. Army and Navy have apparently already confirmed."

Tamasu feigned levity. "Overkill is an interesting choice of words, especially since the reason for testing is to make sure we kill no one."

No one laughed. Heinrich's silence confirmed the point.

Satisfied with the evidence, Mass plucked his reading glasses from his face and tucked them away. "The design is elegant, practical, and we have top geneticists making sure it's foolproof. If anything, I would think we'd be using this time to finalize our plans for the 2nd Protocol. The 1st one should be old business by now."

Tamasu leaned forward. "There was no consensus about the 2nd Protocol."

"Precisely," snapped Mass. "That's why we need to discuss it. We need to finish debate, make a decision, and implement 2nd Protocol as soon as possible. We may not yet agree if additional protocols are necessary, but we must move forward."

Labon baited his older rival. "Maybe we should take this one step at a time. We're still months away from releasing anything. First we need to prove what we're doing with 1st Protocol will delay fertility."

"And what would be proof for you? Waiting a whole generation to find out if we succeeded? You don't seriously expect us to sit around, doing nothing else but meeting like this for ten or twelve years, waiting to see if the 1st Protocol turned out as planned?"

"We're talking about global impact – prudence is non-negotiable."

"Don't be ridiculous. That's short-sighted and everyone here knows it. If we wait a generation it could be too late to do anything. Look around! We do this to *avoid* a crisis of global impact. We can't remain indecisive, straddling the world's tipping point forever."

"You were correct to call for action in phases. But each one takes time."

Mass' temper flared. "At this rate, none of us will live long enough to see our plans come to fruition. And if we don't do it, who will? Already we've wasted twenty years trying to move people to action without the full strength of conviction behind our efforts. Even our successes barely scratch the surface of what needs to be done."

"You don't have to remind us how important this is…"

"But you have no sense of urgency."

Labon stiffened. "Wrong – our urgency is not careless."

Mass stood. "Is that what this is about? Placate the careless one with something that takes a generation to implement?"

"We didn't pick delayed fertility as the 1st Protocol – you did."

"Correct. And it's called the 1st Protocol because it's meant to be the first in a series of stages – stages that I now see you have neither the will nor the foresight to implement in a timely fashion."

"Accuracy in what we do is just as important as speed."

Mass' frustration boiled over. "I don't see why we're having this discussion. We already agreed in principle that the 1st Protocol was needed." Mass pointed at the TV screen. "Why else did we go to the trouble of establishing the alibi if we weren't willing to take action?"

"Of course we agreed. But that doesn't mean we've got every critical detail locked down." Labon sat back down. "Let's take our time and do it right."

Mass headed across the room.

"Where are you going?" asked Tamasu.

Mass composed himself as he stopped briefly at the open door. "Goodbye gentlemen. It's time to see what can be done without Group meetings."

The conference room filled with discussion. Some members stood in shock. One member ran after Mass.

Tamasu approached Labon, "No one's ever left The Group before."

"Let him go." Labon now saw the way it had to be. Mass would be held at arm's length. It was a liberating but dangerous development. The liberation was immediate, the danger only a potential. But in the moment, it was easier to accept the freedom of having Mass out of the Group than contemplate the full scope of the menace he might become.

In time, the men of The Group settled down. Given the outburst, they agreed they needed to reaffirm their earlier decision. They decided to take a vote – without Mass. The choice was clear. Given what had happened, should they go ahead and implement the 1st Protocol or not?

Labon voted not to implement.

He was not in the majority.

CHAPTER 1

Fourteen Years Later, December 7th
Karolinska Institutet, Stockholm

"So many people!" Riya Basu peered beyond the car's tinted windows into the shifting chaos made even more surreal by the lingering jetlag from her flight out of Hyderabad. Riya was a slight Indian woman in her early forties with a calm and studied temperament. All the attention and commotion were unsettling.

NovoSenectus security agent Malcolm Stowe turned back from the front passenger seat to show Riya his phone. "Never mind that. They don't compare to all the people waiting to hear you. Look at this; millions are expected to watch the streaming video."

Riya glanced at the social networking website and attempted a smile. "Thanks, that's all I need to think about right now – millions of people watching me."

Nighttime was moments away. Riot police stood their ground buttressed by clear shields and black batons. The organized mob of demonstrators jostled back and forth, kicking snow and chanting slogans into a clear but frigid sky. A cadre of activists known only as *New Class Order* mingled and manipulated the crowd.

Overhead, news and police helicopters hovered. Search beams shot down, casting fidgety blue-white spotlights. Sporadic clashes turned violent and the first arrests were made. Rumors circulated in the restless swarm; the honored guest was arriving. Peak time had come for agitation and invective.

Swedish officials were determined to keep the road leading into the renowned medical university open for traffic. The world would be watching all Nobel Prize events but none more than the one taking place today.

Dr. Riya Basu's lecture on her breakthrough genetic life-extension therapy was eagerly awaited by the scientific community. Some naysayers claimed her prestigious prize had been awarded primarily because Nobel custom would require her to give a lecture to explain what she had done. Given the military-grade secrecy maintained around her project by corporate benefactor NovoSenectus, this one lecture might be the nearest anyone would ever come to hearing the revolutionary procedure explained in detail – or so they hoped.

No one knew how much Riya would be allowed to say. The experimental life-extension procedure was not available commercially even though it had been demonstrated with lab animals and trademarked under the corporate label *GenLET*. What had started out a decade earlier as research into old age was now, depending on which side you took, either the fountain of youth or the harbinger of nightmare scenarios for humanity.

Adding to the controversy was the reclusive billionaire behind it all. The announcement twelve years ago that Eugene Mass would build his brash but exceptionally private biotech company in India's Knowledge Park known as Genome Valley was analyzed suspiciously by some. Why the sudden, massively expensive plunge into pure research, especially biotech? Mass had never expressed any such interest before. It wasn't where he made his billions. It wasn't his expertise.

Moreover, it had been rumored that nearly three-quarters of his net worth was committed to the venture. There were no investors other than Mass so he didn't have to publicly answer the most basic business question – where was the payoff? To recoup his investment, pundit economists estimated that Mass would have to price whatever NovoSenectus finally produced such that only the rich could afford it.

At first, Mass had responded on a website created to handle public relations. According to company literature, the corporate name said it all – *NovoSenectus* – Latin for *new old age*. The crafted message on the company website satisfied many but not everyone. In time, even the most stubborn of lingering doubts began to dissipate. After interviews of his polished spokespersons, strategically-timed press releases, and feel-good commercials fronted by darling celebrities, Mass' intentions had been made clear to all – by targeted repetition.

In the end, there was no mystery why Mass had a curiosity about everything biotech. It was obviously rooted in a nagging question shared by all. Here was a man in his seventies with an acute and very personal interest in understanding how and why we got old.

Was the unavoidable decline of aging simply another disease to be cured? What if anything could be learned that might improve our later years? These were questions that no one had tackled quite so generously or with such concentrated resources. The concept of creating a "new old age" was noble enough to calm the most wary of speculation.

To sweeten its corporate image, NovoSenectus devoted a branch of itself to the development and free distribution of "many-in-one" vaccines. These were known by their NovoSenectus name MIOVAC. Eugene Mass continued to give away all of them to needy areas of the world. Accolades for his charity work followed in abundance. The gesture was so philanthropic that no one seemed to care that it was the only public thing he ever did. His MIOVAC program had become so extensive that even the World Health Organization noted how unprofitable it had become for any other company to have a substantial presence in the vaccine market.

A larger question remained and it fueled the latest and most virulent of speculations. Would Mass be as generous with *GenLET*? Many hoped so but few suspected it. Some feared the result of any such charity would be explosive overpopulation. Others had darker fears rooted in consideration of who Mass might deem worthy of receiving his coveted life extension therapy. Unless everyone received it, the end-game could easily be a two-tiered society, a new class order.

What-if scenarios abounded. Those who could afford *GenLET* might enjoy an extended life estimated to be more than five times average – up to 300 years. They and their children would rule the world with dynasties only dreamt of in fanciful mythology. The rest of humanity would live lives as before – but not quite.

What would it be like to know that your great-great-great-grandchildren would face the same individuals of an Olympian ruling class who were on the scene today? Some dreaded a future where extended life would become more than an advantage – it would create a new type of society with a new type of human as masters.

The fearful had taken to the streets. Such a new class order had to be stopped.

The riotous disruption was embarrassing to the Nobel Committee but police commanders promised containment. Dr. Basu's lecture would take no more than an hour. During that time the authorities expected to see the worst of the disturbance. That is, until the actual award ceremony in three days.

Staring out the car's other backseat window was Riya's colleague Janis Insworth. A decade younger but a professional equal, Janis was lost in thought. She struggled with a jumble of emotion, the intensity of which surprised her. She had told herself this trip wouldn't bother her. Now she felt overdressed and out of place. She brushed a self-comforting hand through her long auburn hair.

Sitting between the two of them on pins and needles was Janis' thirteen-year-old daughter Alyssa. At first uninspired to accompany her mother on the trip, the excitable teenager was now over-stimulated if not overwhelmed by the upheaval around them.

Janis took her daughter's hand to comfort them both. She told herself a twinge of jealousy was inescapable, only natural. Yes, of course, *GenLET* was Riya's brainchild. But what the world didn't know was how Janis had nurtured it into a practical therapy. Riya rightfully deserved credit – it was her flash of insight that produced the "what." But Janis had cleverly devised the "how." That breakthrough had been kept most secret. There were undisclosed corporate reasons why no one beyond inner circles could know how far along the project really had come. As a result, very little about Janis' work was known outside NovoSenectus labs.

Janis let the sinking feeling flow through her. Of course the Nobel Committee would completely overlook her contribution – after all, they knew nothing about it. Despite all the private conversations and confidential praise that Riya had showered on Janis one-on-one, Janis couldn't help but want to share in the public recognition for the years of work they had shared.

But she was happy for Riya. She truly deserved the award.

Janis turned her head in time to see Malcolm give Riya's hand a squeeze. It was a knowing touch, a shared moment, a communion. Given the pressures of the trip, it looked like Malcolm and Riya needed each other's reassurance so much they were willing to let Janis see what she had suspected all along. They were lovers.

For their own reasons, Riya and Malcolm had kept their relationship hidden. Janis suspected why. It was certain Malcolm would never have been assigned to Riya's security detail if their romantic connection was known by the managers back in Hyderabad. Family ties could cloud judgment. With corporate secrets at stake, it was best to keep such linkages at a minimum. Janis had worked side-by-side with Riya far too long not to notice what the shared look and hand squeeze confirmed. Again, she was happy for Riya.

The driver carefully navigated the gauntlet lined by police and stopped at a side door leading to the lecture hall. It took only seconds to rush everyone inside. Led into an anteroom just off the main hall, the women were left alone while Malcolm conferred with university staff.

"Is this happening?" Riya teared up.

Janis gave her a hug. "Take a deep breath. Everything's going to be fine."

Riya complied but chuckled nervously on the exhale. "I don't know. Someone should warn them – I'm a geneticist, not an entertainer."

Malcolm reentered the room. "It's time. Whenever you're ready."

Knowing the two of them would appreciate a moment alone, Janis took Alyssa by the hand and led her towards the lecture hall. "We'll be in the front row. If it makes it any easier, pretend you're giving the lecture to us. Either way, enjoy yourself out there – you deserve it."

Riya's smile wavered. The last thing Janis saw before closing the door was Malcolm and Riya reaching for each other.

The lecture hall's tiered rows of seating were filled to capacity. The overflow portion of the audience sat on steps forming the aisles or stood several layers deep at the back. Janis and Alyssa were escorted to their seats before the speaker's podium. With their appearance there was increased murmuring around them. Janis noticed how the speaker's podium had been adjusted lower to accommodate Riya's height. On the large wall screen before them, the first slide of Riya's program blazed in promise of her near arrival.

A university professor stepped before the microphone. A member of the Nobel Assembly and associate member of the Nobel Committee for Physiology and Medicine, he did the honors of introducing Riya.

The laureate took the stage buffeted by warm applause. Embarrassed by the ovation, Riya kept her eyes downcast as she opened the folder containing her lecture notes. In time, she looked up with renewed confidence, emboldened by a friendly smile.

"Thank you. Thank you all for being here today." She hesitated and let her eyes sweep the throng before her. "First of all, I want to express my appreciation to the Nobel Committee for this honor and to NovoSenectus for making the work possible. A special appreciation goes out to my friend and colleague, Janis Insworth, who I believe shares in this honor." Riya motioned to Janis in the front row. "Janis has been with me from the beginning. In coming years, when the full story is able to be told, I have no doubt that Janis will also stand where I stand now."

Janis was taken aback. She'd never expected such a direct statement of support. Riya gestured and waited until the audience offered Janis a round of applause. Janis stayed seated and nodded, her tearing eyes locked on the sincerity of Riya's smile.

Riya picked up a laser pointer and glanced back at the wall screen. The title slide switched to an image of a graveyard and a veritable sea of headstones.

"So what's the problem we're trying to solve? Do we want quality of life for as long as we live – or do we want to live forever? These are questions that go far beyond the technical science of what can and can't be done in the laboratory. But first we have to understand our own mortality. Is it even possible to dispassionately analyze the fact that we are going to die? How long do you want to live? Do you want quality or quantity or both? Everything living in nature declines and dies. Is this because we're supposed to decline as we age? In other words, is there a good reason for this – and even if there is, would it be possible or desirable to change it for some better reason?"

Stopping to take a deep breath, she searched alert faces. Her next statement would be controversial and her pause only emphasized the seriousness of its implications. "Twelve years of research led to evidence. Evidence led to theory. Refined theory posited the question: what if the decline of aging was not inherently natural to the exclusion of other possibilities? What if biological decline with age was merely an artifact of an accidental event that happened to DNA billions of years ago? If such a flaw were found, would it be unnatural to repair it? Learning from the flaw and taking it one step further, one had to ask: would it be unnatural to exploit the flaw's insights if such a thing meant life extension?"

Riya switched to the next slide. It showed a graph that plotted increasing life expectancy for humans throughout history.

"Clearly, with the rise of intelligence, we humans have increased our life spans. Up until now, we've done this without any systemic approach to do so. Does this mean it is in our nature to live better and longer lives? In ancient Greece and Rome, the average life span at birth was 28 years. In the early 20th century, the average varied between 30-45 years. Today, it approaches 70 years. Of course, measurements of life expectancy versus life span are different qualitatively. They are not the same thing. Rates of infant mortality, disease and war can skew the statistics, but given any measurement, one has to admit we humans are living longer. And the longer we live the more we wonder – how long of a life is possible?"

Riya turned with laser pointer in hand and froze, distracted by a sudden commotion. Shouts rang out from one of the stepped aisles leading to the stage. A young man and woman wearing bright green ski masks rushed down the steps. As they neared the stage they threw gold-wrapped chocolate coins at Riya and bounced beach-ball sized inflated Earths off the display screen – the land masses of each continent had been pasted over with human faces.

"Reject the new class order!" yelled the man.

"Life is not for sale!" shouted the woman.

As guards rushed to contain the pair, Riya cowered back behind her podium with Malcolm rushing to her side. The audience turned in surprise but stayed seated in shock. Behind a glass partition at the back of the hall, TV cameras zoomed in.

"Equal life for all people!"

"Stop the rise of the Master Class!"

Wrestled out a side door by guards that had converged from all directions, the man and woman cried out in nonstop protest. In their wake they left a stage and podium littered with chocolate coins and rolling Earths. With the initial disturbance over, the audience erupted in discussion.

The professor who had introduced Riya stepped back to the microphone. He called for calm and order and apologized for the disruption. In time, Riya returned to the podium. Her hands shook as she turned a page of lecture notes. She paused over prepared remarks before deciding to leave them and speak freely.

"I'd just like to say – of course I'm aware of the controversy surrounding my work. I believe a debate would exist whether or not a prize was involved. I want to make it clear that I fully support discussing the merits and dangers of anything we do. Constructive questioning is always good. There *should* be controversy about science. We are a species that has it within our power to remake the world around us. That sort of power needs to be enlightened by healthy debate and guided by reason and moral clarity. I truly believe there is much to learn and benefit from life extension therapies. But it should come as no surprise that I personally support a moratorium on its commercial use. We should wait until a reasonable consensus about its application can be agreed upon. I am not one of those who thinks consensus is impossible – not when it's in everybody's self-interest to secure it."

Riya paused to read the reaction of the audience. Her silence was met with spontaneous applause. Riya picked up the laser pointer again and managed a smile.

"I guess I should get back to my lecture. It's not like we have all the time in the world..."

The reference to limited time was answered with scattered laughter.

Riya turned just as the crack of a gunshot split the air. The bullet hit her in the upper chest. The impact tossed her back again the wall. The laser pointer spun out of her hand and crashed to the ground. Riya dropped to the tiles like a rag doll. In reflex, the audience gasped, winced, then ducked into their seats. Shouts of "Oh my God!" and "No!" were broadcast to the watching millions.

Janis pulled Alyssa to the floor and dropped down on top of her to shield her. Malcolm rushed to Riya's side and cradled her in his arms. From floor level Janis could see Riya's head turned towards Malcolm. Her unblinking eyes fixated upon his. Her lips moved. The expression on her face was of distress, astonishment, and finally release.

The auditorium erupted in pandemonium. Some people cowered while others bolted to get away. Police blocked the exits to ensure the shooter couldn't escape. Guards rushed to an area where audience members had gotten into a scuffle. It was a false alarm – only a man reaching for his phone.

Janis was paralyzed by protective fear, unwilling to let go of Alyssa or leave the floor. Across the tiles towards them ran a rivulet of blood. Alyssa shook and panted beneath her. Paramedics rushed in and pushed Malcolm back from Riya's lifeless body.

Malcolm staggered back, stunned that the woman that he loved was gone.

Guards helped Janis and Alyssa to their feet and hustled them towards the anteroom. Janis broke their grasp in detour to the podium. She grabbed Riya's notebook and clutched the lecture notes to her chest. With an arm around Alyssa, she hurried to the exit. The lecture was over as quickly as it had begun.

No one had learned how to extend life – they'd only witnessed how to end it.

CHAPTER 2

Jubilee Hills, Hyderabad
Andhra Pradesh, India

The teakettle screamed. Dinner sat ready on the table as a TV droned in the background. Janis Insworth raced to the stove, haunted by sounds from a faraway lecture hall. Before her eyes, visions of what might have been dissipated in the steam.

"Alyssa!" The call went unanswered. Flustered, Janis headed down the hallway to her daughter's bedroom. Through a crack opening in the doorway Alyssa could be seen wearing ear buds. Despite the private roar of music, she lay on her bed stone-still and staring at the ceiling.

Janis pushed in and gave a wave to attract attention. "It's time to eat."

"I'm not hungry."

"OK, don't eat – come out and keep me company."

Janis returned to the kitchen. She knew Alyssa would find an appetite once she sat at the table. In a minute or two she'd appear; she always did. Janis poured tea but the cup nearly overflowed as a news report shifted her attention.

"...police in Stockholm are testing the weapon they believe was used two days ago in the murder of Nobel Laureate Riya Basu. The .44 caliber handgun was discovered in the pocket of a coat left behind in the famed lecture hall. The shooter remains at large. So far witnesses have given conflicting accounts of the final moments before the renowned geneticist was gunned down before a live audience with millions watching by webcast..."

Alyssa shuffled into the kitchen space. "Have you seen my..."

"Shhh!" Janis held up a hand.

Adjusting pajamas, Alyssa stared into space. "You already have company."

"...speculation mounts about the one responsible. One university guard admitted privately that evidence points to the environmental activist group, New Class Order, the same group that organized the violent demonstration outside the lecture hall. Attention is focusing on two NCO members, a man and a woman, who somehow breached security and disrupted the lecture immediately before the fatal shot was fired. Off the record, sources close to the police say they now believe that disruption provided the diversion that distracted security staff and allowed the shooter to take up position."

Mumbling, Alyssa opened the fridge. "How can you listen to that?"

Janis sat at the table, her eyes diverted to the broadcast.

"...In a statement issued on its website, NCO adamantly disavows responsibility for the crime. Meanwhile, French authorities acknowledge they have begun questioning a former NCO member who claims he has proof the radical group is hiding the truth."

Alyssa's aimless foraging drew Janis' attention.

"What are you looking for?" After no response, "Everything's on the table."

Janis muted the TV and switched from remote control to fork.

"I can fix something else if you want."

Alyssa faced the open fridge, frozen with indecision, her back to her mother.

Janis endured the silence between them until it turned deafening.

"Alyssa, are you all right?"

Still distant, Alyssa closed the door and slunk to the sink for a glass of water.

"If something is bothering you, we should talk about it."

"Yeah, what good is that?"

"What do you mean? Is it about the trip?"

After a sip, Alyssa emptied the glass into the sink and snapped, "I told you I didn't want to go."

Janis sighed. "I'm sorry about what happened. I know you're worried."

"Whatever."

Janis stood. "We should talk. It's not good to hold it all inside."

"There's nothing to talk about."

"Yes there is." Janis caught Alyssa by the shoulder on her way past. "We need to stick together. It's just the two of us."

A nerve was touched. Alyssa pulled away. "Sure, and what happens now? What if they come after you? It's not like we're hard to find." Alyssa was angry even as her eyes filled with tears.

Janis reached out for her. It was hard to hear her fear and pain. But it was good not being shut out. Maybe Alyssa was opening up after days of being withdrawn.

Before Janis could speak, the doorbell rang. Exasperated, she glanced at the clock. That was all the time Alyssa needed to hurry to her room. With her went an opportunity for something both of them needed. Now it might not reappear for days.

Aggravated, Janis anguished over the timing of the unknown visitor and considered not answering the door. No one was expected. The last thing she needed was to face some overachieving investigative reporter who had hunted her down. Despite anxiety, a nagging curiosity and rising intuition drove her forward.

Through the peephole, she spied a fisheye view of Malcolm Stowe.

"Malcolm!" The door swung wide. "What are you doing here?"

"May I come in?"

"Of course."

The bald-headed powerhouse of a man lurched forward with an energy that was fidgety, anxious, hurt, driven. His words were uncharacteristically hushed but the acerbic wit and British accent were intact.

"Sorry for bothering you at home. I didn't find you at the lab."

"I took the day off."

"Just as well. The place is becoming unrecognizable."

"What do you mean?"

Janis sat on the sofa as Malcolm paced. He was eager to share something but suddenly was thinking twice about stopping by. Janis stood up.

"Would you like some tea?"

"All right." He followed her into the kitchen.

"I'm surprised you've returned to work so soon."

Malcolm leaned back against the counter and watched Janis pour. "It couldn't be helped. There were things I needed to do."

"How are you holding up?"

"The only saving grace is that it still doesn't seem real."

"I still can't believe it. So what did you mean – *the place is unrecognizable*?"

Malcolm raised his eyes and the two of them locked gazes. He spoke in a whisper. "They've locked me out of Riya's office. I'm not allowed to collect her personal effects." Pausing to read Janis' reaction, he leaned in closer. "Security has been reshuffled and I've come out on the bottom of the deck – *me* of all people!" He recoiled. "You don't seem surprised."

A bit embarrassed, Janis guessed there was no better time to broach the topic. "Crime investigations are *usually* locked down – especially around those who were *involved* with the victim."

"How long have you known?"

"Since that night."

Malcolm nodded and looked away. "And the whole thing was televised. It's not the way Riya and I wanted it, that's for bloody sure – but what were we supposed to do? It was necessary. The insulation around *GenLET* forced us. You know how it is – working in that lab is like serving solitary confinement. Riya and I never would have gotten time together if we had gone public. There's no mystery about it."

"It's unfortunate but hiding behind secrets looks suspicious. Maybe some people wonder – what else were you two keeping hush-hush."

"What else? Whatever for?"

"You above all know how paranoid they are about corporate espionage."

Malcolm shook his head. "It's more than that."

"Really. Then tell me. You came here so you must trust me."

"Can I?" Malcolm's gaze searched her face.

"What do you want from me?"

Janis was willing to settle up and call it an evening. If Malcolm wanted a shoulder to cry on, that was one thing. If he was after more, he'd better get specific.

After a long draft of tea, Malcolm could no longer hide his game face.

"A week before the Stockholm trip, I spent the night with Riya. She was agitated, preoccupied, not herself. I asked her what was wrong. She wouldn't tell me. Then she got a phone call. She raced upstairs to take it. She shut the door but I followed her. I managed to hear her side of the conversation."

Janis took a breath to calm her nerves. "You sure you want to tell me this?"

"Whoever she was talking to was someone at NovoSenectus. Everything was jargon, the kind only someone in a staff position or higher would understand."

"All right. So what?"

"Halfway through the conversation, Riya couldn't take it any more. She got upset – furious like I'd never heard her before. She accused them of bastardizing her work. She wanted to know why she was being kept in the dark. She lectured them in security procedures and rattled off a covert passcode like it was memorized."

"How do you know that?"

If telling secrets was the way to keep Janis engaged, Malcolm was more than willing to impress her with his frankness. “You may think I’m a glorified security guard. Not so much. Only one thing could tempt me to leave the British Special Air Service – a lot more money but more importantly, an even greater challenge.”

“I didn’t think there was anything more demanding. So what are you saying?”

“All you need to know is this – for the last nine years I’ve been trusted to do whatever NovoSenectus needed done.”

“Anything? Why would they need someone like that?”

“Listen – two days ago Riya got shot and now I’m persona non grata.” Malcolm’s temper flared. “Don’t tell me all of this is because we were fucking.”

Janis felt uncomfortable. He was in her house and now she wasn’t sure who he was or what he might do. She needed to mollify the situation.

“OK. It doesn’t sound right. Maybe there *is* something odd going on.”

“She knew a type of passcode even I wasn’t aware of – how and why?”

“*GenLET* has the tightest security. She was top scientist. Maybe…”

“There’s more to it than that. On the phone, she also demanded to know why she wasn’t told about an *agent* being selected.”

“Agent?”

“Odd isn’t it. NovoSenectus selects an agent and I don’t know about it.”

“Is that really so odd? Do you expect to be privy to *all* corporate business?”

“You worked with Riya every day. You were friends. Ever take her for a spy?”

Janis couldn’t help but laugh. “It doesn’t make sense.”

“So what would?”

“Why not ask your boss.”

“My boss isn’t available.” Malcolm paused for effect. “I was hired by Eugene Mass. I’ve had no other boss.”

“I don’t know…that’s wild.”

“Is it really that hard to imagine? A man like Mass maintains his personal security separate from anything NovoSenectus does – but it’s all for the same cause. It’s all about maintaining interlocking rings of containment. Now do you understand? Me being on the outside – it’s not natural. Something’s up.”

“You should have confronted Riya – asked her about the phone call.”

“I did. She didn’t appreciate anyone tiptoeing to her door to listen. She told me she didn’t want to talk about it – she couldn’t. She said it was better if I didn’t know. Then she threw me out.”

Head spinning with possibilities, Janis walked around the kitchen table. “So what’s this about? Why are you telling me all this?”

Malcolm stepped forward in front of Janis to force her to stop. “I need to know one thing – how can I contact Colin.”

The name shot to the heart of Janis. She hadn’t seen her ex-husband for thirteen years. The mention of his name in this context shot a wave of vertigo through her. “Colin?” Her voice reduced to a whisper.

“I know – hear me out.”

Janis shook her head and fled into the living room. “You’ve got to go. I can’t do this.”

“Wait. You’ve got to listen.”

"I don't have to do anything. I've heard too much already."

"All right. I know this is hard. The last couple of days have been difficult for both of us. I'm not asking you to talk to him. *I* need to contact him."

"What for?"

"Didn't Colin work with you at USAMRIID?"

Rising defenses shot cold through Janis. Her work at the United States Army Medical Research Institute for Infectious Diseases in Maryland was a long time ago. It might as well have been another life.

"Why are you asking me questions when you already know the answers?"

"Do you know where he was reassigned?"

"Even if I knew, that information would be classified. Of course, if I did know, that would make me a covert asset too."

"Was he reassigned out of the country? Was that the reason you two split up?"

Janis felt her heart race. The nature of Malcolm's questions inclined her to suspect the worst. Why else display such passion? Why else explore such topics? "What are you doing?"

"I'm not trying to entrap you if that's what you're worried about."

"You still work for Eugene Mass – you just said so."

"Listen, we're on the same side here. I'm the one who's been locked out."

"Naturally. It makes sense if you had to get this to look real."

Malcolm fumed. "What do you think is going on here? You really think I came over here to pretend estrangement from Mass just to see what information you would give up?"

Janis stepped to the front door. "Trying to hide in plain sight won't help."

Malcolm stood his ground, hands on hips. "I don't believe it. You really think I'm playing you."

"Either way, I don't want to get involved." She opened the door.

"Do me a favor."

"Sure. I'll forget you ever came over tonight."

"If you can get into Riya's office, would you bring me her personal effects?"

Janis didn't need time to consider it. "You should go."

Sensing that Janis had reached her limit, Malcolm nodded and stepped over the threshold and into the night. "Thanks for the tea." He never turned back.

Janis shut the door and turned the deadbolt. She spun around and leaned back with her eyes closed. What was real was lost in a flurry of thoughts. She let the silence settle around her. For a moment, being alone was a comfort. Then a chill set in. Trying to make sense of what just happened left little room to be positive.

Pushing off without finding a sense of relief, she stepped through the living room, turning out lights as she went. She left the food on the table and walked down the hallway. At Alyssa's door she stopped. The light was on but Alyssa was fast asleep. Even if she wanted to talk to Alyssa now, Janis didn't have the strength. She decided to put the food away and head to bed.

Maybe in the morning all the nightmares would be gone.

CHAPTER 3

Kasu Brahmananda Reddy National Park
Jubilee Hills, Hyderabad

Another redial. Janis pressed the cell phone to her ear. A meandering peacock crossed her path. Late afternoon sun filtered through polluted air and casted an orange-brown sheen over the nature trail.

No answer. Same as a half hour before. This time Janis let it ring.

Steps ahead but within sight, Alyssa aimed her camera at something of interest. It was an animal, not moving. Possibly dead. From spots on its lithe body, Janis guessed it was an Indian civet.

"Don't touch that."

"Don't worry."

Janis regretted calling out. No doubt Alyssa would take it as treating her like a child. After the interruption of their conversation at dinner the night before, Janis had hoped the dialogue between them would restart. Another terse exchange was not helping.

Why call out to warn Alyssa? Janis scolded herself and fumbled for an excuse. Last night's mention of USAMRIID by Malcolm had brought back a flood of memories. Maybe she hadn't realized how much her time working at Fort Detrick, Maryland impacted her – was still a part of her.

Thoughts of a classified briefing on the 2003 SARS outbreak in Asia came to mind. Many at the time believed the causal trail of the epidemic led back to the Masked Palm Civet, a cousin of the dead mammal being photographed. Old news.

Janis restarted her stroll to calm a swirl of emotion. She tried concentrating on little things in nature that otherwise would have gone unnoticed. It was no use. Everything she thought or felt led back to intrusive questions and a need for self-examination. It was exactly what she wished to avoid, but Riya's murder was fresh in mind. With it came a palpable sense of mortality and the impulse for life review.

Having such a large park so near their house was a luxury in such a sprawling metropolis. Over the last decade, Janis had witnessed a steady urban surge that left open spaces like KBR Park a premium afforded by only the more affluent neighborhoods. The rising promise of available jobs in sprouting tech industries had made the city of Hyderabad a mecca for the young, the industrious, the opportunistic.

Time had sped by and this year, Alyssa became a teenager. More than a decade ago, Janis arrived in India with a newborn and painful memories of a brief marriage. She clung to the chance to do important work, to understand the bio-mechanisms of life and aging. In actuality, now it seemed more likely she had come to the other side of the world to escape an ethos and lifestyle that clashed with her youthful idealism.

In the decade since, those fires of altruism had been tamped down by the reality she watched taking shape around her. Maddeningly, everyone in her adopted home increasingly wanted what she had run away from. What was once a second world settlement had metamorphosed into a burgeoning city of four million consumers, eerily remote-controlled in many ways by an unquenchable desire for development, progress, and a higher standard of living.

It had been all too easy to watch what was happening and recoil with righteous contempt. Signs of contagion abounded. Everywhere could be seen the virulent symptoms of the disease – cell phone towers, sky-high stacks of corporate cubicles, an insatiable lust to consume and become affluent, the oppressive metastasizing of a mass-produced, global culture taking root, ever more oppressive in its hypnotic insistence to be noticed and define the priorities of life for all.

In many ways, local life had turned into a dreamlike but kitschy reality show whose theme song might feature ancient Hindu and Islamic prayers set to a hip-hop beat. The purist in her reviled the worst parts of it. But now, awakening self-doubt overshadowed her. Rooted in the horror felt at the pace of transformation around her, she had to face a tacit hypocrisy. Strolling through her posh neighborhood, made comparatively rich by the esoteric high-tech arts of genetics, who was she to cast aspersions on the progressive changes enveloping the developing world?

Aged beyond her all-too-easy militancy of youth, Janis could now confront the enemy within. Admittedly, there were undeniable benefits to the encroachment of self-labeled progress that surrounded her. She only had to look to her daily routine to find ample examples, conveniences she wouldn't want to be without. No longer was it a surprise that those tainted benefits fed into the best and worst of a predictable, universal, and unchanging human nature – even at the cost of Nature herself.

What had she learned in her youth? Ideologues at the Ivy League college had taught her that the American Dream was conjured up by oppressors and exploiters. Pragmatists at USAMRIID had taught her that the rule makers abided by no moralistic convention or measure of restraint. Despite international agreements, the insect politics of expediency and self-interest would prevail. "Dual-use" bio-security projects ensured that anything studied for defense in the light of day would easily find offensive applications under the deep cover of sanctimonious night.

The last couple of days had taught her that nothing, no one was safe or secure.

"Hello?" crackled in one ear.

The familiar voice was discordant to her thoughts yet salve for the soul.

"Mom?"

"It's so good to hear you."

"You too. I called a little while back but I guess you weren't up yet."

"I was up. I took a walk to the lake. Just got back. It's a beautiful morning. Crisp but clear."

"How's the snow?"

"Not bad. Roger came by yesterday and plowed a path to the road. I didn't need the snow blower done around the house – not deep enough for that. What about you? How are you holding up?"

"OK. I'm still not sure about Alyssa."

"Don't worry. It'll take time. Like I said the other day, the main thing is – you're with her. Taking time off, being together; that's the best thing you can do for her right now. After all, you just got back."

"I know. It's still hard to see her this way."

"So what have you two been up to?"

Janis watched as Alyssa strolled farther ahead with camera swinging by a strap at her side. "We got up late, went out for lunch and a movie. It was a good distraction. Now we're at the park. We both needed to get out of the house."

"I know you probably think keeping busy with work is the best thing to do but my offer still stands. If you want to take a leave of absence and come this way for a visit, I'd love to have you two stay with me. It would sure warm up the place."

"I'll think about it."

"It'd be fun for Alyssa. How long has it been since you took her to the snow?"

Janis thought back to a vacation in Europe. "It's been a while…a couple years."

Walking and talking, Janis noticed the nature trail up ahead bending between thick vegetation. Intruding on her memories of Switzerland snow was the uneasy realization that Alyssa was scooting around the bend and out of sight. Janis' attention drew sharply present with a burst of disquiet, a sour twinge from a sixth sense.

On the phone, Mom was relegated a few time-sliced fragments of awareness.

"Mom – I'll have to call you back. Love you!"

Janis cancelled the call as her pace quickened down the trail. "Alyssa."

Sights and sounds from moments before on the periphery of Janis' attentiveness were singled out. In sudden recall, the tandem jog of two men could be seen. A jogging track ran parallel to the nature trail in this area but it was mostly hidden by plants. The men had paced themselves, neither running or walking. Their footwear was oddly non-athletic.

Janis broke into a run. "Alyssa!" The call went unanswered.

Around the bend, a parent's worst fear was realized. Through a break in the trees the joggers could be seen hustling a struggling Alyssa to the street and into the back of a waiting car.

"No!" Janis screamed and sprinted into the brush towards them. Her outburst only alerted the kidnappers of pursuit and energized them to move more quickly.

Alyssa cried out and fought them as best she could but the two men flanking her held her by the arms, nearly lifting her off the ground. Her shouts shot flat against the empty expanse of deserted park and indifferent road. The car raced off before the men got the back door closed.

It only took a few moments and she was gone.

Janis ran into the street, her heart bursting, her yelps of disbelief and pain calling out for help to anyone who would listen. In the distance, scooters, cars, and three-wheeled taxis negotiated a far intersection. Accelerating through the traffic maze, the getaway car disappeared around a corner. Janis was left pacing in shock as the horns of oncoming traffic ignored her pleas and demanded the right-a-way.

Dashing in the direction of home, Janis dialed the police. She shouted into the phone while running. The operator demanded she calm down and repeat herself. Neither went well. By the time Janis plunged across her threshold and paced crazily from living room to kitchen, enough had been said to bring the police to her door. Waiting for them was an eternity.

Out loud to no one, she tried to invoke the magic of denial. "This can't be happening!" Too shocked to cry, she shivered, unable to sit but too overwhelmed to stand still.

When the police arrived, they asked for details about the men, the car, their direction of travel. Trying to concentrate, to remember, only made Janis relive the trauma. Officers checked the house to make sure nothing else was disturbed. They assured her they would do whatever they could to bring Alyssa back. Janis wasn't convinced it would be enough but she had to act as if she hoped it could. The detective left a patrolman to watch her street and guard the house for a while.

She still felt violated, vulnerable, devastated, heartbroken.

When the front door finally closed, she discovered how unprepared she was to be alone. Surrounded by silence, the crushing certainty of what had happened weighed down upon her. She had to surrender to the truth. Tears filled her eyes. No longer was she able to stand. Collapsing on the couch, she lay limp, the mother's heart inside of her imploding.

Alyssa was gone.

Even to think such a thing was truth and fiction all at once. She had to admit the reality of what had happened but couldn't. Hanging onto hope that everything would be fine was unbelievable but necessary. What to do next? All she had left was raw emotion and tormenting questions. Why Alyssa? Why not her? What did this terror have to do, if anything, with the horror that had taken place in the Stockholm lecture hall? Why of all people did they target an innocent girl?

A fog of despair ushered in night. Janis fainted, awoke, then fell asleep. At that moment it was the only way to escape the pain. She lost track of time and found herself two hours later in the dark. In a pocket, her cell phone was ringing. She raced to answer, thinking it might be the police with news. Caller-id displayed a lab co-worker's name. She let the call go to voicemail.

She held the phone with numbing indecision. What to do? The answer came as an impulse more than a decision. Fingers quivering, she dialed the one person who might know something more about what was going on.

Hearing her voice, Malcolm ramped into gear. "Jesus! I can't imagine what you're going through."

"You've heard?"

"It's all over the news. Sounds like the police are turning the city inside out looking for her."

"Can you meet me? We have to talk."

"I'll be right over."

"No – somewhere else. I need to get out of here."

Malcolm named a spot, a favorite dive – a restaurant with privacy enough for conversation. She hurried out and drove there straight away. Every minute mattered. Anything Malcolm knew might prompt a spark of recognition, a wisp of hope, a crucial clue to help unravel the plots in play.

There was nothing else she could do about the police investigation; it would have to run its course. Given the revelations from Malcolm the night before, maybe she needn't leave the crisis only in police hands. The thought of it fed her desire to be proactive. Her intuition needled her to focus and pursue anything the authorities either didn't, couldn't, or wouldn't do.

Malcolm insisted on a back booth upstairs. A lone candle lit the table. Ordering food and drinks was easy. Starting conversation was awkward. The contentious way their last meeting ended lay between them like raw meat they were forced to share.

Malcolm remained reserved, if not distant. Janis felt out on a limb, naked.

"After last night, I wouldn't have guessed we'd be doing this now."

Janis felt cold in the warm booth. "After today, I see last night in context."

"Ready to be more suspicious?"

"I'm prepared to do whatever it takes to get my daughter back."

"Be careful of desperation. Crafty ones use such things as tools against us."

"You mean people like you."

He sipped his drink. "Yes, like me. I admit it; but then I confessed as much last night. I'm not the one pretending here."

"What's that supposed to mean?"

"See it from this side of the table. You and Riya spent more time together over the last ten years than the most committed husbands and wives. And yet you still claim complete ignorance of any extracurricular mischief Riya was into."

"I don't care if you believe me. I came here for a simple exchange of facts. If you know something that in any way can help me get Alyssa back, then tell me! My daughter is my only agenda. You're not the one at risk here."

"You sure of that?"

"It's patently obvious – your agendas are not up front. Mine are."

"This is a shitty way to start a collaboration."

"Don't try to elevate what's going on here."

"Look – I shared more last night than I needed to. I thought you'd understand – *from context.* I don't care a flaming fuck if a mere mention of Colin's name rattles the romantic princess in you. Your choice not to move on after thirteen years doesn't concern me. Fact is, finding Colin might help get to the bottom of why Riya was murdered."

"From my side of the table, believing that is a leap of faith."

Malcolm leaned forward. His whisper across the candle was on fire. "Would it help if I told you I got it from a reliable source."

"An unnamed source, no doubt."

"Wrong. I have witnesses."

"Who?"

"You – along with millions of others…if they watched closely enough."

"What are you talking about?"

"Right after Riya got shot, I was holding her. She whispered to me."

Janis thought back and a blast of cold acknowledgment flowed through her.

He was right. The repeating mental image kept her mute.

"You had to have seen it. You were on the floor only a few feet away."

"That doesn't prove that anything she said was about Colin."

The food arrived. Malcolm waited until the service staff were gone.

"Listen, I came here because I thought we could help each other. Maybe not. Maybe we should eat our meal and leave it at that."

Dejected at the prospect of walking away empty-handed, Janis glared across the table. "What are you saying? You won't help me unless I tell you about Colin?"

Malcolm chewed and talked. "It's tit for tat. We both want something, only you don't trust the messenger and you bloody well won't believe the message. That's a piss-poor way to go about collecting information."

"So it's the prey's fault for not seeing the chameleon. For you, it's a defect in the prey, not the chameleon's advantage."

"Believe whatever you like. As long as you think I'm running some game on you, I don't see how we can do business. It's as simple as that."

"A game makes far better sense. According to you, Riya was up to something. I was her closest colleague. You work for Eugene Mass, owner of NovoSenectus. Now that Riya's dead, making me believe you're on my side might be the only way to find out what Riya was up to. The corporate bosses need to know, don't they?"

Malcolm shook his head. His face drew taut, his eyes unblinking. "I've probably already told you enough to get me killed. If any of this gets back to certain people, there'll no place for me to hide. How do I know you won't make the call – tell NovoSenectus everything, let them know I have reason to suspect…"

"Suspect what?"

"Tit for tat, remember?"

Frustrated to the point of action, Janis snapped. "I don't know where Colin Insworth is! When I was pregnant with Alyssa, the asshole was offered another position in bio-defense. Whatever it was, it was way above my security clearance."

"So what was the problem? Are you telling me they insisted he get a divorce?"

"No, they didn't have to. I'd seen enough of what happens around secrets. Even at the low level I was at – things got twisted."

"Sounds reasonable. You didn't want that kind of life."

"He did." The pause was anguished. "He got to be on the inside of whatever they were doing. The way he acted, the offer would put him on the inside from the ground up, based at the core. For something like that, giving me up was a price he was willing to pay."

"You thought he'd choose you. You bluffed and lost."

"Yeah, and for a long time I sat around wondering – what does that make me? Hopelessly romantic or just clueless?"

"You never forgave him; that's one thing. But you also never let it go."

Tears welled up. "It doesn't matter about me. I handled it. But some things are not worth the price. Some things aren't forgiven. He chose a covert assignment over knowing Alyssa. He got a cushy classified title; what did she get? She's different because of it. I'm certain of it. I'm reminded of that fact every day."

Malcolm put down his fork. "Ever hear the word Senex – S-E-N-E-X?"

Janis poked at her food. After a wait, she offered a shake of the head.

"It's Latin for *old man*." Folding arms on the table before him, Malcolm hesitated before saying any more. He considered the dice he was rolling. If Janis knew anything more, this was no time to let up on her. Any second she could crack.

"Riya's last whisper spoke of somebody called Senex. She said Senex was her contact – at GeLixCo."

Janis' reaction was transparent. Malcolm knew mention of GeLixCo would drop a bomb. GeLixCo was the foremost North American corporate rival of NovoSenectus. The adversarial relationship between them went way back.

Janis sat blown away with nothing to say.

"I checked with someone reliable, a source I'd had for a long time. They say Senex is a codename. It was assigned years ago – to *Colin Insworth.*"

Janis was stunned. The idea that Colin was somehow assisting Riya pass information from her lab to GeLixCo carried airs of disturbed unreality.

"Before she died, Riya told me she'd made a computer backup. With her last breath she gave me the password. She said she'd hid this backup at GeLixCo offices in Puerto Rico. She said Senex was her contact." Malcolm reached across the table and grabbed Janis' hand. "You see now why I have to trust you?"

The rush of it all crushed down on Janis. It was too much to fathom. Riya and Colin involved in corporate espionage – together? Riya had known about Janis' past, the divorce, even knew that Colin had chosen a new title over his family. It was hard to imagine Riya ever being civil to Colin let alone trusting him with her life.

It didn't make sense. If any of this was true, why would Riya contact Colin? How would she ever have managed it? If anything, Colin would have made first contact. His position was that deep, guarded, and insulated. There was no way Riya could have reached out to him and succeeded.

Not unless he wanted to be found.

But why? Whatever could be on the secret backup?

Janis searched Malcolm's face for a telling sign. "What do you think they were up to?"

"How much is 300 years of life worth?"

Janis physically recoiled from the suggestion. "No – I don't believe it. Riya selling *GenLET* secrets?"

"Only the two of you knew everything. If somebody wanted extended life, there were only two people to get it from. If they didn't target you, it had to be her."

"I worked with Riya every day. You loved her. You don't really believe that, do you?"

"Get me a way to contact Colin and let's ask him. Either that, or I need to find some way to read what's on that computer backup in Puerto Rico."

"I told you – I know nothing about Colin that's current."

Malcolm grabbed her other hand. "You want to know who has Alyssa…why they took her? Think about it. You are the only other person who knows all of *GenLET's* secrets. That fact is no secret. My God, Riya praised you at the start of her lecture. Everyone knows who you are and what you know."

"Nobody's contacted me."

"What do you call the unfortunate episode in the park?"

"I don't believe Riya was like that. If you knew her as a lover, I'm surprised you'd even consider it."

"All people have layers. Even those closest to you don't show everything."

"The police think the kidnapping is somehow connected to Riya's murder. They believe NCO is behind both."

"I'm suspicious of quick and easy answers – especially from authorities.

Everything I've seen tells me the truth is never that one-dimensional."

"It's clear they want to put pressure on NovoSenectus. NCO doesn't care about grabbing *GenLET* secrets for themselves – just the opposite. They want to shut the whole thing down."

"So what do we know for sure? Nothing. Even more reason to find out what's on the computer backup. Once we read it, I think we'll find the motive. The motive will tell us who's behind this. Murder or kidnapping, it doesn't matter. To answer both, we have to figure out why Riya did what she did and what it means."

"Why Puerto Rico? I didn't even know GeLixCo had a presence there."

"They have a research facility. Very few know about it."

"Sounds remote. An awkward place to do that type of business."

"Not so. Puerto Rico's the perfect place. It's a territory of the United States; it's not a State – it doesn't have State restrictions. If a Federal agency needed a free hand to do whatever they wanted without State interference or oversight, Puerto Rico would be the perfect place to set up shop."

Janis pushed her plate away. "Colin would never leave government service to go work for GeLixCo."

"Who said he did? Bio-defense projects are carved up and farmed out by grant to universities and private labs all the time – over 1300 of them in the U.S. alone. Fragments of bigger secrets are hidden in plain sight. Only the Department of Energy, the Army, Navy, or the National Institute of Health know how to put the pieces together. GeLixCo probably worked on a piece of something. Colin provided oversight for the government."

"That's a big leap. Even if true, it wouldn't explain why Riya got involved."

"Is there anyone else you know, someone with a line into GeLixCo or Colin?"

Janis shook her head. "No one. I'll check, but I don't expect to find anything."

Malcolm eased back. His chest deflated.

Janis looked up from her drink. "What are you going to do?"

"I have no choice. I have to find out what's on that computer backup."

"If you read it, will you tell me?"

Malcolm hesitated. "You want your daughter back. Is that *all* you want?"

"I want Alyssa – and whatever else is good for her and me. I still work for NovoSenectus – just like you."

Malcolm paid the check. "It might be easier not knowing certain things."

"Easier, but not smarter. I want to know."

"No matter where it goes?" Janis nodded as Malcolm stood. "I know someone who might be able to help. It's the only way but it's risky."

"In what way?" asked Janis.

Dropping a tip on the table, Malcolm leaned in closer. "Sometimes mercenaries make money – coming and going." The look on Janis' face prompted an explanation. "He'll charge me for access. But if he's real hungry, he'll tell Mass what I've done – and charge him too."

"You're willing to go that route?"

"Is Riya dead?" Seething with rage, Malcolm turn to go but twisted back, his face draining blank and cold. "To get justice for her, do I have a choice?"

CHAPTER 4

Early evening
Mt. Pleasant, Maryland

Faye Gardner pivoted from her open refrigerator with chilled bottles of Pinot Grigio and sparkling water in hand. Tall, blonde and lean, she sashayed to holiday music from another room. "Do the honors?"

Comfy on a stool, friend Sophia worked the cork free and refilled Faye's glass with wine then topped off her own Pellegrino. As the refrigerator door swung shut, an embedded TV came back into view. The old movie they were half-watching neared its end. After a sip, the credits rolled and the two of them returned to preparing dessert tapas at the kitchen island.

These were the first moments alone for the two of them since Faye's dinner party began. As good friends, they relished the chance to share a bit of fun. And yet, they were close enough to recognize a moment of quiet awkwardness between them.

The discomfort passed quickly but left behind was a regretful realization. They were far more accustomed to workaday encounters in the lab with each other at Fort Detrick – under far more serious conditions.

"I think you're thoroughly enjoying being out of your comfort zone."

Sophia was amused at herself for being so matter-of-fact.

Faye feigned astonishment. "I know. Why haven't we done this before?"

"You didn't have this house to show off."

"You think it's too much, don't you. I mean, for one person." Faye set to work piping chocolate ganache.

"I don't know. If anything, it sends a message."

"What? Overachiever? Conspicuous consumption? Be kind."

"More like hopeless workaholic." Sophia laughed. "No – it says something else, perhaps something even *more* sinister."

"Oooh! Mysterious. I'm listening."

Sophia's pause belied second thoughts. "Maybe lavishing yourself with all this room is a way of saying you desperately want to fill it up."

Faye turned coy. "Nonsense. It gives me an excuse to go find furnishings. You know what a slut I am for antiques."

"Funny choice of words."

"Besides, it's a good investment."

"Like Jacob?"

"Here we go…" Faye cast a weary eye. They'd been down this path before.

"I just want to see you happy. How many years has it been?"

Faye looked up. Outside, beyond the window, three men laughed and struggled in the cold to hang Christmas lights. Faye singled out one man in particular.

"What does it matter? He and I are like bread and butter."

Sophia giggled her sipped drink. "Oh my God yes, creamy-dreamy – but where are all the little croutons?"

"You're bad!" laughed Faye. She couldn't help but glance at the pleasantly obvious poof of Sophia's tummy, now four months along..

"Yes, of course! And I thought you had similar aspirations."

"I have time."

"Oh really. What clock are you watching?"

"It's easier for Dave and you. You two work a building apart. Nobody travels."

"You think that's an accident? Making something easy doesn't just happen."

"Do tell…"

"Well, for one thing, unlike somebody I know, I never started dating the first traveling salesman I met on a far-flung vacation."

"He's not a traveling salesman."

"Whatever he does, he travels."

"I thought you were a romantic?"

"I am!"

"Well, wasn't it you who said *love picks the time and place*?"

"Sure. But a true romantic wants to do more than date."

Faye licked a dot of chocolate from her finger. "He asked me."

"Really!" gasped Sophia.

"I just haven't said yes."

"When did *this* happen?"

Sporting a sly grin, Faye reached for her wine. "Two years ago."

Sophia groaned away her heavy disappointment.

Caroline returned from the bathroom. Caroline and Jack were new neighbors from across the street. Caroline strutted into the kitchen ready to be put to work.

"What can I do to help?"

Faye pointed with her piping bag. "Serving trays are right there. We can start loading them up."

Sophia checked the window. "Oh, look! The lights are on. The guys should be in any minute."

As if on queue, the mud room door opened with a whoosh and clamor of male voices. After a stomp and a shake and a shedding of heavier coats, the men rejoined the party with renewed appetites. Jacob, Jack, and Dave lost no time sampling the nearly done desserts while regaling the women with their macho misadventures in the name of holiday cheer.

Jacob hugged Faye from behind. She wiggled to his touch and kept filling the serving tray. With six people in the kitchen, it was easy to be distracted by multiple conversations. Before long, the playful banter reached a crescendo.

Faye looked up, reacting to a joke, but her eyes diverted to the TV on the refrigerator door. A news bulletin flashed across the screen, along with a face she recognized. Her own smile faded. She reached for the remote control to raise the volume. Others in the kitchen took note of her concern and quieted to see what had happened.

"…the kidnapping took place in a park not far from where Janis Insworth and her daughter Alyssa have lived for the past three years. Witnesses say two men forced the thirteen-year-old into a car and sped off while her mother braved traffic to chase them down the street…"

Jacob stood at Faye's side. "What is it?"

Faye held a stoic pose. "I know them."

Sophia looked to Faye and caught her eye. Sophia understood more than anyone else from conversations past.

Faye raised a hand to ask everyone to wait so she could listen.

"…coming so soon after the murder of Nobel Laureate Riya Basu, this latest crime draws attention once again to New Class Order, an organization well known for its violent opposition to life-extension research. Authorities are not saying if they have evidence to prove the killing and kidnapping were committed by this same radical group, but insiders point to the timing of events and the linkage among targets to infer such a scenario is likely. NovoSenectus has released a statement expressing outrage and concern. It is offering a substantial reward for information leading to Alyssa Insworth's safe return…"

The levity once filling the kitchen was gone. In response, Faye felt she owed her guests an explanation. She lowered the TV's volume.

"Janis and I went to college together. For a while we worked at USAMRIID on the same project. Then we went our separate ways."

The others waited while Faye collected her thoughts and stuffed her feelings. It was obvious her recollections were about a best friend – who wasn't anymore.

"I met Alyssa once, years ago. She was only seven. It was strange. Janis brought her to this conference in Geneva…some biotech thing. I forget."

Sophia waited to see how much Faye was willing to tell. With Jacob standing at Faye's side, Sophia assumed the part about Colin Insworth would not be told. Such a thing would be indelicate. The fact that Janis had captured the man Faye had once loved, had baby Alyssa with him, then let him go – that was not the kind of story likely to come out at this or any other dinner party. For Sophie, if nothing else, the rawness of Faye's emotion only reinforced the deep-seated reasons why she kept love relationships at arm's length.

Faye lifted a dessert tray and headed for the living room. "That's a shame. I hope everything works out. I hope they find her."

The dinner party regrouped around the fireplace but the mood was irretrievably altered. The dessert and wine were soothing, not celebratory. As conversations drifted, issues behind the news boiled to the surface. Differences of opinion were inevitable. Everyone managed to remain civil in spite of strong opinions. Knowing where to place blame, finding the source of evil behind current events, it all came down to the way one looked at things. It was certain: nothing was going to be decided this evening, only contrary lines drawn.

"They really like going after NCO, don't they?" noted Jack.

"Criminal tactics always detract from a valid message," answered Dave.

"The real crime is letting everyone believe they're going to get life extension."

"That's for sure. Someone really has the public snookered with that one."

In round-robin fashion, guests added to the debate. The TV news report had touched a nerve with everyone, not just Faye. She kept quiet and suffered through the less-than-festive exchange.

"From what I hear, NovoSenectus wasn't even looking for life extension. They stumbled on it while studying old age."

"Whatever. I just don't trust billionaires."

"Even those who give away their billions?"

"What's a billion here or there to Eugene Mass? You think he misses it?"

"Miss it or not, his MIOVAC Program gives out millions of doses of vaccine."

"Yeah, I guess with his money he needs all the tax write-offs he can get."

"By percentage of income, he probably gives more to charity than all of us combined."

Caroline spoke up. "I read something the other day that said life extension was the tip of the iceberg. They're planning all sorts of things with genetics. If you're rich enough, your children will have it all – night vision from owls, better hearing from dogs, better muscles from cheetahs, who knows what else."

Sophia grinned. "It'll give a whole new meaning to being *hung like a horse*."

Dave followed up while the laughter subsided. "The next thing to watch are *synthetic* genes. Real gonzo stuff. Sky's the limit. Crazy shit like flame-retardant skin. Imagine being able to scoop up liquid nitrogen with your bare hand."

Jacob eased back on the sofa. "I think the whole thing is overblown. Everything's expensive when it's first developed. Look at cell phones or flat-screen TVs. Not everyone could afford one when they first came out. That didn't split up society and make a *Rich Super Class* like NCO is worried about. In time, everything gets around. It's the economies of scale."

"Those are economic decisions." Jack reached for another piece of dessert. "Life extension is political. You really think the power elite are going to hand out 300 years of life to everyone in the Third World? Are you kidding? No way. That's the dirty little secret they don't advertise. They know the Third World is too busy surviving to watch what could happen. Those who are watching, people like us, they've got us believing we'll make it into the club. We think poverty will be the only 'pre-existing condition' that denies *GenLET* coverage. Not so."

"Where's the poverty line?"

"Unfortunately for us, it depends on who draws it. You know it won't be us."

"Where would the elites like Mass draw it?"

"It's not going to work if some get *GenLET* and others don't."

"Why not? It's been that way for a long time. People at the top have always had advantages the rest of us don't. Why not this?"

"It's always been crony socialism for the rich and free enterprise for the poor."

"When was the last time the IRS sent a member of Congress to jail for tax evasion? How many small farmers have off-shore shelters to avoid estate taxes?"

Sophia tired of the debate. "Is anybody even sure they want to live 300 years? I don't know about you, but sometimes it's hard for me to find things to do on a weekend. My God, what would I do with three centuries in my appointment calendar?"

Dave was the only one not chuckling. "Check out some of the stuff on NCO's website. They lay it out clear as day. The perfected new world order will only have two classes – first and second."

"What about the Third World?"

"It's never mentioned, as if it doesn't exist."

"It won't exist once the developing world raises everyone's standard of living."

"Sure thing – like the Earth has the resources to do *that*."

"Think about it. With life extension in play, what makes more sense – a slower or quicker turnover of the second class? A quicker turnover – of course. You don't want those under you with the same length of experience and longevity as you. That would make them dangerous; they'd start to think they were equals."

Faye's phone vibrated in her pocket. It was a welcome diversion from the debate. The text message was from her boss at Fort Detrick. With a glance, she knew it was cryptic and ominous.

C-Value Imperative / NBACC

The message was easy to decipher. NBACC was the National Biodefense Analysis and Countermeasures Center. *C-Value Imperative* was a code Faye had learned but never had seen used before. It directed Faye to call in immediately on a secure line. It signaled something had happened and everything around it was locked down. She was to act natural and tell no one.

Faye excused herself and hurried down the hall to her home office. She shut the door behind her and raced to open a safe built into the wall. Reaching in, she found the secure phone, the one she never had to use before.

She pressed "1" for speed dial and connected to voiceprint identification. She spoke clearly, saying her name, employee number, and repeating the text message. Not only the content but the order in which she spoke mattered. She waited for authorization, then relay to the appropriate extension.

The other end of the line picked up. Once a connection was made, an automated female voice gave notice. This conversation was being recorded.

"Dr. Gardner?" The unknown voice was heavy with the gravitas of rank and the urgency of its mission.

"Yes?"

"Sorry to disturb you. It was necessary. Where are you?"

"In my home office."

"Are you alone? Can you be overheard?"

Faye glanced back at her closed office door. On the other side, muted holiday music mixed with muffled conversation from the living room. "I'm alone."

"You've been specially requested for reassignment. Your expertise is vitally needed in a Project currently underway."

"What project?"

"I'm not at liberty to discuss it. A TS-4 clearance has been granted for you."

"TS-4?" Faye knew Level 3 was Top Secret. She had never heard of Level 4.

"Special circumstances. I cannot say much more, other than The Project is currently working to avert a major crisis. If you accept reassignment, you'll travel tomorrow morning to a new work location. It's unknown when you'll be able to return."

"What do I tell relatives and friends?"

"As little as possible. Simply tell them you have a temporary assignment elsewhere. Beyond that, you're still waiting to be briefed."

"Will I be able to contact anyone from The Project site?"

"There's a short list of allowed contacts. Immediate family members. Email and phone calls are allowed but no snail mail, no packages. All communications are screened and subject to redaction or additional restriction on a case-by-case basis."

"What about my current work in Building 1425?"

"A liaison will be assigned as go-between to help with transition. Direct communication between you and your old worksite ends with this call."

Faye fell silent despite a flood of questions. It was no use asking them now. An answer was expected, regardless.

"Will you accept reassignment?" The voice assumed her sense of duty and purpose was intact.

"Yes." Faye heard the answer from a place outside herself. A part of her wanted to go. But that was the part that never needed answers to the hard questions.

Faye expected the conversation to abruptly end with travel instructions for next morning. Instead, the voice stumbled over its first awkward pause.

"There's one other matter…I was to cover it only if you said yes."

"I'm listening."

"Your new station chief – will be Colin Insworth. Do you have a problem with that?"

Air caught in Faye's throat. She cleared it with, "Why should I?"

"Normally, people with histories together wouldn't be assigned to this Project, at least not in the same core compartment."

"What history are you referring to…" Faye felt exposed. She had no idea such personal information was tracked. Fifteen years after the fact, why would such a thing matter anyway?

"We needn't go into it. Just be aware, an exception has been made only because your skills are unique."

Faye fought off a flush of defensiveness. Any hint in her voice would only validate their suspicions. "So what are you asking?"

"All we need to know is whether or not this will be a problem."

"No problem for me." Immediately, she regretted the emphasis on *me*.

"Fine. Give your name to the guard at the main gate of Joint Base Andrews Naval Air Facility tomorrow at 0900. You'll be directed from there."

"How should I pack?"

"Bring as much or little as you like. Be assured, whatever you need will be provided. If you want, don't pack at all. Any other questions?"

"No."

"Then welcome to The Project, Dr. Gardner. Thank you for your service."

The line went dead. For a few seconds, Faye could only stand and listen to the silence. A core of isolation like no other enveloped her.

She had been a part of secret projects before but this was different. Way different. Neither anthrax nor Ebola, nothing had ever required the invocation of *C-*

Value Imperative. It was somebody's way of prepping her for what would come. They needn't say more to stress the seriousness of the matter. Fragments of the voice replayed in her head – "*avert a major crisis...an exception made...special circumstances*."

It told her nothing. She knew better than to read too much into the obvious.

She locked the phone away in the safe and started back to her dinner party. At the closed office door, thoughts of Jacob made her waver. He expected to spend the night with her. Should she still let him?

Tomorrow was Saturday. On other weekends when he stayed over, they often slept in the next morning. It was one way they managed to stretch intimate time together. But that wouldn't be possible now – or would it? How long would it take to get to Andrews? When should she tell him she had to go?

Worse yet, what would she say?

Questions came faster than answers.

The voice on the phone had made everything sound so matter-of-fact. It was nothing of the sort. It was complicated and difficult. The need for secrecy made everything so damned uncomfortable. She felt her life slipping out of her control.

It was the nature of a crisis; little respect was shown for human lives.

Thoughts of separation, of stress and the potential horrors to come swept through her. Her expertise was vitally needed. But that expertise played out behind the maximum confinement of a BSL-4 lab. Bio-Safety Level 4 was required in only the most dangerous of situations. Her imagination ran riot. Whatever could have happened? A possible pandemic? A looming biological terror attack?

If it was going to take work in a BSL-4 lab to avert the crisis – that only proved to her how extraordinary the danger truly was.

She took a deep breath but teared up anyway. There was no way of knowing when – or if she'd ever be back. Anything was possible but in her line of work, that wasn't good. Her mind was made up. If nothing else, the sweep of events wouldn't rob her of one last night of normalcy. Jacob would stay the night.

But more than that – she'd make sure they made love all night long.

CHAPTER 5

0918 Hours
Joint Base Andrews Naval Air Facility

An icy wind drove diagonal sheets of rain into sleet gathering on the windows. Clutching Gore-Tex over a pantsuit, Faye exited the black SUV and sprinted for the jet's fold-down steps. Holding the brim of his cap in place, her escort, an Air Force Colonel, followed behind with one black suitcase in hand.

Scurrying up the steps, Faye could see the jet's blue and white fuselage had only two markings. One stretched above six oval windows and boldly announced – *UNITED STATES OF AMERICA*. The second was the distinctive U.S. Air Force insignia, a white star and red-and-white stripes against a blue field. The insignia emblazoned the rear-mounted engine.

An open door and uniformed flight attendant waited at the top step. Faye hurried inside to find a fleeting sense of relief. The Colonel handed her suitcase to the attendant then shook her hand in parting. To her left, the cockpit door was open. Two pilots, a flight engineer, and a communications systems operator prepared for takeoff. At her service, the male flight attendant was pleasant but all business.

"Will you be needing anything out of your bag during the flight?"

Faye hadn't even considered it. "Ah…no."

"Very well. I'll stow it away. May I take your coat?"

With a quick unzip, she handed it over.

His hand directed her onward. "Mr. Insworth is expecting you in the second section, just beyond the first partition. The door panel slides to your right. If you need any help with it, let me know."

"Thank you."

Faye stepped farther back into the jet. The interior was functional but plush. It was designed for business but no comfort was neglected. She hadn't expected to be on a commercial flight but this went beyond anything anticipated.

Entering the second section, a familiar voice directed her. "Close it behind you. We want our conversation private."

The moment she dreaded had arrived. To suppress any show of emotion, she concentrated on a clinical inspection. She turned from the closed section panel and assessed the man walking up the aisle towards her.

She had hoped he'd be completely different; if possible, unrecognizable. As it was, he was older but so was she. Except for graying sideburns and a few more pounds around the middle, he was the same man she remembered. If anything, she sensed layers of experience had added a maturity once lacking.

The reality of working together again, possibly traveling alone, all of it pressed a nerve that forced quicker breaths. Before her was the man she had loved so many years before, loved with an innocence a woman could only offer once. And yet standing there, she was acutely aware of being sore from a long night of lovemaking with Jacob. The awkward juxtaposition rose to a blush, even as she reminded herself

– it was resentment, not love that she harbored for Colin Insworth now.

"Thank you for coming, Faye."

She nodded and waited to hear more.

"I know this is awkward – for both of us. More so for you since it came out of the blue. I've known for a couple of weeks it might come to this."

Faye realized she was going to have to say something sooner or later. She decided to divert her discomfort onto something else besides the two of them.

"Are we the only passengers?"

Colin nodded.

"So why the fancy ride?"

"This particular C-37A is usually reserved for DHS or DoD officials. I told my boss you're a priority. When I explained why – he sent this."

Colin led back to a seating area. He sat in a swivel rocker on one side of a table littered with paperwork and motioned Faye into a matching seat on the other side. As soon as she settled in, Colin dropped into a much more serious tone of voice.

"As a matter of fact, going someplace is only half of the reason for us to be sitting here. Call it what you will – this compartment functions as a shielded enclosure, a TEMPEST/EMSEC chamber. The chance of eavesdropping on us, electronically or otherwise, is virtually impossible. I needed a place to get you up to speed on what we're facing. We have to be absolutely sure what we say can't be overheard. Of course there are other places we could go to do the same thing but this does double duty – it also flies. By the time we get to The Project site, in a few hours, you'll be fully briefed and ready to go. There's a lot to cover."

Faye glanced out the window and noticed the engines hadn't been started.

"Do we have to wait for the weather to improve?"

"No. We're waiting for a decision from you."

"I don't understand."

"You've had since last night to think about this. Not a lot of time but I don't want to obligate you based on one phone call. Some secrets, once they're known, become too important to risk. It may sound melodramatic but sometimes it's true – lethal force has been authorized. Once you hear certain things, there's no going back. If for any reason you have second thoughts, I want to be sure you have one last chance to change your mind."

Faye noticed that the black SUV remained parked next to the jet.

Colin watched her search the rain.

"If you're in, there's no getting out. You can retire, you may quit, but once part of The Project, you'll always be part of The Project. A TS-4 security oath is a lifetime commitment regardless what you decide to do. It's strictly enforced. TS-4 is a special classification of SCI-Access – Sensitive Compartmented Information. Its primary purpose is to restrict subjects and programs not publicly acknowledged."

Faye looked Colin in the eye. "You said retirement is possible – even quitting?"

"Sure, but certain things are binding forever."

"Such as…"

"You can never acknowledge the existence of The Project or its work or your participation – even if parts of it should become public knowledge. No matter what you know, those outside The Project should never suspect from your actions that any crisis exists."

"What about family and friends."

"What about them?"

"Is a normal life ever possible?"

Colin waited before answering. Faye surmised no answer to such a question came easily. "In time, sure. First things first." He leaned closer across the table. "I can't emphasize this enough – your background uniquely qualifies you to help us. We're at a critical point. I hope you decide to stay but I understand if you don't. I'm sorry I can't tell you more to help you decide."

Faye had already made up her mind the night before. Rehashing the risks now served no purpose. Everything Colin said was to be expected. It was simply the disclaimer on the back of the adventure package ticket.

"I'm in. Let's get on with it."

Colin settled back and pressed a button on the intercom panel. Moments later, the jet's door closed and the engines started. The escort SUV made a U-turn and sped away across the tarmac. Clearance from the tower was immediate. Taxi and takeoff were executed as one smooth motion.

Faye turned her gaze to watch Washington D.C. disappear in the distance. Up through rainclouds soared the Gulfstream V. It wasn't until they reached cruising altitude in clear skies that Colin was comfortable enough to share secrets.

He poured coffee for the two of them. "Would you like breakfast or anything before we get started?"

"What do *you* think?" Her bristling answer startled even Faye. Was she really that annoyed at Colin? One wouldn't expect a fifteen-year-old grudge to be so close to the surface. Maybe it was his insistence on being so cordial that made her snap. In her experience, such things were out of character for him.

Luckily, Colin had taken her answer a whole different way.

"I think you'd rather find out what this is all about." He turned away to fetch something from a metal suitcase. He sat back down holding a small device in front of him. It looked like a cell phone.

"Taking my picture?" asked Faye.

"Looks like it, doesn't it."

After thumb-punching a few buttons, he reached across the table and set the device in front of her. Her gaze dropped to the small screen. On it was a database readout detailing Dr. Faye Gardner including photo, current address, government work status, and biographical background.

"What is this? My personnel file?"

"No." Colin pointed to the device. "Pick it up. Point it at me the same way then push the button on the side."

Faye complied. Within seconds, a database readout on Colin Insworth appeared on the screen. Faye considered the possibilities. Her mind raced.

"So what is it? Facial recognition?"

"No." Colin grabbed the device. He punched more buttons and handed it back.

Colin's name remained at the top of the screen but below it now was a graph.

Faye recognized the graphing technique but couldn't imagine how it related. Peaks along twin horizontal measures were labeled with numbers and an X and Y.

"STR Analysis..."

Colin sat back down. "Yes. Short Tandem Repeat. Those are the thirteen core STR loci that make up my genetic profile."

"You accessed the FBI's CODIS database?"

"No. We generated our genetic fingerprints using this device."

"That's impossible..." It came out, even as Faye saw the facts were otherwise.

"Scan any skin surface and the generated record is submitted to The Project database. If the record exists, a hit is returned to the screen. If it doesn't exist, the record is added and populated with photos and data as they come available."

Faye felt compelled to entertain her disbelief. "To do such a thing, nuclear DNA has to be extracted...precise polymorphic regions have to be amplified...and that only happens with two kinds of electrophoresis."

"Gel or capillary. Sure. Outside of The Project, I'd say you're correct." Colin held up the device. "This is the first thing you must know about."

Faye was in awe. "But it never touched us. It did it so fast..."

"This is RIDIS – *Remote Infrared DNA Identification Scanner*. It comes in many sizes, configurations, and capabilities. This is the most compact one so far."

"Infrared..."

"Far infrared and terahertz radiation is used. Among other things."

"Anybody can be ID'd just by pointing this at them?"

"That's the idea. The range is getting better all the time. Using a new type of laser, they scan from aircraft. Soon, they plan on doing this from orbit."

"Incredible."

"About twenty years ago, DARPA went looking for a way to improve on the CODIS database. Grants were awarded for proof of concept and various subsystems. Several grants went to universities. One was awarded to GeLixCo, the biotech company. It took a couple of years, but eventually GeLixCo had some success. That's when I was recruited as a liaison between them and The Project."

A flash of recognition filled Faye's face. She stiffened.

"That's when you left...USAMRIID." Faye avoided the obvious reference to Janis. Her pause before saying USAMRIID had said enough.

Colin noticed her reaction and took it as a sign. The past was a large part of what they were going to have to work with. He'd have to deal with it sooner or later. His mood shifted. Pensive and somber, he summed up his confession.

"The past is what it is. In the last two weeks I've had to push a lot of that aside. That doesn't mean I'm free of it either. I'm the first one to second-guess the choices I've made. It doesn't get easier, looking back, wondering how it might have been. I did what I did. I was a different person then. I see that now. I was more full of myself – and less complete. I'm sorry for what that meant for those around me. I don't know what else to say about that."

Faye fought back tears. "Some people would say you have a lot of nerve."

"You're right; some would." Colin repressed the urge to say more. "Others would realize there must be a serious crisis to force me to do this at all. You don't know the half of it."

Colin's frankness took Faye by surprise. She said nothing; she couldn't.

To deflect both of their emotions, Colin got back to business.

"Fifteen years ago, a GeLixCo team in Puerto Rico had a breakthrough. When DARPA combined that breakthrough with other work universities had done, government scientists realized that remote scans could return much more than Short Tandem Repeats. A person's entire DNA signature could be captured."

"Just as quickly?"

"Not at first but now, yes. Certain people above DARPA decided to keep it under wraps. They wanted a pilot project to test the limits of what was possible without civil rights constraints. Once the scope of the technology was proven, they intended to lift an appropriate level of secrecy and develop commercial applications. They expected a path of normalization for RIDIS just like GPS had gone through."

"That didn't happen."

"No. The RIDIS database grew quickly in secret. The advantages of keeping it that way – just one more year, then another year – it all became too seductive. After a while, it was hard to imagine how they'd ever be able to admit the truth without it looking bad. Too much had happened beyond the law. The issue was kicked down the road. Future administrators would have to deal with it."

"What size of database are we talking about?"

"Now? North America, Europe, huge numbers beyond. One-third of humanity."

"In one database, verified by a quick scan?"

Colin nodded. "We've been collecting data for over ten years. We've coupled RIDIS scanners to ATMs, airport security scanners, even the eye test machine where you get your driver's license. Every baby is added to the database at birth. Push a button in some elevators and you've been scanned. Go through a toll booth or a revolving door, a record of ID is tabulated. Swipe a credit card and the machine scans you. If a timestamp is included with any one of these, movements can be tracked. We don't have time to go into all the ways RIDIS scanners are being used."

"So what do you do for The Project?"

"They put me in charge of the database."

"Sounds all-encompassing. What exactly does that mean?"

"I'm responsible for the data's availability, integrity, and survivability."

"But you're not talking about a simple identification database – you're sitting on the collective genetic information of humanity."

"Exactly what I told my bosses several years ago. I couldn't believe the limited way they were using the data. Taking real time IDs of people without their knowledge was one thing. But they hadn't bothered to do any genetic trending or comparative analysis of the data itself."

"What a waste." Faye gazed at the RIDIS device in hand. Disenchantment stained the marvel of it.

"I asked for permission to run a pilot project. All I needed to get started was a supercomputer and a couple geneticists to guide individual studies."

"They turned you down."

"No. They gave me everything I wanted – and more."

"There's a problem with that?"

"Call it a crisis."

Colin sat back. He let the severity of the moment build.

"Six months ago we discovered something in the data – something we didn't want to believe. At first we were certain it had to be caused by data corruption. The more we looked at it, the more we hoped we could prove ourselves wrong. We've busted our asses ever since." He activated an electronic tablet and turned it around. His tone was grave. "We're not wrong."

Faye took tablet in hand. Onscreen, classified internal memos were labeled *USAP*. She had only heard rumors of *Unacknowledged Special Access Programs.* Legend had it black material like this didn't exist. The Congress, the Joint Chiefs of Staff, not even the President had access to such material or knew of its existence.

All the memos confirmed what Colin said.

"As best as anyone can tell, the DNA trend is confirmed..." Colin hesitated, bracing himself and preparing Faye for the impact. "...children under the age of fourteen will be sterile when they reach puberty."

Faye's expression was blank with disbelief, then shock.

Colin drove home the point. "All children...everywhere."

The weight of what Faye had heard pressed in on her. Could such a thing be true? It couldn't be, could it? Colin continued to speak but she barely heard him now.

"If true, as we believe it is, the world is producing its last human generation."

"That can't be!" Unable to accept such an apocalyptic concept on face value, Faye launched into questions. "Why are the parents OK? They reproduce."

"We aren't sure. But we think we've found a couple markers that give a clue."

"What markers?"

"We discovered them only two weeks ago – Ghyvir-C virus markers. That's where you come in."

Faye's thoughts rushed back fifteen years to the last project both Janis Insworth and she worked on at USAMRIID. They were testing a new giant virus found in the wild – the Ghyvir-C Virus. Faye had even suggested the Ghyvir name. Not knowing what to call it at first, she had lab staff label related items *GHYVIR*. It was simply shorthand for *Giant Hybrid Virus*. It was hybrid because the giant virus had another, smaller virus inside of it, a parasite virus generically known as a *sputnik* virus.

As Faye collected memories, Colin continued.

"As you know, the virus swept the world fourteen years ago. Today, it's found on every continent. Oddly enough, in that time it's resisted mutation. As best as we can determine, parents who are infected with Ghyvir-C produce sterile children."

"No, that's not right!" Faye struggled to remember specifics from her USAMRIID lab work years ago. "Ghyvir-C turned out to act like a rhinovirus – it produced nothing but a common cold. That's why it's called Ghyvir-*C*. The 'C' is for common cold."

"That's right. A common cold – in the parents. No tests were ever done to determine what exposure might do to their future children."

"Rhino viruses don't act that way. Something's wrong. It doesn't make sense."

"You sound like my boss. Certain people want to keep these wild ideas under wraps until absolutely proven. They fear mass hysteria."

"They're not convinced by the data?"

"Exceptional claims require extraordinary proof."

"What would it take?"

"I'm guessing your knowledge of Ghyvir-C and my access to RIDIS."

"How can you be sure the effect is sterility?"

"We've done tests. All the children have the same something happen to them between the fourth and sixth weeks of fetal growth. That's critical time in the development of their reproductive cells – the germ cells."

Faye held her head in hand and closed her eyes. "I was told we were trying to *avert* a crisis. That's a lie – the real secret is – the crisis has happened."

"No, what you were told is absolutely true – we are desperately trying to avert a crisis. But the crisis isn't sterility. It's extinction."

Faye absorbed the impact of Colin's admission.

"Project Administers are between a rock and a hard place. By accident, their secret, illegal database may have stumbled upon a monumental crisis. But to openly research if the crisis is real, they would have to admit to the world what they've been up to. That's a problem; one they're still wrestling with. What if they come clean and it turns out to be a false alarm? You see why they want absolute proof."

"If this is true, every scientist in the world needs to be enlisted to find an answer. This is too big, too serious for bureaucratic games. If the clock is ticking on the last generation, there's no time to lose. To hell with petty secrets!"

"There's more to it than just getting world scientists involved. We have to counterbalance added research with the damage to society that would be done if news of this got out. Imagine the social consequences if people thought humanity was facing its last generation. What would happen to family structure, planning for the future, people deciding to get married or have children? It's hard to imagine the panic and fallout – increases in crime, suicides, disruption of social order – the fabric of society might unravel. With no future, many would live in the moment in reckless ways that could bring down everything. I'm not sure if Project bosses are doing the right thing – but considering the alternatives, it's not the wrong thing."

Staring out the window in shock, Faye could only mumble.

"Where are we going?"

"Dugway Proving Ground, Utah. We fly into Michael Army Airfield. The Proving Ground is about eighty miles southwest of Salt Lake City…"

"I know where it is," snapped Faye.

"You've been there?"

"No, but I've heard about some of the things that have gone on there."

"There are always lots of stories…"

"Yeah, hundreds of open air tests secretly conducted in the '50s and '60s. The bacteria and viruses were known to cause disease in humans, animals, and plants. Nobody knows to this day how many people in the surrounding area were exposed."

"Don't worry about open air tests. The RIDIS database is kept underground."

Faye pulled her concentration from the clouds to look Colin in the eye.

"Don't you find that ironic – RIDIS is buried."

Chapter 6

NovoSenectus Corporate Business Park
Hyderabad, India

The sense of relief was brief. Janis Insworth exited through a revolving door and entered a covered, elevated walkway leading to the parking structure. Behind her sprawled a bustling biotech campus, its glass and metal buildings arranged as spokes around a central administration complex. Much of her professional life had been spent in those buildings. Now the sight of them weighed her down.

She hurried across the skybridge, unable to keep her gaze from following the manicured flower beds and walking paths laid out below. The parklike grounds always had been a refuge from the intensity of work performed inside the sterile labs.

Now they were haunted.

The walking paths had been a favorite place for Riya and Janis to stroll. The gardens were a seasonal joy that brought to mind the cycles of life, the very thing they were studying. At first when they started walking together, work issues were the topic of conversation. In time, as they drew closer, personal stories were shared, along with dreams for the future.

In the place where friendship had blossomed, there was no sign of it now. Janis pulled back her gaze to focus on the parking structure. Her steps quickened.

With car in sight, Janis answered her cell phone after checking caller ID.

"Malcolm?"

"Janis, can you meet me? Right away."

"I'm on my way to police headquarters to find out about Alyssa."

"Can it wait?" Malcolm's voice was agitated, insistent.

"What's going on?"

"I can't tell you on the phone. Where are you?"

"I'm leaving NovoSenectus."

"What are you doing *there*?" His rushed words bordered on accusation.

"I picked up a few things from my office."

"Is that all?"

Janis held back an answer and debated the wisdom of offering the truth. She unlocked her car and sat inside. "They offered me the Director of Research post."

As both knew, that had been Riya's position on the *GenLET* Project.

"What did you tell them?"

"I requested a leave of absence. I simply can't concentrate right now under the stress of everything."

"Good. That's perfect."

"What do you mean?"

"There's something I have to show you. You need to see this."

"Is it what we talked about?"

"Meet me at the railway station parking lot by Sanjeeviah Park. It's off Necklace Road."

"I know where it is."

"Come straight away. Make sure you're not followed."

Malcolm hung up before Faye could say anything more. Sitting in the car alone, she felt the parking structure close in around her. She searched the open spaces for others who might be watching. Her eyes settled on a small half-dome of black plastic mounted on the concrete ceiling nearby. It was elevated above the spot where cars entered and exited the structure. Behind the obscuring black plastic was one of the many ever-watchful security cameras.

Janis started the car and drove away at slower than normal speed. As she headed out on the road, she watched the rearview mirror. The ride to the railway station took twenty minutes. It was more than enough time to imagine the best and worst and contemplate the unimaginable.

At Sanjeeviah MMTS Station, Faye pulled up alongside Malcolm's parked car. He sat and waited while she got out and walked around to his passenger side door and got in. It was the middle of the afternoon and few other cars were around. Another train wasn't due for a while. It was a public place but it was unlikely they'd be disturbed.

Janis was direct. "What's so important that can't wait?"

Malcolm was stone-faced, wound tight enough to be facing combat. He reached into the back seat and grabbed a laptop computer from the floor.

"I know why Riya was killed." He opened the computer between them and began to type. "This changes everything."

"You got into that place in Puerto Rico?"

"Remotely. I bought access to a back door."

"Were you able to download Riya's backup?"

"Part of it. Maybe a third. Something happened; I got kicked off the network before I could get it all." He glanced up and scanned the area around the car.

"What about GeLixCo? Can they trace the connection back to you?"

"I did what I could to prevent that. Nothing's foolproof. I'm not positive they detected me. I hid behind several hops; the routing was complicated. Any one of several nodes could have dropped me." Malcolm stopped typing. "This is it. The downloaded copy still requires the password. It took me a while to figure out the right format."

"I thought Riya told you the password."

"She said it was our anniversary." For a moment, Malcolm softened to explain. "She called the day we met our anniversary. June 3, 2006 – a Saturday."

Janis watched Malcolm's fingers type out SA632006. The moment he finished, a blank file folder onscreen populated with unencrypted files.

Malcolm scanned the list looking for one in particular.

"We can't stay here long. You can read all this later but right now there are a couple of things you should see."

A span of five documents opened, each one offset and on top of the last. Malcolm turned the laptop to face Janis. As her eyes raced down the page, Malcolm rushed to give details.

"Riya wasn't a spy. She got into something she wasn't supposed to see. Then she made the mistake of confronting the wrong people about it."

The next moments crashed over Janis as waves of information overload. She listened while her eyes disbelieved what they read.

Malcolm forced a summary through rising pain and anger.

"Riya discovered certain parts of *GenLET* were being passed to a secret lab in Austria. She must have stumbled on it by accident and was curious. When she dug deeper, she found out the Austrian lab was preparing a *select agent.*"

Janis interrupted. "*Select agent* – that's what you overheard on the phone. You said Riya was upset because they were *selecting an agent*."

"It was right there all the time. I missed it."

"With all the talk of spies, a bio-defense meaning slipped my mind."

"We both missed it."

"A *select agent* – a biological agent that is or could be *weaponized*."

"They're planning on having a startup company in Shaanxi Province, China produce it for them." Malcolm pointed at a document. "It's right there – the place is in the Baoji Hi-Tech Industrial Development Zone."

Janis felt flushed even as a chill went through her. "What does *GenLET* have to do with a biological weapon?"

"A trickier question is why would Eugene Mass want to produce one."

"Mass?"

"He's behind the Austrian lab. I also think he was on the phone call I overheard with Riya."

"What exactly are they making?"

Malcolm pointed to another document. "It's called the 3rd Protocol."

"But what is it?"

"An influenza virus – designed to take out six billion people."

"What!" Janis thought she had heard wrong.

"The mission statement is clear. The 3rd Protocol is being designed to selectively, surgically collapse human population. Thin the herd. The goal is a world population stabilized at 500 million – and kept there."

"This can't be real…there must be some mistake."

"Don't you see? Riya knew too much. They couldn't take the chance of her going public."

"You're saying Mass had her killed?"

"The simplest explanation is usually correct. Riya was in a position to expose his plot and I know from the phone call she didn't like what she'd found. At the same time, New Class Order has been winning over hearts and minds around the world, creating doubters about life extension therapies. The elegant solution was to take her out and have NCO blamed for it."

"There's more to it. I still think NCO knows something about Alyssa. It doesn't make sense for Mass to kidnap her." A swirl of possibilities spun Janis dizzy. "*GenLET* has nothing to do with an influenza pandemic."

"From what I read, the Austrian lab is not interested in *GenLET* directly. It's after the ingenious way you devised to deliver the therapy so quickly."

"Nothing about my work is a weapon."

"You developed a way to genetically alter bone marrow, the place where blood is produced. That little bit of magic convinces the body to produce a continual, slow-release of *GenLET* therapy agents over time – directly from the marrow. Riya even predicted when news of your work got out, you'd be the one with a Nobel Prize."

"I don't understand. What does bone marrow have to do with this thing – this 3rd Protocol?"

"The 3rd Protocol's pathogen needs a way to target the overall population based upon individual blood markers. What better place to target blood than bone marrow? As twisted as it sounds, the reasoning is egalitarian. They want the more populace ethnic groups affected by the 3rd Protocol more aggressively."

"The virus is being engineered to profile by race?"

Malcolm nodded. "Mass consulted a series of whitepapers put out by something called 8-Ball."

"8-Ball?"

"Yeah. Here's one of their studies. It concludes…"

Malcolm read from the screen.

"…the most equitable method of population collapse would take into consideration the proportional segments of ethnic diversity. By definition, the most numerous people produce the greater portion of the population problem facing the Earth. To be just, a larger carbon footprint, nationally or ethnically, would by necessity require a comparatively larger share of pruning."

"He's designing a virus that racially profiles to ensure the same ethnic diversity after the population collapses?"

"And something in your work makes that possible."

"That's crazy. What the hell does he think he's doing?"

"According to the plan, it's necessary to save the Earth."

"Murdering six billion people!"

"The 8-Ball studies include all kinds of simulations and projections, even contingency plans for post-collapse scenarios. One study points out that 60% of the world's population is in Asia, 40% in China and India alone. That's why it recommends releasing the agent first in Asia, especially in large seaport cities. They've done a lot of research on swine and bird flu, anything where genetic data transfers from animals to humans…"

"Zoogenic agents…"

"He wants it to look that way. It'll be a good cover story."

"My God…"

"Do you have any idea what 8-Ball could be?"

Janis strained to focus. "No. I don't."

"Mass uses whitepapers sponsored by 8-Ball to anchor what he's doing. I'm not certain, but it looks like Mass isn't working alone."

Janis thought back. "There's only one thing I can think of – but it couldn't have anything to do with this."

"You never know…"

"Back at USAMRIID, when I worked there, they had this thing in Building 527 – a test sphere. It had many names but everyone knew it by its nickname. 8-Ball."

"What was it?"

"A huge biological warfare chamber, a testing facility; they called it the *one-million-liter test sphere*."

"A million liters – that's quite a test."

"It's a relic. The whole thing was decommissioned long time ago. They only keep it because it's the largest aerobiology chamber ever constructed. It's on the National Register of Historic Places."

"What rubbish!"

"It has to be something else. The 8-Ball test sphere has nothing to do with this." Janis navigated to another document.

The ring of Malcolm's phone startled them both. He answered it; the conversation was brief. Janis continued to cycle through open documents.

"Who's that?"

Malcolm was grim. "NovoSenectus. They need me for an assignment right away."

"Were you expecting this?"

"My work is far less predictable than yours. It's hard to say."

Paging through windows on the screen, Janis inadvertently brought up a saved copy of an email. As quick as her eyes could scan, they fell upon a word that shocked her.

"What's this?"

Malcolm craned his neck to get a look. "Oh, I forgot to close that. It's an email from an old contact. Why? What's the problem."

"What's this list of words?"

"It's just a list of words. No bother."

Janis braced herself. "What contact? Where did you get this?"

"Why do you need to know?"

Janis felt like she was surrounded and had just opened her eyes. "Tell me what this is! Are we working together or not!"

"All right, all right. I know someone who has a hacker on his payroll. The hacker uses searchbots to troll government networks looking for new words. That's all it is."

"What kind of *new words*?"

"Acronyms, jargon, anything really."

"What good are they to you?"

"Everything starts somewhere. If you want to find icebergs, look for the tips. It's amazing what pops up in regular conversation, often unclassified. A simple acronym can be a clue to a whole lot more."

"Who is this person, this contact of yours?"

"You don't really expect me to tell you. What's your problem anyway? If we're working together, as you say, then explain."

Janis took a deep breath. Her eyes riveted to the screen.

"I recognize one of these words."

Malcolm jerked with interest. "Which one?"

"BIOPONORE."

"No shit! What does it mean?"

"I know what it means to me." Janis stiffened as she looked over at Malcolm. "*Biological Point of No Return.*"

"How in the devil do you know that?"

A sour smile creased Janis' lips. "You won't believe it."

"Try me."

Janis admitted, "I made up the word – over twenty years ago."

Doubt shocked Malcolm's face. "Like bloody hell you did!"

A fog of memory held Janis rapt. "Back in college I made it up to tease my best friend. She liked to study and I liked to party. She thought I dated around too much. I thought she was afraid of men. I used to rag on her about how fast her biological clock was ticking. I laughed at her and said a lot of rude things. I told her she'd never have any children unless she loosened up. I warned her BIOPONORE was coming."

"Charming. What does that have to do with my email?"

"This can't be a coincidence! What are the chances somebody else made up the exact same crazy word?"

"What am I supposed to believe – that your friend is using your word as part of some government project?"

"The last I heard, my friend was still working at USAMRIID."

"Really." Malcolm was suddenly more serious. "The same place that has that thing – the test sphere."

Janis nodded. "8-Ball."

"What's your friend's name?"

"Faye Gardner. We haven't spoken in years."

"Why not?"

"A lot of things. We didn't agree on the dual-use aspects of our work. Later…it got personal."

"Do you think she'd work on something like 3rd Protocol?"

"No! Of course not."

"It doesn't look good. We know Eugene Mass is using research from 8-Ball to plot the collapse of world population. 8-Ball might be his nickname for USAMRIID, the place that has the massive test sphere. Now we find out there's a good chance your friend, who just so happens to work there, might be connected to something called *Biological Point of No Return.* It doesn't take much to connect the dots."

"She wouldn't do such a thing. Besides, you can't actually think the U.S. government is mixed up with Eugene Mass in a plot to kill six billion people?"

"Not the government; maybe powerful elements hidden within. Some things are kept so secret, I doubt even the government knows how they operate or get funding."

"Faye and I may not be friends now but I know her. She wouldn't be a part of this."

"Look at it another way. Maybe some deep-cover research group discovered something about climate change, or the depletion of oil reserves, or an impending fresh water crisis, something big. If a secret branch of government was convinced that a catastrophe was about to hit the planet, who could stop them from deploying their solution?"

"The 3rd Protocol."

"If you had to decide between everyone dying or a preemptive strike to thin the herd and save humanity, what would you choose?"

"You're assuming they would only have those two options."

"It would make sense to move the project offshore, outsourced to a like-minded mogul, someone who could cloak the real work behind something as controversial as life extension. It's the magician's art of misdirection."

"You're talking hypothetical nonsense."

"As hypothetical as scientists being murdered and children being kidnapped? As hypothetical as Riya telling me her contact at GeLixCo was none other than another ex-employee of USAMRIID – your ex-husband Colin? You say he's disappeared. How convenient, especially if he's now working for a deep-cover branch of government."

The references to Alyssa and Colin struck home. Janis decided to force the issue. "We can't be sure. I won't jump to conclusions based on a word on a random list – a list from somebody who got it from somebody else. We need more information and you have contacts. Whoever sent you this email must know more – or they can find out more. The stakes are high enough – you need to lean on them."

Malcolm took back the laptop and closed it.

Janis sensed his reticence was strategic but wasn't sure.

"Who's behind the email? What's going on? All I want is my daughter back! Did somebody put you up to this?"

As Janis broke down into tears, Malcolm grabbed her by the arm

"All right. I'll tell you what I can. Do you remember, years ago, when a group calling itself *Friends of the Ocean* got their hands on plastic-eating microbes and dumped them in the ocean?"

"I think so…"

"The microbes were stolen from the U.S. Navy. The thief was never caught and *Friends of the Ocean* never gave up their source."

"So what."

Malcolm leaned closer. "A few years ago, I got a tip. It led me to some incriminating evidence – evidence that identified the man who stole those microbes."

"But you said the thief was never caught."

"That's right. Since then, I've been leveraging what I know. As long as the thief sends me email with answers to my questions, I sit on the evidence."

"You're blackmailing him?"

"He's in a very sensitive position, with access to all sorts of things. He doesn't want to jeopardize what he has. In exchange, I'm willing to do business with him."

"I don't suppose you're going to tell me his name."

"Makes no difference. It's the same name he and I agreed upon years ago."

"What is it?"

"Knockout Mouse."

"Strange. Any reason for the genetic reference?"

"You'd have to ask him. He came up with the name but it fits him. Over the years, he's impressed me as somewhat of a social mutation. Maybe he sees himself the same way – just an engineered little mouse. He's the mutation that shows us how full functioning we are by comparison."

"Sounds like you two have an odd relationship. Symbiotic yet parasitical."

"In my experience, those two aren't so far apart. The friend of my enemy's enemy is still not my friend. And now that I've told you that, it's your turn. You're hiding something about Colin."

"Why would I?"

"He's the father of your child. You loved him once. You still may. It's only natural."

"We didn't have that kind of divorce."

"Aren't you the least bit curious why Riya named him as her contact at GeLixCo?"

"Of course I am."

"But not enough to ask him."

"Have you heard anything I said?"

"How convenient." Malcolm checked the time by glancing at his phone. "I've got to go."

"Just like that? And what do we do about all of this?"

Malcolm looked Janis up and down. "That's one big fucking question. What do you want to do?"

Janis stared out at nowhere. "I don't know. If in doubt, I go the way I feel. Especially if what I know doesn't make sense."

Janis opened the car door to go but Malcolm stopped her.

"Here – take these." He handed over his laptop and cell phone.

"What's this?" Janis had them in hand but froze.

"I've got this assignment to do. I don't want to risk having Riya's backup found on me. My private phone has emails from Knockout Mouse. I still have my work phone. Keep them for me until I get back. I'll give you a call."

Janis accepted the laptop and phone with a nod.

Malcolm stopped her again as she leaned out the door.

"Hey – it's better knowing what we know."

Janis muted her reaction. She stepped out of the car and held the door open. Within her, a sinking feeling told her the world had changed. The sunlight felt foreign, lighting a place where darkness hid in plain sight.

The impulse to answer Malcolm passed.

She shut the door and walked away.

CHAPTER 7

Near the Forest of Soignes
South of Brussels, Belgium

Plush carpet muffled the hurried steps of Leah Mass. The estate house was large but Leah knew right where to find her husband. With each stride along the hallway, sounds of conversation and family laughter faded from the first floor below. So did the warmer light.

Eugene expected his wife to barge into his study any second. His meditation had overstayed its welcome yet, as the door opened and Leah rushed in, he couldn't move from the window. A dutiful diversion had become a brooding daydream. All sense of purpose was lost on a higher but elusive focus. It was all he could do to watch the last light of day fade from the woods in the west.

"There you are…" Leah pretended her discovery was incidental. "Is everything all right?"

"Everything?" Purposely not loud enough, the word couldn't be a question.

Leah closed the door behind her. She was accustomed to maintaining privacy in the study. She approached her husband from behind and laid hands on him with gentle reserve, as if not to startle him.

"Everyone downstairs misses you."

"I was just about to come down."

Eugene Mass turned and read the concern on his wife's face. She was still a beautiful woman, at least to him. Sixteen years younger than he, she was his second wife and far more of a kindred spirit than anyone he had known.

"I was getting worried. What was the call about?"

"You can imagine." He brushed his fingers through her hair and stepped away.

"I take it the news isn't good."

"Nothing I can't contain." The inference was clear.

"Someone else might know – besides Riya?"

Eugene nodded, prompting Leah's sighs of desperate disappointment.

"I warned you this was not the way."

"Don't start." Eugene tamped down on a simmering frustration.

"You didn't need to go down this path. It's so unnecessary."

"Under normal circumstances, *none* of this would have to happen." Restless, Eugene searched his desk for answers that couldn't possibly be there. "You said it yourself – we live in a time that forces good people to embrace drastic measures."

"The whole situation's drastic! That's not what I'm talking about and you know it. You're risking so much more by this foolishness. Doing nothing would have served us much better."

"Where's the guarantee? There's no way of telling what might have happened if the information got out."

"You have resources. Who is everyone going to believe? It's far better to force them to prove a negative than give them positive evidence by trying to cover it up."

"I can't take that chance. Our work is too important."

"You can't afford to be this obvious. Where does it stop?"

Leah was the only person in the world who dared talk back to Eugene. For her love and his sanity, he allowed it. With his focus now on diffusing the situation, he held back the impulse to argue. There was still a family dinner party to return to and a daughter and son-in-law downstairs who shouldn't guess anything was wrong.

"Don't worry. All we need is a little more time."

His attempt to calm Leah only shifted her mood from irritated to sullen.

"It wouldn't take much to ruin everything we've worked for."

"Soon, none of this will matter. Remember, we're building a sustainable future where once there was none. This isn't just about us; there's a whole world at stake."

Leah said nothing at the one time Eugene thought she was primed to do so. He turned to read cues from her body language. "This isn't like you. Why worry when you know I have the resources to do what's necessary?"

Exasperation drained from Leah's voice. In its place was something sour and dreadful. "The real horror is that Riya was just the first of so many more to come."

Leah's confession was a truth too raw to be stated so frankly. What it implied was not something Eugene liked being reminded of despite his commitment to the plan. For what it made him feel, he resented Leah's sudden sense of revulsion. A compassionate but exaggerated conscience should never overrule a clear, altruistic vision of what needed to be done. In reflex, his resentment turned flippant.

"Every remodeling project starts with demolition."

The reference was distasteful. "Don't talk like that. You make it sound so wooden and impersonal."

"We've gone over this a thousand times."

"There's sanctity to sacrifice. That's what it comes down to. The sacrifice of many for the greater good. For our children. I hate to hear you be so debased about it."

"If there was another way…if the world had time…"

"The necessity wouldn't be so clear. I know. You've told me."

"Why go into this again? We both agreed someone must take action – someone with the power and means to do something on the scale required."

"It's not about that. I agree something needs to be done. I have issues with how you're going about it. We're going to have to live a long time with the legacy of how this was done. I want that legacy to be a blessing, not a burden."

Eugene was suddenly incensed. His voice fell to a whisper. His anger was not directed at Leah, but everyone he had witnessed giving little but lip service to the crisis enveloping the planet. "Same old story. Everyone wants to be at the feast – but no one wants to get their hands dirty killing the beast!"

For the sake of their evening together, Leah thought better of snapping back.

Eugene stepped around his desk in a huff and sat down. "After a lifetime of trying everything else, I see no other way. No one else is stepping up. I love the fact you have sensibilities. But to get through this, you need to love the fact that I don't. How else is anything going to get done?"

Eugene didn't expect an answer but he hoped for one.

Instead, there was a knock at the door. “Grandpa?”

The child’s voice belonged to Jayden, their nine-year-old grandson.

Leah retreated to the door and opened it. “Here he is.” She braved a smile in the presence of innocence.

The boy idolized his grandfather for the way he doted over him. Jayden shuffled into the room, enthused to be the center of attention. “I’ve got the billiards table all set up. Are we still going to play?”

Leah headed out the door with an eye on Eugene. “See you downstairs.”

Seated behind his desk, Eugene nodded and watched the boy approach.

“Mom said not to bother you but I didn’t think you’d mind.”

Eugene patted the boy on the back. “Not at all.”

“What are you doing?”

“Just some work.”

“You have to work *tonight*?”

“I got a phone call I had to take.”

Jayden snooped on the desk and jiggled the computer mouse, canceling the screensaver. An open document blazed on the screen before them.

“What’s that?”

Eugene leaned back. “A speech I’m working on.”

“Who’s it for?”

“A university. They asked me to talk to the students.”

“What about?”

Eugene considered an appropriate way to sum it up. “A lot of things – how the present becomes the future. What happens to those who ignore the past.”

Jayden strained to read the title, then pointed at it. “How do you say that?”

“The Anthropocene Dilemma.”

“That’s a funny word.”

“Anthropocene is the period of time we’re living in right now. Just like the dinosaurs lived in the Jurassic Period – right now is the *Anthropocene* Period.”

“Oh…” Jayden’s confused lack of interest spurred Eugene to explain.

“This is the time in Earth’s history when human activities for the first time are having a big impact on the whole planet. We’re using up the Earth, the oceans, we’re changing the weather and making it hard for all the animals to live. There are so many of us and we’ve gotten so good at what we do, we’ve become a bad thing for the Earth. We have to realize if we hurt Mother Earth, we hurt ourselves.”

Jayden fidgeted. “So what’s a dilemma?”

“It’s when you’re trapped in a place with only two ways to go – but neither way gets you out of the trap.”

“So what do you do?”

“With any luck, you won’t have to worry about that. Grownups are going to fix that problem before you’re old enough to care. Come on, let’s go downstairs.”

“Great! More time to play! I bet I can beat you this time!”

Eugene stood and led the boy towards the open door. For the next hour, the old man would try to lose himself in the moment – enjoying the present without a care for the unthinkable future it was becoming.

CHAPTER 8

Spanish Wells Plantation
Hilton Head Island, South Carolina

A restive ocean gave fair warning in the darkness beyond the three-acre estate. Curtis Labon strolled through the damp air, relishing the sting of its chill. Something more purifying than refreshing could be found in cold discomfort. He pressed his steps forward and let the late hour induce a bitter reflection. He didn't believe in sin – odd how self-imposed penance felt good.

There was no escape from thoughts of Noah, his son away at college and now suddenly estranged. It was easy to explain why; harder for the heart to understand in ways that led to acceptance. The reason seemed clear; the all-consuming idealism of youth. And yet, thinking back on a busy life, Curtis couldn't shake the rising dread that it might be due to something more.

Blame altruism. Any protest sign outside meetings of the G20 or WTO would sum it up. The boy didn't understand how his father could be part of the Hydra strangling the planet. No matter what anyone did to throttle the monster, it always managed to grow another head. Global governance, corporate multinationals, NGOs were used as shills in a shell game of power and money. Corruption, avarice, and self-interest had been refined into functional specs and standard operating procedures. Nothing existed outside the rigged zero-sum game.

As the beast fed, his father had become rich. In the eyes of his son, being rich, by itself, was enough of a stigma. Worst yet, Noah had only recently discovered how the family fortune had started. In his son's eyes, biopharma had been bad enough, but adding to the riches by mining oil sands from ore deposits in the Athabasca region of northern Alberta, Canada was being dirty rich in the worst way.

Curtis quickened his steps along the path. The hypocrisy of both sides was infuriating. With experience, he had recognized it for what it was. The unholy excesses of the rich elite were legend. But that was only half of the saga. The very people who held the most righteous contempt for the Hydra were also the ones most addicted to the lifestyle, gizmos, and conveniences the beast made possible.

The boy's world view was simplistic and naïve. But like a child's innocent remark, it held a kernel of truth. On the other side, the Hydra was only a beast insomuch that human nature was beastly. Neither side had the answer. Both sides framed the problem. Regardless, Noah had disowned him.

Curtis' mind raced, his heart even faster. It felt like finally arriving only to discover he had everything except the one thing he wanted most, the one thing that couldn't be bought. Some things were hard to admit even if no one else would ever know. A life lived well was not always a life lived to its greatest potential, its highest calling. Curtis had no escape from searing self-judgment. Years had flown by and what had he done? Too often he had acquiesced in pursuit or enjoyment of comforts instead of working through what he knew to be right.

He could claim relentless reality had jaded him. He could argue it's easy to be idealistic when practical facts are skewed or ignored as unimportant. Even if he was right, it was still an excuse. Sick with himself for a life of slipping into patterns, becoming complacent, he pushed forward under the solitary cover of night.

Somehow he had to devise a means for atonement.

Behind him, an old world masterpiece of a house was ablaze with light. At the end of the cobbled trail, a covered dock was dimly lit by a full moon sliding higher behind a haze of marine air. Along the wide stretch of prime waterfront, the lap and toss of salt water announced the undisputable border between worlds. In nature, things could be that certain, unlike the world of man.

Behind a post near the end of the dock, the tip of a cigarette glowed red. A human form took shape and snapped Curtis' reverie. It was a disappointment to find he wasn't alone. It was some relief when Hasuru Tamasu appeared in the mist. Curtis could deal with Hasuru. Not so if the master of the house, Herr Heinrich, had appeared. Curtis was apt to become overly frank in the late hour. Heinrich would never appreciate that level of honesty.

Hasuru made an indolent show out of blowing smoke at the moon and Curtis caught an acrid whiff. "Still polluting the air I see…"

Hasuru didn't move. "It's OK. This tobacco's *organic.*"

Curtis didn't laugh. His lingering self-judgment had a momentum. Hasuru was dead serious which was even more pitiful, especially since there was something infuriatingly meme-like about the illogic. Tribal knowledge had reduced human society to a cargo cult, awash in the certainty of its enlightened delusions, ever at the ready with ditto-headed catch-phrases and aphorisms in place of critical thinking.

Hasuru registered Curtis' lack of humor as disapproval but ignored it.

"What happened? Did Heinrich kick you out of the house?"

Curtis stopped alongside Hasuru, faced the ocean, and shoved hands in pockets. "I'm surprised he invited me."

"He believes business should be done in privacy and comfort. It's the way he likes it."

"This place is nice. Not sure if it suits him."

"He got a good deal on it – from a Senator."

"Just in the neighborhood, eh?"

"Not quite. They have some new thing together."

"Such as?"

"Green software. For government. Something for the smart grid. Senator Rigis is heavily invested."

"I didn't know Heinrich was into software."

"He isn't. But he just acquired a company that designs smart sockets, smart meters, home automation network interfaces, all kinds of monitoring and control gadgets. Rigis wants to be sure the right software gets into the new devices."

"As a Senator or an investor?"

"Is there a difference? Heinrich talks a lot about dynamic energy pricing, load scheduling, automated control of equipment. Between us, I think it must be something else."

"Why's that?"

Hasuru laughed. "Because he talks so much about it."

"Strange. He's usually so reserved."

"You watch. He'll bring it up at the meeting tomorrow. He'll tell The Group it's all about efficient energy consumption, reducing greenhouse gases."

"More power to him."

"Exactly. I'd do the same. Lock in as many investors as possible now." Hasuru took a long drag on his cigarette. "Position correctly and command the future."

Hasuru's words tugged at Curtis. Inexplicably, the hour seemed too late for such blatant bravado. For Curtis, the ebb and flow of self-judgment couldn't decide whether to cover up the truth or reveal the lie. Moonlight on the waves and the invisible horizon wasn't helping. An impulse came over him to reveal the truth but cover up the lie.

"It's hard to command something I can't imagine."

"I don't imagine the future. Imagination is now. The future is fallout."

The statement was sharp, matter-of-fact flat, a punctuated Zen koan. The harshness of the response and its clarity called for silent consent or an escalating challenge. Curtis saw no other way to avoid the trap. He personalized it.

"I imagine Dr. Riya Basu saw herself in the future."

Mention of the name threw Hasuru off stride. "That was a tragedy." He recovered and looked at Curtis. "It proves one thing. It's not the future that's uncertain. It's the present."

Curtis kept focus. "It made no sense."

Flicking ashes, Hasuru faced the water once again. "That's what you get when the foolish and pointless joint forces. *New Class Order* is the worst kind of scourge. It does evil in the name of good."

"Don't be so quick to judge."

"Why? You know something?"

"Like I said, it made no sense. NCO didn't kill Riya."

"How can you be so certain?"

"I'm the one who's been doing the heavy lifting getting *GenLET*."

"As I remember, you were more than willing to volunteer."

"Someone had to."

"You took it personally when Mass bought NovoSenectus. To hear you talk back then, he picked biopharma just to compete with you."

"Nonsense. We all thought he might run off and do the unthinkable. That was the real worry."

"As time went on and he didn't, what was your reason then?"

"Same as yours – *GenLET*."

"I always thought stealing his secrets was one of your guilty pleasures. You make it sound like a burden."

"Admit it, many within The Group have become silent partners."

"You mean inactive."

"Yes. Inactive but still sitting at the table."

"What's your point?"

Curtis searched the mist. "How long have we been a Group? Thirty…forty years?

The message has gotten diluted. Do we even know what it is we're after?"

"If we wanted to do easy things, anybody could do them."

"Just as anybody can go through the motions."

"What would you have us do?"

"For one thing, pay more attention. Something is going on. NCO didn't kill Riya. Mass did."

"Mass?" Hasuru started to pace the dock. "Don't be ridiculous."

"Oh, really? I know for a fact it was a professional hit, paid for by Mass. The shooter is back in Algiers. The money was laundered through the Grand Caymans."

"How do you know so much?"

"I know where to look and I've paid a high price to find out. Call it a side benefit from years of stealing secrets from Mass."

"But Riya was his top scientist. Why would he do such a thing?"

"That's all I'm asking you to do – *ask the question.* If it's true, then there has to be something going on. Why would Riya betray him – to traffic in *GenLET* secrets? That's hard to believe after so many years of service. But if she did, who would she be working with? It certainly wasn't us and we haven't heard anything. Something that big would have shook the ground. Something bigger may still be buried."

"I don't know. NCO had motive and opportunity."

"Beware of packages wrapped too neatly."

"But *GenLET* isn't finished. He needed her…"

"He has other scientists. Isn't it odd that Riya's closest colleague had her daughter kidnapped. How about that for leverage."

"It's easy to concoct conspiracy theories. Just as easily, the feeble-minded believe them."

"And the Emperor has no clothes. Listen, I'm not drawing any conclusions one way or another. I don't know what Mass is up to – but we have to face the fact; he's up to something. We can't rule out the worst-case scenario."

"After all these years?"

"Maybe it took him this long to get ready."

"I don't think so. He's obsessed with long life now."

"*GenLET* is a recent success. Wasn't he always the one worried we wouldn't live long enough to see our plans come to fruition? Now that he has long life within reach, he can go back to the original plan."

"I need more evidence…"

"Fine. But you should know, if evidence is found, we're going to have to decide a few things. Not just you and me – the whole Group."

"What do you mean?"

Curtis moved in close. "We can't let him have his way with the world. We might have to put the rabid dog down."

Hasuru froze then turned away. "That would be going too far. We'd be no better than him."

"It's what I'm going to tell The Group. Consider this your heads up."

"I appreciate that." Hasuru flicked his cigarette into the waves. "Good night." He stepped away along the path until receding darkness swallowed him.

Curtis stared off towards the house before turning back to the ocean. Renewed solitude meant the return of his bitter reflection. In no time, thoughts of Noah wrapped around the burnt end of Hasuru's cigarette. Somewhere in the dark it floated, now part of the natural landscape.

Curtis knew what his boy would say. Like a save-the-planet poster, facts and statistics flashed into awareness:

People discard over 4 trillion cigarette butts every year.
Nearly 30% of all cigarettes smoked end up as litter.
Over 500,000 tons of pollution per year.
Butts are made of "synthetic polymer cellulose acetate" and never degrade.
In 12 years they might begin to break apart.
Within an hour of contact with water, cigarette butts leach chemicals.
Cadmium, lead, arsenic are common, along with hundreds of others.
Many are eaten by whales, birds and other marine animals.

Curtis had to walk. Everything came back to human nature.

Was it beastly or divine – or something else?

Was it a cancer consuming the planet or the reason the Earth existed?

Was it too far gone or something worth saving?

Either way, would it ever be in anyone's self-interest to do what was necessary for the common good in the time allotted? It was only human nature to encompass both sides, the problem and solution, and everything in between.

Curtis strolled back through the damp air.

He no longer felt the sting of its chill. He was used to it.

All around, a restive ocean gave fair warning.

CHAPTER 9

Dugway Proving Grounds
Tooele County, Utah

The uneasy silence had lasted many miles. Flat and arid spaces under a dusting of snow surrounded them as far as the eye could see. Faye Gardner felt sick to her stomach, a queasiness brought on by anxious thoughts following the in-flight briefing. No matter where she looked, specters of what might be were unavoidable.

The trip out from Washington D.C. had changed her. It was chilling how quickly the world could transform. As respite for her nerves, she clung to distraction and anything more mundane than the pressing questions troubling her.

"Does this road have a name?"

Lost in thought at the wheel of the Humvee, Colin Insworth hesitated before answering. "Stark Road."

"Not very original."

"I give it points for accuracy."

Faye studied the contours of a mountain range up ahead to escape the sameness of the ride. "How far do we have to go?"

"About twenty miles. The east side of Granite Peak." Colin swept one hand to the southwest. "This section is called GPI – Granite Peak Installation. It covers 250 square miles of the Proving Grounds."

"There's more?"

"A million acres. The whole thing's larger than Rhode Island."

Faye's response was kneejerk and humorless. "Impressive, except most things are larger than Rhode Island."

"I guess so – even test sites for weapons."

The added context hit Faye and left her pale. "You don't mean that."

"What?" Colin shot her a glance, his eyes hidden behind sunglasses.

"What kind of testing goes on out here?"

"Back in World War II, the Korean War, the War Department tested all kinds of things: chemicals, biological agents, flamethrowers, smoke bombs, flares. They even built mockups of German and Japanese villages to test the effectiveness of incendiary bombs."

"What about now?"

"The mission is defensive." Colin's attention shifted back to the road. "Part of that will always be preparation for what the other guy might do."

Faye looked away from Colin, out the passenger side window. "It makes sense. If you want to find out how to stop a bullet – first you need some bullets."

"It's not quite that simple."

"How else would you explain it?"

"I don't. You can read all about DPG on its website – dugway.army.mil."

"You can't be serious."

"What do you expect? No one knows more than they're supposed to know."

The Humvee slowed. Colin turned off onto a smaller dirt path that stretched arrow-strait on a sharp diagonal into nothing. Faye marveled at the lack of road signs or markers of any kind since leaving Michael Army Airfield.

"I'm glad you know where you're going. I wouldn't want to get lost out here."

Colin accelerated and a fine cloud of dust trailed the vehicle. "If you want some real fun, try doing this at night."

"Impossible."

"If you're not prepared." Colin tapped a GPS readout. "Passive transponders are buried at key intersections. Each one becomes a beacon for an authorized signal."

"I take it those are used for something more than navigation."

"That's right. I wouldn't advise driving in certain places unless your vehicle can light up the beacons. Same with the airspace – it's restricted as far up as you can go. Dugway is part of the larger Utah Test and Training Range with controlled airspace that includes Hill Air Force Base to the North."

More miles passed by. The dirt path led to an even less travelled trail in the shadow of a mountain. Flanked by low-lying scruff of vegetation, the Humvee followed the trail to an encampment at the base of rocky foothills. Two structures were visible; a single-wide trailer and a windowless building three stories high and thirty feet square with a flat roof.

In between the structures was a parking area in the dirt with room for a half dozen vehicles. Off to one side, away from either structure, a flat and level square of land sat open, cleared of vegetation; a platform awaiting something.

Colin parked on the mountain side of the taller building. It was the only side with a door. Faye got out and stretched her legs. The drone of the Humvee's engine was gone and the full impact of the surrounding stillness closed in. Faye hugged her coat close and braced against the freezing temperature.

"Strange place to keep a database."

Colin handed her a holographic dog tag on a chain.

"Here, wear this. Along with your palm print, it's your ticket anywhere within the facility. The palm print takes fingerprints and a RIDIS scan."

Faye slipped the chain over her head and eyed the flat-top building. "There's more to this I hope."

Colin stepped off towards the lone door. "This way."

"What's the trailer for?"

"Temporary quarters for anyone not authorized to go below."

"Why would such people even be out here?"

"Lots of reasons." Colin pointed at the flat and level square of dirt. "When fully operational, helicopters can shuttle personnel in and out. The pilots have no business below. Also, surface security teams sometimes need a forward command post."

Colin stepped up to the three-story building and opened the door. Faye followed him into a bare lobby. The small, austere space was just enough room to wait for the elevator while shielded from the weather.

The elevator door opened without any visible security check and their descent started. Faye searched but there was no buttons to press to select level or floor.

She fingered her dog tag. "What about this? Don't we have to be cleared?"

Colin stood solid beside her. "Anybody can go down. Clearance is only needed to come back up." The elevator door opened upon a vault-like structure under video surveillance. "This is the Landing Zone. It's blast-proof. Sensors detect a variety of chemical agents. Once the elevator door opens, the elevator is grounded until our passage through here is complete."

Colin moved forward and placed his open palm on a metal plate. He stepped aside for Faye to do the same. Moments later, a negative-pressure airlock door opened to their right. Faye followed Colin down a narrow corridor as the airlock door thudded closed behind them with a pneumatic hiss.

"This is where we get the final scan. Pressurized doors on either side seal this space shut if anything is detected while we're in here."

"You mean weapons?"

"Anything."

As they approached the far side, another airlock released. On the other side was a guard station. Grim with duty, the armed guard nodded both of them through. Again, Faye lifted the dog tag from around her neck.

"I guess somewhere back there this got scanned."

Colin continued down a hallway into an office area. "All you have to do with that is wear it. You never know where it's needed, so have it on you all the time."

The office was staffed with a skeleton crew. The administrative area bordered a series of corridors leading to various labs. From directional signage, Faye could guess their purpose. As they walked, the message on the signs added up.

"I thought you said this was about RIDIS – the DNA database."

"That's right."

"Why do you need a Level Four safety lab for a database – especially a lab like this, hidden underground? I thought we were going to the place where you work."

Colin shook his head. "As you said, this would be a strange place to keep a database. Besides, databases can be accessed from anywhere via secured connection. The actual location of the RIDIS database is classified above your security level." Colin stopped and turned back to Faye. The weight of his task was upon him. "As we discussed, your expertise is not in databases; it's in Ghyvir-C."

Faye walked up to a lab door and looked through a small window. A pair of researchers in lab coats worked at elevated tables. "We're talking about a virus that causes the common cold. This place was designed for Ebola or smallpox. What's a lab like this doing out in the middle of nowhere anyway?"

"It's here in case it's needed."

"In case it's needed? This place was set up to work on dangerous biological agents in secret. When is *that* needed?"

"When is anything needed? Some things you can't prepare for at the last minute. This had to be built – just in case. As we now know, the unthinkable can happen. It's a good thing it's here."

"What about the Geneva Protocol of 1925 or the Biological Weapons Convention of 1972?"

"An empty lab breaks no treaties. This was built as a contingency. In times of crisis or war, there isn't time to start from scratch."

"I get it. Above ground, everything is defensive. There's no such thing as dual-use. Below ground, facilities are in place to weaponize on a moment's notice."

"It's only common sense. To do anything else effectively would be unilateral disarmament. The time for preparing for a crisis is *before* it happens."

"You expect me to believe sites like this exist and are never used to assess offensive capabilities?"

"Believe what you want. What you see here doesn't prove a thing other than the government likes to spend lots of money."

"There's only one reason for a site like this."

"Conduct a search – you won't find any hot agents stewing in Petri dishes."

"No – those are probably warehoused down another dirt road, guarded in another hole."

"What you believe and what you can talk about are two different things. Remember your oath. I'm not going to get into speculation."

"This still doesn't make sense. You said *RIDIS* was kept underground."

"It is. Somewhere. Not here. We have a connection to it."

"I don't need a BSL4 lab to find out why a common cold virus causes sterility."

"No, you don't." Colin stepped up to her and looked her in the eye. "But you'll need a lab like this to engineer Ghyvir-C to undo what it's done."

The true motive for being added to The Project hit Faye. Colin couldn't have said it more clearly but her first reaction was to deny its import.

"What are you asking me to do?"

"You heard me. We're facing global panic if news of this gets out. We're facing extinction if we don't fix it. The powers that be have decided. If sterility is proven correct, as I know it will be, then the best way to handle both problems – panic and sterility – is to undo the problem the same way it came about, by stealth from a natural cause."

Faye stormed away down the hallway. "I'm not going to engineer a pandemic."

"We have no choice."

"You can't mitigate the risks. The chance of something even worse going wrong are too high."

"What's the alternative? If you found a fix, how would you deliver it? Do you want to go on the evening news and explain it to everyone, tell them to line up for a government-issued shot? Don't forget to bring their children."

"You can't be sure of unintended consequences."

"What about the consequences we *can* be sure of? Sterile children are reaching puberty. How long will it be until the world notices the drop in teenage pregnancies? Project research has identified at least three groups that are already red-flagging early statistics."

Faye bolted into one of the unoccupied labs. She paced before biological space suits hanging in an open locker. "This is all about keeping secrets, isn't it."

Colin stood his ground and followed her with his eyes. "Think about it. Some secrets *should* stay secret. It's a good thing."

"You can't just release something like that on the world. Once in the wild, the chance of mutation leaves the door open to any possibility – most of them bad."

"I've read the reports – how Ghyvir-C resists mutation. That's one of the anomalies that kept research on the virus alive all this time. We don't understand how it does it. Oddly enough, its ability to resist mutation seems engineered."

Faye paced. "I don't know."

"We have to find out what caused this. Once we do, we have to take extraordinary measures to reverse it. If everything gets done without the world knowing, all the better."

A cold silence fell between them. Colin dropped his gaze to the floor.

"You're at a pivot point. You've been given a unique opportunity. Think of the consequences if we do nothing. How often do you get asked to make the ultimate difference is something so critical? What kind of outcome do you want to see?"

Faye halted and let her sight roam the range of advanced bio-lab equipment around her. She thought of New Year's Day only weeks away. The flow of time suddenly seemed borrowed for everyone. "What exactly do you want me to do?"

Colin stepped closer and lowered his voice.

"We need three things. First – confirm our findings that sterility exists. Second – diagnose how and why this happens. Third – engineer a way to reverse the effect in a package that can be delivered by a sputnik virus."

"Why a sputnik?"

"That's how we think this whole thing started."

A realization swept across Faye's face.

Colin nodded. "You're right – the common cold doesn't cause sterility. As you're well aware, inside Ghyvir-C is a sputnik, a parasite virus. We believe something with the interaction between the two viruses causes sterility. We need you to discover what that is and then figure out how to reverse it…"

Colin left the thought hanging for Faye to complete.

"…then all that's left is to decide how to deliver it around the globe."

Colin nodded. "Without alarming anyone."

Faye felt her heart race. "It's hopeless, ridiculous, not possible."

"Then we better get started."

Faye couldn't smile. "We'll need to isolate the sputnik."

"Already done."

"Sequencing should be done on regional samples of the parasite. We need to determine if the sputnik shares Ghyvir's resistance to mutation."

"Good idea."

"The markers you found need to be correlated with the RIDIS database."

"As we speak."

"Sounds like you're already onto this."

"I have a good team but we're few in numbers. None of us have the direct experience you've had with these two viruses."

"Can we get more people?"

"Not likely. They'd have to pass TS-4 security. By design and necessity, group size is meant to be limited."

Faye walked back into the hallway. "Where do I sleep?"

Relieved she was onboard, Colin stepped to another elevator. "Right this way."

CHAPTER 10

Jubilee Hills Police Station
Hyderabad India

It was the ragged end of a frustrating day. Janis Insworth walked into Road Number 18 Police Station for the third time in one afternoon with failing hope and little expectation. Each visit before resulted in delays, excuses, claims of more pressing business, finally promises to have word for her later.

This time her arrival drew an immediate response. She was escorted directly upstairs to the office of Detective Inspector Syed Koteswara. Instead of feeling buoyed with optimism, the prompt attention gave her reason to pause and fortify herself. No news is better than bad news.

"Please, sit down. Thank you for your patience."

Koteswara's manner was cordial. Nonetheless, Janis could tell he had troubling business to attend to. She sat across from him and watched as he shuffled paperwork on his desk. He was a stocky man with a fresh haircut and a wide mustache.

"Excuse me, I'm still getting settled in the new building. It's quite something, don't you think?"

"Yes, it's very nice." Anxious to be on with it, Janis restrained the urge to press him for information right away.

Koteswara perused an open file while he talked. He was obviously filling time to give himself a chance to catch up on the latest report.

"Yes…we were all excited to move in. You might have heard on the news about the gift of 50,000 rupees given to the police by Sri Hari, the famous film actor. We bought furniture with it." After a pause to read, he gazed up from the file and looked Janis up and down. "That chair you're sitting in was purchased with his gift."

"Very generous of him."

His gaze, all over her, was too noticeable. He wanted her to be aware of it. If his intent was to deliberately make her feel uncomfortable, he'd succeeded. Maybe he wanted to bring her emotions to the surface. See what, if anything, she might be hiding. A sexual innuendo was out of place. His reason had to be elsewhere.

He leaned back. "This is a neighborhood police station. As you know, your case is being handled by SIT, the Special Investigation Team. They've asked me to be point of contact on the case. The truth is, we're understaffed. There are only four Inspectors and 12 Sub-Inspectors in SIT for all Hyderabad. Each neighborhood gets by with less."

"I realize that but I was told there might be promising leads."

"Who told you that?" As Janis hesitated over the name, Koteswara waved it off. "It doesn't matter. The Assistant Commissioner believes the future of this case is out of our jurisdiction."

"How can that be? My daughter was kidnapped in this neighborhood."

"Yes, but the promising leads you talk about all suggest Alyssa was taken out of the country. All we can do here is reconstruct past history. Finding her is a future event that must be pursued somewhere else."

"So is that it? You do nothing more?" Her voice quaked with emotion. "You're just a messenger because SIT has given up?"

"It's understandable you're upset…"

"Damned right! My daughter was taken in broad daylight. I gave you a description of the men, the car, the direction of travel…"

"Be assured, we are ready to work with any outside agency…"

"What about local connections to the kidnappers? What about following up on how they got her out?"

"This was done by professionals. They knew very well how to hide their tracks. Of course we will investigate any new information as it comes up. I have to be honest with you. We don't expect much in that regard."

"I can't accept that. I was told there would be an investigation of money transfers to anyone associated with the group New Class Order. Certain individuals were arrested for vandalism of NovoSenectus property. I was told there would be background checks…"

"All well and good. Some of it has been done. Some of it is in the pipeline."

"The pipeline?"

"There is a method to police business. You really must trust us on this. We are still in contact with Stockholm authorities and we've begun checking with local airports to have them review any irregularities with non-commercial flights."

"So what am I supposed to do? You don't have any more information for me. Where do I go for help now?"

"Investigations take time. The main thing is not to despair."

On the verge of tears, Janis stood to go.

Koteswara leaned forward. "There is one other thing."

Janis froze then turned back with curiosity as Koteswara checked his notes.

"Inspector Sudarshan would like to see you at Central Crime Station tomorrow morning at ten o'clock for a deposition."

"You need a sworn statement from me?"

"It's been requested of anyone who was with Malcolm Stowe during the last few days. You saw him on several occasions, isn't that right?"

Janis recoiled. However did he know that? "Yes, but why Malcolm?"

"Haven't you heard?" Janis gave a shake of her head. "Oh, I'm sorry. I thought you knew. Malcolm Stowe died late yesterday."

Janis felt faint and sat back down. "How?"

"An automobile accident."

"What time?"

"Late afternoon."

"Where? What happened?" Janis was dazed.

"It was a single car accident in an area quite a ways west of here."

"I don't understand. Why do you need depositions if it was an accident?"

Koteswara rocked back and forward in his chair. "It seems Mr. Stowe did special security work for your employer, NovoSenectus. Were you aware of that?"

"I knew he was a Security Agent. I assumed he protected the corporate campus but I didn't know his role for sure."

"According to the company, he had in his possession a variety of sensitive items that must be returned. They want to find where he might have left the material as soon as possible."

"Are they suggesting someone has this material improperly?"

"No, nothing of the sort. As a security agent, Mr. Stowe was privy to many things the company would rather not share with competitors. Some things would be tempting to any thief. Malcolm's accident was so sudden, naturally there are loose ends. They just want to be sure everything he had is properly returned."

"You need sworn statements for that?"

"The company wishes to be thorough – just in case anything comes up later that involves an Intellectual Capital Property Crime."

"Do you have any idea what's missing?"

Koteswara rocked forward and stopped to check the file. "Looks like standard items. The same things every employee would have to turn in – cell phone, laptop, cardkeys, access badges."

"I see..." Janis stood to leave once again. "You said Inspector Sudarshan..."

"...ten o'clock at Central Crime Station. Shouldn't take more than an hour." Koteswara scribbled something on a slip of paper. "Here, in case you have any questions, you can email the inspector directly."

Janis stepped forward and read the paper as she took it in hand.

sho.ccs@hyd.appolice.gov.in

She nodded at him and he nodded back. There was nothing more to say.

Janis couldn't speak. Her mind raced too fast. Shock and surprise, terror and dread; another colleague was dead and it felt like a trap was being set.

Koteswara wasn't on the level with her. What did NovoSenectus tell the police? Were they playing it straight? Maybe they didn't care if Malcolm's death looked like a murder. What was the last assignment given to Malcolm? Did they lure him to a remote place west of the city expecting no loose ends? Did they ransack his house after they couldn't find the missing items in his car? Did the police even check his house? How did Koteswara know Malcolm was with her recently? Had she been followed to the train station?

The appointment at Central Crime Station was a more immediate concern. What would be asked of her tomorrow if she showed up? What could she say?

Janis crossed the lobby of the police station and hurried into the light of day feeling as if she had escaped. The police were only doing their duty.

NovoSenectus had made the whole matter look like a legitimate concern. Mass' corporation was a major corporate presence in the city, employing thousands. It was easy to leverage the police to do its bidding. It all appeared so matter-of-fact. No wonder Koteswara toyed with her, gauging her discomfort. Everyone suspects something more – even if everyone has to pretend otherwise.

Aware someone might be watching her, Janis slowed her pace walking to her car. She got behind the wheel and waited for a semblance of composure that didn't come. She couldn't tell the police the truth and there was no future in trying to live a lie. Riya and Malcolm had both died because they possessed certain information.

Now she had the laptop.

That made her the next target.

Janis drove into traffic with an aimless need to move forward. Stunned with indecision, she followed traffic for an hour without settling on a destination. Where to go now? Home was no longer a sanctuary. Work was no longer a safe haven. In the trunk of her car, in the space where the spare tire should be, Malcolm's laptop and cell phone lay wrapped and hidden in a blanket.

Powerful forces would kill to have those things. But getting rid of them wouldn't help. Not now. Janis had to assume that Eugene Mass wouldn't take chances. Anyone who had discovered his plan must be eliminated. No loose ends. Even if she did the unthinkable and drove to NovoSenectus to turn in the missing items, she was sure the result would be the same. Within hours, she too would have some sort of accident.

An hour and a half after leaving the police station, Janis was still on the road, driving in circles looking for a way out. Night had come to Hyderabad but it offered no rest. Nothing was left for her there. She would surely die if she stayed. Koteswara had confirmed it – Alyssa was out of the country. If she was ever going to be found, Janis needed to leave the country too.

Janis turned the wheel in the direction of the airport. She felt that one simple action dividing her past life from an unknown future. Suddenly, the two of them were very different things. Her old life was gone. She knew that now. It would never come back. There was nothing left but a future she must take day-by-day. It was a decision she was forced to make. She was only beginning to realize how stark and sharp-edged life could be when forced to survive on those terms. The detective had summed it up; finding Alyssa *is a future event that must be pursued somewhere else.*

She parked in long-term parking and bought the first ticket she could get going anywhere in Western Europe or the States. The nearest departure was a flight to Miami with connections in Bengaluru and Paris. Flight time, nearly twenty-eight hours. She sat waiting on the concourse not knowing if she would go all the way. She wasn't sure where she was going at all. Running away, it didn't seem to matter.

Clutching the laptop with cell phone in pocket, she was handed back her ticket stub. She hurried onto the plane and belted herself in her seat. For the first time in her life, an airplane seatbelt felt like security. Her eagerness to be in the air was tormented by delays on the ground. Her worst fear was seeing airport security come on board to take her into custody. Did anyone know she was at the airport? She paid for her ticket with cash from an ATM but was someone tracking bank transactions? Nervousness bordered on paranoia.

To distract herself, she opened Malcolm's laptop. It powered up out of hibernation just where he had left it. With fingers hovering over the keyboard, Janis wavered. What now? The keyboard exuded a power, a potential force for good. How would she wield it?

She brought up Malcolm's email client and opened a new email. Checking his contacts list, she selected the one person she was most interested in having a discussion with.

Knockout Mouse.

CHAPTER 11

West Shore Road
South Hero Island, Vermont

A shroud of gray over a slab of white. Beyond the trees, the winter sky hung low over frozen Lake Champlain. Janis knew these roads as childhood friends. Driving them now, as necessary as it was, felt like a betrayal. As if coming with her on this trip was a loss of innocence to mar a place she knew only as paradise.

Dashboard vents in the rented Jeep Wrangler gushed heated air but little comfort. The ride up from Albany had been a crucible of reflection. She never liked long drives. Her mind was always too restless for them. But compared to the interminable airline flights into Paris, Miami, then New York, she shouldn't complain. At least the act of driving required a diverting concentration and focus.

Around a familiar bend in the road, there appeared a welcomed sign that she had arrived. It still stood, just as she remembered it as a little girl, just as it was the last time she saw it several years before. Crafted in wood and painted white with light blue lettering, the sign announced the entrance to *Bright Hope Farms*.

In times past, Janis' grandfather had raised horses on the vast property. Her mother and father had used it as a fair weather getaway from the businesses they co-managed. Some of their happiest times were spend there. With Father gone, Mother gravitated to it as the place to live out her years. It was as close as she could get to him now. Surrounded by a sometimes senseless world she no longer felt a part of, Mother had found in solitude a refuge if not consolation.

Janis slowed the Jeep and shifted into four-wheel drive. The long traverse down the narrow lane of compacted snow and ice gave her a sense of stark contrast. Most of her memories of this place were forged in the warmth of summer. In her fondest memories, the wooded areas were so much brighter and full of vibrant foliage. Wild flowers dotted the landscape. Now those places were locked away under a mantle of frost and fallen leaves.

Smoke rose from the chimney of the main house. Janis parked the Jeep alongside a wood pile and turned to the backpack on the seat next to her. She had bought it at Charles de Gaulle airport, along with a change of clothes and a tin of Calissons d'Aix almond candy. Add Malcolm's laptop and the clothes on her back. These were the sum total of all the physical possessions she had left in the world.

The front door of the main house opened and Janis snapped alert. Grabbing the backpack, she exited the Jeep and took the frigid walk to the porch.

Sara Rushton stood in the doorway with arms folded against the chill. The gray-haired woman offered a brave smile in welcome but her eyes were sad. She had heard enough bad news. Janis had shared incredible details of her harrowing tale. Calls from public phones during her recent layovers were a disturbing confession. Sara was ready for some good news but didn't expect it. Seeing her daughter again was good news enough. For now.

Mother and daughter hugged and kissed in the doorway before Sara hurried them inside where it was warm.

Janis felt suddenly out of place. “Thank you for letting me come here.”

“Nonsense. You belong here. It’s so good to see you.”

“You too. But I don’t want to put you in danger.”

“Don’t worry yourself. You need someplace safe.”

Janis dropped her backpack on a couch. “I’m not sure that’s possible anymore.”

Taking a moment to look around, Janis was overcome. The child in her was home. All the tension of the last thirty hours roiled up. Her abrupt tears were enough to trigger the same in Sara.

“What’s wrong?”

Janis fought to form the words. “I should have made time to visit more. I got too lost in my work. I’m sorry.”

“What are you saying? Your work is important. I’m the one who made things difficult. I can live anywhere but I hung onto this place in the middle of nowhere. I’m delighted and thankful you got away as much as you could.”

Janis wiped her eyes. “It’s all turned into a mess, hasn’t it?”

“Don’t give up hope. There are still possibilities.” Sara took her by the hand. “Come on, let’s get you settled in and have some tea.”

Janis nodded and managed a smile. Mother showed her to her room upstairs. Of course Janis knew the way but Sara wanted to watch her daughter’s delight in finding it just as she left it.

All of Janis’ senses took inventory. The scent of jasmine and honeysuckle sachet came first. Then the sight of a double bed, a dresser and desk, a cedar chest she used to call a hope chest. The feel and exact placement of comforter and pillows, jewelry box and favorite dolls were confirmed. Janis felt at one and yet removed from it all. She stepped to the window and remembered all the dreaming she had done from the special vantage point of youth.

“I’ll let you freshen up. I’ll be in the kitchen.” Sara retreated downstairs.

Janis took her time. To be surrounded by the youthful energy of when she had been Janis Rushton was a luxury to be savored in the moment. She hoped the feeling would somehow recharge her spirit and shore up her resolve.

She took off her coat and slipped Malcolm’s laptop from the backpack. With a renewed thirst and curiosity, she headed downstairs.

“Is that it?” Sara eyed the laptop as she would a WMD.

Janis nodded and sat at the table with fingers on the keyboard.

Sara brought tea. “Have you heard anything back?”

“I’m checking now.” Janis waited for the email client to load.

“From what you said, it sounded like you don’t know who this is.”

“I know Eugene Mass wants him blackmailed. That’s enough.”

“I thought you said the other man, Malcolm was the one doing that.”

“Yes but Malcolm told me Mass was the one who gave him the tip in the first place. Malcolm wouldn’t have found Knockout Mouse if it wasn’t for that tip.”

“I don’t like it.” Sara poured from her teapot. “You shouldn’t have anything to do with Mass anymore.”

“It’s too late for that.” Incoming mail populated the screen. “Here it is.”

"He answered?"

"Why not? He thinks he's writing to Malcolm."

As Janis read silently, Sara got up and looked over her shoulder.

TO: malsto
FROM: km
SUBJECT: RE: urgent

Is this a joke? As if you don't know.
OK you bugger, I'll play along.

Answer #1 is André Bolard.
Lives and works in Marseille. Escapes to Port Frioul.
What else you wanna know – the thickness of his dick?

Answer #2 is a snore.
Genetic study of an endangered breed of Loggerhead turtles and their food sources in Atlantic Ocean habitat. Currently hush-hush because of possible involvement of a certain GAMA dropped in the Sargasso Sea 15 years ago. (You have a shitty sense of humor asking me this one.)

Sara's eyes widened. "My, my. A foul and testy sort, isn't he? Whatever did you ask him?"

Janis stared at the screen, rereading for innuendoes.

"I wanted to know where I could find the leader of New Class Order. I also asked him to report back everything he could about a new government project called BIOPONORE."

"There's a project called that?"

"Apparently."

"I haven't heard that word for twenty years – not since you and Faye came up here on summer vacations from college."

"I've never used the word since."

Sara thought it through. "Why were you asking about that? You don't think Faye is mixed up with any of this, do you?"

"I can't be sure of anything. I needed to find out."

"That's ridiculous. Faye would do no such thing."

"Mom, people change. Faye stayed at USAMRIID, remember? There's no telling what they have her doing now."

"Well, she certainly isn't trying to kill six billion people. I'm surprised you'd even consider it."

"*Biological point of no return.* You can't get more clear than that."

"It's about turtles! They're endangered. You have your answer."

"Sure. I guess so."

"Why do you care about this André Bolard fellow?"

Janis vacillated on sending a return message then closed the laptop.

"If NCO took Alyssa, then he has the power to let her go. If they don't have her, I bet they have a good idea who does."

"So what's the plan? Walk right up and ask him?"

Janis stirred sugar in her tea. "Yeah, something like that."

"That's not a plan. That's wishful thinking at best. More like suicide."

Janis stood and paced to the kitchen sink to avoid her mother's glare.

"You don't understand. I don't have options."

"Yes you do. You're not alone."

Janis turned and snapped, "What would you have me do? Go back to Novo-Senectus? Or maybe go to the government – how do I know they're not 8-Ball?"

"You can contact Faye."

"Faye! Huh! That's like contacting the government."

"That's not true. She's your friend. Tell her how serious this is."

"She *was* my friend. Not now. Not for this."

"She'd understand. I know she would. She might know something that could help."

"We haven't spoken in years. The last time wasn't pleasant."

Sara sat down and shook her head. "You two used to be so close…"

"Lots of things *used* to be."

Sara couldn't contain her bitterness. "Everything was all right between you two until Colin entered the picture."

"Leave him out of this!"

"I know. I should shut up. No one can tell you what you don't already know. You like to find things out for yourself. Always did."

"I'm not going to stop until I find out what happened to Alyssa. If that means leveraging this laptop to win her release, so be it."

"Leverage?"

"Sure. NCO hates Mass. They want to stop his plans for *GenLET*. They'd love to get their hands on Riya's computer backup and expose Mass. Nothing would give them greater pleasure. If it's that valuable to them, I'll trade the laptop for Alyssa."

"Oh, Janis, no – you're in way over your head."

"I have to use the only thing I have. I have nothing else."

"All you're doing is pulling yourself in deeper – a sheep among wolves."

Janis reopened the computer and inserted a flash drive in a slot.

"The truth needs to get out. If the government is working with Mass, the world needs to know about it. I would rather NCO take the credit and the heat for exposing 3rd Protocol. I get Alyssa, Mass gets taken down, and NCO gets the glory."

Sara nervously watched Janis at the keyboard. "What are you doing?"

"I'm making a backup. If anything should happen to me or the laptop gets lost or stolen, the information won't be lost."

"I don't want you to do this. You need to reconsider."

Janis stood and kissed her mother. "No. I need to get everything ready. Is the boat house open?"

"Yes." Sara stood, saddened with the weight of things to come.

Janis headed for the living room. "I guess I'll take a walk. I need some time alone

– to think."

Sara followed her to the stairs, pleading. "What if Malcolm really had an accident? What if it wasn't murder? Maybe NovoSenectus wants their things back for security reasons, just like the police said?"

"You don't get it. Malcolm knew he was in danger; that's why he gave me the laptop. Riya was hiding a secret from NovoSenectus for a reason."

"You can't be sure about anything. Maybe Malcolm stumbled into something else. Don't you think it's strange that all the damning evidence about Mass and this 3rd Protocol was found at GeLixCo? Those two companies have been bitter rivals for years."

Janis stopped her stride. "I can't believe you're sticking up for Mass. Why would Riya be on the phone with him, angry about a select agent? What about the secret lab in Austria, the arrangements with China? She was the one who told Malcolm about GeLixCo. Was she deluded too? And what about Colin, her contact – why is he involved? I know for a fact he still works for the U.S. government – the child support garnishment proves it."

"I'm just saying, what if all of this is something else. How do you know it wasn't GeLixCo that killed Malcolm? He broke into their Puerto Rico office? Maybe they don't want something to get out or be traced back to them."

Janis strained for an answer.

Sara came closer, armed with a key doubt. "What if NCO were the ones who killed Riya just like all the media are saying? Do you really want to go over to Marseille by yourself and confront Bolard? Why would he listen to you?"

"I have something he'll want."

"And why wouldn't he kill you for it?"

"If he wanted me dead, he would have done it at the Nobel lecture, the same time as Riya."

"You didn't have the laptop then."

"Bottom line, I think he knows where Alyssa is. The police in Stockholm and India insist everything on the kidnapping points to NCO."

"It's crazy! You can't risk your life over such guesswork!"

"You said I can't be sure of anything. You're wrong. I'm sure Alyssa is gone. I'm sure friends have died violently and something evil is going on."

"But there's been no ransom demand – no contact about Alyssa at all. What kind of kidnapping is that?"

"There's been no ransom demand made to *me*. But I'm not the one who can stop *GenLET*. Only Mass can do that. I would expect negotiations for Alyssa to be private, between NCO and Mass."

"And Mass wouldn't let you, the mother, know this was going on?"

Janis headed up the stairs. "You make it sound like Mass cares. You're the queen of 'what if.' Well, what if Mass doesn't care if Alyssa is ever returned."

Sara stood at the first floor landing with nothing more to say.

CHAPTER 12

Granite Peak Installation
Dugway Proving Grounds, Utah

An emergency meeting was scheduled sixty-six feet below the desert sand. Faye Gardner walked into the empty conference room expecting more. An active video display emblazoned one wall dark blue. One of twelve chairs was pulled back from an otherwise undisturbed table. Spots of brightness from track lighting bathed the large oval. One ceramic coffee cup was the only evidence that anyone else had been invited. Faye halted in solitary surprise as another door opened.

Colin Insworth returned to the room holding a remote control. A rare terseness equaled his haste. "Close the door. No one else is coming."

Faye did as he asked then took a seat. "What's this about?"

"This." Standing between pulled-back chair and table, he pressed a button on the remote control. Two pages of a document appeared on the video display.

Faye recognized them right away. "My report…"

"Yes." The affirmation was laden with a mélange of emotion difficult for Faye to distinguish. Colin sat down and ran fingers along his salt-and-pepper beard. "It differs from the official record."

"I wrote exactly what happened. What's different?"

"Yesterday you were wondering why I wouldn't let you read any of the case files from fourteen years ago."

"It's an odd restriction if you want me to get up-to-speed."

"Not so odd if it exposes discrepancies. I asked you to write out what you remember so I could compare it with what USAMRIID has on file."

"Go on," prompted Faye.

"The two accounts are identical except for a couple of things. Your report says a lab worker was accidentally exposed to the virus."

"That's correct."

Colin stared down at the bare table in front of him. "You claim that lab worker was Janis." He shot Faye a glance but Faye said nothing. "You say she was quarantined."

The fact that Colin's surprise involved Janis rocketed Faye through an emotional minefield. Any response now would be awkward. There was nothing to do but attempt a dispassionate review of the facts.

"It was Ghyvir. We didn't know what to expect so they held her in isolation. She was there for weeks. The confinement triggered a quite serious bout of claustrophobia. We were quite worried. That's not in the record?"

"None of it." Colin stiffened and switched the view to USAMRIID documents.

"You believe me, don't you?"

Colin fought back the twin demons of rising feeling and strategic complication. "I don't disbelieve you."

Colin's hesitation spurred Faye to think it through. "Why would they take that out of the report? As terrible as it was, the accident turned out to be a good thing. We had a human test case, something that was unthinkable otherwise. We dodged a bullet, but it proved to be significant. Despite how odd the virus was, we knew it produced the common cold. Nothing more."

"Your report called it *remarkable*."

Colin's overtone was rife with innuendo. All of it lost on Faye. He was hiding something but considering where they were, it was to be expected. His silence on the matter was pointblank. Her need to explore the wound between them was uncertain.

"It was remarkable because normally common colds are caused by the smallest of viruses. This was something new. Ghyvir was a giant virus but it matched the other 99 types of human rhinoviruses in critical ways. Ghyvir also uses a six-stage lytic cycle. It penetrates a host cell, injects its own nucleic acids, and the host mistakenly copies the viral acids instead of its own. The copies fill up the host until its membrane splits. The copies are then free to go infect other cells. Janis caught a cold. The pathology was critical to our understanding of the virus."

"Critical." Colin stood and paced to the video display. "But not in the report."

"It could have been important to hide the truth. As panicky as everyone was at the time, maybe they didn't want to admit that a BSL4 accident had taken place. The public outcry about that might have led to more regulation, more restrictions on biodefense programs across the board. They could easily leave it out. It wouldn't change our conclusions."

"The Ghyvir incident was a big deal at the time, wasn't it?"

"It was all over the media. Unfortunately, news stories only fed the hysteria. A giant virus, never seen before, had been found in the Arctic's Beaufort Sea. Within days, researchers in South China also found it in recycled greywater, the kind used for irrigation. We knew then the exposure was global. People were worried."

Colin groused. "Truth is stranger than fiction. For the most part, news is fiction. The fact is – the public understood little about giant viruses."

"Many had never even heard of them."

"With all the terror threats at the time, everyone was invested in speculation."

"Retelling the history of giant viruses made for bad television. It was rare to hear anything about *Mimivirus*, the first giant virus ever discovered – or *Mamavirus*, the one found in a cooling tower in Paris, or *Marseillevirus*. The fact that those giant viruses were uncovered long before Ghyvir didn't seem to matter."

"I remember. There was a lot at stake, especially at USAMRIID. It wasn't the only lab looking into Ghyvir. The competition involved much more than bragging rights. That was a topic of conversation at your worksite, wasn't it?"

Faye nodded. "It was suggested more than once that it would be better if we could announce right away that we understood what we had. No one wanted to look like they were taken by surprise."

"Get to the answer first. That kind of thing can make or break someone's career."

Faye watched as Colin stopped pacing to face her. She noticed his silent pause and the way his eyes fell upon her before asking, "What are you getting at?"

He didn't blink. "Were primates used to study Ghyvir?"

"They weren't needed. Giant viruses typically infect amoebae, not humans."

"But Ghyvir was peculiar. Even the research ship that saw it for the first time noticed how different it was. All precautions were to be taken until you knew how it acted. I checked – your lab did make inquiries about primate availability."

"As it turned out, we didn't need to go that way – the accident with Janis precluded it."

"I see. That saved a lot of time – and aggravation."

Faye burned as his inference bordered on allegation. "If you're accusing me of something, be clear about it."

"Sticking with the facts – the official report says monkeys were used."

"Not in my lab."

"*Your* lab?"

"The lab I was working in."

"Did you and Janis ever argue about the use of monkeys?"

"At USAMRIID, Janis and I argued about a lot of things. That proves nothing."

"I had another lab worker from that time questioned. He says you and Janis argued quite a bit. He even remembers one time overhearing Janis accuse you of doing anything to advance your career."

"That's right," snapped Faye. "That's what she said. I said a lot about her too – that doesn't mean any of it's correct. Janis and I were on a collision course from the day we started at that place. Work on Ghyvir was her breaking point; it soured her to USAMRIID overall. The forced confinement left an emotional scar. She thought the way Ghyvir was being handled was suspicious. She was certain something wasn't right. When I didn't share her paranoia, she started distrusting me too."

"You were the one working closest to her – so what gave her those ideas?"

"Who knows. She accused me of knowing something about the dual-use nature of our research, something I wasn't telling her. She hated the idea that any of her work would be used to make a weapon. The idea that I would be a silent partner in any of it was too much for her."

"You thought she was jeopardizing the research, didn't you? You'd lose out on the competition to find the answer first. That would set back your career and future. She was being unreasonable."

"Nonsense. We both distrusted our bosses. I wasn't blind and I certainly wasn't naïve. I always assumed there was more to it but I had no idea what it was. She thought I did. I told her we were both at too low a level to know such things – or to care. It didn't matter to me so I didn't pay attention to the little things. She did – to a fault."

Colin walked back to his chair and sat down. He leaned back, emboldened to be direct. "Did you rig the lab so Janis would get infected?"

"You're out of your mind!"

"I don't know. Am I? At that time, not long out of college, you wanted to advance your career. She was too idealistic for you – no monkeys, no weapons. She picked a time to be difficult just when you wanted to shine."

"She was my best friend. How dare you suggest I'd do such a thing!"

"Isn't it true you thought the virus was harmless? You went on the record in an early report, before the accident. You had an opinion on the matter. You thought

Ghyvir would act as a rhinovirus or a giant virus – in either case, you predicted it would be found relatively harmless to humans."

"That doesn't mean I'd prove my point by turning my best friend into a guinea pig."

"Your best friend? The same best friend who lured me away from you."

The personal reference struck too deep for Faye. She was more angry than hurt – and the hurt was unbearable. "That's insane! I would never expose anyone like that, for any reason. Besides, some dogs don't have to be lured into the next yard. They don't mate for love and have no sense of decency."

Colin calmly responded with his most potent blow. "Did you know she was pregnant at the time?"

"Did you?" Faye tapped into a reservoir of womanly rage. "Or were you too busy pursuing your next conquest?"

"You know damned well Janis and I had been married three months by then."

"Does it matter?" Faye's animosity was palpable.

"Janis was at least four weeks pregnant at the time of the lab *accident* – if it was an accident."

"How can you be so sure of that?" Faye had to wait for an answer.

"It had been that long since she and I – were together."

Faye stared him down. "Is that normal for newlyweds?"

A wrenching finality came over Colin. There was little left to say but what there was spoke volumes. He leaned forward with arms on the table.

"It sucks when it takes a marriage to wake up. The fact is – I married the wrong woman." Without saying it, Faye knew his most bitter truth was about her.

Faye digested what she heard with leaden indifference, a full heart, and a careless disregard for the little voice of what might have been. She looked away from Colin, disgusted. "No. She married the wrong man. You don't know what marriage is. You certainly don't know how to be a father."

The final blow was landed. Colin drained of all fire, all resolve to confront her. He reached for the remote control and switched off the video display. Standing, he picked up his coffee cup. His manner was all business but his energy was defeated.

"We both deserved that." He walked to the door. "Maybe now we can get on with the work. There's more I need to tell you. But not now. I'm going to the surface. I won't be available. I'll call you." He hurried out the door.

The emergency meeting ended as abruptly as it had begun.

Faye sat in the empty conference room, expecting more.

One of twelve chairs was left pulled back from an otherwise undisturbed table. Spots of brightness from track lighting bathed the large oval. An unbearable tension lingered in the room. It was the only evidence that anyone else had been invited.

Sixteen years of unfinished business between them had gone by in a blink.

Faye felt like crying but couldn't.

She sat a long while, astonished. A solitary surprise of instant reflection petrified her. Not sure of her feelings, her breaths quickened around a realization.

There was nothing left – of what she knew was no longer there.

CHAPTER 13

Marie-Louise Square
European Quarter, Brussels

Eugene Mass eased back on the heated leather and waited for his driver to open the black Bentley Mulsanne's rear door. It was the middle of the afternoon but weather kept traffic light. They had made good time from Mass' office to the rendezvous site. Buttoning up his topcoat, Mass took a moment to reflect. Looking around, he was dismayed.

A dusting of snow had drained color from the familiar row of Art Nouveau residences. Their elongated windows and ornamental spires reached for a grey sky without inspiration. Once decorative arches and moldings now seemed pallid and excessive in the cold. Across the street, a frozen lake was ringed by frosted trees. Everywhere around him, the bloom of nature was in retreat and the encroaching works of man appeared pitiful.

The skyline was a disheartening contrast of architectural styles. New concrete blockhouses squatted next to 19th century charmers. Looming above the unlikely pairings were the glass and steel monoliths of finance and government. In their false glory they exuded the arrogance and narcissism of global enterprise. Mass knew it all too well. He was a part of it. He was also in the best position to bring it down.

As the heart of the European Union, the once great European Quarter was considered by Mass to be a governmental ghetto. It was a place where neglect and lack of planning met a callous infatuation with anything new. The evidence surrounded him. Bureaucratic expediency and the lust for mindless profit had run roughshod over the lessons of history and civilizing culture.

This street had come to symbolize the world for him.

No wonder he found it so easy to come here in secret to plan its reordering.

The car door opened and Mass stepped into the cold holding his gloves.

"I expect a longer session today but I may have to leave on a moment's notice."

The driver doubled as bodyguard. "Yes, sir." Mass was accompanied to the front door of the residence but not inside. He had a key; there was no need to knock.

Mass headed up the stairs right away. He ignored the elaborate furnishings, the fine paintings and exquisite woodworking. Even though he had supervised their installation, today they seemed out of place for the work at hand. A sterile operating room with scalpels and needles would be more fitting. The patient was dying but in denial; the disease was aggressive. Only drastic amputation would save the body. The burden of being the one who had to do it was a crushing but humbling reminder that without moral conviction, facile chance alone guided individual fate.

At the fourth floor landing, Mass found the door to the room at the front of the house open. He stepped into the scent of fresh-brewed espresso and bathed in the light from slanted windows in the vaulted ceiling. He knew the place from frequent visits but took inventory anyway. What was once a bedroom for children was now an office, a meeting place where surgeons conspired to launch a bloody intervention.

It was time to revisit the tryst.

"I've been waiting for you, lover." It was a voice of inflated machismo reeking of sarcasm. It belonged to the handsome man on the sofa.

"If you mean we're all fucked, I'm inclined to agree." Mass shed his topcoat and helped himself to a cup of Jamaican Blue Mountain Peaberry. He stood at the window and wallowed in his disgust.

The voice fell out of character. Its true accent was a blend of far-flung experience. "We don't have to do this today if you're not feeling up to it."

"I know damned well what we need to do. Putting it off won't make it any easier." Mass turned to face a lounging man half his age. Years of their private collusion had made Mass as much friend as boss. Sometimes the casualness between them felt too familiar. Other times, Mass was thankful for someone he could interact with man-to-man. Someone who wasn't afraid to call bullshit to his face.

Javier Francisco was not his birth name but it adorned his American passport. An expat twice removed from Cordoba, Spain, Javier had run the full spectrum of a colorful life. From male model to drug runner, from soldier to bouncer, from activist to private operative, the man was a caldron of energy and contradictions.

It now seemed a lifetime away. Mass had recruited Javier off the streets of Marseille. Back then, by day he did dirty work for *Friends of the Ocean*. By night he worked at a techno-dance club tending bar and exercising his dick with anything young and willing. In exchange for his loyalty, Mass promised a lucrative income and membership in an exclusive club. Club members did dirty work for Mass.

Javier had once stood on the deck of the environmental research ship PaxTerra wearing a windbreaker and green ski mask. He had shoved a handmade sign at the camera announcing *Operation Mermaid's Tears*.

Shadowing André Bolard had been Javier's first assignment. Since then, he had become an essential resource for coordinating business that by necessity must remain secret. Javier shared Mass' vision for a stable and ordered future. More importantly, Javier needed to be where the action was, on the inside track, in line to be rewarded.

To protect the final stages of the overall plan, Mass had set him up in this residence as a kept man, the object of Mass' philandering desires, the secret tryst into bisexual bliss that was sure to be discovered. Once rumored, the salaciousness of it had blinded an orgasmic press to the real motive for their occasional get-togethers. Never substantiated but made guilty as sin by investigative journalists, it provided the perfect cover.

Ironically enough, the ruse had been the suggestion of Mass' wife, Leah. She felt the future was too important for pride and held no illusions what would work. Both of them were too rich and too old to cling to monogamous fantasies. That would be their story. Racing each other to the bottom, the world's media would believe it and propagate it. The indoctrinated masses would be teased to distraction.

Mass took a seat in a favorite overstuffed chair. "Where are we?"

"Where would you like to begin?"

"Tell me about Malcolm."

Javier lifted a leg off a coffee table and straightened up. "We can't be sure if he discovered more than Riya. Whatever he knew, Janis has to know. She never showed up for the deposition. Indian police can't locate her."

"And the laptop?"

"Gone."

"We have to get to her first."

"Just like Malcolm?"

"No! We can't afford that kind of sacrifice if we can help it. Not again." An agony discharged through Mass. "She's too valuable in the lab. There's more to do on simplifying the delivery of *GenLET*. There's still a chance she'll come around. We need her to finish her work on the rapid therapy method."

"That's a huge gamble. If anything leaks out…"

"I know. Prepare countermeasures just in case."

"This sucks. So much exposure over one fucking memo! We don't even know if she has the damned thing!"

"We have to assume she does. I'll have Indian police coordinate with Interpol. Wherever she's running, we'll bring her back. NovoSenectus will press charges. We'll make it about intellectual capital."

Javier pulled on his upper lip and nodded.

Mass felt a prodding sixth sense. "I'm surprised she hasn't gone public already. What is she waiting for?" A silent gap filled with concern. "We've been acting on the assumption we know more than she does. What if she knows something else? What if she's *been told* something else?"

"What can she know?"

"You tell me. That's your job."

"There's nothing. Riya had good reasons to keep her in the dark."

"Don't avoid the fucking issue. Somebody kidnapped the daughter. Alyssa is leverage but for what? Did Janis run out of India or was she taken out? If she was taken out, was it willingly or by force? Does somebody want *GenLET* secrets as ransom? What could we be missing?"

"Isn't *GenLET* too complicated? She can't have it all in her head."

"She knows enough."

"She has no access to NovoSenectus to give anybody the details."

Mass felt the weight of holding the prize everyone wanted. "If you locked Robert Oppenheimer in a room, you wouldn't have the atomic bomb. But you'd have the next best thing."

"We'll find her."

Mass was all boss as he stared at Javier. "We better. She can hurt us two ways."

"So what if we get into a situation."

"Say what you mean."

"If it comes down to it, when does she become expendable?"

"You already know the answer. Tell me."

Javier hesitated. "To preserve the plan, we're *all* expendable…" He looked up at Mass with a wry smile. "…at least down to 500 million."

Mass had a second cup of espresso. He let Javier's affirmation of 3rd Protocol linger in the room undisturbed. It was a good reminder for both of them. Cup in hand, Mass stood at the window. His gaze saw nothing in particular. He was tired of looking upon a troubled world. With that in mind, he grew intensely serious.

"What about Goodwin Diye. Have we set up the necessary financial accounts?"

"Everything's in order. Finances and legal instruments."

"Double check it. Goodwin Diye must be in place; it's imperative. It's the only insurance I have that things will get done. Anything new going on with vaccines?"

"The 3rd Protocol extension to MIOVAC is ready."

"Does that include halal inoculations?"

"Of course."

"Good. We can't overlook any detail. One-fifth of humanity is Muslim. Devout Muslims will not permit themselves to be injected with vaccines grown in pig cells or alcohol. When something is permissible by Islamic law, it's halal. We must provision accordingly."

"It's being done."

"Do you have anything else for me?"

Javier thought a second. "You wanted me to keep an eye on The Center for Earth Awareness – one of Curtis Labon's think tanks."

Mass squinted and snickered. "Imagine that. He has more than one."

"He's lobbying all nations to sign the Population Neutral Policy Treaty."

"In a revised state no doubt. He's tried that before."

"This one is more aggressive."

"Give an example."

"The new treaty would make all foreign aid contingent upon the receiving country's government adopting certain Population Neutral Policies."

"Such as?"

"It requires all women of child-bearing age implanted with a treaty-approved birth control device. Governments would issue permits when women can get pregnant. Permits would be decided by lottery. To be eligible for the lottery, certain criteria would need to be met."

Mass looked down on the snowy street below.

"A remarkably old idea. And I imagine a spectacular failure."

"It's applauded at all the international conferences…"

"And ignored in the legislatures."

"It's gotten a lot of attention. Their newsletter has twelve million subscribers."

"No doubt. Everybody likes to hear what someone else is doing to solve the problem. It makes them feel so much better about doing nothing at all themselves." Mass strolled back to his seat. "It's an odd state of affairs. Progress nowadays only defines how bad the problem is. Did you know that Iran is the only country where contraceptive classes are required for men and women before a marriage license can be obtained? In India, only people with two or fewer children are eligible to run for election to local government. China is the only country with a one-child policy – that alone has prevented 400 million births, a massive weight on the planet."

Javier sat in reverential silence. He had seen Eugene Mass like this before. It was often at his lowest point that his loftiest idea came forth.

Mass smiled. As was his habit, he rubbed his right temple to feed energy to his thoughts. "So much for old business. Let's begin with what comes next."

CHAPTER 14

Bright Hope Farms
South Hero Island, Vermont

Sara Rushton entered the boathouse knowing where to look for her daughter. Stretched out on a bay window couch with blankets over her legs, Janis was engrossed with a webpage open before her. The mid-day view of Lake Champlain offered an unchanging palette and little movement. The occasional Pine Grosbeak or Snow Bunting flew by but Janis no longer noticed them.

Sara broke the studious seclusion with an offering. "How about some lunch?"

"Sounds good. Thanks."

Sara set the covered plate down. "My guests have gone – if you want to come back to the house."

"I've kinda settled in here for now. Did you have a nice visit?"

"Oh, sure. Whenever they're down this way from Swanton, they like to see how I'm doing. They love to talk about their road trips. Sorry it took so long."

"We got the Jeep in the garage just in time."

"I don't think it would have been a problem. They're harmless."

"I know. It's just better if no one knows I'm here."

Sara motioned to a color printout on a stack of research. "What's this?"

"A map. Knockout Mouse volunteered it in his last email. He said Bolard is back at home. The map shows where in Marseille I can find him."

Sara sank into a nearby chair. "I thought you reconsidered that."

"What gave you *that* idea?"

"It's been several days…"

"I was waiting for word Bolard was back in town. Let's not get into it."

"You know how I feel."

"I know but nothing's changed. I've scheduled a flight out later tonight."

"You didn't tell me about this."

"I just confirmed the tickets. I was going to tell you as soon as I finished here."

"There's nothing I can say to change your mind?"

"Sure there is. You can tell me Alyssa is up at the house, waiting to see me. You can show me proof that Eugene Mass has given up on this plan."

"All right. Do as you wish. If there's anything I can do, I'm here. But I think you're going to need help. You're jumping into a complex, chaotic situation. Worst yet, you're trusting everything to circumstantial evidence. I can't believe you accept what this shadow, this Knockout Mouse sends you. It's anonymous hearsay."

"The facts I know are strong enough." Janis looked out across the lake.

"Something else is bothering you. What is it?"

"It's nothing. Just something I have to decide."

"About Marseille?"

"No."

"Tell me. I need to know what's going on with you. How else can I help?"

Janis considered holding back but couldn't. "I discovered something else on the laptop. It's everything Malcolm used to access GeLixCo."

"The backdoor into their network?"

Janis nodded. "I wonder if it still works. I imagine they've plugged that hole by now."

"You're not thinking of trying it, are you?"

"I don't know. Don't worry. I wouldn't do it from here. When Malcolm did it, he disguised his route. I don't know how to do that."

Sara scooted to the edge of her seat. "Janis, listen, you really have to think this through. Holding what someone else stole is one thing. Stealing more yourself takes it to a whole different level."

"You don't have to tell me. I know what it would mean."

"Then why involve yourself so deeply?"

"Because Malcolm didn't get all of it. He told me so."

"You said there was a good chance he got cut off because they detected him. Look what happened to him."

"There's more to Riya's story. There's a reason why she needed to hide what she did. More of the truth is still out there."

"The truth. How much worse can it get? If the part you already have is true, you already know what Mass is planning."

"Riya hid certain things for a reason. I have to know why."

"You can't protect yourself if you go down this path. No one can."

"I told you – I'll wait to do it in a public place, a web-hotspot somewhere."

"None of this makes sense. What about Bolard? Do you intend to walk right up to him with the laptop and try to make a deal?"

"I've thought it through. I can get two safety deposit boxes when I get there. I'll put the laptop in one and take the key to the other, empty deposit box to the meeting. If he takes the key away from me without making a deal, he gets nothing and I'll know he's a liar. If he's serious, he'll get the real key when I see Alyssa."

"All that does is give you a false sense of security. Besides, it's amateurish. He'll see right through that."

"Then give me a better idea."

Sara raised her voice. "Go to the FBI. Go to Faye. Drop the damned laptop in a mailbox someplace and be done with it. I don't know. Just don't sacrifice yourself on a wild goose chase."

"It would be easier to take your advice if I knew you could follow it yourself. I don't think you could; not if I was the one kidnapped and you had this laptop."

"No, you're wrong. Rushing to do something might make things worse. And doing something foolish wouldn't prove my love for you." Sara got up to go. "I'll be up at the house if you need anything." Sara stepped out of the boathouse.

Janis was alone with her thoughts. She needed to refocus away from her mother's objections and doubts. She gazed at the laptop screen. Ad banners flashed but she was inured to them. The title of the article she was reading attracted her eye.

"*Nature's Built-in Limitation on the Number of Times Human Cells Can Divide*." Her attention drifted down the page, catching passages here and there.

"Replicative Cell Senescence in human fibroblasts...the stopping mechanisms are poorly understood...changes in the structure of the telomeres seem to be the cause... telomerase promotes the formation of protein cap structures that protect chromosome ends... human fibroblasts are deficient in telomerase, their telomeres shorten with every cell division...their protective protein caps progressively deteriorate...the result is DNA damage at chromosome ends."

The road to *GenLET* had started back in 1961 when Dr. Leonard Hayflick at Stanford University discovered that human cells could only divide a limited number of times. No more than 50 divisions were permissible by nature. Based on 50 divisions and barring lifestyle issues, Dr. Hayflick calculated that the maximum lifespan for humans, as programmed by nature, was 110 to 120 years. That was how long it took for that many cell divisions to occur in the body.

It was a natural fact that had fascinated Riya Basu. Aging was programmed in nature and human cells aged by a calculated degeneration of DNA. Somewhere, something had fashioned telomeres to be a burning fuse. As time passed and the fuse burned down, a human life would near its end. At first, cells would become more susceptible to deterioration, then organs would be less able to defend themselves, less resilient, more feeble and prone to disease. Time and DNA damage took its toll.

It was ironic. Scientists had always thought the lack of telomerase in most human cells was a protection from damaging runaway cell growth, such as what happens in cancer. Then they discovered most cancer cells had regained the capability to produce telomerase. Cancer cells maintained telomere function as they proliferated. Cancer cells didn't undergo Replicative Cell Senescence like other human cells. Somehow cancer had figured out how to beat the life cycle system.

Janis closed the laptop. The flood of lab work she had done with Riya came back to mind. It was overwhelming. Cancer had figured out how to beat natural limits. But in doing so, it had turned itself into the unspecialized cell, a damaging law unto itself. The majesty of *GenLET* was figuring out how to harness the iconoclastic cancer cell, learn from it, then merge it back into the natural order in a way that didn't turn off aging – but slowed it to a crawl. The irony doubled back on itself. Who would have ever thought that cancer, the great killer, would hold the final key to the fountain of youth?

Janis had been so deeply concentrating, she failed to notice the man at water's edge. His movement up the shoreline had been slow but steady. Suddenly distracted, she shifted her gaze, only to find the man staring up the bank at the boathouse. A chill ran through her. She felt paralyzed but needed to run. Whoever he was, he was trespassing on *Bright Hope Ranch* property. There was no legitimate reason for him to approach the main house from the beach.

Janis wavered. She had no phone. She could hardly call the police even if she had one. Should she run to the house with or without the laptop? Or stay put. She might endanger Sara by leading him there.

She slid off the couch and scurried across the floor out of view of the window. She knew the bathroom's pocket door was loose. She scampered to the bathroom doorway and buried the laptop in the wall behind the door. There was only one way out of the boathouse. The front door. Just then, a knock was heard.

CHAPTER 15

The Boathouse
Bright Hope Farms

The knock sounded again. This time, more playfully. Five knocks…then two.

Janis edged back into the main room, aware the stranger knew she was there. He had seen her. No way could she pretend otherwise. She paused and looked for a weapon. Should she open the door? If she didn't, would he break in anyway?

"Janis! It's all right. I just want to talk." The voice sounded casual but resolute. The man knocked five times again and waited for Janis to answer with two of her own. Instead, she opened the door.

The man was not what she expected. Shorter and unimposing, he was a rumpled stray with a rugged but cartoonish face, an oddball waif in his 40s that carried the airs of an idiot savant. He wore a drab wool coat over black jeans with sneakers that had seen better days. On his head was a Black Hawk camouflage toque with built-in headphones.

"Can I come in? It's fucking cold out here. It's winter you know."

Janis stood her ground. "Who are you? What do you want?"

The man blew hellacious noises into a handkerchief. "What do you want from me – soul searching? I'm Knockout Mouse. Who else would I be?"

Janis took a step back. "Knockout Mouse!"

The man invited himself in and stepped past her. "Don't ask me to explain myself. You're the one on the hook here."

Janis closed the door and stood back against it ready to reopen and run.

The man gave himself a tour of the boathouse's main room. "You should really be more careful. I imagine Eugene Mass has half of the goons in the world out looking for you."

"I have no idea who you are. There's no reason to believe anything you say."

"That's quite a declaration." He picked up the printout of the map of Marseille with key locations pinpointed. The map was right where Sara had seen it and Janis had left it. He waved it in the air then set it back down while enjoying a little bluster.

"Don't tell me you're like those women in bars or clubs – oh so suspicious of the men they meet. They wouldn't think of giving any of those men their personal information. After all, they just met and all they know is what they see. But those same women will go home and post detailed profiles of themselves online or chat with people they *can't* see and gab away everything." He dropped the map. "If only you were as cautious about your email habits."

Janis flinched at the oversight. In her haste to hide the laptop, she had neglected to hide her research. "How did you find me?"

"It was easy once you opened this map. It contains a web beacon. It calls home when it's opened. That call was all I needed." Sitting down, he lounged back and got comfortable. "You're lucky Malcolm disabled the tracker on his laptop; otherwise, you'd be in deep shit. NovoSenectus would have you strung up by now."

"What are you doing here?" Janis remained standing at the door.

"You have no idea how important you are, do you?"

Janis said nothing.

"No, I didn't think so. Maybe if you knew a few things it would help."

"I've been told I know too much already."

"You can never know enough."

"This was forced on me. It's not my idea."

"Join the pity party. Everyday is forced on us. It's the curse of being alive."

"All I want is my daughter back."

"You don't act like it. I think you're lying."

"My friends have been murdered. My daughter taken from me…"

"But you ran. That makes you look guilty – of something. For the past week you've been impersonating a dead man – a man with a sticky past. I knew something was screwy with that first email. It didn't sound like Malcolm."

"I needed to get to NCO…"

"Oh, yeah, I know why you did it. Don't bullshit me. There's more going on. Why the fuck are you going to Marseille?"

"I told you."

"Like I said, you have no idea how important you are. When I found out who was emailing me, let me tell you – I had a spasm of joy you wouldn't believe."

"What are you talking about?"

"Riya's dead. You are *GenLET* now. You can make it work. You know the dirty little secrets NovoSenectus hides in India. Only you know how to finish *GenLET* and make it work in mass production. You are the key to the Rapid Therapy Technique. What the hell are you doing – *trading GenLET* for your daughter? Maybe you already did. Is that why you need the map? Are you going there to pick her up?"

"I don't have to tell you anything."

"No, you don't. But then, you won't find out anything either. I'd rather be sitting here than standing where you are. You have no idea what's involved – or how bad it can get. Did you hear about the merry little troupe in Malaysia? Some say they work for the Chinese. They claim they just acquired *GenLET* for themselves. News of it came out today. I hope you know what you're doing. I suspect you don't."

"That's preposterous! I wouldn't give *GenLET* away to just anybody."

"Even to get your daughter back? Honey, that's the way it looks. And let me tell you, the people I represent aren't one bit happy about it – because they stole it first. In their minds, everyone else has signed the *Life Extension Non-Proliferation Treaty* – in spirit, if you know what I mean. You think you pissed off Eugene Mass. He'll have to get in line."

"Who do you represent? Who are these people?"

"They've been working together a long time. I used to think they were working for something important."

"You work for them?"

"I've done a little bit of everything for them over the past twenty years."

"They have *GenLET*?"

"And Mass doesn't know it. Ain't that a bitch. The life extension club has more members than he planned. But then, you knew *that* was going to happen. The rich and powerful were always going to find a way to get it from him. But that's as far as it goes. You trading it away for your daughter could blow the whole thing."

"What thing?"

"The new class order! *GenLET* for the rich and global governance for everyone else. Wake up! Just because Bolard is a clueless prick doesn't make him wrong."

"But how can *I* blow the whole thing?"

"Because you don't fucking care who you give *GenLET* to – just as long as you get Alyssa back. Isn't that right? What kind of Boy Scout do you think André Bolard is? How fast do you think he'll put *GenLET* on the open market? How many times can he quickly sell it before everyone realizes everyone has it? Is Malaysia celebrating too soon or did you really give it to them? I need to know."

"Relax. Marseille isn't about *GenLET*."

"If you have a way to prove that – The Group would be most appreciative."

"The Group?"

"They don't have a name. Of course, they've had nicknames. Your boss likes to call them 8-Ball."

Janis stepped back. Tears filled her eyes. "Oh, my God!"

"What part of that sent you ballistic?"

"You work for 8-Ball…!"

"It seems my reputation precedes me. Do we need a time out here?"

Janis jerked open the door and ran outside. In her fear and confusion, she dashed parallel to the shore, into a wooded area. Knockout Mouse chased after her. Kicking up snow as they went, they entered a small clearing a minute later. Being out-of-breath forced Janis to realize there was nowhere to go. She stopped her running but was still shaken.

Knockout Mouse kept distance from her but approached cautiously. "All right. Let's settle down. This isn't the Iditarod and I'm not Hannibal Lecter."

Janis gasped for air. "Stay away from me!"

"I don't know who told you about 8-Ball but if it was Mass consider the source. You're running away from *him*, remember?"

Janis was shivering cold but shaking from nerves. "It's the same thing…" Janis gasped for air. With hands on hips, she walked in circles. "You want the same thing…"

"Life extension…"

"No!" Anger erupted at the evil being planned. Janis faced Knockout Mouse and shouted. "The 3rd Protocol! A '*most equitable method of population collapse*,' isn't that right? Zoonotic agents that preserve '*proportional segments of ethnic diversity*' when the time comes for global pruning."

Knockout Mouse had heard a ghost. "The *3rd* Protocol?"

Janis continued on a tear. "You have it all planned, don't you? Simulations and projections, contingency plans for post-collapse scenarios."

He stepped up and grabbed her by the shoulders. "Where did you hear about a 3rd Protocol?"

Janis jerked away from him. "Don't act so innocent. I know for a fact you're part of it."

"Part of what? Where did you hear this?"

"I read the white papers 8-Ball published. I've seen the plan!"

Knockout Mouse grabbed her once again. "The Group has never had any plans for a 3rd Protocol."

"I don't believe you."

"What did you find out? What is Mass doing?"

"Riya saw it – that's why she was killed. Malcolm recovered the proof. That's why they murdered him. I guess you're here to finish the job."

"I came here about *GenLET*."

"Are you telling me you know nothing about a 3rd Protocol? That's a lie!" Janis started running further into the woods.

"Goddamn it! Listen to me!" Knockout Mouse gave chase. He raised his voice. "I don't know of any *3rd* Protocol – just the 1st and 2nd."

With that, Janis halted and turned around. "1st and 2nd? There's more?"

Knockout Mouse kept his distance. "Let's go back and get warm."

"Answer me! There's more?"

He threw his arms up. "If there's a *3rd*, did you really think it would start there? Come on, we both have a few things to tell each other."

"Why should I tell you anything?"

"Do you want to stop Mass or do you want to stay alive?"

Janis was perplexed. The dilemma left her mute.

"You might think those are your only options. Keep to yourself on this one and they certainly could be." Knockout Mouse started back towards the boathouse.

Janis stood in place, her legs wet and cold, her arm wrapped tightly across her chest. "I would never team up with you!"

Knockout Mouse kept going but called back. "It's mutual interest, nothing more. Fuck the team thing."

Janis was curious. The boathouse was warm. She headed back.

CHAPTER 16

The Boathouse
Bright Hope Farms

Knockout Mouse made himself at home. He kicked off wet sneakers and left them to dry over a floor heating vent. He moved through the space as if he lived there. Shedding his jacket, he set to work in the kitchenette making coffee. Janis could see he was on edge and needed something to do with his energy. He spoke to himself at first, a stream of consciousness sounding as much wounded as enflamed. Janis caught only a part of it.

"...Everyday, something new for the wicked, while paradise is always the same. Some would rather have pride in hell than share in heaven's shame..."

Janis took a folded blanket from the couch and wrapped it over her shoulders. She stepped to the edge of the carpet where the kitchenette began and watched as Knockout Mouse gripped and re-gripped a kitchen rag as absentminded relief.

"'Millions long for immortality who do not know what to do with themselves on a rainy Sunday afternoon.' I wonder if Susan Ertz would have wanted GenLET."

"Who is Susan Ertz?"

"A British author you haven't read. Doesn't matter. Tell me what you know about 3rd Protocol."

"You came to me. You first."

"Is that the way it's gonna be? Show me yours or I won't show you mine?"

"You work for this Group, this thing called 8-Ball. I know for a fact 3rd Protocol is based on their work. For me, that makes you complicit with Mass."

"Mass left The Group years ago, before he bought NovoSenectus."

"He was one of them?"

"Nine members minus one – 8-Ball."

"It doesn't matter when he left. The policy work done by The Group calls for population collapse. Don't try to deny it."

"The Group's plan calls for *Phased* Population Reduction – not collapse."

"That's not what I read."

"It's not what it seems. Nothing is. A year before 9/11, the Pentagon conducted a training simulation called MASCAL. They trained for a passenger jet flying into the Pentagon. That doesn't mean the military had advance knowledge of 9/11."

"Some people think so."

"All right. Bad example."

"Why did Mass leave The Group?"

"Progress was too slow. Group successes were minimal. He thought the *inconvenient truth* about what was happening to the planet was a call to action – not education or legislation. Mass was the one who came up with the idea of Protocols to begin with. It was his compromise between unacceptable extremes – doing nothing or mass murder."

"Killing six billion people is not a compromise!"

"The 3rd Protocol is pure Mass – unrestrained by The Group."

"Admit it – 3rd Protocol is no surprise to you."

"The Group always knew the worst-case scenario was possible. But Mass was so worried he wouldn't live long enough to finish his work, The Group thought his pursuit of life extension had kept him fully occupied. It was always wishful thinking on their part. As years went by, it became easier to believe."

"So what are the Protocols?"

"I told you. Phased Population Reduction. They're targeted changes to the human genome to stop the world's population from doubling every fifty years. That trend is clearly unsustainable."

"What kind of targeted changes?"

Knockout Mouse clutched the washrag one last time then tossed it in the sink. "Gradual. Explainable. Acceptable without panic. Natural looking if possible."

"Such as?"

"It took a lot of think-tank study before anyone felt comfortable giving the green light to anything. Mass hated the endless analysis. In the end, The Group agreed the safest way was to target young and old first. People in the prime of life had the clout and awareness to resist – even when it was for their own good."

"Young and old. I don't understand."

"Attack the problem from both ends. Delay fertility in the young and put a cap on lifespan for the old. 1st Protocol would delay fertility until age 25. The 2nd Protocol would cap lifespan at 70."

"Unbelievable! How could they take it on themselves to do such a thing! Who do they think they are?"

"The voice of reason. The answer to the *Tragedy of the Commons*. The wise ones who have chartered a course between animal ethics and Armageddon."

"They think it's reasonable to limit a human life to 70 years?"

Knockout Mouse shrugged. "It was that or go with Mass and do it his way."

"There *are* other choices!"

"Oh, really? What? Mess with people's cherished reproductive rights? Hand out condoms to the Third World? Teach abstinence to poor people in countries with high infant mortality rates, people who reproduce like rabbits because they're worried there won't be anyone to take care of them in their old age? Mass got fed up with half measures."

"What about The Group?"

"In their plan, the 2nd Protocol would be reversible – once the world's population reduced to its optimum level."

"And who gets to set that?"

"The Group believes reason and logic should determine it. There have been many studies of MVP, the Minimum Viable Population size. A lot has to be considered. What is critical mass to ensure the common welfare and exclude inequality? What level preserves cultural and bio-diversity? What standard of living should be expected? At what average per-capital energy use would human society and the natural planet both be able to thrive?"

"It's as simple as that, huh? Crunch the numbers, come up with a formula, dispense the logical remedy. No qualms. No debate."

"When your jet is going down, don't quibble over the shape of your parachute."

"So what MVP did they come up with?"

"The Group never agreed on a number. For Mass, it was five hundred million."

Under her blanket, Janis shivered. "*Maintain humanity under 500,000,000 in perpetual balance with nature* ...the first principle on the Georgia Guidestones."

"Whatever. Like minds come to similar conclusions. University professors have published articles saying the same thing."

A wave of deep feeling swept through Janis. It was a grief-like sinkhole of pain for all that could happen. She had to retreat to the main room and sit on the couch.

"Just the thought that someone could plan all of this..."

Knockout Mouse followed her. "Oh, they did more than plan it."

A dagger of disbelief pinned Janis in place. "They went through with it?"

A nod from Knockout Mouse. "1st Protocol's complete."

Janis' mind raced into denial. "But there's no sign of it."

"Funny you should say that. Shadow research funded by The Group is about to be released from independent sources in Japan and Germany. Didn't you know that animal studies have confirmed that a cocktail of chemicals in the environment are responsible for the drop in teenage pregnancies around the world?"

"What do you mean, *shadow research*?"

"The Group knew 15 years ago this day would come. When it did, society would need plausible science to explain and temper the blow. They planned these studies as untraceable yet ready to be released at the proper time. That time is now."

"Why now?"

"Because 27% of the world's population is below the age of 15. All of them have parents who were exposed to the 1st Protocol. None of those children will be fertile until the age of 25."

Janis bolted from the couch. The blanket dropped from her shoulders. She lunged at him. "You mean that's it! The bastards actually did this?"

Taken back by the power of Janis' approach, Knockout Mouse could only nod.

"All the children...my Alyssa!" The certainty hit her. He was serious.

Knockout Mouse was stone-cold. "Fait accompli."

In a fit of shock and rage and a mother's terror, Janis slapped him across the face. "How dare you! How could you!" She slapped him again and sobbed openly. "This can't be happening! No! Who in the hell do you people think you are!"

Knockout Mouse stood by, restrained but jittery. Janis paced like a caged animal. She shook her head over and over and searched for answers at her feet. "All of humanity! The future of everything!"

He rubbed away the sting from the side of his face. "It was released fourteen years ago. In all that time, there have been no bad side effects."

"The whole fucking thing is a bad side effect! It's nothing but stupidity and somebody's outrageous arrogance! They probably don't believe in God but they damned well want to be one, don't they!" Janis could no longer stand. She sat on the edge of the couch with her knees together, hugging herself. "How does it work?"

"The key change is made in the parents, by viral infection. The process completes before the children are born. Fetal germ cells are modified. From then on, the trait is inherited."

The final blow hit Janis. She looked up at him with a fatalistic stare. "It's passed on…to all generations?"

Knockout Mouse was mute and motionless. He could see Janis was on the edge of losing it again. He waited in silence while the full weight of her awareness settled around her. This time he could see a profound sadness overtake her.

"You did it to the children!"

"The children grow up knowing no other way. The parents will live their lives and eventually die off. Affecting the parents would have increased the possibility of public resistance. This way, the Protocols will be in place before anyone realizes what's happened. It's the Boiling Frog Syndrome. In The Group's position papers, it's referred to as *an application of the doctrine of the inevitability of gradualism*."

"The 2nd Protocol. Have they done that too?"

"They're about to. That's why I'm here. That's why you're so important."

"Me?" Janis was a limp rag, ready to be grasped.

As Knockout Mouse sat down next to her on the couch, his attitude shifted. A pure and determined sincerity blunted the sarcastic edge. "I was just a kid in college when my father got me a job doing research for this new think tank. Back then I thought we were the vanguard of real change. I remember the first Earth Day and the national contest to come up with a recycling symbol. Everyone now knows what that green triple arrow means. It's universal. It's ironic because *triple green* has always been the go-code for anything done by The Group."

"So what's changed?"

"That's just it – not much. I thought progress was that simple. The Group did too. A lot has happened, not much of it good. Everyone's become someone else. Over twenty years my faith in the process drained away. I see it clearly now – The Group is no better than Mass. They've stolen *GenLET*. They're ready to implement the 2nd Protocol for everyone else, capping the lifespan, while they live 300 years and lead the *New Class Order*. The only difference between Mass and them is Mass doesn't hide behind altruistic rhetoric and euphemisms. They are diplomats with a velvet glove and secret timetable. Mass is an insect that knows to abandon the hive when it means survival."

"Why don't you leave them?"

"Why don't people leave bad marriages? Commitment and fear. I know nothing else and I'm afraid of what might happen if I ran off the ranch."

"They'd kill you if you quit your job?"

"Oh, I'm sure it wouldn't be a Group decision. One or two of the more paranoid ones would meet in a corner; they'd want to be sure. Leave no loose ends. Who knows. It's more likely than not. I definitely know too much about them and what they've done."

"Why are you telling me all of this?"

"Whatever happens, I have a sense it's all coming to an end. Whether that applies personally or globally, I don't know. Face it, humanity is the Incredible Wobbly Tower. We all suspect it's about to fall. It's too far gone to stop it, but there are still things we can do to soften the blow."

"How?"

"I can get you the base to the 2nd Protocol – before they release it. You may be able to devise a way to inoculate humanity against it and any future phases."

"What future phases? I thought you didn't know about the 3rd Protocol."

"That's right, but The Group left the door open. They have other ideas. Nothing as formalized as the 2nd Protocol – the one you must stop."

"That's crazy! You're asking me to genetically engineer something and release it on the world. If I did that, I'd be no better than them."

"A bullet has no morality, only the person using it. You'd be stopping them."

"It's out of the question. Why not just expose The Group and their plan?"

"Be real. They're too well insulated. They maneuver within layers of disinformation. They buy influence and create cover stories that become the history books used in schools. I could never pin them down. I'd be shuffled out the side door with the media clowns and conspiracy bloggers."

Facts and opinions cascaded across Janis' mind. She had to stand and walk away from him. Knockout Mouse leaned forward, sitting on the edge of the couch.

"If Mass is using the same base, maybe you can stop them both."

"Are the 1st and 2nd Protocols based on *GenLET*?"

"No."

Janis paced. "Then he isn't using the same thing."

Knockout Mouse raised up. "He based 3rd Protocol on life extension? How does he collapse the population with life extension? That doesn't make sense."

"As best as I can tell from what Riya discovered, he's harnessed apoptosis – programmed cell death. By using metagenomic techniques, the 3rd Protocol convinces the body's immune system that *all* body cells have severe DNA damage. The body naturally views DNA-damaged cells as prone to becoming cancerous. In effect, the body sees its own DNA as a cancer and triggers apoptosis in all cells. In a convoluted way, he's used *GenLET* to craft a cancer of DNA."

"Insidious little fucker, isn't he."

Taken with a new angle, Janis turned back to face him. "What about the government – is the government involved in this? Are they partners in any way?"

"Yes and no."

"What does that mean?"

"Good and bad come in all shades. Some people have been planted in key places, many others co-opted, many more bought off with grants, tenure, or a civil service paycheck. Most don't know the master they serve."

"If you have to dance around the answer, you must be lying."

"There is no yes-or-no answer to some questions. As far as the government is concerned, Mass and The Group feel the same way. Governments are too dimwitted, lethargic, corrupt, and self-serving for something like this. Elected officials are the intellectually and morally bankrupt reflections of the populaces they serve."

As long as Knockout Mouse was being so talkative, Janis went to the next question on her list. "Did you steal a GAMA from a Navy lab years ago and give it to the *Friends of the Ocean*?"

His eyes widened at the non sequitur. “Ah, that’s close to the truth. I had someone else steal it for me and I *sold* it – I didn’t give it to LALO. The whole thing was a stunt to provide cover for the 1st Protocol. LALO didn’t know they were being used. They enjoyed the publicity. Meanwhile, the suicide gene from the GAMA was put into the 1st Protocol Base.”

“And you got blackmailed.”

“It was a sensitive time between me and The Group. I couldn’t afford a screw-up, especially one with exposure that came so close to them. As time passed, the blackmail perpetuated itself. The things I had to divulge to keep the original secret only forced the deception deeper.”

“You must really want to bring them down. Why else would you tell me all of this? You couldn’t be setting me up for something, could you?”

“Only wingbats and moon-nuts would be so foolish.” He checked his watch. “Hey, I’ve got to go. I’m not used to being out from behind the wall this long.” He put on his coat and shoes.

“Just like that you’re out of here?”

“You know how to reach me. Think about what I said.” He opened the door to leave. “You are important. You could be the lynchpin that blows this whole fucking thing wide open. You know what’s going on, you know *GenLET*, and I can get you the 2nd Protocol. Imagine it – there’s no one else in the world like you…” He smiled a wicked smile. “…and there’s seven billion fuckers out there – and counting!”

He shut the door and scurried off down to the shore. Janis stood at the window and watched him hurry along the water’s edge until out of sight.

She turned and faced the empty boathouse. The smell of overheated coffee filled the air. Then it hit her – they hadn’t poured a single cup. She switched the brewer off but couldn’t bring herself to dump it out.

On pins and needles, she rambled back and forth. Her ears rang as if she had heard a loud noise before abrupt silence. It was all too much to know what to do. Without another plan, she went through the motions. She retrieved the laptop from the pocket door wall, gathered up her research, then headed back to the main house. There wasn’t time to tell Sara what had happened, who she had met, if indeed he was who he said he was.

Janis left the tin of Calissons d'Aix almond candy with a note to her mother on her bed. The note was more of an apology than an explanation. She hoped her mother would take it as it was intended – an act of love.

Sara would find it later – when Janis was in the air, on her way to Marseille.

CHAPTER 17

Hotel Azalai Independence, Ouagadougou
Burkina Faso, Africa

The beat-up Peugeot 505 skidded to a stop at the hotel entrance. Curtis Labon climbed out of the bush-taxi's front seat and squinted into a dry wind. A fog-like haze moved through the city. The gritty *Harmattan* had been blowing steadily out of the north for two days, a rare occurrence at this time of year. Flights were grounded. His one-day visit to attend a World Health Organization symposium had become an unexpected detour into a sub-Saharan alternate universe for the marooned.

Only two things were good about being stranded.

Temperatures had dropped and he had met Djamila Baye.

The taxi roared off, leaving Curtis holding onto hope tempered by a growing sense of being unsettled. If it wasn't for his chance meeting with Djamila and their unlikely conversation, he wouldn't have learned what he did. If he hadn't been able to speak fluent French, their connection would have been impossible. So many things had aligned. Most importantly, if he hadn't convinced her there was a legitimate reason to keep their liaison secret, he wouldn't have taken the chance at whatever she might bring him today.

Djamila was a local health worker. She was also a part-time researcher, employed by a multilateral development bank. Her job with the MDB was just as much a demonstration of the bank's commitment to the Maputo Protocol, the African charter on women's rights, as it was of interest to their Analytic and Advisory Services Division. Unlike most *Burkinabè,* Djamila possessed a key qualification. She was literate. No doubt her unique contribution was highlighted on their website.

Curtis hurried inside the hotel lobby and dodged the reservation desk. A pathway off to one side led to doors that opened onto the pool area. He paused there, sickened yet invigorated with the clandestine way he had to proceed. He was taking a big chance. If only the instinct to follow through wasn't so strong.

A gust of wind rippled the surface of the water at the deep end. The movement reinforced a feeling. He should have been long gone from here. After one more conference in another country, he would have been heading home by now.

Ever since the dust storm arrived and departure time came and went, it felt like he was living a parallel reality. Another possible pathway into the future had been struck for the world. Priorities had shifted. There was no going back.

For all mortals, time moved in one direction only. Where it was going was anyone's guess, but everyone's destiny. For Curtis, the question remained; how much of that destiny was preordained? How much of it was blind chance? Where was the human element in between? JFK had said, "*Our problems are man-made, therefore they can be solved by man. No problem of human destiny is beyond human beings.*" Curtis had once championed that quote. Now he was not so sure. Now it seemed there might be some messes that none of us were ever going to clean up.

The pool area was deserted, the lounge chairs abandoned. It was an odd place to meet, given the weather, but it had been the best place he could think of on the spur of the moment. Djamila wanted to meet at some place close to the Ministry of the Economy. He wanted to be sure she wasn't followed but he was no secret agent. In a crude way, a circuitous route passing through hotel property and then to a nearby restaurant made sense at the time. Now it was lame and needlessly devious.

He stepped outside, expecting someone to appear from the shadows but no one did. Maybe she had changed her mind. Perhaps she'd reconsidered the propriety of what he had asked her to do. He'd at least walk the area to be sure. At the far end he wavered between continuing on to the tennis courts or heading back the way he came. As he turned back, she appeared from a sheltered area under a thatched roof and quickly caught up to him.

"Good day, Mr. Labon."

"I hope you weren't waiting long."

"Not at all. I just arrived and was checking around."

"Shall we go?" Curtis led the way. Without drawing attention to himself, he searched the area for eyes upon them. There were none. So far so good.

"I thought we might go to the Algerian restaurant on the corner."

The change of location didn't faze her. "That would be fine."

The street was a clogged clutter of cars, motorbikes, bicycles, and pushcarts. Curtis wove a path along and through them until arriving at the restaurant's covered porch. They were seated right away. The place was sparse with patrons. Using the weather as an excuse, Curtis asked for a table farther back from the entrance.

Djamila was a bit nervous and overly polite. Her research work had exposed her to a variety of situations but she was still uncomfortable meeting a man for lunch who wasn't her husband. "Thank you for meeting me near by work."

Curtis tried to relax. "I prefer it. Hotel Libya is convenient for meetings at the convention center, but too remote from the center of town. It's good to get out."

"I hope your visit here has been productive."

"Progress comes in many disguises. Sometimes it's recognized only with hindsight."

"I still don't quite understand what you were telling the delegate from WHO the other day. It sounded like you have an organization but it hasn't formed yet. How does that work?"

Curtis preferred a short lunch and even briefer discussion. He liked Djamila but the longer they were together, the more he felt at risk. He had one goal and the sooner it was obtained the better.

They ordered something light and then he dealt with her question.

"The goal of my organization is to form other organizations around the globe. It's called COPE, *Communities of Population Expertise*. It's based on the CoE Networks convened by the UN's Department of Economic and Social Affairs."

"Oh, I see. You organize people locally so they can discuss population issues."

"Exactly. The goal is to move beyond discussion, of course."

"How so?"

"I believe a concerted effort needs to be undertaken to handle world population trends. Reasonable measures should be adopted into the Millennium Development

Goals. Each area of the world faces different issues, but the problem is global."

"Sounds ambitious. You do this apart from your corporate work?"

"Yes. COPE is a separate, non-profit venture of mine."

"Commendable. But from what I hear, none of the current Millennium Goals have been reached. If you add another one, do you think it will have a chance?"

"What's the alternative?"

"True." She wasn't convinced but it would have been rude to explore the truth.

Curtis was anxious to get on topic. "So…how did it go at the health clinic?"

"Oh, you mean the blood sample?"

"Yes." All his hopes hung on her next words.

"I couldn't get you one of the glass slides from the blood differential test."

Curtis deflated but then she added, "But I did get some blood. It's not stained or prepared for study." She produced a small box from her pocket. Inside was a small vial of blood. "I verified it was taken from the same patient."

Curtis was greedy to find out if she had gotten everything. "And the vaccine?"

"Yes, that too. For a while, we kept the evidence for the police. The stolen box contained many small patches. In all the confusion, they weren't going to miss one."

"You said *patches*?"

"Yes, this new vaccine is quite different than anything I've seen before." She produced a sterile pad in its clear protective pouch. The pad was small and square, about the size of one wrapped condom.

Curtis recognized it right away. "Microneedles…"

"Really?"

"Yes. The center of the sticky side…right there." Curtis pointed. "It's coated with a hundred microneedles. They're very short but after they pierce the skin, they dissolve and release the vaccine. The whole absorption process completes in anywhere from thirty seconds to five minutes."

Djamila handed over the box and vial to Curtis. A rush of accomplishment filled him. He was excited and worried all at once. The deed was done.

"What happened to her – the patient?"

"She was ceremonially washed and shrouded then buried right away. It's required by Islamic custom."

"And her husband?"

"He's still in police custody."

"You said they tracked him down far north of here."

"Yes, in Gorom-Gorom. It's where her mother lives. When the woman first got sick, she went home. That's when her husband broke into the storehouse. He heard it contained new halal vaccine that had just arrived. Rumor said it was a conjugate vaccine, targeting several diseases. He claims he was desperate to save his wife and thought it would help. He didn't know about the restriction. I think the police will eventually let him go."

"What restriction?"

"We got instructions that said this vaccine was not ready to use. We shouldn't use it until we were told it was all right. That's why we locked it up."

"Is that typical?"

"I don't know what's typical. I know several medicines in the body at the same time can cause bad interactions. Burkina is in the part of Africa known as the meningitis belt. Bacterial epidemics usually arrive with the dry harmattan winds, like now. Many people have just received their immunizations for meningitis. It's prudent to do things in proper order."

"That's what you said before. So what's your opinion? Do you think the vaccine is partly responsible for the woman's death?"

"It's a possibility. Not that the vaccine is bad. I don't think that. But it is certain we were told not to give it to people – not yet."

Curtis flipped the sterile pouch over and examined the patch sealed inside of it. A characteristic logo was evident. He read the fine print at its edge – MIOVAC.

"As I told you a couple days ago, that's why we need to keep this quiet, between you and me. We wouldn't want people to panic. Those who already received their meningitis vaccine might get worried. Those who haven't received it might refuse to take it. We wouldn't want that."

"No, that would be bad." Djamila nodded in agreement.

"I can have this quietly studied in a lab – one that has advanced tools. That is the only way to be sure everything is all right." Curtis smiled at her. "You've been a big help."

Djamila was concerned. She motioned to his face. "Your nose. It's bleeding."

Curtis dabbed his napkin on his upper lip, then held it up against one nostril. "It must be the humidity. With these winds, it's dropped so low."

Djamila looked away. "I hate to see blood. I know it's strange to say, me working in a clinic. I guess in the clinic I expect it. I'm sorry."

"No problem." Curtis quickly put vaccine patch and blood vial in pocket. "So tell me, what sickness did the woman have? What was the cause of death?"

"The doctors aren't sure. They believe it was some kind of non-specific lower respiratory infection."

"Non-specific?"

"I know her lymphocyte count was next to nothing. The doctors said with such a suppressed immune system, just about anything would have killed her."

"They checked for other things, didn't they?"

"Of course. Diphtheria, tetanus, pertussis, tuberculosis, measles, hepatitis B, poliomyelitis, and naturally this time of year, meningitis. All came up negative."

Curtis was intrigued. "…a minor bacterial infection."

"With all the terrible things one can catch in this country, it's odd this woman should fall victim to something so benign in comparison."

"Maybe it was HIV."

"No. They ruled that out."

"Interesting."

They finished their meal and went their separate ways.

Two days later, Curtis was finally able to fly out of Ouagadougou. He landed in a Mediterranean state where he chartered a private jet. If his instincts were correct, he could waste no time getting his precious cargo to the lab.

The *rabid dog* might be bearing his teeth.

CHAPTER 18

Granite Peak Installation
Dugway Proving Grounds, Utah

Colin Insworth stepped out of the elevator and hurried outside only to pause. His eyes lifted to view a sunset obscured by a storm gathering in the west. The desert sky was streaked with high clouds faintly painted in shades of fading sunlight. A stillness encircled the three-story, flat-roof structure behind him. Across the dusty parking area, the windows of the single-wide trailer were dark. No one was in sight but that didn't matter. Security knew that Faye Gardner was out here somewhere.

The open desert left few places to hide. According to sensors, Faye was nearby. She had passed through the airlock tunnel twenty minutes ago. Video cameras had recorded her movement through the landing zone a minute later. At the time, guards were alert to her movements but not alarmed.

An occasional trip to the surface was not uncommon for newbies to Granite Peak. It took awhile for some to get used to working in a buried lab. Some people just needed to see the sky again. Others felt the pull of open spaces. Whatever had prompted Faye's race to the surface, one thing was certain: she couldn't go far without losing herself in a lot of nothing.

Colin stepped to the single-wide trailer and wound his way to its other side. Just as he suspected, Faye was off to herself, facing a darkening east. She sat on a berm of dirt that marked the end of level grading. It was obvious she had been crying. He forced his approach to be casual. Making it seem incidental was a stretch.

"You found my secret place to think."

She glanced at him but said nothing. Her gaze returned to a far horizon.

Colin found a sandy place to sit next to her. "I take it you didn't come up here to watch the sunset. What's wrong?"

She leaned her lips against a clenched fist. "You don't know?"

Colin looked away from her. "There's lots of things I don't know."

"You expect me to believe that." It wasn't a question.

"After the last couple of days, I'm not sure what to believe anymore."

Each with their own thoughts, a brief silence fell between them. Colin decided to confront what he thought might be the issue.

"I stopped off at the lab. I heard about your concerns."

"Oh, really…"

"The sputnik virus inside of Ghyvir-C is getting a lot of attention."

Faye erupted. "Can you drop all the bullshit and tell me flat out what we're dealing with? Was sterility a biological accident or a planned event?"

"What? Where are you getting this?"

"Don't lie to me, Colin! You've got me studying the damned thing. Did you think I wouldn't find out?"

"Find what?"

"The suicide gene inside the sputnik – it's not natural to that virus. The damned thing was engineered. It contains a gene patented by the Army in 2001."

"That patent was *after* Ghyvir-C was discovered."

"So what are you saying? The gene didn't exist and the Army didn't have it before the patent?"

Colin took a moment to carefully choose his words. "You studied the virus fifteen years ago. You're surprised by this?"

"The big scare back then was about Ghyvir, the giant virus, not the sputnik inside of it. At USAMRIID, we were *directed* what to study. As far as we were told, the sputnik was just a parasite. Our research concentrated on the giant virus. A giant virus that caused the common cold in humans was big news. The fact that it had a parasite didn't seem to matter that much. Our primary lab studied Ghyvir-C. We were told another lab would look at the sputnik."

"We know now that thinking was wrong. The parasite is the key. It has to be."

"But there's no interaction between the two of them. I checked. There's nothing symbiotic about Ghyvir-C and its sputnik. The sputnik gets a free ride until the right time to reproduce. Then it hijacks the giant virus and replicates until it causes Ghyvir to split open, releasing thousands of sputnik copies."

"That's where we have to look for answers."

"You expect me to believe a suicide gene, engineered by the military, accidentally got loose and somehow, randomly in the wild, wound up combined into a neat little package inside a brand new giant virus? All this was natural?"

"I expect you to find out how it works and come up with a way to defeat it."

"We know this thing resists mutation. You think *that's* natural?"

"Why couldn't it be? It might be something new. You said yourself that a giant virus causing the common cold was new."

"You're not going to tell me the truth, are you?" Faye looked away.

"If you think I know everything, you have a problem right away."

"It's common sense, Colin! If you see a thousand-piece puzzle all put together in front of you, it's reasonable to assume it didn't fall out of the box that way."

"What do you want from me?"

"Tell me what's behind this. Because it's not normal. Somebody designed it!"

"That hasn't been proven."

"What do you think I've been doing? I've proved it! This sputnik is smart enough to know it has to affect the germ cells of the unborn. But it targets them before they're even conceived! It installs in the parents an epigenetic mechanism that cleverly orchestrates a series of 'snips,' single nucleotide polymorphisms. The way it makes swaps in base pairs is not casual or random. It hijacks the very thing that makes one human genetically different from another. Then it makes sure its disease gets inherited. All of this executes in proper order, directed at a single purpose."

"What does that prove? Most viruses are single-minded. They all seem targeted at a purpose. That isn't evidence someone planned it that way. All viruses come from nature."

Faye was emphatic. "Up until now."

"Nature can be nonlinear and chaotic – or deliberate and precise. Finding either one doesn't prove anything was engineered."

"You can't mean that. You know the business we're in. You know what's possible. Project talking points might work on the public, but not on me."

"Admit it, there's just as much design in Ghyvir-C as there is in DNA itself. Complexity doesn't prove design. If that were true, we'd all be Creationists."

"Viruses may come from nature but the way these two were put together had to be planned. Why are you fighting me on this? Why won't you admit it?"

"And then what? You'll have your excuse to quit The Project? Is that it?"

Faye's anger flared. "You wanted me to confirm that sterility existed. I did that. Now you want me to figure out how it happens but you're keeping me in the dark. We both know there's more to this. I can't work blind with my hands tied."

"You have everything you need – you have the viruses; you have RIDIS. History at this point is a footnote we can ignore. It won't make a hell of a lot of difference one way or another how we got here if we can't find an answer."

"You're making my work harder. Knowing what caused this mess, how it got put together is vital. Don't you understand? This thing was crafted! You know it and I know it. If you expect me to *reverse* engineer it, then seeing some historical blueprints would help."

"Believe me, they wouldn't." The statement was as much confirmation of Faye's claim as Colin was willing to admit.

"How convenient." Faye stood and escaped a few steps into the desert.

Colin remained seated. He leaned forward, his forearms on his legs. "I don't like this shit anymore than you. I certainly don't know anymore than I need to know. Just like you. But it doesn't matter. I keep at it because we have no choice – not because I believe everything my bosses tell me."

Faye folded her arms. She shook her head in disgust.

Colin noted her rebuff. He stood and came to her side. There was a tension, a distressed confession in the way he murmured. "You're not special, you know. We all have our feet planted firmly in mid-air."

Faye held silent. She glanced to read Colin's rigid expression.

"Keep this to yourself," started Colin. "But I have my own doubts, even with what I know. I've learned some things in the last couple of days I wasn't supposed to. It's one of the fortunate hazards of leading a project like this – sometimes people assume you have clearance for things you really don't."

Faye's concern was piqued. Her head turned in interest, even as she held silent.

Colin's gaze shifted between faraway reference points in the darkening desert. "It started with a memo attached to an email I was copied on. I don't think the memo was meant to be sent to everyone; at least not to me. Maybe they thought it didn't matter. It was only one word that caught my attention."

Faye's resistance to conversation melted away. "What word?"

"Manhattan."

The obvious jumped to mind. "Is the city being targeted?"

"It's not about New York. It's about Kansas."

Faye rushed through possibilities. In context, Manhattan could only mean one thing. "N-B-A-F." She spelled it out.

Colin nodded confirmation. The *National Bio and Agro-Defense Facility* was a new BSL4 lab being built by Homeland Security in Manhattan, Kansas. When ready, the 520,000 square-foot facility would employ 300 biodefense workers. Bio-Safety Level Four was mandated only for work with the most dangerous agents, the ones posing the highest risk of fatal disease in humans. The ones for which no treatments or vaccines existed. NBAF would soon take its place in the heartland.

Colin's hesitation drew Faye out.

"That lab isn't supposed to be operational for another two years."

"For the most part – it isn't."

"What did the memo say?"

"It only mentioned Manhattan in passing. Nothing specific. But it was obvious a project related to what we're doing is underway in Kansas."

"Related? How?"

"That's what I didn't know. So I checked around."

"How could you check without exposing what you know?"

"It's an advantage of doing this for so long. The human web. Over the years, I've made some friends. Everyone knows their compartment. If you discover key compartments, you can deduce a lot about structure."

"Structure?"

"Function follows form. The fact that Manhattan, Kansas has *any* crossover with our compartment is telling."

"But what are they doing there?"

"It doesn't make sense." Colin took a breath. "They're studying animals."

"You think that's related to us?"

Colin turned to face her. "They're studying the *fertility* of animals."

"What does that have to do with sterility in humans?"

"Exactly. And what's the rush to do it at a place still being built? It's not supposed to be open for two years. I can't figure it out."

"And you can't ask about it."

"Of course not. I'm not even supposed to know. That's the strangest part. Why would a study of animals rate a higher security clearance than I have – especially if it's related to what we're doing?"

"Maybe it's not more important. You just don't need to know. It's like what you told me – *you have everything you need* for your work. Why do you want to know more? Would it make a difference? In my case, you don't think so. I guess others think the same about you."

Faye's sarcasm struck a nerve. Colin raised his voice. "They've *decided* not to tell me. It's strategic. But I was *ordered* not to tell you. That's the difference!"

"So you admit it – there *is* more to this!"

"Isn't that what you believe anyway? There's always something more. The closer we get to anything, the more complicated it gets. I don't have to tell you that." Colin paced farther into the desert.

Faye pursued him. "If you know something, tell me!"

"I can't."

She grabbed him by the arms and spun him around.

"Then I want out! I can't do this!"

"No. You can't walk away!"

"Why not? Are you going to threaten me – tell me *lethal force* is authorized?"

"You can't leave. The clock is ticking. You know what'll happen if we don't set this right."

Faye started to cry. "Things haven't been right for a long time."

"What's that supposed to mean?"

"What's the point? It's obvious nature didn't do this to us. We did it to ourselves. Maybe in some weird way this is what's supposed to be. Maybe time was up for our species anyway."

"What's gotten into you?"

Faye turned away. "Leave me alone."

"This isn't like you. What's happened?"

Faye's shout carried into the desert. "I'm pregnant!"

Hugging herself, she hunched forward and sobbed. She braced herself as if a sudden impact was about to double her over.

Colin was blindsided. All his previous certainties evaporated. He had completely misread why Faye had come to the surface to be by herself.

"When did you find out?"

Faye was in pain. "Does it matter?"

"Your physical exam…the results came back today." Faye gave a nod. Colin took slow steps to narrow the gap between them. "I don't know what to say."

"I don't expect you would." Faye's open palms couldn't wipe away the tears streaking her face fast enough.

Colin let the barb pass over him. "I guess I deserve that."

Faye's thoughts raced back to a snowy evening in Mt. Pleasant, Maryland. Long after dinner, the guests had finally left. Jacob tended the fire in the living room. Faye's mind was made up. The sweep of events wouldn't rob her of one last night of normalcy. She invited him to stay. They had made love all night long. Something so real and sweet had landed in a barren field of lost dreams.

She had said Jacob and her were like bread and butter.

Sophie had asked, but where were all the little croutons?

Faye's face was leaden but tears persisted. "This is somebody's idea of a cruel joke." Bubbling emotion caught in her throat. Sarcastic humor mixed with anguish. "I avoided having children all these years. And *now* it happens." She struggled with a laugh. Bitterness filled her tone. "Don't say it. Better late than never."

Colin rested his hands on her shoulders. She resisted his touch for only a moment, then caved into him. She buried her crying face into his chest and hugged him tight for comfort. Colin hugged back as a friend but it couldn't be denied; the ex-lover in him was there too.

They had not been this close to each other for so long. Both had forgotten how good it felt. A jumble of shared sensations confused them both. The incongruity of it all only heightened the irony of Faye's sadness. This was no time to act out over her lingering love for Colin. She would always love him but they would never be together. Was that why she never married?

She was carrying Jacob's child. Life had moved on. It was now about other people, other things. The moment was now consumed by an unborn child marked with a terrible distinction. If nothing was done to stop it, the last generation of humans would walk the planet. Her child would be one of them.

The care and comfort of the embrace softened Faye's anguish. She could speak again. Her rage and grief gradually diffused as thoughts turned reflective. Steeped in the pathos of the moment, she recalled a simple action taken days ago.

"On the jet ride out here, you asked me to fill out a form."

Colin thought the comment out of place but acknowledged it.

"One thing you wanted me to do was fill in a name for my cover project."

"That's right – in case someone tries to snoop into what you're doing, The Project needed to set up a mock reason why you're away. The fake secret means nothing but it has to appear real. We made your secret program work all about endangered sea turtles. If any snoopers find the cover secret, they're usually satisfied and look no farther. One secret covers another."

"Did you see the name I picked for my cover project?"

"No. We were too busy talking."

With her head against his chest, Faye closed her eyes and uttered the word as if it was a sacred invocation. "BIOPONORE."

"That's it?"

Eyes still closed, Faye whispered, "Yeah."

Colin snickered. "That's odd enough to be real."

Faye opened her eyes. "It's real enough – that's what's odd."

"Oh, yeah? What does it mean?"

Faye closed her eyes again. She could feel Colin's heartbeat against the side of her head. The pulse of it filled her ear. She paused while fast-forwarding through her college years. The rhythm of times past transfixed her.

Colin prompted, "Does it mean anything?"

In the desert, night was only minutes away. Once again, tears filled her eyes.

In a flash, a flurry of thoughts passed through her mind – she should tell him how Janis made up the word as a way to needle her in college. How Janis had goaded her with tales of dying childless because Faye had avoided any entanglements with men. How such a life would leave Faye with regrets as her baby clock ran out and she found herself beyond the *biological point of no return.*

It was a funny story, a sad story, a true story of girls who had lots of life and love ahead of them. But it was a story she could not tell Colin – him of all people.

"It's a made-up word. It's real if we let it be..."

Surrounded by nothing, an uneasy silence deepen until Faye found the courage to honestly finish her thought. "Today, for the first time, it feels real."

In the moment, their embrace became everything.

CHAPTER 19

Hall 1, Marseille Provence Airport
Marseille, France

Bienvenue.

Janis Insworth rushed past the welcome sign wondering if the message was meant for her. She had researched and plotted out her stay in Marseille long before the wheels of Air France Flight 7664 touched down at 2:35 PM. Now that she had arrived, all she wanted was to get in and out of the city as quickly as possible.

The airport concourse was a blur of people. Janis paused to get her bearings. The harried connection at New York's *JFK* and customs inspection at *Charles de Gaulle* in Paris had taken their toll. Burlington, Vermont was fourteen hours behind her. It might as well have been a dream. The conversation with Knockout Mouse still swirled within. Impossibly real, the odd little man and agonizing bits of his horrific tale had only added context and validation to the nightmare scenario outlined on Malcolm's laptop. Even more reason to see this through. Janis walked on.

Beleaguered by worried thoughts, she hurried to execute her plan as if only its completion could provide relief. She drove herself forward. Tortured by raw feeling, she was intent on finding an area away from the bustle where she could sit and work. In the haze of the moment, her plan looked more and more like a frantic wish complicated by uncertain detail. She had landed in a new city, on a new day. Standing among strangers, it now seemed like another life altogether.

Janis pressed on, dismissing clawing doubt. She wouldn't give in to the idea that adrenaline and irrational hope alone were empowering her to go through with this. She fought to explain away such things. It must be the time shift, the change of language, the unfamiliar location. Her heart raced. Everything inside and around her conspired to make the simple act of moving forward suddenly surreal.

The wisdom of her strategy had weakened while crossing the Atlantic. Strapped into her seat, she had felt like a prisoner of onrushing events. Sleepless through the night, there had been too much quiet time at 35,000 feet alone with her thoughts. Desperation was giving way to prudence. She dismissed it as nerves and ignored the little voice inside of her that knew better.

At least the time spent at her mother's place had allowed her to gather trip details she'd need. With so much as stake, there was no time for guesswork. If something unexpected came up now, she'd have to deal with it and move on. Her fervent desire was for any surprises to be manageable. There was no time to worry about all that could go wrong. She had to concentrate.

She found an empty seat in a designated Wi-Fi hotspot and got to work on Malcolm's laptop. She'd rehearsed the access procedure several times. It was 10:25 a.m. in Puerto Rico. The workday there was in full swing. She hoped the flow of business at the target site would help mask her activity.

GeLixCo's network was distributed among several locations but only the head office had VPN access to the research section in Puerto Rico. Malcolm's contact had managed to get him the proprietary client software for the head office's Virtual Private Network. Malcolm had automated a script to load the client and log in. All Janis had to do was run Malcolm's script.

That was the plan. But she had never run the script all the way through. Malcolm had inserted a prompt that stopped execution right before the username/password combination was entered. If she selected *yes to continue,* connection to GeLixCo's network should complete.

She hesitated and looked up from the keyboard. A businessman and a pair of students sat across the way, each buried in their own work. Outside, a jet roared up from the tarmac and angled for the sky. An airport service announcement droned in the background; the pleasant female voice and her fluent French was common on the concourse, but to Janis in the moment, all of it felt out of place. Passengers headed every which way. None of it mattered. Her next move would be a crime.

Was she willing to take it that far?

The need to know was too great. Riya had died for this information. Janis pressed the Enter key on the laptop. Connection was made. After authentication, the client software opened a directory listing. A group of named folders populated a window. All of them were on a partition named *RABARCHIVE.* If the first three letters were Riya's initials, it made sense; otherwise, Janis had no idea what the word might mean.

There was no way of knowing how much time she had. Downloading as much as possible was vital. Once the data was on the laptop, she could read and sort through all of it later. She recognized two folders that Malcolm had already acquired. She skipped them and selected everything else. In a few movements, she had the copy process started. A progress bar crept agonizingly towards completion. It was barely halfway done when the window closed and the VPN client threw up an error message. The connection had been terminated at the forty-eight second mark. She needed at least a minute and a half to get all of it.

Janis shut down the connection to the airport's Wi-Fi and powered down the laptop. She wanted to check inside the copied folders to see how much she was able to get but she dare not take the chance. Not here. She'd wait until she got settled in at her hotel. First she had a call to make and it had to be from a public phone.

She stuffed the laptop into her backpack and hurried downstairs. It took only a minute to locate a phone by the check-in area. Her hand shook as she fumbled in her purse for the number to dial. Knockout Mouse had supplied the contact information. She had carefully vetted all of it. The number connected to a yacht brokerage located on *Quai du Port* in the old harbor section of the city. Janis wasn't sure what André's role at the brokerage might be. It would be the height of irony if the radical activist behind such groups as *Friends of the Ocean* and *New Class Order* was earning his living selling the rich their pleasure craft.

The number rang and a man answered in French. Janis forced her voice calm. "I'd like to speak with André Bolard, please."

Responding to her English, the man paused before answering, "Just a minute."

For Janis, after the long trip, any more of a wait was an eternity. She huddled closer to the public phone and tried to ignore the commotion around her.

"This is André. How can I help you?" The voice was deep, silken, and businesslike. It exuded confidence and sophistication along with guarded warmth.

"Mr. Bolard, my name is Janis Insworth. I believe we can help each other."

"Say that name again…"

"Janis Insworth. I am looking for my daughter."

"I'm sorry. I can't help you."

For Janis, the answer was clumsily abrupt. His flat reaction to her identity was telling. "Even if I can help you?"

"How so?"

"I have information on Eugene Mass."

"What kind of information?"

"The kind you would desperately want. Information you'd be willing to exchange my daughter for."

"I don't know what you're talking about."

"Maybe you don't, but I believe you know people who do."

"Where are you calling from?"

"I'm in the city. I'm prepared to make a trade."

"I've heard about you. You expect me to believe you do this on your own?"

"Yes."

André laughed. "It's hard to believe one woman would be so bold."

"Why? Do you think it's dangerous to meet with you? Or perhaps your opinion of women is antiquated."

"You have me mistaken for someone else."

"That's right. You sell yachts. To meet with you, I should want a boat."

"You should desire an unparalleled luxury craft." The sarcasm was apparent.

"Of course. The pleasure of yachting is…priceless."

"Yes, it is."

"So is my daughter. Along with the information I have. Don't you want to know what Mass is really up to?"

"I'm sorry. This is the business line. I need to free it up."

"Naturally. Some business can't be done over the phone. I understand."

"I really must go."

"I *am* interested in a pleasure craft. If you'd like talk about it, I'm going to be down along La Canebière later today."

"That's good." The remark was dismissive.

"If you think you can help me find something nice, I'd appreciate it. I'll be at the carousel near General de Gaulle Place at seven o' clock. I'm eager to see what kind of business we can do."

The line went dead. Janis stood on pins and needles. Had she said the right thing? Would André come to the carousel? If he thought the phone line was tapped, wouldn't he suspect a meeting along La Canebière to be a trap? No doubt her knowledge of how to make contact had him spooked. To locate him so precisely, she had to be working with someone else. Would hunger for information overcome his concern? She'd know in a few hours. Until then, there was no time to dawdle.

Exiting the airport in a taxi, Janis drove to the Sofitel Marseille Vieux-Port Hotel where she checked in under her real name and arranged for a safety deposit box at reception. All the while she critiqued herself. Her steps across the lobby were way too fast. Her voice much too tight. Her manner suspiciously constrained. She wasn't acting like a tourist. The hotel staff had the appropriate smiles and demeanor but she fretted about the impression she had left with them.

She then took another taxi to the HSBC Private Bank on Avenue du Prado where she arranged for a second safety deposit box. She was hoping to be in and out but instead she was shuttled aside to a bank officer who had to verify her New York office account. His innocent questions made her feel guilty. She couldn't help being defensive. She hoped he would chalk it up as just another arrogant American.

Finally, she returned to the old harbor section of the city where she checked into the Hotel Alize under an assumed name. She had never done such a thing before. She paid in advance in cash to avoid having to show a credit card. The reservationist looked her up and down and showed surprise when she requested a single room. He wasn't bashful about showing suspicious that a solitary woman such as her would request a room for cash and not be entertaining someone.

Her fifth-floor room at Hotel Alize overlooked the Quai des Belges seawall with a view that had inspired artists such as Cézanne and Monticelli. The outdoor fish market was not active at this time of day, but a steady stream of traffic and tourists added diversion and color. She took in the view for a second. Only one thing captured her attention. She unpacked the laptop and opened it on a small desk near the window. Her burning curiosity would not wait any longer.

The file folders copied from GeLixCo appeared on the screen. She opened one named UDIF. In it were dozens of documents and spreadsheets. They bore scientific-sounding names but nothing Janis recognized. Another folder was named TZ. Inside of it, more lab documents and spreadsheets. One by one, Janis checked the creation dates on the files. All of them were in a timeframe fifteen to sixteen years ago.

A third folder was named CA-CC. Inside of it were over a hundred documents. Janis opened one called *CA-Base*. It was a boilerplate template for *Integrated Test Results Reports*. Janis scanned the page and noted blank sections for items such as *pilot test summary, acceptance criteria review, issues/workarounds, endorsements,* and *approval signatures*. She closed the document.

Her eye gravitated to another file called *CA-Abstract*. She opened it and read the three-page summary authored by Riya Basu. It detailed a *Conformity Assessment* being done for the *UDIF/TZ Project*. UDIF was defined as ultra-definition infrared. TZ referred to terahertz radiation. The goal of the *CA* was to secure a *Conformity Certificate* to ensure that specifications and standards were properly established for a new DNA analysis process. The final process should be easily interoperable and extensible. Eventually, it would need to pass review by the Department of Defense's Biometrics Management Office (BMO) and the National Institute of Standards and Technology. Mention was made of DITSCAP, the *DoD Information Technology Security Certification and Accreditation Process*.

Janis recoiled back in her seat. None of this was what she expected. This was not about Mass. There was nothing here about 3rd Protocol. This was a project Riya had worked on at NovoSenectus before Janis had gone to work for them. This project had studied the effect of focused radiation scans on DNA samples. The project was apparently such a success that it needed to develop ongoing ANSI NIST/AFIS standards. Whatever was being developed was intended for wide and common use among the defense, homeland security, and intelligence communities.

Janis read aloud from the abstract.

> "The Biometrics Fusion Center (BFC), a subordinate unit and technical arm of BMO, will validate vendor performance claims, determine if technologies meet approved standards, and use testing and evaluation metrics and merits to achieve an acceptable and reasonable level of comparison considering variables (e.g., false match, false non-match)."

Over the next hour, Janis opened each document and read them. The gathered facts centered on DNA analysis and a covert project to develop a quick and accurate means of confirming a person's identification. Greedy for detail, Janis snatched acronyms and phrases from the text and added them to her overall impression. The scope was beyond anything anticipated. Some items she could recognize from similar methods and procedures employed at USAMRIID. Many others were new.

> "…Second-Party Testing to be conducted in Puerto Rico."
> "…addendum to the Common Biometric Exchange Formats Framework."
> "…pilot test group comprised of approximately 3.8 million military personnel including uniformed military, DoD civilians, and contractors…"
> "…must adhere to Subcommittee 37 (SC37) JTC1 guidelines…"
> "…conformance testing completed at a stateside Common Criteria Laboratory."
> "…data compression will be based on the new extension of the Wavelet Scalar Quantization algorithm…"
> "…Performance Reporting Mechanisms – Receiver Operator Curve, Detection Error Trade-off Curve (DET), Cumulative Match Curve (CMC)…"
> "…Collection Steps are as follows: Extraction / Quantization / Amplification / Genotyping / Interpretation of Results / Database Process."
> "…Performance Metrics – False Acceptance Rate (FAR), False Rejection Rate (FRR), False Match Rate (FMR), False Non-Match Rate (FNMR), Failure-to-Enroll (FTE), Failure-to-Acquire (FTA)."

In between the lines, Janis gleaned a greater impact. Each document added detail and weight to her understanding. It was clear – eighteen years ago, GeLixCo had been awarded a grant by an undisclosed agency of the U.S. government. GeLixCo was allowed to outsource part of the project to save money. NovoSenectus in India was selected as a partner. That was years before Eugene Mass bought the company.

Back then, Riya was a rising star at NovoSenectus. Drafted into the project, her first role was establishing standards-based specifications for DNA material scans using various mixtures of UDIF and TZ radiations. She showed managers such promise they added her to the implementation work phase. Details of that phase were missing from what Janis had managed to copy from the archive.

But the most telling fact was not in the archive. Janis knew it already from her work with Riya. Work on *GenLET* first started due to a radical new process for DNA analysis that Riya had developed.

Or so Janis had thought.

That analysis had jumpstarted the techniques that made the rapid progress on *GenLET* possible.

Janis remembered starting work at NovoSenectus and her first days with Riya. Riya's new technique just so happened to involve the scanning of various DNA samples using modulated controlled bursts of electromagnetic radiations. In proper proportions, blends of focused radiation could provide a clean unzip of DNA's double helix for purposes of analysis.

In light of the GeLixCo archive, it was evident that Riya had borrowed technology developed on the UDIF/TZ Project for her own uses. If so, then the genesis of early progress on *GenLET* laid squarely in the work originally done at GeLixCo in Puerto Rico – work secured by a U.S. intelligence agency for a whole other purpose. When Mass bought NovoSenectus two years later, the billionaire inherited the technology Riya had taken – illegally.

No doubt the UDIF/TZ Project required a confidentiality agreement, possibly a security oath. But having worked with Riya, Janis understood the dynamic all too well. Riya had been seduced by the science. She cared little for what she saw as the artificial divisions between the control of information and the greater need for human progress. Riya would have had no problem justifying the use of what she had learned on one project to help another – regardless of one nation's attempt to keep the discovery to itself.

Of all things to discover, Janis had found evidence that Riya Basu had been guilty of dual-use duplicity in the application of biodefense secrets. Such a thing was the very reason why Janis had left USAMRIID. It was the one thing she thought she was free of working at NovoSenectus.

Janis could only surmise what had happened in Riya's last days. It was easy to see how she would have been panicked over what she discovered Mass was planning. Who could she turn to without giving herself away? Malcolm said she had told him SENEX was her contact. Knockout Mouse had said that SENEX was a codename that Colin Insworth had used. Had Riya turned to Colin because she knew him from long before – on the UDIF/TZ Project? That fact now appeared certain.

For Janis, it all came together in a personal way. Was it possible that UDIF/TZ was the mystery project that Colin had left USAMRIID to work on? Colin had left her at the same time. Janis felt a chill run through her. It was all too close for comfort. It looked like UDIF/TZ was the project he couldn't talk about with her but wanted to join. It was the main thing they'd argued about. It was the one thing they'd both used to justify their divorce.

Janis sat back in her chair and stared at the screen. The once unbelievable was now overwhelming. All this time she had worked alongside Riya and never knew – Riya had probably worked with Colin secretly long before working with her. But Riya had never said anything about knowing Colin. Given the secrets that Riya had illegally taken to start *GenLET*, Janis now understood why.

As Janis sat, she focused on the long list of file names in the open folder. By now, she had opened and read all of them. Except one. That file was not a document. It was an image. It was the only thing she hadn't looked at yet.

Emotionally, she'd reached a completion point. She opened the image with a sense of being thorough, not expecting much. To her surprise, it was a picture of a document, a dated fax saved as an image. She sat forward to get a closer look. The document was a handwritten memorandum. Alarmingly, its creation date was only weeks old.

To: *Javier*
From: *EM*
Subject: *Trigger*

It should be an accident. Something at a bio-defense lab. Manhattan would do nicely. Draw attention and resources there. Lots of blame to go around. Headlines to make it a circumstantial fact.

We can use Oliver. He'll jump at the chance.
No love lost between him and Labon.
3P will be a fait accompli.

As always, wait for my sign
– green, green, green.

Janis read the memo over and over. Each pass only confirmed her rising horror. *3P* had to refer to 3rd Protocol. So many details were written in such a little space. It was quite unlike the other material Malcolm had downloaded from GeLixCo. This was not dated years ago, not abstract or philosophical. This was blatant and operational. This contained clues and provided names – and it ended in an ominous way that corroborated what Knockout Mouse had said.

"…triple green has always been the go-code…"

A chilling snap of intuition hit Janis – this was the main thing Riya had hid.

This shifted everything in the population collapse white papers out of the realm of the hypothetical. This was confirmation detailed enough to loose one's life over.

Frozen in her chair, Janis didn't know whether to rush to tell someone what she had found or run far away and hide. Either way, it didn't matter. Despite how utterly spent she felt, it was time to head out.

Time to store the laptop in the bank's safety deposit box.

Time to visit the carousel. Time to meet with André Bolard.

CHAPTER 20

Sheldonian Theatre
University of Oxford, England

A twinge of annoyance pierced the composure on the face of Leah Mass.

For the third time during her husband speech, his cell phone vibrated in her purse. Why Eugene hadn't turned the blasted thing off before the event she couldn't understand. She glanced down at her program and contemplated the title of the evening's lecture: *The Anthropocene Dilemma.*

A hot and cold sweat blanketed her. Even more puzzling than Eugene's phone habits was the sharp edge to her irritation. Her nerves had been on hair-trigger release ever since she received a *GenLET* therapy treatment earlier in the day. Of course she couldn't speak to anyone about it. She dare not go to a hospital during this trip for fear doctors would detect such a procedure had been done. She took a breath. Despite a slight faintness and nausea, she needed to maintain poise and self-control.

Thank goodness today's treatment was the last in the series she and her family would have to endure. Several therapies over the past few weeks had taken a toll. Meanwhile, the lab staff assured her everything had gone well. She was probably just tired from all the running around and the rushed flight from Brussels.

Straightening up, Leah kept attention focused on her husband. He had been looking forward to this opportunity for weeks and she was proud of him. Someone needed to deliver impassioned testimony to indict the way humanity was conducting itself. It was such a vital message and rightfully deserved the center of attention.

She was glad it was being captured on video and happier that members of the press had been allowed in. A heavy police presence kept the majority of *New Class Order* demonstrators at bay. It helped that the authorities had seen fit to close Broad Street out in front of the four-hundred-year-old meeting place.

Seated in the theater's front row, Leah held a posture matching the regal and urbane décor. From extra chairs at ground level to the highest row in the gilded balcony, a thousand students and honored faculty members comprised a largely sympathetic audience. Suited but refusing to wear a tie as always, Eugene Mass used no notes as he drove home his points with piercing eye contact.

Some in the audience were not prepared for the intensity of his presentation. With sideways glances, Leah watched their faces. Most bore the smugness of youth. But here and there, beneath the tribal in-crowd exteriors of superiority and cool, their inner children were realizing the nightmare was true.

From the darkness of their dread, the voice of Eugene Mass filled the hall.

> "...In closing, I'm faced with the problem of summing up. Facts alone do not stir anyone to action and yet facts give us the clearest picture of where we are and what we must confront. Some of you may want to do something to help. Most of you suspect you are impotent to make a real difference given the enormity of the entrenched and powerful forces

aligned against you. The tides of human nature seem intractable.

And so, all I can do is sum things up the way I see them.

Years ago, a vaccination team from the Centers for Disease Control landed in Nigeria as part of an aggressive campaign to eradicate smallpox from the African continent. To their horror, they were met by angry people with knives. As it turned out, the vaccination team had never heard of *Shapona.* It's an African word meaning 'overlord of the Earth.' The local Yoruba people were furious. These strangers intended on waging war against their deity – a *smallpox god.* It was vital that *Shapona* control his realm with smallpox. Smallpox wasn't a disease; it was an instrument of divine judgment, a necessary indicator of *Shapona's* disapproval.

From New York to Shanghai, from Cape Town to Helsinki, each in our own way – we all have our personal *Shaponas.* No matter how progressive we think we are, a primitive core is harbored within everyone. All give energy and devotion to idols of our collective passions, however our individual cultures may define them. The question is – when the time comes, how easily will we stand with knives in our hands when the forces of reason come to rescue us?

Those who worry about an approaching tipping point are blind to the precarious world we live in. We're already off balance. The *Anthropocene Dilemma* is not something we can pass on to a future generation to solve. One generation blaming another at this point is juvenile and misses the point. Everyone alive today has a responsibility and a stake in this. Any person alive has a carbon footprint and represents one part of the problem. The planet is dying – not by the mayhem of a megalithic machine but by billions of tiny individual cuts. Each one of you is a cut. So am I.

Anyone who intends on having children must ask themselves hard questions about what constitutes sustainable development. Time for blame is over. Now we must act.. It will not matter if we restrict family size to one child if the polar ice caps melt, the oceans rise, and food production is wiped out as the planet's temperature soars.

Take China, for example. It's already the world's largest emitter of gases that warm the planet. It risks the melting of the Himalayan glaciers and disrupting major rivers and the nation's water supply but it shows no signs of restraining its CO2 output. If anything, it's increasing. China is building new coal-fired power plants at an astounding rate – one a month, every month.

From what I've seen in humanity's binge with itself, the sobering facts are ignored. But I need to say them. I know they may wash over you, but like the sea of humanity they describe, ignoring them will not make them go away.

Every day, 2.7 million babies are born.

At any given time, 100,000,000 women are pregnant.

27% of the world's population is below 15 years of age.

50,000 years ago, the world's population totaled 10,000. Think about that. There were only 10,000 humans on the planet and they were concentrated in one tribe living in Africa, a region where the Kalahari Desert now stretches across Namibia. Today, the San Bushman tribe still lives there. But the world has changed.

It took 48,000 years, until 1804, for the population to reach 1 billion.

Just 150 years later, by 1927, that number had doubled to 2 billion.

Just 50 years later, by 1974, that number had doubled to 4 billion.

Just 50 years later, by 2025, it's estimated that number will more than double.

We have reached the point of unsustainability.

The Earth simply cannot support a continued doubling of population every 50 years. We don't have the energy for it, the fresh water for it, the food for it, the vital mineral resources for it.

Frankly, we don't have the civility nor instincts for it.

To drive home the point, consider this…

If all of human history is represented by one year, then

– In January – the first ape appeared;

– In October – the first ape-man began walking upright;

– On 28th of December – modern humans arrive;

– On 31st of December – members of that single tribe of humans leave Africa;

– By January 1st – we've populated the entire globe.

The U.N. estimates our numbers will reach 9.2 billion by 2050 if we maintain our current trajectory. I ask you – how do we satisfy the twin aspirations of improved material life and ecological sustainability for 9.2 billion people?

To put it another way, let's relate energy usage with standard of living.

The total planetary energy consumption of humans per year right now is 13 trillion watts or 13 terawatts. If you'd like a standard of living that allots only 3 kilowatts per person, a 6-terawatt world would allow for 2 billion people, about the number of people alive in 1930. For a higher standard of living, how about a world with 1.5 billion people using 4.5 terawatts of energy. In the year 1900 there were 1.5 billion people on the planet.

Maybe we should halt population at 14 billion and convince everyone to be satisfied with a per capita energy use of 7.5 kilowatts. By the way, 7.5 kilowatts is about the average consumption in most rich nations. By comparison, 7.5 kilowatts is only two-thirds of average consumption in the United States. But I digress. A world like that would need 105 terawatts of power, eight times what the world uses today. Clearly, a recipe for ecological collapse.

The fact is, one billion people are too poor, hungry, or diseased to develop themselves. Every year, ten million people die simply because they're too poor to stay alive. Some people look to foreign aid or revolutions in technology to save us. But the track record there is dismal.

A few years back, The World Bank estimated that *flight capital* out of sub-Saharan Africa for one year totaled $95 billion. If you're not familiar with the term *flight capital*, it's the amount of money siphoned off from foreign aid by corruption.

It's estimated that over the past fifty years, 2.3 trillion dollars has been given out around the world in foreign aid. Divide that among the 3 billion people in the developing world over the past sixty years, it amounts to 13 dollars per person per year.

In the same period, $17 trillion were spent on the U.S. military.

There are three hundred million sleeping sites in Africa needing protection from malaria. Anti-malaria bed nets cost one dollar per year. By quick calculation, $1.5 billion would pay for bed nets for all of Africa for five years.

Meanwhile, the U.S. Pentagon spends $1.7 billion *per day*.

Worldwide, nearly 34 million people now live with HIV/AIDS. The medicine to keep the disease in check costs 40 cents per day per person or about $14 million a day for all 34 million. That's $5 billion a year for everyone infected around the world.

Meanwhile, in the United States, $3 million is being spent on pornography *every second of every minute*. That's $13 billion a year. Worldwide, $100 billion a year is spent on porn.

Don't get me wrong; I'm not picking on the United States by any means. There are plenty of other examples from other countries. For purposes in this regard, the United States is simply the gold standard for comparison. Each year in the United States…

$1 billion is spent for breast augmentation.

$25 billion is invested in videogames.

$17 million is spent on Viagra for auto workers at General Motors.

Pharmaceutical company Pfizer markets *Slentrol*, a successful dog-obesity drug that costs $2 a day. Eli Lilly & Company sells *Reconcile* for 'canine separation anxiety.' Another company has sold 240,000 pairs of *Neuticles*, a patented testicular implant for animals who've been neutered. The fake testicles sell for $1000 a pair and promise to restore a pet's *natural look and self-esteem*. It's just one part of the $41 billion Americans spend on their pets each year – that alone is more than the gross domestic product of 130 countries.

We humans have our priorities. Too bad they're at odds with reality.

In the last half of the 20th century, advances in agriculture increased grain production by over 250%. This was heralded as a great thing. The only problem was, as a result, world population grew by four billion since then. Worst of all, much of this agricultural revolution had to be accomplished with fossil fuels. Natural gas to produce fertilizers, oil to produce pesticides, irrigation powered by hydrocarbons.

As economies of the world have grown more interdependent, fertility rates in the world's poorest areas have skyrocketed. In the poorest regions of Africa and the Middle East, populations are doubling every generation. There is no world stability when such a demographic bulge incites despair and violence or adds to poverty, unemployment, and mass migrations.

Our century is the time when it all changes. We can either allow the perfect storm to hit us or make the hard choices now. The problems of growing populations, falling energy sources and food shortages will converge by 2030. Food reserves are already at a fifty-year low. And yet, the world will need 50% more energy, food and water by 2030. By 2050, the world will need 70% more food to feed an extra 2.3 billion people. This is not my alarmist rhetoric. This was reported by the United Nations' Food and Agriculture Organization, the FAO.

And so, the time for half-measures and token efficiencies is gone. Compact fluorescent light bulbs will not save the planet. Don't get me wrong. I'm not against conservation measures. Of course there must be smart electric plugs in homes with strict usage governors. I'm all for computerized trip monitors on cars with high fines for inefficient travel. Things like that must be the norm, but those are just the beginning of what I like to call the *New World Harmony*. But none of it will be possible until humans are back in accord and proportional balance with nature.

My grandson came to me the other day and asked me what I was working on. I explained *The Anthropocene Dilemma* to him this way. We're living in a time in Earth's history when human activity for the first time is having a major impact on the whole planet. We're using up the Earth, the oceans; we're changing the weather and making it hard for animals to live. There are so many of us. We've gotten so good at what we do that now we've become a bad thing for the Earth.

We must realize – hurting Mother Earth is suicide.

All considered, I can only come to one conclusion. Humanity needs an intervention of epic proportions if we are going to survive. For the sake of generations unborn, we are somehow going to have to devise a way to conduct an intervention on ourselves. No one else can do it. It will be the hardest thing we've ever done. Will it be worth it?

Consider this.

The Jurassic Period lasted *fifty million* years. And yet, the dinosaurs are gone. Maybe in the distant, evolved future, some intelligent lizard-insect hybrid will look back upon *The Anthropocene Period* with bewildered curiosity. How could the bygone human species attain so much so fast – but have it all end after only *fifty thousand* years? How could they be called *intelligent* and yet miss so many blatant signs of their own demise?

They must have been infected with narcissistic mass hysteria. Somehow their very own intelligence had become a mental disorder. They believed themselves too clever to be governed by natural laws, cause and effect, or even basic common sense. Of course, they didn't realize this. How could they? According to them, their place within the circle of life

> was preeminent and assured. They could mate and procreate to their hearts' content. To be human meant one was *entitled* – in so many ways.
>
> I thank the Department of Sociology for its kind invitation to speak to you this evening. I ask all of you to consider the lifeboat we've all fallen into. We now face a terrible storm in the middle of an unforgiving sea. What will be do? Will we drift into oblivion – or seize ethics and practical values to guide us?
>
> At such a pivotal time, true words can be harsh. Necessary actions might seem severe. But without them and our resolve to see them through, none of us will reach the distant shore."

Eugene Mass stood at attention. His stature and sudden silence punctuated his words. With solemn intensity he searched the faces in the audience one last time. Fervently, he soaked in their reaction. Only when he was satisfied with the study of their faces did he nod to signal the end of his lecture.

The audience, comprised mostly of students, responded with a standing ovation. A commotion of side conversations erupted to bolster the impact of the applause. Media members jockeyed to take still pictures or find the next best setup position for their live-action cameras. Reporters wrestled with bodyguards in an attempt to get a word of immediate reaction from Eugene for their microphones.

Leah Mass sighed and smiled at her husband. As she stood in place before her seat, Eugene stepped forward and took her by the hand. He led her into the center of attention with him and put his arm around her in solidarity. Only then did he manage a smile. He received the affection of the audience with expected grace and humility.

Eugene stepped towards the exit while shaking the hands of university deans positioned closest to him. Pleasant but assertive, one reporter managed to poke a microphone over a professor's shoulder. He yelled above the hubbub.

"Mr. Mass…that was very dramatic…you defined the problem, but how do you answer critics who say you offer no real answers?"

Eugene stepped between Leah and the media assault but the protective move placed him square before the microphone. Mass couldn't help a condescending smile as he made his way past.

"You had time for one question. It's a shame you wasted it belaboring the obvious."

Husband and wife clung together as they aimed their way down a narrowing gauntlet for the door. For security reasons, guards hustled both of them out of the hall in the direction of a waiting limo. They were handed their coats which they hurriedly put on as they hit the crisp air. Outside, a dusting of snow blanketed everything. A twilight sky brooded grey above them as they dashed for the car.

Flanking bodyguards shielded them. Dozens of photoflashes sparkled from behind the police lines. Then an arcing brilliance attracted everyone's attention skyward. A Molotov cocktail landed in the street in front of the limo and erupted in flame. A second later, another firebomb was thrown from the roof of a building across Broad Street. It landed in the street on the far side of the car.

Guards reacted quickly by shoving Leah and Eugene into the limo's backseat.

Panic and chaos exploded as spectators and police ran every which way. The limo driver revved the car in reverse and gyrated the vehicle back to the next corner. On the way, a pedestrian was clipped by the rear fender and left injured in the street.

Eugene and Leah were alone in the backseat. The driver and bodyguard controlled the escape in the front seat on the other side of soundproof privacy glass. Within a minute, the limo was on the road towards London with a police escort in front and behind. Leah slumped away from the window, doubled over.

Eugene reacted to her position. "Are you all right?"

Leah nodded but said nothing.

"What is it?"

Straightening up, Leah squeezed Eugene's hand. "I'm just a little tired."

"You can rest on the plane."

Leah smiled weakly. "You know I don't rest on planes."

"At least the worst is over. The treatment's done."

Leah pulled away from him. She knew he was speaking of *GenLET* but after the speech she had just heard, his comment seemed out of place. *The worst is over* – how comforting lies could be, even when she knew in her heart what they were.

Nothing more was said until London city limits when Mass' cell phone vibrated once again in Leah's purse. She plucked it out and handed it to Mass.

"Here – this thing was going off all during the speech."

Eugene answered it curtly and turned his attention to the oncoming city lights.

"I told you not to call me on my private line."

The man was insistent. "I thought you'd want to know right away."

"Know what?"

"The laptop was used again."

Mass tensed and leaned forward. "For what?"

"The same thing. Another download."

"Shit!" Mass pumped his fist against the window. "What is wrong with those people? Can't they secure their network? Where are we now? Any chance we can get an MD5 Hash? We need to know if that memo got out?"

"No way. It happened so fast; no chance for a digital fingerprint."

"Damn!"

"What do you want me to do?"

Mass held a steely gaze out the window. For the longest while, only his labored breaths could be heard in the phone. When he finally spoke, it was guttural, determined but fatalistic. "Find out from Oliver how soon he can be ready. We need to accelerate the schedule."

Mass pressed disconnect and threw the phone on the seat between him and his wife. Leah held her breath.

"Was that Javier?"

Mass nodded.

Leah turned away. She watched outside as the city rolled by.

The *New World Harmony* edged closer. Necessity was not always kind.

Her eyes filled with tears.

Chapter 21

Curtis Labon's Estate
Quebec Province, Canada

"So. What's the mystery?" Heinrich pushed away his empty breakfast plate.

Curtis Labon excused the service staff by motioning for privacy in the atrium. As the doors closed, he reached for tea. "I'd rather wait until everyone's arrived."

Hasuru Tamasu studied Heinrich's reaction. "It would only complicate things to start a discussion now. The whole Group should participate."

Heinrich settled to one side. He managed to smile. Toothpick in hand, his mouth widened as he dug deeper. "You two have already talked about it, haven't you? Whatever it is." The German was not so much perceptive as he was familiar with the longstanding friendship between the other men.

"What of it?" Feeling empowered at home, Curtis saw no reason to be coy.

"Nothing..." Heinrich bit down on the toothpick then let it dangle from his mouth. "...except you could be using this time to convince me."

"Whatever for?"

"You didn't call this meeting so abruptly just to go over regular business."

Hasuru tried to make light of the rising situation. "I didn't know there *was* such a thing as *regular* business anymore."

"Let's see..." started Heinrich. "For whatever you're planning, you'll need five votes for a majority. Without my vote, I predict you'll only be able to muster four. The delay in some people getting here is already sending a message, don't you think? I wouldn't be surprised if one or two of them don't even show up."

Curtis paused. Heinrich was right. Any new proposal would be a hard sell to The Group, even with new facts on his side. With the advent of delayed fertility, most Group members had become risk adverse. Even at the best of times, the radical proposal he had in mind would not sit well among the Group. But it couldn't be helped. He could act alone but Curtis knew that Group cohesion going forward would be irreparably harmed by unilateral action by any one member. A consensus was not needed to move forward with the plan – but forward as a Group.

Heinrich eased forward. It was as if he had read Curtis' mind. "I don't see why we go through the formality of voting anyway. Times have changed. We'll all do what we have to do regardless. You've proven that."

"If you had any problems with my actions before, this is the first I've heard of it." Curtis' attempt at nonchalance went unnoticed.

"You have a way of getting what you want – despite advice to the contrary."

"Such as?"

"People are starting to notice the drop in teenage pregnancies. Delayed fertility will soon take center stage. The World Health Organization, among others, are quite interested. Already, some at the fringe are becoming alarmed."

"As we expected."

"Yes, that's why we agreed years ago, when this time came, we'd have independent research ready. We need to give people another reason for what's happening, something that doesn't lead them to 1st Protocol – and to us. Hasuru and I, through our agents, have managed to get our research out on time. You have not."

"Releasing simultaneous studies would be suspicious. If I remember correctly, our plan was to stagger publication."

"Not beyond the point when it's needed. The truth is – you insisted on having your part done by a government agency in the States, despite the advice of The Group to keep such things with private institutions.

"I already had biodefense contacts. It wasn't a problem."

"You mean you didn't expect it to be a problem. My sources tell me you've had several run-ins with your boy in Kansas – Oliver Ross. You're not seeing eye-to-eye on the scheduling of several animal studies. You think he's dragging his feet."

"It's a procedural matter, nothing more."

"*Government* procedures, to be precise. The kind of procedures you wouldn't be bogged down with if you'd followed Group advice and kept the study private."

"The extra hassle is worth it. Private studies convince some people. Government studies convince others. We need both. We agreed simultaneous research would be suspicious but leaving the government out of the loop will also look peculiar. They're bound to research it anyway. This way, we control the results."

"I'm still not convinced you're in control of Ross. The man is too high maintenance to be on the team."

"Oliver is my concern."

"He wasn't even your first choice."

"He was available when I needed him. Don't worry. I'll handle it. He's at a new facility. Some of it is still under construction."

"Excuses," snapped Heinrich

Hasuru turned to the German. "Since we're on the topic of disrupted schedules, what's going on with 2nd Protocol? Last year you said we'd have it by now."

"That was best case." Heinrich pushed back from the table. "You know very well what we're up against. Capping lifespan is more challenging than delaying fertility. Hitting a precise age is the most difficult thing of all. We have to be patient if we want to lock it down."

"Is there something about a 70-year cap that's a problem?"

"A cap at any age would be difficult. It's not the age; it's the precise timing."

"But it's going to happen," prompted Hasuru.

"Difficult, not impossible." The answer was immediate but without conviction.

"So, you've figured out how to accelerate the aging process?" asked Curtis.

"What's to figure out? It's the flipside of *GenLET* – the easier side. I like to call it *RevLET – reverse* life extension therapy. Thanks to Malcolm Stowe's split loyalties between spying for Her Majesty and accumulating pounds sterling, his work procuring *GenLET* for the Crown also gave us what we needed."

Curtis tensed. "Your mercenary is dead. And that's a problem. With Malcolm gone, our line into NovoSenectus is shut down."

"We have what we want. It's just as well. Malcolm went off the deep end after his girlfriend died. Last time we spoke, he was ranting about a bio-lab in Austria."

"What lab?"

Heinrich laughed. "*My* lab – the lab where we were working on 2nd Protocol."

"Why didn't you tell us about this?"

"It was a non-issue. I handled it."

"Handled what?"

"Malcolm claimed Mass was preparing to collapse the world's population using my lab. Something so ludicrous didn't require Group involvement."

"Did he report this back to British intelligence?"

"I think not. He wanted to confront me with it first. Poor man. Blinded by the need to explain Riya's death, he lost grip and critical focus. He became gullible."

"Gullible enough to suspect you and Mass might be working together?"

Hasuru added, "Maybe he took your denials about the lab with a grain of salt."

Heinrich laughed. "Me? Working with Mass to collapse the population – and at the same time stealing his *GenLET*? Hardly."

"What else did Malcolm say?" asked Curtis.

"Does it matter? The man was obviously deranged by grief. More importantly, he was paranoid. He felt NovoSenectus was freezing him out. He'd gotten used to being on the inside of their top security. Suddenly, he was out of the loop. It didn't occur to him that a non-professional association with Riya Basu might have something to do with that."

"Is that what you told him?"

"No. You can't reason a man out of something he has not been reasoned into. It had gotten emotional with him. That mindset is immune to logic or common sense. He badly needed his explanation to be true."

"You had to tell him something."

"I told him to take some time to get his head on straight. I can't afford unstable people in sensitive positions. I know what's going on in my lab. Eugene Mass has nothing to do with it."

"Is it so impossible?" Hasuru squinted. "You got to Malcolm in NovoSenectus. You convinced him to supplement his income while stealing secrets for the Royals. Likewise, why couldn't Mass have someone in your lab in Austria?"

"That's preposterous. Stealing secrets is one thing – developing a major pathogen, with all that would entail – that's something else. Malcolm was a spy at NovoSenectus – but he was one person – he wasn't running a major lab project to develop a superbug. That's what he claimed was going on in Austria."

Curtis sat up straight. "Malcolm was a trained agent – British Special Forces. He may have been lining his pockets working both sides against the middle, but he wasn't deranged. What else did he say?"

"I only half-listened after that. He wasn't making sense. He had just watched Riya Basu gunned down right in front of him."

"His job was to be on the inside – and you ignored what he brought to you?"

"Oh, I didn't ignore it. I'm not stupid. Just in case, I moved 2nd Protocol work out of Austria, to another lab."

"If you weren't concerned, why bother?" asked Hasuru.

"The way Malcolm was acting, I couldn't rule out that Mass had put him up to it.

I knew there was no way Eugene was running a major bio-weapons project out of my lab. All the same, I wasn't going to fall for one of his tricks."

"Like what?"

"Isn't it obvious? Our work could interfere with Mass' plans for *GenLET* and his *New World Harmony*. What if we successfully release 2nd Protocol? What if we manage to cap lifespan *before* Mass has a chance to extend life for everyone he's invited to his fountain of youth party?"

Hasuru looked to Curtis. "He's right. We weren't a threat to Mass until now. It didn't matter until we got near to having 2nd Protocol ready."

Curtis stiffened. "If Mass knows the project status of 2nd Protocol that well, then he *must* have someone on the inside. That would prove your project's been compromised. Who knows how far it goes?"

"A mole is one thing," noted Hasuru. "But there's no way Mass could be hiding a whole project in Heinrich's lab. I'm more interested in what else Mass is up to."

"Sabotage." The German elaborated. "To sabotage 2nd Protocol, I figured Mass might be motivated to let some vile rumors about himself fall into the hands of an intelligence service – the Brits or Americans, probably."

"He probably still has contacts," noted Hasuru. "When Mass bought NovoSenectus, I heard they were doing some secure government contract work."

Curtis would only add, "I'm familiar with it."

Hasuru turned his attention back to the German. "The leak would need to be plausible. Beyond scrutiny."

Heinrich offered, "Malcolm Stowe was handy – and vulnerable. His assignment from London was to get next to Riya Basu in order to get *GenLET*. Unfortunately, he got in bed with her in a way that affected his judgment."

"What about sabotage," prompted Hasuru. "You said 2nd Protocol."

Heinrich continued. "Yes, well, all these on-purpose leaks would lead to my lab in Austria. Before you know it my lab would be investigated and 2nd Protocol would be exposed and linked back to us. Mass would be cleared of suspicion while eliminating 2nd Protocol's threat to his timetable."

"He'd also have a bit of revenge on us," added Curtis.

"It sounds like Mass." Hasuru explored the implication. "Exposing us would create a cover story. If anybody cried wolf about him after that – few would listen."

Curtis added, "At least long enough for him to carry out plans to bring the population down."

Heinrich laughed. "You two sound like Malcolm. His rants were helpful in motivating me to move 2nd Protocol work out of possible harm's way, but that's the extent of it. Face it. Mass is consumed with *life extension*, not mass murder. It's been that way for ten years. The older Eugene gets, the more desperate he is to live longer. It's all he thinks about."

"Did you hear his speech at Oxford last night?"

"Oxford of all places – no."

"You need to hear it. You're right, Mass wants to live longer – but he wants to do it in a world where humanity is back in balance with nature."

"Don't we all…"

"But Mass intends to get there in a single generation."

"Even sooner," added Hasuru ominously. "He sees fewer people as the only answer to a slew of converging crises."

Curtis was quick to add, "For Mass, population collapse serves another purpose besides rescuing the planet. It's the surest way to bring about global social reordering. After something of such magnitude, those who have advance warning will be prepared to pick up the pieces and enforce a newly designed social order."

Hasuru added, "And Mass has *GenLET*. He'll live a long time to see his global plan implemented the way he wants."

Heinrich was bemused but interested by the other men's fervor. "Really. Even if this were true, he's not the only one with *GenLET*. We still have skin in the game."

Curtis returned to his central point. "Years ago when Mass walked out he said we had no sense of urgency. We watched him agree with André Bolard – that desperate acts were needed to save the planet."

Heinrich shook his head. "You will not convince The Group to move against Mass, if that's what you're up to." Heinrich stared at Curtis. "Too many members have followed the squabbles between you two over the years. Anything you suggest will be seen as a personal vendetta. Nothing more. At this point, you're not only personal rivals; more importantly, you're business competitors."

"You're right. I came to the same conclusion months ago." Curtis stood and strolled to the window. "But that was before my trip to Africa."

Heinrich glanced at Hasuru in puzzlement then back to Curtis. "The connection escapes me. Is this about COPE, your Communities of Population Expertise?"

Curtis glanced away from the window. He looked to Hasuru for a sign. Should they broach the mystery topic before everyone was assembled? The conversation's momentum made it a foregone conclusion. Still, Curtis needed to see buy-in.

Hasuru's nod was infinitely shallow – but evident.

Curtis turned from the window and walked back to the table. Leaning forward on closed fists, he unloaded in Heinrich's direction.

"A couple days ago, a woman in Burkina Faso died after receiving a combination MIOVAC vaccine delivered by microneedle. This new batch of vaccine is being stockpiled on three continents but healthcare workers have instructions not to use it. Not yet."

"So how did she get it?"

"A worried husband was desperate enough to break in and steal it."

Heinrich remained puzzled. "Are you saying the vaccine killed her?"

"No. It's more complicated than that."

"You're sure it's MIOVAC – from Mass."

"Yes." Curtis sat down across from Heinrich. "I got samples, including blood."

"Such timing," quipped Heinrich. "Such luck…"

"More like fate."

"The analysis is complete?"

Curtis nodded. "The vaccine didn't kill her. The vaccine is MIOVAC's standard combination package – but we found something new in the preservative used with the microneedles."

Heinrich's interest was piqued. "The preservative?"

"Only someone familiar with the 1st Protocol base would recognize it."

"What is it?"

"A catalyst designed to work with a *new* Protocol. A key for a missing lock. The design copies work done at MIT. The catalyst is a nanoparticle, wrapped in a time release agent, then covered in a water molecule to disguise it from the body's immune system."

"What's the point?"

"In the presence of the new Protocol, and only then, the key matches the lock. Nanoparticles are released."

"Then what?"

"The immune system shuts down – giving the new Protocol a clear shot at the body."

Heinrich took a moment to let it sink in.

Hasuru reiterated. "The preservative is a trigger for an immunosuppressant. The vaccine was designed to be normal unless it interacts with this new Protocol. In this case, it didn't work out that way."

Curtis was adamant. "The lab is certain of it. We spotted it because we know what the 1st Protocol base looks like. Anyone else would miss it. They'd only see a new preservative for a microneedle delivery system."

Heinrich wavered. "So this has nothing to do with the woman's death."

Curtis shouted. "No! That's not the point. Don't you get it? There's no reason for Mass to design a key without also designing the lock. This is being staged in preparation for something, something big."

"What exactly? If Mass is staging a new Protocol, what does it do? Did you find out?"

"No, but from the vaccine it's designed to work with, we know it's clever and elegant. If a pandemic hits and people rush in panic to be immunized, it'll be the vaccines that suppress the immune system. That'll make the new Protocol's job that much easier."

Hasuru drove home the insidiousness of it all. "Those who aren't killed right away by the Protocol will be at the mercy of tuberculosis or diphtheria or meningitis or any one of a dozen diseases that kill millions around the world. What better way to collapse the population?"

Curtis added, "What better way to confuse the world as to what's going on."

Heinrich was somber. "Can I see your results?"

"Of course."

Curtis emphasized, "We don't have immunity to a new Protocol. But you know Mass has to have engineered one for a select few."

Hasuru grimaced. "Have you considered the fact that he might know that *GenLET* secrets have gotten out but he's not concerned; he knows a new Protocol will likely eliminate anyone else who acquired it without his approval."

"Malcolm might have been right after all," mused Curtis. "We can't let Mass get away with this. If there's no other way, we have to take him out."

Heinrich took in a deep breath then released it. "The mystery is revealed."

"I see no other way."

"I see your concern, but you'll never get The Group to step over the line. They won't go that far."

Curtis locked gazes with the German. "He's going to do it. You know he is. What choice do we have?"

After a deathly silence, Hasuru asked Heinrich, "What exactly did Malcolm tell you Mass was working on?"

Heinrich said nothing for a long while. When he finally spoke, he dropped his gaze to his empty plate.

"3rd Protocol."

CHAPTER 22

General de Gaulle Place
Marseille, France

The spinning carousel cast a warm glow into winter's twilight. Sounds of children's laughter blurred against the pulse of city streets. Paces away from the frivolity, Janis Insworth stood beneath a street lamp hugging her coat close. Turning away from the sting of cold ocean air, she watched as pedestrians flowed up and down La Canebière.

Behind her, a male voice drew near. "Waiting for someone?"

Startled, Janis turned to find a man standing inches away. His demeanor was relaxed but serious. English was his second language, Marseille his home. Taken by surprise, she said nothing. All at once, nerves took over. Her mind went blank.

His hands dug deeper into the pockets of his charcoal pea coat. He shrugged.

"Pardon me. I'm supposed to meet a woman here. She's in the market for a luxury craft. A boat."

As he turned to go, Janis found her voice. "Yes, that's right!"

The man changed direction. "Janis?"

She nodded.

The man took a couple steps away. "Let's walk." He glanced up into the glare of the streetlamp. "Standing here might be…bad for business."

Janis held her ground. "Where to?" Her suspicion was obvious.

"Rue Saint-Ferréol. Lots of shoppers. Very public."

The Rue Saint-Ferréol shopping promenade was only a block away. Janis was familiar with it from an excursion earlier in the day. She felt it would be safe. The two of them walked side-by-side. Unsure of the situation, she said nothing.

The man was suddenly cordial. "Is this your first visit to Marseille?"

"Yes."

"You've come a long way. What made you think of coming here?"

"I think both of us have something the other one wants."

"Whatever we've got to say to each other should be done quickly."

"Agreed. I don't want this to take longer than it needs to."

They turned down Rue Saint-Ferréol, a narrow straightaway lit by shop windows on either side. The man slowed the pace. His attitude hardened.

"You've got me curious. That's the only reason why I'm here. What could you have that I would want?"

Janis turned and stopped at a shop window away from other shoppers. The man drew to her side and pretended to window shop. Janis spoke in whispers.

"You've had a hard time convincing people that life extension is a bad thing."

"Sooner or later, people have to wake up. The fact remains, only the rich and powerful will get it. When they do, there'll be two kinds of humans – gods and mortals."

"Why do so many people believe they are going to be one of the gods?"

"People are deluded. Hope is a strong force."

"And you think your tactics so far are going to convince them otherwise?"

"I bring attention to the fact: seven billion people aren't going to get *GenLET*."

"I take it you don't believe in the *New World Harmony*."

The man was gruff. "That's code for a new social order, the final solution, the complete management of man. Thanks to people like you."

"Me?"

"Scientists are naïve. They'll create anything just because they can."

"Then we give it to people like Eugene Mass. Is that it?"

With mention of the name, the man's anger flared. "Why are we here?"

Janis turned from the shop window to face him. "Mass is preparing to collapse the world's population. I have proof. I'll give it to you in exchange for my daughter."

"Whatever would he want to do that for? His thing is life extension."

"I guess he wants to live a long life – in a new kind of world. In some ways, he agrees with you. People are killing the planet. His solution – fewer people."

The news took the man off-guard. He turned and walked away lost in thought.

Janis paced along at his side. "Riya Basu discovered the plot and was killed to keep it from getting out. Same thing with Malcolm Stowe."

"That's not what the tabloids are saying."

"What are you talking about?"

"I did an internet search on your name today. I found several sources that claim the three of you were in a love triangle. They say jealousy killed Riya."

"That's ridiculous!"

"All the same, it's out there. By the way, Indian authorities are still eager to talk with you. They don't like the fact you ran out on them."

Janis' mind raced. "That's convenient for you, isn't it?"

"It's not a bad thing."

"What about the police in Stockholm? They've gone on record saying they believe members of New Class Order killed Riya."

"Yeah, well, that's no longer their only possibility."

"Did New Class Order plant these rumors about me?"

"Why should we take the fall? We didn't kill Riya."

"I should believe that?"

"Why would we do such a thing? It's bad PR, driving people away from our message."

"It's more complicated than that. Admit it – there are radical elements within New Class Order you can't control."

"All I care about is what the police and the public believe."

"So shift the blame."

"Shift it back where it belongs, on Mass and the people who work for him."

"But why me?"

"It's perfectly plausible, all about sex and violence – the public will eat it up."

Exasperated, Janis shook her head. "All you've done is make it harder to expose what Mass is planning. Now, people won't know what to believe."

"Doesn't matter. People think they believe what they want to believe. In reality, they believe what they're told. Fortunately for me, they like sordid tales."

"What's more sordid than murdering six billion people?"

"You have proof of that…"

"Riya had proof. Before she died, she gave it to Malcolm."

"But Malcolm is dead."

"Before he died, he gave it to me."

"If I were you, I wouldn't like that progression. No wonder you want to get rid of this thing you call proof."

"I want my daughter."

"So I've heard."

"And you want to bring down Mass. I have the way to do it. Pretend all you want but your campaign against *GenLET* isn't working. You need something else."

"I take it you won't trade your proof until you get your daughter."

"That's right."

"I'd need to verify this proof. How do I know what you have is genuine unless I have a way to confirm it?"

Janis produced paperwork from her pocket. "I've brought sample redacted pages, enough to demonstrate its value."

The man stopped walking, turned, and drew closer. He took the offered pages and stepped closer to a shop window to read them.

Janis studied the changes in expression on his face. Curiosity became genuine interest, then surprise. Wiping his face clean of emotion. he handed the pages back and walked on. Unexpectedly, there was an aura of menace and mischief about him.

"I have to confess. I didn't search the Internet for you. There are no stories out there about your love triangle. I made that up."

"I don't understand…"

He smiled. "I wanted to see how you'd react. I needed to impress on you the importance of this. You'll leverage anything to get your daughter back. Likewise, I'll leverage anything to move my agenda forward."

"Are you threatening me? Cooperate or you'll spread rumors of a love triangle to implicate me in murder?"

"You came prepared to negotiate. So did I."

"Riya's proof is all I've got to give. What else do you want to negotiate for?"

The man restarted their walk. "You're a scientist. Eventually, you'll go back to the lab. There's still work to do. You need to perfect *GenLET*."

Janis was wide-eyed. "You want *GenLET*?"

"No. But I want to know what's going on with it. I want regular reports on its status. What's possible, how it works, its limitations, its weaknesses."

"How does that help you?"

"I'm a realist. I hold no allusions about my chances at stopping the powerful few from getting what they want. When they do, the game will change. With it, so will the rules. I need to know what I'm up against and how to fight it."

"I'm not signing up to be your source of information forever."

"Then we have no deal."

"Do you want the proof or not?"

"Sure I do. But that's not all. If you want your daughter, I need assurances you'll give me ongoing reports about *GenLET.* I need someone on the inside. I need to know what's possible with life extension, and what isn't – the same way Eugene Mass knows it. That's my offer. Take it or leave it."

"You're admitting you have Alyssa…?"

"I'm telling you I can get her for you."

"How soon?"

"When can you have all the pages – without redaction?"

"Tonight."

"Very well. Meet me back by the carousel at 9 o'clock."

"You'll need to bring something that proves you have access to Alyssa."

"No problem. But let's be straight about this. I want the proof but I also want ongoing reports from you. If you're not willing to do both, don't bother coming."

Janis nodded and the man leaned in closer. "And don't think you're going to get your daughter and forget about the ongoing reports. Do that and you'll see love triangle stories popping up all over the Internet."

"A kidnapper and blackmailer…"

The man's sudden grin became a grimace.

Just then, four men in suits converged on them from front and back.

In French and English, they shouted orders. "Arrêt! Restez où vous êtes. Police! Turn around. Show your hands…"

"What is this!" The man stiffened as two detectives grabbed him by the arms.

"You're under arrest…both of you." One of the men flashed a badge.

The other two plainclothes officers took hold of Janis. Before she could speak, both of them were hustled back down Rue Saint-Ferréol under the watchful gazes of startled shoppers and passerby. With a relentless urgency, the detectives rushed Janis into the backseat of an unmarked car. The other two officers frisked the man with her and put him in a separate car. Janis craned her neck around in time to see the other car driving off in another direction.

"Where are you taking me? What's this about!" Her cries were ignored.

Silent, the detectives sat out the ride with steely-eyed determination. Down side streets and into an underground parking structure they flew. After a ride in an elevator and escorted walk down a hallway, Janis found herself in an interrogation room facing a metal table. It was bare except for one object – Malcolm's laptop. Seeing it laid out by itself stunned her with waves of panic.

The door opened and a middle-aged man in suit and tie strolled in. In his hand was an open file folder. Closing it, he looked up. "Janis Insworth…"

Incensed at being ignored in the car, Janis breathed heavily and said nothing.

"A tourist in our fine city, I suppose…" Janis kept silent. The man sat down opposite her. "For a tourist, you keep company with the oddest people."

"Who are you?" demanded Janis. "What agency is this?"

The man dropped the folder onto the laptop and eased back. "Direction Centrale du Renseignement Intérieur. You would call it the Central Directorate of Internal Intelligence. My name is François Dufray."

Janis offered, "I have no idea what this is about. I've done nothing wrong."

Mr. Dufray used one fingernail to pick at another. "I'm not here to arbitrate right and wrong. I'm more concerned with what's legal and illegal."

"I want to talk to a lawyer."

"Of course, in due time, I recommend it."

"I want a lawyer now!"

"I'm afraid it doesn't work that way. Not here. Not now."

"What am I being charged with?"

"Did I say you're being charged?"

"You arrested me."

"We took you into custody. You're on an Interpol watch list. We've been following you since your arrival."

"If that's true, why didn't you pick me up when I first arrived? You must have known about the watch list when I went through customs in Paris?"

"We were curious to see where you would go – what you'd do."

"So why end it tonight?"

Mr. Dufray was flippant. "We've seen enough."

"What you saw tonight proves nothing."

"Maybe, maybe not. But it's time to put an end to it."

"Nothing is going on."

"What was your purpose in coming to France?"

Janis said nothing.

"You told the custom's agent in Paris you're on vacation. You then flew to Marseille, checked into two separate hotels and acquired two safety deposit boxes. Into one of those boxes you deposited this laptop. Only hours later you met with a representative of the radical group New Class Order. Now, tell me, whose idea of a vacation is that?"

"I want to talk to a lawyer."

"Oh, you should. When you get back to India, it's the first thing I recommend."

"India?"

"Yes, the authorities in Hyderabad want you extradited. Apparently, this laptop doesn't belong to you."

"It was given to me – for safekeeping." Janis felt the last shred of her plans unraveling.

"Ah, safekeeping. Why, because it's valuable? It's odd you should risk international travel with it, don't you think? Unless you were going to use it to make some kind of deal."

Janis slumped in her chair. "You don't understand…"

"I understand intellectual property rights. I understand corporate espionage." Mr. Dufray turned the laptop over and rubbed a thumb over an affixed asset tag. "NS-L31-4186. NovoSenectus laptop model 31, sequence number 4186."

"That's right. I work for NovoSenectus."

"Is this your laptop?"

"It doesn't matter."

"Oh really. Have you checked with NovoSenectus on that? Do you think they want a laptop from one of their top security agents falling into the hands of New

Class Order? Did you know a global search has been underway for NS-L31-4186?"

Janis felt her nerves take over. She began to shiver. Tears filled her eyes.

"It's not like that. I just want my daughter back."

Dufray casually dropped the redacted pages taken off her onto the table. "So you admit stealing the laptop in hopes of bartering the release of your daughter."

"No! I didn't steal it. He has to be stopped!"

"Who?"

"Eugene Mass!"

"Why would Mass want to kidnap your daughter?"

"No!" shouted Janis. "He wants to kill six billion people!"

Bemused skepticism furrowed Dufray's brow. "Really. And New Class Order is going to stop him. Is that what you were told tonight?"

Janis held her hand to her head. "They didn't tell me – I told them!"

"Now I'm confused. But, of course, I find most wild excuses like that." Dufray glanced at his wristwatch. "The local authorities will be here at 9 o'clock to take you to a holding cell. In a couple of days, extradition paperwork will be complete and you'll board a flight back to India. My job will be done."

The mention of 9 o'clock sank heavy on Janis' heart. That should have been the hour of the follow-up meeting and exchange – the laptop for Alyssa. Janis had been so close to securing a deal with New Class Order. Suddenly, all hope swept away and an arrow of pain shot through her.

Out of a mother's hurt, an upwelling anger blinded her judgment.

Needing to vent, she jumped up, reached across the table, and grabbed Dufray by the coat. "Do you know what you've done! I was so close! Now what will happen to her? You bastard! You don't care what they do with my daughter!"

Mr. Dufray recoiled and grabbed Janis' wrists, preventing her attack. He pulled her hands away from him and held them at arm's length.

"Theatrics aren't going to save you, Ms. Insworth."

Just then, a guard who heard the outburst rushed in to secure the situation.

Mr. Dufray picked up the laptop while Janis was handcuffed. He paused on his way out. "I'm sorry about your daughter but the ends rarely justify the means."

Janis's rage ebbed away. "What's going to happen to André?"

"André?"

"The man I met with – André Bolard."

Mr. Dufray raised an eyebrow. "You think you met with André Bolard, the leader of New Class Order?" Dufray gave a laugh and shook his head on his way out.

The deceit was complete. Suddenly, it made sense. André Bolard would never risk himself when a foot soldier of his organization could be rehearsed to fill in.

The guard led Janis one way down the hallway. Mr. Dufray walked in the opposite direction. At a reception area, he was met by an associate.

Dufray handed over the laptop. "Here, take this to forensics. I want a full report on what they find. This has to be done tonight, before we hand her over."

"Yes, sir." The associate nodded and started to hurry away.

"Tell them, not a scratch...," Dufray called after him. "It's important. If we looked at nothing – it must seem that way to a trained eye."

Chapter 23

Granite Peak Installation
Dugway Proving Grounds, Utah

The bottom of the hole.

That's what computer technicians called it. At the lowest basement level reached by elevator, the data center evoked a morbid fascination for most staff members of Granite Peak. The fact that only the freight elevator went down that low was just part of it. Universally, the place made reluctant visitors feel claustrophobic if not creepy.

Few people had reason or inclination to visit the bowels of the buried facility. Something about being that deep and isolated, that surrounded by the sameness of penetrating cold and a slight electronic hum evoked feelings of the grave. Some said even if you knew you were down there alone, it didn't feel that way. You certainly didn't want to be alone if you could help it.

Faye Gardner reassured herself. Much of the basement's macabre mystique was inflated by bored specialists who liked being seen as a rare breed for braving duty assignments in such a place. In fact, the sealed-off data center was an elaborate raised-floor cocoon with low ceilings and super-chilled air. Nothing to fear.

The place was abandoned most of the time, except for an occasional visiting technician seated at a console or making a system tweak to one of the precisely racked components. Automated systems and the impressive array of sensors kept computers and redundancy systems operational. If all was working as it should, nothing and no one else was needed.

Faye had seen *the bottom of the hole* only once. That visit was brief but she'd been more than happy to take the elevator ride back to her laboratory floor. Today's visit would be as much a surprise for Colin as it was when Faye was told by security she could find him there. The more she thought about it, the basement might be the perfect place for the discussion they had to have. What better place to give a sense of the way she felt about the inscrutable project that had taken over her life.

The elevator doors opened and Faye stepped into the LZ, the security Landing Zone. From here, she could access the raised floor directly or head off to the side into a storage area or back farther into the darkened power plant.

After a RIDIS scan, Faye stepped up as doors slid open granting her access. Down an aisle between rows of imposing lockers of black Plexiglas, Colin stood behind a technician seated at a console. Startled by the arrival of a visitor, Colin turned. He was even more surprised to see who it was.

"Faye – is everything all right?"

"I was told I'd find you here. I have something that couldn't wait."

"What is it?"

Faye drew her arms in close around her to ward off the cold. She glanced at the technician. Colin took the hint and sent him away. Once the young man was beyond the LZ, in the elevator, Faye felt she could speak freely.

"I've made a discovery. I wanted you to be the first to know."

"You haven't shared it with anyone in the lab?"

"No, no one."

"Why keep it from them?"

"I need to hear from you what's going on before I get them involved."

"What's going on? I don't understand…"

"You know I've been studying everything we have on Janis. Now that I have the complete virus – with sputnik intact, we're making progress. As we suspected, Janis' Ghyvir-C infection explains a lot about how the viruses work together."

"Good so far…"

"When I started this, I assumed my research fourteen years ago at USAMRIID was just a starting point. We know the common cold doesn't cause sterility."

Colin sat back on the console desk. "OK. So, what's the discovery."

"You said Janis was pregnant at the time of the infection."

"That's right. Frankly, I still don't see how you missed that fact back at USAMRIID. You had to do blood work on her…"

"We went over this already," snapped Faye. "At the time staff were on a tight regiment. Our research was restricted. We were instructed to operate within narrow parameters."

"Sounds like standard procedure to me."

"No. We all thought it was odd, Janis in particular. She was sure we weren't being told everything. I told you – she suspected a dual-use project for weapon development. That's why as soon as she got well and we released her from quarantine, she quit. When she left, we weren't on speaking terms."

"It doesn't matter now. Go on."

Faye stepped closer. "We know the virus doesn't sterilize the parents. But it does something to the parents that affects the children. The children wind up sterile."

Colin nodded, waiting for Faye to bring herself to the point.

"…so I got the idea of pulling up everything I could about Alyssa."

Hearing his daughter's name struck a nerve in Colin, both personal and professional. He kept quiet even though he suspected what was coming.

Faye was intense. "Janis was pregnant with Alyssa when she was in quarantine. So I checked the RIDIS database and every other source I could find. The results are conclusive. Of all the parents carrying the Ghyvir-C marker, Janis is the only one to have a child with a genetic variance from the others. Alyssa carries a different marker from all the other children with Ghyvir-C parents."

Colin said nothing.

Faye was startled by Colin's lack of response.

"You realize what this means? Alyssa might be the only child of her generation to be exposed to the Ghyvir-C marker – and not be sterile!"

"That's a relief." Colin stood and took a breath. "We were hoping you'd come to an independent verification of what we've known for a couple weeks."

Faye felt a chill down her spine. "You knew this?"

"We found out just before you got the call to join The Project. It's one of the reasons why we wanted you on the team."

"What's the point of keeping me in the dark! How am I supposed to work?"

"I don't make the rules of who gets to know what."

Faye spun around, incredulous. "That doesn't make sense! Everyone on this project is handcuffed by ridiculous security rules!"

"Including me! You were there fourteen years ago. Until you told me, I had no idea Janis had been infected or was placed in quarantine. Someone scrubbed that from the record, remember?"

"But you knew Alyssa wasn't sterile!"

"We knew she carried a unique marker. We weren't sure what it meant."

"But you suspected it."

Colin shouted back, "I didn't know Janis had been infected in the lab! There are lots of kids in the RIDIS database who aren't sterile. Any child conceived before their parents got infected with Ghyvir-C is normal. As the virus spread, more couples were affected. The RIDIS database shows the trend line. It took a few months before all live births contained the marker. Alyssa was born in that closing window of time when it was still possible to have a normal pregnancy. We had to be sure!"

"There's more to it than that! Janis is a special case, her infection's unique."

"How so?"

"I told you. USAMRIID removed the sputnik. The giant virus I studied fourteen years ago was missing its parasite. Janis was infected by a modified virus. Her infection was a rare if not singular event."

The realization hit Colin. "That's right…and the sputnik is the key element."

"Janis passed the Ghyvir-C infection to Alyssa when she was still a fetus – but it got passed without the interaction of the sputnik being present."

"So how would that work?"

"Don't you see? Alyssa was exposed to Ghyvir-C in utero. Her system either developed or received antibodies to the giant virus before she was born. She also got her mother's immune response. As she grew up, like everyone else she was exposed to the fully-functional Ghyvir-C in the wild, the one that contains the sputnik. But by then her system already knew how to attack it. With Ghyvir-C under attack, the sputnik inside never got a chance to go viral inside of her."

"And that explains why Alyssa isn't sterile…?"

"In part. It also explains why Alyssa's future children might be protected. Like her, they won't be sterile."

"That's a whole other line of testing…"

"Janis and Alyssa are the key! Their systems might contain the exact combination of elements we need to reverse sterility. The modified virus that infected Janis gave Alyssa the key marker. It's unique. No other child has it. We need to study both of them."

Colin paced back and forth before facing Faye again. "We might have to make do with just one of them."

"Who?"

"Alyssa. According to my boss, The Project has her at a place called The Nest."

"What!" Faye was enraged and nonplussed. "You kidnapped Alyssa!"

"I didn't kidnap her. The Project did. Once I showed them her RIDIS markers were different from everyone else's, they knew she was special. We had to protect her."

"Protect her from what?"

"Riya Basu had just been killed and Janis worked with her. Some people might be crazy enough to want sterility if they found out it had happened. If there was any chance Alyssa was the key to this, we couldn't leave her out in the open. We weren't certain what was going on inside groups like New Class Order. We had to secure her just in case. Like you said, we needed to study her."

"And kidnapping was the only way? When were you going to tell Janis about this? Were you ever going to tell me? Didn't you think this might have a bearing on my work?"

"I was told it would be better if we tried working out a solution without you knowing."

Faye crossed her arms and looked away, refusing to engage.

"They needed your expertise. They weren't sure how you'd react."

"Perceptive of them – the bastards."

Colin held up a hand of truce. "Before you go off on this, let me explain."

"What – more acceptable lies? Another necessary cover story?"

"You have to understand, the kidnapping was a spur of the moment thing. Lots of ideas were floated on how to gain access to Alyssa. Some inside The Project wanted to approach Janis; get her approval to do some testing. Others wanted to bring Alyssa in using trumped-up medical excuses. Nothing clicked."

"Did you even try?"

"It seemed certain whatever we did would only have people asking too many questions. Above all, we weren't going to risk exposure. If anyone snooped into why we needed Alyssa, our excuses had to hold up to scrutiny. The truth about sterility had to stay a secret to prevent a panic. The decision got put off."

"Until Riya was shot. Then you saw an opportunity."

"It made sense. Everyone's attention was on NovoSenectus and New Class Order. Blame for the kidnapping went right to them. But we had to move fast. We never had plans to do it but it turned out to be the perfect cover for getting access to Alyssa for as long as we needed."

"Meanwhile, you put Janis through hell and blindfolded the very people like me who need to figure this out!"

"It had to be done."

"Oh, really? Well, here's something else that needs to be done. I need to go back home. I need to get away from here."

"Now, wait – let's think about this."

"If you've got anything to say, say it. Otherwise, I know what I need to do."

"It's not that easy."

"Yes it is. I won't work under these conditions!"

"I don't believe you'll walk away, not when you know sterility is real."

Faye shouted, "What else are you hiding?"

"It's not your place to design security for The Project."

"I don't even know what The Project *is* anymore. Do you? Have you figured out why there are animal fertility studies in Manhattan, Kansas? What else are they keeping from you?"

"I looked into it. There may be an answer for that."

"Like what?"

"There've been some studies coming out in scientific journals explaining the drop in teenage pregnancies around the world. The studies claim there are chemicals in the environment that appear to be causing delayed fertility in some mammals."

"*Delayed*....fertility."

"They say the findings are preliminary."

"You don't actually believe that, do you?"

"At this point, we can't discount anything. It would make sense for The Project to run their own trials on animals just in case. It could be a factor in what we're seeing. If so, we have to isolate it and determine how it fits in."

"Where were these studies done?"

"I'm not sure...Germany, Japan. The only study like it in the U.S. that I know of is in Manhattan, Kansas."

Faye heaved a sigh. "I don't get it. We already know why there's a drop in pregnancies. It sounds like another cover story. Something else must be going on inside The Project."

"Nothing that I know about."

"That's not reassuring."

"At least it explains one thing. To do my job, I don't need to know about the lab in Kansas. There's nothing sinister about me not being told about animal trials in Manhattan. As it should be, everyone knows only what they need to know."

"Your bosses aren't scientists. How do they know what I need to do my job?"

"You're not the only scientist working on this. I imagine everything you find is being routed to The Nest. Someone, somewhere is probably putting it all together."

"That makes me sound pretty expendable. There should be no problem letting me go home."

"It doesn't work that way."

"Then we have a problem."

"What can I say to convince you?"

"For once, you can tell me the goddamn truth! Tell me what you know about this or I walk. I won't be kept in a box, fed lies, and made to wonder if I'm helping to save the world or ruin it."

"I don't know what you want to know!"

"You picked the wrong person to team up with. I know you. I can tell when you're holding back. We've been too close to think you can lie to me."

"Nothing I say will make any difference. The children will still be sterile."

"I don't care. I want to know. Tell me or take me to the surface. I'll walk out of here. I swear it. At this point, I don't care how big the desert is up there. It'll be on your head."

The two of them glared at each other. Faye was heartbeats away from bolting.

Colin blinked first. He spun a chair around and offered it to her.

"Here. You better sit down."

Faye held up until she sensed the offer was genuine. As soon as she sat down,

Colin leaned back on the desk opposite her.

"What I'm about to tell you I'll deny. You want to know? So be it. I still think some things are better left alone."

"I don't need your disclaimers. I get it."

Cut short, Colin nodded his acceptance of terms. He took a long breath and looked up at her with an expression drained of emotion. It was a game face, hollow of feeling like she had never seen before. It seemed fitting in such a place.

"Fourteen years ago, I was liaison between an intelligence task force and the RIDIS project. My work was at GeLixCo in Puerto Rico. Because of my USAMRIID background, I got recalled to Washington to be briefed on a special assignment. Little did I know then, but that assignment was where a deeper side of The Project began."

"I thought The Project was all about the RIDIS database."

"That's my part of it now. It's been so much more."

"Go on…"

"I was told with high confidence that someone was using a lab in another part of the Puerto Rico complex to synthesize a new virus combination. The two labs were strictly insulated from each other. We didn't know who was behind it, but it was obvious they planned on releasing it worldwide."

"What was the point? A pandemic?"

"Yeah. What else could it be?"

"So why didn't the Feds just shut them down?"

"Maybe we should have. The problem was, if we had done that the only people we would have stopped were the mercenaries, the bit players. My bosses wanted to catch the masterminds behind this. By letting the lab stay open and watching it, infiltrating it, we hoped to find out more about who or what was behind it."

Faye was ahead of him. "So what went wrong?"

"We didn't find out about some key information until it was almost too late. We thought the U.S. lab was the only place working on this. It turned out they had several locations, all but one in other countries. We were blindsided. By the time we got confirmation, we discovered their schedule to release the pandemic was farther along than we thought. We had the impression they were midway; in fact, they were almost finished."

"You didn't move in and stop it?"

A shake of the head. "By then, shutting them down wouldn't have made any difference. The plot was international. Any one of the other labs would have completed the plan. We couldn't get to them all. Luckily, the U.S. lab was their synthesis point – that's where they merged what the others had done."

"What happened?"

"We did the only thing we could. We hatched a plan to sabotage the final agent."

"Wouldn't they find out and just start again someplace else?"

"That's why we had to do it in a way they wouldn't suspect. We wanted them to go through with their plan – only, we had to make the released agent harmless."

"How did you manage that?"

"We substituted a benign payload – into the sputnik."

"Sputnik! You're talking about Ghyvir-C!"

Colin nodded.

"You knew Ghyvir-C was engineered all along."

"The difficulty was – it wasn't engineered by us."

"So how was it supposed to work?"

"As you'd suspect. The common cold was the best way of spreading the virus. The sputnik parasite went along for the ride. It was designed so Ghyvir-C going active in a host would signal the sputnik to hijack Ghyvir-C. That's when the real damage would start."

Faye stood and paced. "Wait a minute. If you sabotaged it, then why are we here? Why are we facing sterility in children?"

"You've hit upon the big question."

"You don't know?"

Colin's half-shrug was noncommittal. "We had operatives on the inside. At the last minute, they switched payloads in the sputnik. Everything went as planned. The benign agent replaced the deadly one. Ghyvir-C got released. For fourteen years nothing happened – nothing but the common cold. There was no pandemic. For The Project, that was success. It appeared our sabotage worked."

For Faye, another piece of the puzzle fell into place. "Until a few months ago. That's when you found the sterility markers in RIDIS."

Colin nodded. "Only weeks ago we traced the markers back to Ghyvir-C."

"Maybe you're looking in the wrong place. Maybe those studies about a chemical in the environment are right. What if it's not sterility, just delayed fertility."

"Don't patronize me. You've been in the lab. You've seen the markers. We've done enough test cases on children. You know sterility is real."

"Then why is the *National Bio and Agro-Defense Facility* doing animal trials? You're still holding something back."

Colin shouted, "I've told you what I know!"

"Don't lie to me, Colin! It doesn't add up. What are we really dealing with? If you succeeded in stopping them fourteen years ago, then what is going on?"

"You want to know what's going on? Extinction! Is that clear enough for you! Stop chasing your tail. All the dirty little secrets in the world won't change the fact that unless we do something – the last human generation has been born."

For Faye, the gaps filled in. "I see now why back at USAMRIID we were under such a tight regimen. Janis was right – it was all about dual-use. They gave us a modified virus because The Project didn't want us to inspect their benign sputnik. But why? Why hide something so benign from their own government lab?"

"Don't overthink it. There were good reasons to separate the two viruses. It wasn't sinister – it was simply good lab procedure."

"Is that the way you were told to spin it?"

Colin stepped close to confront her. "Listen, we need you here to help solve this. It's got to be done with or without you. What good is it to win the point and lose the game? Arguing with me may give you some satisfaction, and you can go home and pat yourself on the back for being so assertive – but how long will that last? How long can you sit and home, doing nothing, and watch the children grow up?"

Faye was torn between storming out and staying.

Colin added, "In a few months, your baby will be born. Are you going to be all right with that?"

Tears filled Faye's eyes.

Colin didn't let up. "You have a choice. You can sit at home smug, knowing you won the argument – or you can help do something about this. What's it going to be?"

The silence between them raised the intensity to an unbearable level.

For Faye, something about being that deep, that isolated, that surrounded by penetrating cold and impersonal electronic hum evoked feelings of oppressive dread.

She had truly reached *the bottom of the hole.*

She gathered all the strength she had left and stared back at Colin. "If you want me on The Project, I have one condition…"

"Name it."

"Janis and Alyssa need to be part of the research. I want access to *both* of them."

"You expect me to bring Janis into this?"

"What's the matter? Afraid to face her after what you did to Alyssa – what you did to *her*?"

Colin flinched and redirected off topic. "At my level, I can only deliver so much."

Faye failed to steady her nerves but her voice was strong. "*Impress* it on your bosses – if they want to solve this, they need *both* of them. Now take me home. I'll come back when my terms are met."

She stormed off in the direction of the Landing Zone.

Colin stood flatfooted for a second then followed her into the elevator.

During the ride to laboratory level, the silence between them only deepened.

CHAPTER 24

NovoSenectus Corporate Business Park
Hyderabad, India

Standing at his ninth-story office window, Eugene Mass looked down on the unexpected arrival with a mixture of confusion and annoyance. A black Suburban with tinted windows trailed the limousine along the circular drive. Security cameras pivoted at the corners of the central administration building's rooftop and tracked progress of the cars nearing the south entrance.

The guards had called ahead to give Mass advance notice. He had done nothing with the lead time other than wait. Without more detail, there was nothing else to do.

When forward motion stopped, suited bodyguards exited the Suburban and took up point positions around the limousine. The limo driver scurried back to open the rear door. From the back seat stepped Mass' wife Leah in a uncharacteristic hurry. Obviously, the energy given her steps belied a matter too important to heed doctor's orders to stay at home and rest.

With everything in his day, the unanticipated visit forced Mass to reconsider the decision to bring his wife with him from Brussels. Leah had joined him in India so corporate scientists could treat her mysterious chronic fatigue. She had struggled with it since completing *GenLET* treatments. Doctors had followed up with tests and trial prescriptions as much as she wanted. All the while, they informed Eugene they believed the ailment was psychosomatic.

Not dissuaded, Leah was certain her symptoms proved she was having an adverse reaction to all she had gone through to secure a greatly extended lifespan.

As Mass watched Leah strut towards the building's entrance, he reflected on the next hundred years. After receiving *GenLET*, *'til death do us part* took on challenging new potentials and problems. He sighed at confirmation of a reality he suspected but had hoped to avoid – even the gods have issues, after all.

He turned from the window and glanced across his work desk without inspiration. Moving on, he stepped into a sitting area on the other side of the room. He fixed himself a drink and waited for the inevitable. He could only guess what new emergency had prompted Leah to need face-time with him.

A female voice sounded on the intercom.

"Mr. Mass, your wife is on her way up to see you."

Eugene took a sip of scotch. "Very well. Hold all calls and appointments until further notice."

"Yes, sir."

Two sips later, the door opened.

In came Leah with a distraught but determined face.

"Eugene...," she gave him a brief hug. "I'm sorry; this couldn't wait."

"You couldn't call?"

Leah froze as if affronted. "Aren't I welcome?"

Already exasperated, Mass closed his eyes. "All I meant was, it might have been better to rest." He opened his eyes to find Leah settling on the couch. "How are you feeling?"

"I'm beside myself. Haven't you heard?"

Mass restrained the sarcasm of asking if those statements were meant together. "I've been a little busy."

"I told you something was wrong. I should have listened to my intuition."

"Hold on, now – start at the beginning."

Her eyes filled with tears. "It's Jayden!"

Eugene felt her concern and drew near. He sat on the couch and took her hand.

"What about Jayden?" Mass expected to hear that his nine-year-old grandson had suffered an accident.

Leah was overcome by all the emotion bottled up during the limo ride.

"You've got to put everything on hold! Something isn't right!"

"Put what on hold? What are you talking about?"

"*GenLET*...3rd Protocol. We can't be sure of any of it."

"*GenLET* is out. We've already given or sold it to so many. What does that have to do with Jayden?" Mass held her by the shoulders to calm her. "Just tell me. It's all right. When did this start?"

"I went to the clinic; I had palpitations."

"This morning?"

"A while ago...I just came from there."

"Go on..."

"I was in the office, telling them how I felt when they got a call."

"About Jayden?"

Leah nodded. "The results came back from his post-therapy tests."

"Post *GenLET*...," Mass confirmed.

"Something isn't right genetically. They found an anomaly."

"What exactly?"

"Something's abnormal." Leah bent forward and sobbed. "They say he's sterile. He'll never have children."

Mass took a moment to let the news sink in. He settled back.

"That makes no sense. How do they know this? He's only nine years old..."

Leah's temper fought her grief. "Something's gone wrong with *GenLET*. I just know it."

"What did the clinic say?"

"What do you expect? They aren't going to take the blame."

"Just tell me what they said!"

"They said no way. It's not their fault."

"What's the reason? Did they explain?"

"Of course! They compared genetic material taken from Jayden before *GenLET* therapy and matched it with his test results. They found the same genetic variance before and after. They claim that proves Jayden was sterile before he got *GenLET*."

"Then *GenLET* didn't cause it. If they had this before, why didn't they see it?"

"According to them, they only do this kind of exhaustive review when they confirm the therapy is complete. They said there's no reason to do the same review before treatment. It's a comparative test; before, there's nothing to compare."

"You don't accept that?"

"I know what I feel. There has to be more to it. How can they explain it away so fast? It doesn't seem right."

"Why, because you want it to be so much more?"

"The best thing to do is put everything on hold. We have to take time to look into this. We need to be sure."

"It's not that easy." Mass stood and sauntered to the window.

"Of course it is!"

"I know you're upset, but let's think this through…"

"A lot of *GenLET* research got used in 3rd Protocol." Leah's statement was an accusation.

"We've already gone over this. Neither one of us are scientists. We can't tell them how it works. If they're certain *GenLET* isn't involved, we have to trust the evidence."

"I have chronic fatigue for a reason…now this."

"The doctors say the fatigue has more to do with you than anything."

"It's *not* all in my mind."

"Nobody else receiving *GenLET* reports the same symptoms."

"*GenLET* is something new. It could go wrong in each person *differently.*"

"Leah, please…I don't have time for this. There's too much to do."

"Your grandson is sterile! Aren't you the least bit concerned how that happened?"

"How does *any* birth defect happen?"

"Birth defect! Now who's jumping to conclusions? You said you're not the scientist, so stop all of this until they have the evidence."

"I'm sorry but there's too much at stake to put everything on hold."

"The schedule is ours to make; no one's forcing us to do anything right now."

"Janis Insworth has been taken into custody in France. They're preparing to extradite her back here."

Leah was confused. "But that's good news."

"Not necessarily. We didn't get to the laptop first."

"But they'll bring it back with her, won't they?"

"Yes, but we don't know who's been looking at it. You know the French won't pass up the chance to examine it."

"What was she doing in France anyway?"

"Trying to make a deal with André Bolard."

"My God!"

"All the more reason why we must accelerate the schedule, not slow it down."

"It's that damned memo again!" Leah stood and paced. Anger dried her tears.

"It's the only thing that can hurt us."

"If you hadn't been so sloppy to let Riya get a hold of it..."

"She was more resourceful than I thought."

Leah stood and paced. "That wasn't it. The whole plan was flawed. Whatever possessed you to think that baiting her was a good idea in the first place?"

"I needed to find out who she was passing information to, where it was going, and what they were using it for. I needed to give her something to find. Why not make use of it?"

"She was a corporate spy. She should've been handed over to the authorities."

"She was our top scientist. Losing her meant *GenLET* might not get finished."

"So you fed her lies that only complicated things – especially when some of the lies were true! Admit it, you were trying to be too clever."

Mass turned from the window to confront his wife. "If it wasn't for that one memo, we wouldn't be arguing about this. Nothing else Riya transferred to GeLixCo can hurt us. Nothing on the laptop matters but the memo. For chrissakes, it has my initials on it – it names Javier, Oliver, Labon, and the lab in Kansas."

"What about the rest? You put out there the whole plan!"

"It mentions 3rd Protocol – so what? There's nothing going on in Austria and there's no deal with the Chinese. The white papers on population collapse were published years ago from think tanks funded by The Group. Anyone using that information will be crying wolf. If anything, The Group will have to duck and over. That'll delay their 2nd Protocol which is want we want. The exposure on us will only *protect* our plan. If someone else comes after us with conspiracy theories, they'll look ridiculous. Mixing the truth with lies can only insulate us."

Leah looked to the floor. "You never found out why Riya betrayed us…"

"No sense going into that." Mass stood his ground. "We'll never know. After 3rd Protocol, it won't matter."

Leah steamed silently for a moment. "What are you going to do about the memo?"

"There's not much I can do. We have to assume it's already out there or soon will be. If we had gotten to the laptop first, we'd have more maneuvering room. As it is, I see no choice but to give Oliver the go-code."

"With all that's going on, that's your only concern?"

"The crisis isn't going away. If we wait longer, more can go wrong."

"And what about Jayden? What about our dynasty carrying forward?"

Mass was brutally pragmatic. "His parents now have hundreds of years together. Lots of time. We'll have other grandchildren."

Leah looked up and stared at her husband. "You're no scientist, but somehow you know for a fact that the same *birth defect* won't happen again? You'd rather rush forward than wait and be sure."

Mass couldn't dispute her point. It was easier to placate. "I'll have the lab look into it. If you want, I'll have every *GenLET* recipient tested. Will that make you feel better?"

Leah felt no closure. "Don't do it to make me feel better. Do it because it's too important not to get right. This is our future – and now there's so much more of it."

Leah waited for an answer that didn't come. She took a step closer to Mass.

"If you get this wrong, we're going to have to live with it a long, long time." Leah headed for the door. "Think about that."

With Leah gone, Mass shuffled back to his desk and sat down. Motionless for a minute, he let the conversation settle and his business focus return. Before him was keyboard and monitor. On impulse, he did a search on his name. Dozens of news articles and blogs returned, most detailed the arrest of Janis Insworth; they named Mass only peripherally as her boss at NovoSenectus.

As Mass scrolled down the search results, one article from a Parisian scandal sheet caught his eye. He clicked on it and read a translation. Scanning the text, he caught the gist of the article's salaciousness – and accuracy.

> "…Janis Insworth worked alongside Riya Basu, the murdered Nobel laureate,
> …the laptop was found in a safety deposit box not far from where the *GenLET* scientist met with a representative of New Class Order,
> …Indian authorities claim the laptop contains sensitive intellectual capital from NovoSenectus and belonged to Malcolm Stowe, a security agent for the biotech firm who died under suspicious circumstances,
> …a source within the Hyderabad Police headquarters says Eugene Mass, owner of NovoSenectus, is anxious to get the laptop returned,
> …the Central Directorate of Internal Intelligence is in possession of the laptop,
> …so far there's only wild speculation about what secrets the laptop might contain."

Mass reread passages from the article. With each pass over them, he couldn't help but feel anxious about the way the course of human events stewed in its own self-serving pettiness. It would take so little, something so minor, to interfere with all he had worked for.

Meanwhile, *The Anthropocene Dilemma* was waiting to be solved.

A calmness of conviction came over him. He was suddenly imbued with the righteous perspective of a reluctant savior. Humanity and the planet needed him. Above all else, he wanted to live to see a healthier earth, a better humanity.

The conversation with Leah receded. It seemed long ago and far away.

He opened a desk drawer and reached in for a private phone.

Before he pressed a speed dial key, there was the slightest pause.

Leaning back in his swivel rocker, he waited for his man to answer.

"Yes, what is it?" It was Javier.

Mass was firm. "Pass it along…*green, green, green.*"

From Javier, a moment of hesitation, the shock that this was real.

With a press of a thumb, Mass ended the call. No answer was needed.

He dropped the phone into the drawer, stood and made strides to the window.

The black suburban and limo were in the distance.

Mass watched them disappear.

Filled with a rush of passion and purpose, he raised his sight and squinted at the all-powerful sun. The future was now. The deed was done.

The New World Harmony had just begun.

CHAPTER 25

Lufthansa Flight 2261
Franz Josef Strauss International Airport, Munich

Janis Insworth looked away from the porthole window and braced for landing. Descending out of a grey sky, the Canadair Regional Jet 700 touched down on runway 26L shortly before 10:30 a.m. The flight was on time. Janis felt out of place.

For a moment, she closed her eyes and absorbed being engulfed by the energy around her. The roar of back-thrusting engines and the forward pull from the plane's braking both felt as if they surged from a protected place inside of her. Strapped in her seat, she reflected on a regret, rawness and longing that ached for release.

If only she could stop or reverse so much of what had happened.

If only she could prevent so much of what she feared might soon be.

But everything around her resisted. The unyielding momentum of events felt fateful, at times fatalistic. Despite determination and clarity, at moments it was easier to doubt, to relent that one was probably helpless to change the course of events, to exist merely as another powerless transient along for the ride.

Her muscles tightened against the feeling even as the roar around her subsided.

Alongside her in Seat 9C, a French air marshal had spent much of the 90-minute flight from Marseille in silence. He remained all-business and duty-bound as her armed escort. His name was Paul but all Janis cared about was what awaited her after being in his custody for three interconnecting flights back to India.

Janis forced deeper breaths. The excited rush of landing had calmed. The plane turned and started a slow taxi towards the terminal gate. Janis anticipated this first layover with unusual dread, enough so that it sparked her intuition. Something wasn't right. She forced herself to settle back. Focusing on the mundane, she hoped a calmer perspective would prevail.

"How long will we be here?" She didn't look at Paul.

He idly glanced past her out the window. "Not long. Next flight's at noon."

"That's the one to Doha?"

A nod. "Five and a half hours. The longest leg."

She sighed and stared up at the fasten seatbelt indicator. She remembered the rest; it stuck in her mind. After another layover, twice as long, the flight out of Doha would put them into Hyderabad at 3:30 in the morning. The thought of it ran cold. There was something about arriving in the middle of the night that didn't sit well. Not where she was going. Not when she knew who wanted her there and why.

She asked the question she'd avoided up to now. "Do you have the laptop?"

For the first time in over an hour, Paul looked her in the eye. He studied her interest with aloofness edged with wariness. "That's none of your concern now."

Janis didn't pursue it. She looked out the porthole and ignored him. Thoughts of Eugene Mass overwhelmed anything else. On the surface, French and Indian officials would make her issue appear to be a police matter. But she knew what was really behind the effort to return her to India. It would never be enough for Mass to simply get the laptop back. He had unfinished business with her.

She wondered how it would play out. Would Mass pretend reconciliation to get her back in the lab so she'd finish streamlining methods of *GenLET* therapy? Would he feign concern and sympathy over Riya, Malcolm, and Alyssa – all the while plotting to make her own eventual demise look like a lab accident or illness? Would he try somehow to use unverifiable news about Alyssa as leverage over her?

What possible excuses could she give for having the laptop, for being in Marseille, for leaving India so abruptly after Malcolm's death? The police would insist on explanations for some of it but Mass would eventually demand to know all. Lying to one of them would only alert the other to her subterfuge. Surely Mass would find out anything she told the police. Confiding in the police the truth about Mass would not work; Mass no doubt had already prepped them to expect her desperation to come out under pressure. The police were used to wild stories and excuses coming from criminals.

The thought of fleeing again seemed far-fetched. But was there a choice? More importantly, even if she wanted to, would that be possible anymore? Mass would have her under constant surveillance. Even if the police dropped all charges, her life might appear normal, but it would really be spent under corporate house arrest.

No sooner had the plane parked at the gate but a flight attendant hurried down the aisle. She leaned over Paul, verified his name then handed him a slip of paper.

"A note from the Captain," she whispered.

Janis watched the exchange between them. Paul stiffened after reading the note. He stuffed the paper in one pocket while pulling a phone from another.

"What is it?" asked Janis.

"I'm not sure." Before she could ask more, Paul pressed the phone to his ear and spoke to his boss in French. The exchange was hushed and rushed. Janis translated as best she could but only gleaned part of it.

There had been a change in plans.

Apparently, it was a surprise to both sides of the conversation.

Passengers stood and gathered belongings from the overhead compartments. The cabin door opened and Flight 2261 disembarked. Paul shouldered his small carry-on. Janis had nothing to take with her; all belongings collected from Marseille's Hotel Alize, where she had registered under an assumed name, were being shipped separately. She left the plane, the only passenger with nothing in hand. The distinction was a nagging reminder of her vulnerability and displacement.

Paul led the way out the cabin door into the jetway. Immediately they were met by an airport guard. Instead of following the rest of the passengers into the terminal, the guard escorted them to a side utility work door which led outside and down a stair onto the tarmac. Jet noise and the whip of cold air surrounded them. At the base of the stairs, an airport security van idled, its side door open and waiting.

As they approached, a suited man stepped out and handed Paul a folded paper.

Paul gave it a cursory look. "My bosses in Marseille know nothing of this."

"Call them again. It just happened."

The suited man sounded American. With an upturned wiggle of an index finger, he motioned for Janis to approach the open door.

Janis started to move but was blocked by Paul's outstretched arm. "I need to see more than this. I don't take orders from this agency." He handed the paper back.

Another man in the van thrust a satellite phone out an open window. "Here, Place Beauvau wants to talk to you."

Janis halted in time to see surprise cross Paul's face. She had never heard of Place Beauvau, but the reference was common knowledge to everyone else. The man outside the van passed the phone across.

Paul took it and had a brief conversation. Mostly, he listened.

Abruptly, the call ended. "Oui, monsieur, tout de suite."

The American accepted the satellite phone back and handed Paul the folded paper again. "Are we squared away?"

Paul nodded as Janis drew close. "Who was that?"

Paul relaxed. "Minister of the Interior, in Paris."

"What's going on?"

"It appears you are in more trouble than I thought. The Americans want to extradite you too."

"Why?"

The man outside the van took Janis by the arm and led her into the van. "It's a matter of national security. Please, we have to go now."

Paul backed away and pocketed the folded paper. Janis took a seat between the two Americans as the door slid shut and the van accelerated away from the terminal.

Janis didn't know whether to be relieved or worried. The detour might be saving her from Mass, but by offering her up for what? The situation was not clear. She turned to the man who had stood outside the van.

"Am I being rescued or extradited?"

The man was matter-of-fact. "We're taking you into custody for transport to the United States."

"What kind of custody?"

The men in the van gave each other a knowing glance. "You have the right to remain silent. Anything you say can and will be used against you in a court of law. You have the right to speak to an attorney and have an attorney present during any questioning. If you cannot afford a lawyer, one will be provided for you at government expense. Do you understand these rights?"

"What am I being charged with?"

"First of all, do you understand your rights?"

"Yes! But I don't understand what you think I've done."

The man had had enough. "I don't have the complete list. It includes violations of Title 18 of United States Code Section 1030, interstate flight to avoid prosecution, aiding and abetting a terrorist organization, espionage, trafficking in state secrets, and interference with an ongoing investigation."

Janis sat back, dazed. The thought of it was too incredible to even protest.

Through the front windshield she could see a small jet waiting on the runway's apron. They were headed straight for it. It carried only one marking, words in blue written above the windows.

UNITED STATES OF AMERICA.

CHAPTER 26

New Year's Eve
Mt. Pleasant, Maryland

"Sophia, can I call you back? There's someone at the door."

Faye Gardner tapped her Bluetooth headset to disconnect and left half-made guacamole resting in a ceramic bowl on the kitchen island. The doorbell rang again. Wiping hands on apron, she strutted through the entrance hallway. It couldn't be Jacob. He wasn't expected for another hour.

She opened the door. Cold air and late afternoon light rushed in.

Colin Insworth stood his ground on the welcome mat. "We need to talk."

Faye recoiled. "What are you doing here?"

"It's necessary."

"It's New Year's Eve."

"Doesn't matter. I won't be long."

Faye hesitated then took a step back, widening the opening to let him in. He moved forward as she turned away and headed back to the kitchen.

"You'll have to talk while I work. I'm in the middle of something."

"No problem." Colin shut the door behind him and followed. "Aren't we all."

Faye busied herself preparing tapas and let Colin find his way to a stool.

"Nice place."

Faye ignored the compliment. "So, what chased you out of your hole?"

"You've been following the news?"

"I have – that's why I'm surprised you're here."

"Really, why is that?"

Faye tapped her smartphone, navigated to a saved page and read from it.

> "Janis Insworth, top *GenLET* scientist and coworker of slain Nobel laureate Riya Basu, was arrested in Marseille last night while meeting with a representative from the radical group New Class Order. Police will not comment more, other than to say they are following up on a request from Interpol to extradite Ms. Insworth back to India for questioning regarding possible intellectual capital crimes connected with Malcolm Stowe, a security agent for NovoSenectus who died in a car accident shortly before Janis left the country."

Colin nodded. "Yeah, that came out a few days ago."

Faye went back to dicing tomatoes and accenting her words with flourishes of the knife. "You know the deal – I come back only if Janis is added to The Project. I don't see how that can happen now."

Colin got up and helped himself to a beer from the refrigerator. "May I?"

"Go ahead, it looks like you need it."

He popped the top and took a swig. "Did you read the speculation swirling around the meeting she had? What was she doing in Marseille? Of all things, why meet with New Class Order?"

"I saw it."

"Then you've seen the shit storm of rumor coming out of this. There's more news being reported about what they *don't* know rather than what they do."

"Typical."

"Except they could be onto something. You know there has to be more to it."

"What does it matter? When did anyone get the full truth listening to the news."

"But you're not just anyone – you know Janis, far better than I ever did."

"I knew her in a different time and place."

"And yet you insist on working with her now."

"Not because of who we were in college. There's no one else in the world with the genetic markers that she and Alyssa carry. It's as simple as that."

"And that's enough. It's nothing personal."

"It doesn't matter; it's what's necessary."

"Regardless. That's pretty cold."

"What do you want me to do – vouch for her? There's no telling how she's changed."

"Enough to commit espionage? Enough to barter state secrets with terrorists?"

With the accusation, Faye stopped chopping. "If you know something, tell me."

"I know the full story isn't out yet." Playing it casual, Colin sat back down on the stool. "I can tell you what the headlines are going to be tomorrow."

Faye set down the knife. "What's happening to Janis?"

"It's bigger than that." Colin nursed his brew and made her wait. "You recall what I said about Manhattan, Kansas?"

"The animal experiments on delayed fertility."

"Exactly. Environmental chemicals in combination that might be causing delayed fertility in mammals – or more specifically, primates."

"So what? I read similar studies out of Germany and Japan. Given the drop-off in teenage pregnancies around the world, there's nothing controversial about that. Sooner or later, people outside of The Project would notice something isn't right. It makes sense they would launch studies."

"Even in the United States – home of The Project?"

"That's a stupid question. You know the kind of security we're talking about."

"That's right. The government is schizophrenic that way – one group studies what another group already knows about. It can't be helped around Unacknowledged Special Access Programs."

"And TS-4 security oaths."

"I'm not talking about *what's* being studied – I'm more interested in *where*."

"Kansas."

"More specifically, the N-B-A-F."

"What's your point?"

"Homeland Security builds a Level 4 biodefense facility in the middle of the heartland. Naturally, there's blowback. Some believe the breadbasket of the United States is the absolute worst place to build such a thing. It doesn't make sense."

"Some people would have an issue no matter where you built it."

"But their question hasn't gone away. This is a place where the government works with the most dangerous agents, the kinds of things that pose the highest risk of fatal disease in humans. Why put such a thing in the middle of your prime area of food and biofuel production?"

"I've read the excuses – cheap land, remote from major population centers."

"And what happens if something screws up – by accident or on purpose?"

"What's your point? Are you saying there's some kind of conspiracy?"

Colin threw back his head and drained the rest of his beer. Setting the bottle down, he stepped up his delivery. "Conspiracy theories wouldn't be nearly as fascinating if they didn't have so many strange and sobering facts on their side. Granted, the conclusions might be daft but that doesn't prove everything is all right."

"What kind of facts?"

"90% of the world's food comes from just 15 plant and 8 animal species. 75% percent of genetic diversity of crops has been lost in the past century. 15% percent of the Earth's land area has been degraded by human activities. It takes 500 years to replace one inch of topsoil lost to erosion. In the past 40 years, almost one-third of the world's cropland was abandoned because of soil degradation and erosion. More than half of the world's population live in urban areas – any disruption to food stocks would trigger a global food crisis in short order."

"What are you getting at?"

"An accident in Kansas would have global repercussions. Food futures would skyrocket. It would get very expensive to eat. Even if nothing serious happened, the scope of BSL4 vulnerability would be exposed. An accident like that would launch an already heated discussion far beyond the theoretical. One accident at NBAF would do more to shut down biodefense and panic world markets than years of worldwide activism could ever hope to do. You have to ask yourself – who would benefit from handcuffing biodefense and causing that kind of panic and financial instability?"

"Are you saying something's about to happen?"

"Something already did." Colin slid off the stool and stepped around the kitchen island to stand nearer to Faye. "Tomorrow the news will say a man named Oliver Ross was arrested in Manhattan, Kansas. The FBI has evidence he was about to create a major biological accident at the site. U.S. agents are claiming they stopped the plot in the nick of time."

"Who is he?"

"A scientist who worked there – researching delayed fertility in animals."

"My God...." Faye absorbed the impact of the news even as she raced to put it in context. "What was he trying to do?"

"He had a virus tailored to infect poultry. If it had gotten out and spread, the poultry industry would have been devastated. The U.S. is the largest poultry producer, about 40 billion pounds of chicken a year. 20% of that gets exported."

"How was he discovered?"

"The French tipped us off – but you won't hear that on the news."

"Marseille?"

Colin nodded. "Something found on a laptop Janis had in her possession. We told the French it's imperative we keep the source of this hush-hush."

"It doesn't make sense. Why would she have something like that?"

"She got it from Malcolm Stowe – who got it from Riya Basu. Riya secretly tried to pass it to U.S. agents – and failed."

"Riya?"

"Yes, she's been very helpful to The Project for many years." Colin's words came low and quick. "Riya's group was subcontracted to complete early investigations of radiation effects, the kind that ultimately went into the design of RIDIS. The only problem was, she decided to borrow classified Project work and use it to jumpstart her own *GenLET* research."

"When was this?"

"Twelve years ago – the year RIDIS went operational and *GenLET* was still a theory. A year after I joined The Project."

"What came of it?"

"We gave her an ultimatum – cooperate or be prosecuted. The United States would not pursue legal action on the security breach under one condition, a condition she must keep to herself. She had to pass regular updates to us on her work. I was named her one and only contact. She knew me only by a codename, *Senex*."

"You blackmailed her?"

"We let her do the work she loved. Of course we wanted something in return."

"She gave you *GenLET*?" Faye was stunned.

"It only seemed fair. Without RIDIS technology, *GenLET* research might have never taken off."

"You don't know that for sure."

"It doesn't matter. Riya knew how valuable RIDIS research could be so she took it despite her security oaths, confidentiality agreements, and Top Secret classifications. All she cared about was the work; it didn't matter who had rights to the technology. She had this thing about her – she liked to say that knowledge should be free. All we did was call her bluff on that one."

"You boxed her in."

"She had a choice. Remain primary scientist and pass along updates to a drop-spot in Puerto Rico, or have her crime exposed and lose any future doing the work."

"How long did this go on?"

"Several years. When the RIDIS database got huge and needed a caretaker, I got reassigned and The Project stopped monitoring the drop-spot. I notified Riya no further updates would be necessary. By then, The Project had other sources of information inside NovoSenectus. It made sense because we suspected that NovoSenectus security was getting close to discovering what was going on."

"And what if they had?"

Colin shrugged. "No biggie. That's why we located the drop-spot where we did. GeLixCo is their prime competitor. It would look like corporate espionage, nothing more."

Faye sat back on a stool, the pieces coming together. "And now this new information about Oliver Ross in Kansas – Riya was trying to pass that?"

"Again, the drop-spot isn't being monitored. It had to be a desperation move."

"And it got her killed."

"It looks that way."

"Are you saying the accident just averted in Kansas was planned at NovoSenectus?"

"How would you connect the dots?"

"Why would NovoSenectus want to do such a thing?"

"We've checked the drop-spot. The information there lines up with what the French told us. It looks like Riya found something disturbing but could only think of one way to pass it along and remain anonymous. After she got shot, it fell into the hands of Malcolm Stowe. He turned up dead but now Janis has been found with it."

"NovoSenectus wants it back. They call it intellectual capital."

"The problem is, we can't be sure what's on the laptop. There may be more than what we found at the drop-spot."

"The French won't let you see it?"

"Not so far. They're debating what's proper. Last I heard they're inclined to give the laptop back to NovoSenectus as rightful owners. We have only one bit of leverage over them."

"What's that?"

"Riya must have been rushed when she accessed the drop-spot. She wasn't careful about where she copied her new material. She put it in an old project directory for RIDIS research. Parts of the research had unique names. Riya worked on a section called UDIF/TZ."

"How does that help?"

"If the laptop contains any UDIF/TZ files, then French authorities can't simply return it to NovoSenectus. Those are classified files – most people even in the U.S. government don't know those files exist."

"Tell the French to erase them before giving the laptop back."

"We'd still have a problem. If classified files are really there, that makes the laptop evidence of a crime. Homeland Security will want to prosecute and will need to enter the laptop into evidence at trial."

"You just said hardly anyone knows these files exist."

"All anyone needs to know is that the content is classified."

"Why would Homeland Security even be aware enough to prosecute?"

"Because The Project wants it that way. Because you need Janis back."

"You're prosecuting Janis?" Colin's silence was confirmation. "You've got to be kidding! What are the charges?"

"Espionage, trafficking in state secrets, aiding and abetting a terrorist organization, interference with an ongoing investigation..."

"What investigation?"

"What the fuck was Oliver Ross doing and who gave him the order? Janis has been sitting on this information. You know how close we came to a BSL4 accident? Riya was trying to pass this information to us – what the hell was Janis doing in Marseille with it? The French think she was shopping it around to people who want to find dirt on Eugene Mass."

"Is this about Eugene Mass? Are you covering for him or something?"

"What planet are you on? It's about Janis and the insanity of what she's been doing the past couple of weeks."

"I can't believe you're going to prosecute."

"We needed an excuse, something to trump the Indian request for extradition."

"You've acted on this already?"

"We have Janis in D.C., secured at Andrews incognito. We intercepted her in Munich; she was on her way to police custody in Hyderabad. If we'd been an hour later, we would have missed our chance."

"Have you talked with her? Is she on The Project now?"

"No. Disposition of her case hasn't been decided."

"Disposition....what do you mean? She's still being charged?"

"That's entirely up to you."

"Me?"

Colin was pointblank and forceful. "You wanted her on The Project. I talked my bosses into getting her. But now you need to convince her. She's going to be valuable to us one way or another."

"What other way?"

"The fallout from this is going to hit everyone. Congressional hearings are a certainty along with a media circus. Senators will want to know how a lone nut almost used a secured BSL4 lab to cause a major biological crisis. What was the scheme, was it part of a larger plan, and how do we make sure this doesn't happen again? Congress knows the public likes seeing a perp walk. Someone has to be held responsible, even if a token offender is trotted out and sent to jail. If Janis won't join The Project, they'll make sure she gets prosecuted."

"You bastard!"

"Are you telling me she didn't do these crimes? She's lucky we need her."

"I can't believe this."

"All you have to do is convince her."

"You're nothing but a goddamn coward! You don't want to be the one to have to tell her about Alyssa. That's it, isn't it?"

"I can tell her. I'll look her in the eye and say I took Alyssa. I'll say pointblank I made it look like terrorist kidnapping. I planted evidence to keep Stockholm police and Indian authorities looking the other way. It wouldn't matter to me – except for one thing. If I walk in and tell her the truth – she'll never join The Project."

Incensed as she was, Faye could say nothing. She knew Colin was right. Janis and he had too much history, more than enough reason to repel each other. Having Colin tell her about Alyssa would cement Janis' heart against anything he wanted.

Faye tried to reason with him. "You don't need to go after Janis. You have Oliver Ross. Isn't that enough justice done?"

"This is too big. Ross might not be enough."

"I don't believe Janis was working with Ross."

"Which Janis are we talking about? The one I have in D.C. or the one you knew in a different time and place? The fact is, Janis had news of the plot and kept it secret; she didn't bring it to the authorities. Why did she have all of this material in her possession if she wasn't involved? The Indians already suspect her in the murder of Malcolm Stowe." Colin sampled one of the tapas. "Between commercials, the public doesn't think that deep; implicating her will be easy."

Pinned in, Faye was stoic but compliant. She lifted her knife and started dicing again. "What exactly do you want me to do?"

"Come to Washington and talk to her. I'll tell you when."

Faye stared him down. "Why do you think I'll have any better luck? The last time Janis and I spoke, we argued about dual-use issues. She quit USAMRIID because she didn't trust what was going on. Now you leave me with this."

"You're the only one that can do it. You're on The Project, you know what's at stake, and once upon a time, the two of you were friends."

"None of that matters now. What am I supposed to tell her?"

"Tell her the truth – and anything else that gets the job done."

"I can tell her everything? Sterility, RIDIS, Granite Peak?"

"Why not? If you're going to work together, she should know what you know."

"Knowing what I know may set her mind against this."

"Just keep focused on what's at stake. Just tell her the truth."

Faye paused to let implications and complications swirl together in her mind. When everything had coalesced, she saw her dilemma clearly.

"I know what's true. I don't trust The Project. But you expect me to convince her I do. Worse yet, you want me to lie to her – and tell her she should."

Colin finished chewing and swallowed. He licked his lips and raised his coat collar in preparation to leave. "Great food. It's going to be a great party."

Faye stood flatfooted and watched him stuff hands in coat pockets.

She said nothing. She wanted him to leave.

He waited until sure she was done with him, then nodded and turned to go.

"I'll let myself out. Happy New Year."

CHAPTER 27

Minutes before midnight
Brussels Airport

A frigid rain beat down on an isolated stretch of tarmac near a perimeter fence. Rolling to a stop, the nose gear of an unmarked Gulfstream G650 came to rest in a puddle. The whine of twin jet engines subsided as Eugene Mass hustled down the steps from his private jet and ducked into a waiting limousine. Before the driver shut the door, Mass settled back, turning to the man he knew would be there.

"Anything new?"

"Nothing good." Javier Francisco's Latin accent was distinct.

Javier was a slumped shadow pressed back in folds of black leather. Mass gave him only a glance, anxious for the car to be in motion.

Javier asked, "Is Leah coming?" The limo sped for the exit.

"She got back yesterday; doctor's appointment."

"Something new?"

"Same thing – chronic fatigue."

"The one thing she never tires of…" From the shadow, a chuckle in the dark.

"Perversely consistent, don't you think?" Mass considered the city lights with no interest. After a series of quick turns, the limo accelerated into traffic.

Checking directions, Javier startled. "Where are we going?"

"I decided against Marie-Louise Square. Not tonight. We'll talk while driving."

"A change in our pattern might draw attention."

"I don't want to be predictable right now."

"What happened?"

"A man with a gun. By luck he missed me."

"Jesus! Where was this?"

"Outside NovoSenectus."

"The guards take him down?"

"Unfortunately. I would have preferred him alive, at least until interrogated."

"Any ideas who's behind it?"

"Hard to say. It's gotten to the point I'd have to make a list." Mass spread his arm across the top of the seat and tapped fingers. "We need to concentrate on damage control. Where's Oliver Ross now?"

"Fort Riley, Kansas. In custody. The feds haven't moved him."

"We need to find out what happened."

"If we're lucky, he got careless."

"Make sense for chrissakes!" Mass' temper flared. "Let's assume for a moment they're not fucking stupid. They have the laptop. They have to have seen the memo. They've got names; Ross, Labon, you, even *my* initials. The exact thing we were trying to avoid has happened. We must manage the shit-spin and find a way to regroup – fast."

"You're out ahead of me. You started with that already."

"What are you talking about?"

"The thing about the poultry virus. All the newswires are saying Ross was about to release a virus that targets poultry."

"That's right."

"But I thought the go-code was for the release of 3rd Protocol."

"I don't tell you everything – by design. Some things are better kept to myself."

"Not now. Not if you want me to keep on top of this. Tell me."

Mass considered options, then relented. "3rd Protocol is designed to look like a crossover disease, from chickens to humans. The poultry virus was supposed to be the trigger, but only the trigger. 3rd Protocol is the bullet. If Ross had let the poultry virus loose, that was the signal for others around the world to release 3rd Protocol."

"The two aren't related?"

"Except in people's minds. We need to create circumstances that point away from us. While we're at it, if we make trouble for those likely to come after us, all the better. Now's the time to put biodefense networks on the defensive."

"I like it. Make them wonder if someone on the inside caused the plague. Except, Ross didn't get that far. No virus got released."

"Yes…well, it may not matter. News of it is out. A seed of doubt is planted. All the Live-at-Five fear mongers will be all over it. The story's sensational enough to dominate the news cycle. It's just as well. "

"How so?"

"They only stopped the trigger but we still have the bullet. They don't know that and we must keep it that way. At least long enough to release 3P."

"So, that poultry virus, the trigger in Kansas – was it for real?"

"The newswires are correct. It's a virus that targets poultry. Surprised?"

"Curious, I mean, what's the point?"

"A real virus creates stronger circumstantial connections to the coming pandemic. Dying chickens makes it easier to believe a deadly crossover flu is from poultry. As a side benefit, disruption of the food supply would only help the population collapse. As expected, some of my friends heavily invested in hedge funds are reacting appropriately to help get the ball rolling."

"How long will it take us to reset for the release of 3rd Protocol?"

"That's up to you. How long will it take you to ensure Oliver Ross is dead?"

A huff of startled air escaped from Javier. "Just like that?"

"We need it done. We can't have him talking. We definitely can't have him testifying. He doesn't know much but what he does know must not go on record. One damned thing, no matter how small, pulls on the next. I'm not going down. I won't have this nonsense get in the way of the plan. I don't care what it takes."

"It would be very difficult. They're sitting on him tight."

"I don't care if they have him up their ass. I'll transfer funds into a special account. Do whatever it takes."

"It's not a matter of money."

"Everything's negotiable. Surely you can find someone who sees the value of looking the other way for a second."

"It's different now. I can't do it directly. As you said, they have my name. We have to assume they'll be watching my every move."

A cell phone rang. Mass checked the call then stuffed the phone back in pocket. "Beguile them with your charm. It's time to innovate."

Javier was deadpan serious. "What if I don't get to him?"

Mass jabbed an intercom button to the driver. "Stop the car!"

The long black limo shot to the curb and halted.

Mass reached past Javier and opened the door opposite him. "Get out."

Javier hesitated.

Mass settled back and prompted with a wave of his hand. "We've finished talking. You know what to do."

Javier gave Mass one last look before bolting from the car. Standing in the street, he shut the door and stared at his warped reflection in the tinted glass.

The rain came down. A moment later the limo accelerated into the night.

Mass suffered the rest of the ride in grim silence. A brooding darkness robbed him of concentration. The forest of Soignes swallowed what should have been his calculated attention on matters at hand. The limo's advance along familiar roads south of Brussels became hypnotic. Giving in to its predictability felt defeatist. Mass tried resisting a shift in mood by imagining the best outcome for an uncertain future.

By the time the long black car had cruised the semi-circle drive and stopped before the front door of the Mass estate, Eugene was ripe to believe any suggestion that promised this night wouldn't go as planned. He walked the entrance hallway shedding a topcoat and musing to himself. A woman would call it intuition; for a man it was just a hunch. One had mystique, yet both were equally potent.

Leah Mass found Eugene in the downstairs study minutes later. Her steps about the room were full of nervous energy. "How long have you been home?"

"Just got in." Drawn to the fireplace, Mass tended the fire, relaxed but studied.

"It's been quite an eventful couple of days."

Leah's leading statement left too much room for sarcasm. Considering what Mass knew was coming, he decided to forgo the opportunity to be clever.

"Yes, it has."

"I see you barely survived your day in India."

"It's good of you to be so concerned."

"Pardon me if I don't fall apart. I know you'd say it's to be expected."

"We don't need to do this now, you know."

Leah shouted, "As a matter of fact, we do."

"As you wish."

"When were you going to tell me?"

Mass said nothing.

"As long as you are going to ignore my wishes, at least you could have the courtesy of letting me know when you decide to reorder the world."

"The plan has never been a secret between us. It's been our plan from the beginning. The exact moment it happens is tactical, not strategic."

"Didn't you hear anything I said to you in your office? I made a simple request. Given the fact your grandson's sterile and I continue to have difficulties, the reasonable thing to do was to order more testing. You completely ignored that and went ahead anyway."

"I told you what the situation was."

"Oh, and what was *I* doing? There's more to this situation than your need to pull the trigger."

"A decision had to be made. The longer we wait the greater the chance we fail. Look at what happened to Oliver Ross."

"That's another thing. What's this about a poultry virus? Since when was a plague on poultry ever part of the plan?"

"The plan was never static. How it gets executed can be improved. The poultry thing was a minor detail. I didn't bother you with it."

"Didn't bother me! Excuse me but Kansas was supposed to be a simple diversion. Why risk the complication of injecting a second virus into the wild?"

"Why waste an opportunity? We need a solid connection, something that connects with what's going on. A diversion is too easily explained away."

"This poultry virus…you're still going to release it, some other way?"

"It may not be necessary now. The world knows it's real. Everyone will suspect the worst when 3rd Protocol emerges."

"So you admit it isn't necessary!"

"I'm suggesting it might work out just the same."

"What else haven't you bothered to tell me?"

Mass finished with the fireplace and found the comfort of a nearby chair. "Tonight I told Javier he should eliminate Ross."

A hand flew to Leah's temple. She shook her head and paced. "Where does it stop?"

"You know very well this is just the beginning."

Leah rushed to Mass' side. "Then let's do it right! Promise me you'll do the testing. This thing with Ross has given us a second chance to be sure."

"We can't scatter our energies right now. We have to focus. Testing would drag on for weeks."

"What's a few weeks when *GenLET's* given us so many added years?"

"Everything could change in a matter of days. Someone might try to stop us."

"You showed me a list of all the 3rd Protocol release sites; they would never find all of them in time. Besides, we'd only be testing people who got *GenLET*."

"Precisely. That's too many people to contact. Each one a risk."

"None of them want to be exposed. We told them to look upon extended life as a secret club."

"But it only takes one to be careless."

"It's the same risk we agreed to when we gave them the treatment. You weren't so worried about it then."

"Where was Malcolm's laptop then? Where was Ross? Besides, what will they think? Being tested might make them worry something's wrong."

"Then don't tell them what the test is for. Say it's a routine follow-up."

Mass said nothing. Leah read his silence as a chance to press the issue.

"We need to take a step back, be sure of what we're doing. Imagine the repercussions if we get this wrong. We're talking about the future of everybody.

Once you release 3rd Protocol, it can't be taken back. What kind of New World Harmony will there be if we have to live hundreds of years with a mistake?"

Mass looked into her eyes, saw the changing expressions sweep her face. He knew his wife too well. She was hiding something. Before he gave in, even a little, he needed to probe. It was best to find out now where this was going. He'd assume the worst and confront her with it in hopes of catching her off-guard.

"Testing isn't the real issue, is it?"

"Of course it is."

"No, there's something else. I see it in you. There's been a change. You're not sure about the plan anymore, are you?"

"I certainly don't want to make a mistake, that's for sure."

"Is that an answer?"

"What are you asking?" Leah shook with nerves.

Mass took Leah's hands in his. He was deliberate and calm about his question. "Have you had a change of heart about the plan?"

Leah hesitated. She felt Mass' withering stare. Her eyes teared up.

Silence shifted allegiances. Mass felt suddenly alone.

"All this talk…the testing…the chronic fatigue, it's all a smokescreen, isn't it."

Leah looked down, said nothing.

Mass roared, "Isn't it!"

Startled by the outburst, Leah pulled hands away and bolted away from him.

Mass reeled back. "My God! I never thought I'd have to fight *you* about this. You of all people! You know what's happening to the world. You know there's little time left to set things right. What don't you understand?"

Fleeing to the warmth of the fireplace, Leah found the strength to yell back. "It all made sense – until people started dying!"

"You knew what had to happen! We talked about this! There's no other way!"

Leah turned from the fire to face Mass. "There has to be!"

Mass sprung from the chair and gestured wildly. "What part of unsustainability don't you understand? Should we do nothing and let the perfect storm be the end of everything?"

Leah stood her ground. Her voice softened on reflection but quaked with its confession. "Watching Riya die did it for me. I sat there in horror while she lay on the floor bleeding. I couldn't imagine – six billion others just like her."

"You know the alternative. Everyone goes. Everyone dies. That's where we're headed. Population doubling, food and water shortages, runaway greenhouse gases, dying oceans, depleted soil, collapse of biodiversity, a state of continual war like you've never seen. The collapse of everything humanity has built in 50,000 years. Is that what you'd rather watch?"

Leah's heart raced. "I know the way I feel."

"But what do you *think*?"

Unsure of herself until that moment, Leah found resolve taking a definite form. As surely as one thing followed another, what lay ahead suddenly seemed clear. "I can't stay with you if you go through with this."

The statement hit the air and shocked them both.

Mass wavered. Leah was too emotional to be saying this merely to call his bluff. “You don’t mean that.”

Leah cried. “I don’t see how I could. Seeing you afterwards would only remind me. Every day, I’d be reminded that none of it had to happen. None of it.”

Mass sat back down. He could see her newfound realization was genuine. Facing the certainty of it left him paralyzed between rage and despair. “Not now. We’ve worked at this for so long. We’re too close.”

Leah stiffened and dried her tears. “Close to what?”

“Everything…”

“It terrifies me.”

“What?”

“Living a hundred…two hundred years in a world gone wrong – knowing it could have been different.”

“It’s already gone wrong!”

“Yes, but I’m not personally responsible for it.”

“We’re all responsible.”

“Maybe but I can’t stop wondering – what kind of trauma would it be to watch six billion people die? You’re asking me to live a long, long time with that. That’s a risk, a burden I don’t want to take on.”

“You’d rather risk doing nothing? You think that’s going to turn out any better?”

Leah headed for the door. “I only have control over myself. I won’t participate – and I can’t stay with you if you go through with it.”

“So it’s never been about the tests – you don’t want the tests any more?”

“Of course I want them. Regardless what you decide to do, we need to know the truth about what we’ve already done. Why is Jayden sterile? And what about the rest of them? We’ve created a secret club. But are they privileged or cursed?”

Unable to say more, Leah quickly left the room.

Mass watched her leave and the room closed in around him.

The crackling of the fire consumed his dreams. A pain and fury enveloped his heart. For all or nothing, for everyone and the two of them, beyond fate, some things simply had to be. Suddenly isolated, he was left to ponder what was next.

The one most dear to him had split his life in two.

One side knew what he must do. The other had a hunch.

Something else must be in store.

CHAPTER 28

Plenary Session of PEACE
United Nations Conference Center, New York

The cavernous room was dotted with faces. Seated at the lead table, Curtis Labon listened as the Assistant Secretary-General for Policy Coordination and Inter-Agency Affairs finished her speech. Distracted by an incoming text message, Labon split his attention long enough to become concerned. A moment later his thumbs relayed a return message – *meet @ 845 UN Plaza 90B 20min.*

Lifting eyes to peer into the relative darkness of the far gallery, Labon caught sight of a conference banner. PEACE – *Population Exposition for the Advancement of a Caring Earth.* Aligned with news just received, the message rang hollow. Just as abruptly, he sensed being out-of-place, sickened at the vestige of hope offered by the assembly around him.

The annual conference he had long sponsored felt mired in the inertia of the day. It was under-energized and over-populated by elite speakers and professional listeners rarely moved to effective action. Messy reality outside the hall suggested only problems had momentum. Labon gathered up his things and headed for the exit. From the podium, a drone of final words filled the room and echoed into the foyer beyond.

"...the profound challenge lies in the fact that most of this population growth will be in less developed countries. Grappling with the greater implications of the global policy dialogue must be the work of current generations. Beyond gathering information and identifying trends, governments need to harness political will, financial resources, and technical innovations on an unprecedented scale. Focusing on current development without a consensus for future maintenance is untenable..."

In the lobby, a young staffer caught up with him. She was energetic and dutiful as an event planner but fragile when it came to a disruptive change in plans.

"Excuse me, sir. Should we expect you at the Parallel Session in Room 6? It follows the break after the next speaker."

Labon kept walking. "And who is that again?"

She glanced at her hand-held device. "...it's the Moroccan Deputy-Minister for Foreign Affairs and Cooperation."

Labon grunted. "Ah, yes. Well, in that case, I have more time than I expected."

"More time?" She tried following both his intent and accelerated walking pace.

Labon gave her a glance then a more thorough once-over. She was quite attractive in her mini caftan dress. An idea occurred to him.

"Do you think your conference mates can spare you for a few minutes?"

"Me? I think so."

Labon guided her out the main exit into the open air. "Good. I need you for the next hour, if you don't mind." They followed a walkway towards the U.N.'s front entrance on 1st Avenue. "What's your name again?"

Buoyed by his attention, she strutted alongside. "Isabella. Isabella Bayner."

"Of course. I'm a bit distracted; you'll have to forgive me." Labon angled them the long way past the busy entrance toward a lineup of taxis waiting for a fare.

A driver hustled around the lead car to hold open a rear door. With an arm around Isabella's shoulders, chivalrously guiding her, Labon waited for the pivot of her shapely legs into the back seat to fortify his resolve. Ducking in after her, he called out to the driver getting behind the wheel.

"Trump One Tower."

The driver did a double take of annoyance. The destination was within walking distance. Curtis slipped a folded hundred dollar bill across the seat.

"Be ready to bring us back in an hour and I'll double that."

Glancing between the two of them, the driver kept wild assumptions to himself and became animated. Labon settled back closer to Isabella than was necessary. She held proper poise with cautious wonder in her expression.

The ride was a catapult along two short city blocks. At the base of the sleek Tower, the two of them scurried past an attentive doorman before waiting only a second at a bank of elevators. Lighting up the button for the 90th Floor, Labon used the rush of their ascent as an opportunity to calm the girl's rising concern.

"I've worked on my closing speech for days but with only hours to go, I'm afraid I'm no more confident about it now than when I started. Maybe you could give it a look. I'd appreciate a second opinion."

Isabella's visible relief was tenuous. "Certainly."

Labon showed a smile. "I don't want it to be too stuffy. I'd like to reach out to a younger audience but I'm not usually the best judge about what works when it comes to that. You understand…"

Isabella held up on commenting. Labon was obviously more savvy than he let on. His excuse for heading upstairs came across weak, making her wary.

Labon entered Unit 90B as if he owned it. Isabella followed as if encountering an enchanted world. The more she saw, the more her reticence faded. Stepping through the breathtaking penthouse, Labon gravitated to the forty-one foot living room. The ceiling was double height; panoramic views from the clear floor-to-ceiling windows were stunning. Isabella wandered, her attention split between sweeping views and elaborate furnishings. Labon spoke as he checked his phone.

"Quite a place, isn't it? I've rented it for the month while I'm in town. It's a bit extravagant but, as you can see, it's convenient to U.N. Plaza. If you'd care to make a bid, they're asking $34 million."

Labon glanced up and noted Isabella's attention to the furnishings.

"The way they've staged it is quite nice. Someone is eager to sell."

Labon saw all he needed from his phone. He headed off down a hallway.

"I have a copy of the speech – this way."

He led her to the master bedroom. She hesitated in the doorway.

Crossing the room, he stopped at a desk, picked up a tablet and tapped it awake.

"If you don't mind, I prefer you read it in here. I have some private business to attend to in another part of the house." As Labon stepped out of the room, Isabella felt more comfortable stepping in.

She accepted the tablet with a nod. "No problem."

Labon closed the bedroom door behind him and returned to the living room. Staring into the view, he waited to answer a knock at the front door. When it came, a woman in a black pantsuit hurried in. She had been there before. Labon knew her as Hannah but also knew she went by other names. Flowing with her was a marked confidence and edgy style, half Special Forces but all Madison Avenue.

He pointed down the hall. "We have company. I'll explain later." Labon led her towards the southeast corner dining room, the place farthest away from the master bedroom. Standing by the window, they drew close.

"Tell me what happened." Labon's calm facade was gone.

"Like I said, your son Noah was arrested in D.C. It started as a demonstration."

"What about?"

"Life extension. NCO wants a moratorium on it."

"New Class Order?"

A nod. "They want a law, something like the thing on cloning."

"So, what's the story? Was Noah just there in the crowd or what?"

"I'm not sure. It doesn't look that way."

"What do you mean you're not sure? You were supposed to be following him!"

"I don't have access to all his social media. He changed plans and was gone before I knew it. He must have received some kind of orders to flash mob."

"Orders?"

"He and several others showed up at the demonstration ready to engage. While most people were marching on the White House, a group of NCO hardliners formed up in Franklin Park. They firebombed a biotech lobbyist office on K Street."

"Jesus!" Labon held a hand to his head. "Don't tell me he was part of that!"

"It's being sorted out. He was definitely in Franklin Park. They've got him on surveillance video."

Labon turned to the view. "My God, what's he gotten himself into?"

Hannah was silent.

"Has the media picked up on this? Do they know he's my son?"

"I don't think so. If it's played right, there's a good chance they won't." She hesitated then finished her thought. "…for now, being estranged is on your side."

Labon paced away from her. "Of all things to get mixed up in…"

"You can't protect him from himself."

"And that's a problem – because I can't stand by and do nothing."

"What do you want *me* to do?"

It took a minute before Labon organized his thoughts. "Find out if he needs to make bail. If so, route money through a defense fund, something he won't connect back to me. Then find out the charges. If there's a prosecutor, I want name and background. We'll take it from there."

"Excuse me for asking, but are you sure Noah would want you to do all this?"

"Doesn't matter. I want to do it."

"Sure thing." Hannah started to go.

"Wait up a second…"

She turned back, expecting additional orders.

Labon shifted away from the window. He looked sideways in the direction of the master bedroom. It was obvious to both of them – he was at odds with himself. Hanging in the balance was a decision he couldn't take back.

Could there ever be stability in playing it safe? Events he couldn't have predicted, out of his control, had redefined his equilibrium. Taking the challenge on, he felt part of himself slipping away. In what remained there was a dense core spinning around the point of no return. From that moment on, future decisions would be easier to make – but harder to live with.

Labon pulled out a dining room chair from the table. "Have a seat."

Intrigued, Hannah sat down. Labon pull out a second chair for himself. He turned it around backwards, straddled it then leaned forward on the backrest.

"You've done private investigation work for me for quite a while."

"That's right."

"I hope we can be frank – just between the two of us."

"I thought we always had."

"Privately, it's safe to say some of the things I've asked you to do over the past couple of years haven't been completely ethical."

"We've agreed on everything."

"And why is that?"

"Let's just say we have an appreciation for what's necessary."

"I like to think it's because neither of us is bi-polar when it comes to judging right from wrong."

"Everyone does something someone else thinks is wrong. There are no saints."

"Exactly. But I wonder – how far does it go."

"What do you mean?"

"What would you say if I asked you to do something no one else but me thinks is right?"

Hannah paused. "How can you be sure of that?"

"Let's just say…"

"Something no one thinks is right – including me?"

"Correction. That's up to you to decide."

"Based upon business we've already done, I'd say the answer is pretty simple."

"Do tell…"

"If I don't think something is right, I won't do it. It doesn't matter what anyone else thinks – including you."

"What if it doesn't matter to you either way?"

"Then it doesn't matter."

Labon stood and turned to the window. "I need someone to disappear." Just like that a line was crossed, a delicate balance broken. To commit to it was empowering.

Silhouetted against the lofty view, Hannah watched him consider the sky. The full import of what he was suggesting hit her. Without more detail, she let silence be her exclamation.

It's better to get some things over quickly. By being blunt, Labon hoped to minimize the impact of what he was asking. He summed up as if what he was suggesting was business as usual between them.

"A man by the name of Oliver Ross has been arrested. You might have heard."

"It's in the news."

"He's being held at a military base in Kansas but sources tell me there are plans to run him through Topeka courts for processing. For the last year I've had him on assignment. As it turns out, he was working for a competitor, one who'd like nothing more than see me implicated and exposed in ways I can't go into. This man must not testify. He needs to disappear. Under the circumstances, suicide seems appropriate."

Hannah's silence returned.

"Regarding the fee – I'm prepared to be appropriately generous." Labon twisted his neck to look back at her. "So, what do you think?"

Hannah stood. "It doesn't matter to me either way."

Labon turned back to the view. "I'm glad you feel that way."

"There are other details to work out…"

"Yes, but right now I need to get back to the U.N. I'll make reservations at Megu for 8 o'clock. We'll do it then. We can go down from here."

"Very well." Hannah started to leave but midway in the foyer turned back with a sudden thought. "You said we had company. Care to explain?"

Labon leaned close. "Remember the name – Isabella Bayner."

Confused, Hannah furrowed her brow.

"Just do it – in case we need it." Smoothing back a strand of hair from her face, he added with a sneer, "What better alibi for an old man's wickedness than more of the same."

Hannah made it to the front door before Labon stopped her.

"Let me know about Noah as soon as you find out."

After a nod, she was gone. Labon steadied himself with a breath. The task had completed quicker than he had imagined. It was time to shift back into the world of PEACE. On the way to the master bedroom, he unbuttoned his collar and loosened his tie. For all concerned, it was time to appear satisfied and relaxed, even if the rising impulse was anything but.

He opened the bedroom door to find Isabella lounging on the bed, reading. The image of her there was suggestive of everything and nothing. Energized by the meeting with Hannah, he was ready to entertain the wildest of possibilities. Anything seemed possible. Something powerfully new within him felt dominant and commanding. How could ordering the death of a man make one feel more vigorously alive? The sense of it was so unlike the morning spent at his conference. In stark clarity, Labon knew – in taking action he had became more potent and prevailing.

"Quite a comfortable spot, isn't it?" He approached the bed.

Isabella turned over and started to get up but on impulse he was upon her. Startled and resisting at first, she succumbed to touches in hidden places. They rolled together and became a tangle of force and submission, joy and pain.

Labon never intended to take her that way, that's what he told himself. Her visit was meant only as a suggestive alibi to cover his time with Hannah. But there was no stability in playing it safe any more. Events out of his control had redefined his equilibrium.

As he climaxed into her, he felt the restraining part of himself slipping away.

Anything was possible – when nothing mattered either way.

CHAPTER 29

Capitol Building
Washington, D.C.

The promise of early afternoon languished, trapped under a mid-January pall. Rushing onto the steps of the Capitol, another news crew jockeyed into position for their live remote broadcast. Restive but determined to complete business in one take, a bundled-up reporter shivered and glanced back at the soaring dome. Camera and sound setup were lagging and his impatience showed. Any distraction helped take his mind off last minute concerns of losing his edge.

"What's up? Did they sweep the streets? Where'd the protesters go?"

"Too cold for them."

"Just when you need them…"

"It's time for their union break."

The field producer took up position next to the camera. She pointed at the reporter. "All right, ready – three, two, one…"

Lifting microphone, the reporter spoke to the world.

"Once again we report from outside Senate chambers where today a second week of testimony began in a special closed-door session. Hearings were hastily organized two weeks ago when public outage erupted over the vulnerability of one of the nation's most sensitive biodefense sites. Oliver Ross, a research scientist working at the National Bio and Agro-Defense Facility in Manhattan, Kansas, was arrested on New Year's Eve while making preparations to release a deadly virus targeting poultry. His motives for attempting such an outrageous act are still unclear. How this plot was uncovered is also unknown. For national security reasons, authorities and Senators at these hearings are keeping silent until testimony concludes and the official report is released. Exactly who might be on the witness list is a topic of continuing speculation. Senate spokespersons have given few statements but all of them have reiterated Congress' determination to investigate thoroughly, prosecute where necessary, and pass appropriate legislation to ensure nothing like this can happen again…"

A lanky man in a gray suit jogged up the steps, passing the news crew. At his side was a slim attaché case. In his ear, a transceiver. In his coat pocket waited a prepared statement, a list of talking points, and a falsified business card. On it, his name was listed as Richard Gains. Today's occupation: attorney.

Richard Gains breezed through security and headed straightaway for subcommittee hearing chambers. The hall was a tangle of staffers, aides to the Senators, and plains-clothed guards. One official photographer busied herself framing strategic shots of selected history. No one was allowed in chambers while the hearing was in session except appointed Senators, testifying witnesses, their counsel, and the official stenographer and videographer.

Richard Gains had somehow timed it perfectly. He approached a pair of doorway sentries and showed ID. A stern woman holding the agenda noted an entry for him on the official calendar and allowed passage. He said nothing to anyone. The guard cracked open the door and allowed him to slip into chambers.

In contrast to everything outside, the hearing room was deathly calm and silent. For such a large room, it was sparsely populated. Elsewhere, so much stillness and quiet might have been relaxing. In chambers, the effect was opposite.

Richard Gains casually wound his way to the witness table and settled in behind one of the microphones. With a quick glance he noted six of eight Senators in place behind an elevated bench. Most were distracted reading notes or leaning back into hushed conversations with assistants. Two others stood mumbling to each other at the far end of the panel.

A corner door opened and in stepped the sergeant-at-arms. Following him were two special agents and a woman immediately recognizable by the tracking bracelet around her ankle. Agents led her to the witness table.

Gains stood and presented her with his business card.

"Ms. Insworth, I've been assigned to assist you today."

Janis read the card but hesitated to sit. "Assigned? By whom?"

Mr. Gains turned on the charm. "As you're aware, these proceedings are under oath. Since you didn't retain counsel, I've been assigned."

"It's an odd time to let me know. We've never spoken."

Gains sat down. "I know this is rushed. It couldn't be helped."

"What can you do for me now? The hearing's about to start." Janis sat down.

Leaning closer, Gains whispered. "We both know they made access to you impossible. But that didn't stop me from doing some research."

"On what?"

A gavel sounded. The chairman called proceedings to order. Preliminary business was entered into the record. Ordered to stand with raised hand, Janis was sworn in.

Senator Delane leaned closer to his mike, eager to commence business.

"Mr. Chairman, in light of our extended morning session, I move that relevant exhibits be entered into the current record pursuant to standard rules of evidence."

"So ordered."

"If I may, I'd like to start off with a statement and a few questions. I believe they will drive clear to the central issue before us this afternoon."

"Hearing no objections, you may proceed."

Delane took his time shedding half-height glasses before staring down at the witness table.

"How could a madman bring us to the brink of a global tragedy? That's why we're here. The question may seem rhetorical but left unanswered, we risk too much."

Janis swept the faces of the Senators, looking for reaction. Concerns about Eugene Mass jumped to mind. She was not prepared for the frustration that followed.

"Oliver Ross is an aberration – but a dangerous one. So far in these proceedings we've managed to firmly establish the obvious – guarding against madness will always be an inexact science."

The Senator picked up the pace with tempestuous vigor. "But if we believe Ms. Insworth's statement to federal agents after being arrested, by concentrating on

Oliver Ross, we are missing a truly maniacal conspiracy of epic proportions. She'd have us redirect our attention to a shadowy plan to murder six billion people. Details of this plan are purportedly on a laptop found illegally in her possession. And what did Ms. Insworth do when she discovered such evil plans? Did she contact the authorities? No. But classified files were added to that laptop. Those files appeared at the same time a corporate computer network was illegally breached. And where did Ms. Insworth go after those classified files were obtained? Marseille, to meet with a minion of New Class Order."

Exasperated, Richard Gains jerked towards his microphone.

The chairman raised a hand. "You'll have your chance, counselor."

Senator Delane skipped a beat. "…the fact is, Ms. Insworth's convoluted claims are a facile diversion, concocted in an attempt to draw our attention from a far more personal and embarrassing truth. She would like nothing more than see this committee spend days untangling all the deceit and misdirection swirling around her. Above all, she craves attention. Is it any surprise? Passed over for the Nobel Prize, traumatized by the deaths of both people in her love triangle, shaken by the kidnapping of her daughter – no wonder she desperately reaches out for attention, for someone to notice her pain and help her."

Fidgeting, Janis glared back at the Senator.

Gains grabbed her by the arm, holding her back.

Senator Delane consulted his notes. "Ms. Insworth, to be brief, I would like to established for the record a few relevant facts. How did you come into possession of the laptop?"

Janis caught her breath to steady herself. Refusing to be provoked, she felt time to set things right grew short. The fate of so much turned on a single word.

"Malcolm Stowe asked me to keep it for him."

"Ah-huh, Malcolm was a security agent for NovoSenectus, was he not?"

"Yes."

"Didn't you think it strange that a top security agent for a global biotech company would hand you his work computer?"

"Not after he showed me what was on it. He was worried certain information would be found in his possession and they'd take it away before he had a chance to act."

"Of all the people at NovoSenectus, why do you think he'd approach you with something so delicate? Was it because you shared a love with the two of them – him and Riya?"

Janis erupted. "What evidence do you have of that? Those are rumors started by New Class Order."

"Why would they want to do that?"

"Probably because they think I set them up! Because they threatened to do the exact same thing if I didn't cooperate with them."

"Despite what you'd like us to believe, your associations within NovoSenectus were not all business. You admit you knew of Malcolm's romantic relationship with your lab partner, Riya Basu?"

"Yes."

"Were you aware he was also an agent of British Intelligence?"

"No."

"Were you aware that Riya Basu had a Top Secret U.S. security clearance?"

"No."

"Were you aware that Malcolm Stowe and Oliver Ross once knew each other, in fact, briefly worked together many years ago?"

"No, I didn't."

"Did you know Oliver Ross was once employed by GeLixCo Corporation?"

"No."

"You've testified in your deposition that it was Malcolm Stowe who first brought you evidence of a plot to collapse the world's population."

"That's right."

"You also claim to have seen a mysterious memo. In this critical memo, someone with initials EM orders a man named Javier to arrange for Oliver to trigger something in Manhattan, something called 3P."

"Yes."

"Is it possible the reference to 'P' in the memo might refer to poultry?"

"Not in context – no, I don't believe so. The reference to 3P matches what other documents called 3rd Protocol."

"Interesting. Did Malcolm show you this memo?"

"No, I found it later, in Marseille."

"Found it? Is that what you call hacking into private computer networks? So you admit that Malcolm never saw the material you took from GeLixCo."

"I'm not sure. We hadn't gone over every document before he died."

"I see. So chances are Malcolm Stowe never had anything to do with this memo. He never showed it to you. As far as you know, he knew nothing about it."

"It was on his laptop, outside of the folders I had downloaded. I assumed he had seen it."

"And if he had, don't you think he would have mentioned it to you? It seems so damning a piece of evidence not to bring it up."

"I don't know. We were rushed. Maybe it *was* part of the second download."

"The one you did – illegally."

"I didn't know what we had; I wanted to be sure before going public. Malcolm said the files were Riya's. She wanted them exposed."

"So she hides them in a classified storage area on a computer network owned by one of NovoSenctus' main competitors. Is that what you expect us to believe?"

"She was passing them to her contact, someone named Senex."

The Senator chuckled. "This is quite a spy thriller. Isn't it convenient that the most damning piece of evidence was seen only by you. Who else might have seen it? Someone we can subpoena?"

"I don't know."

"It's odd. Suddenly, there's quite a bit you don't know. For someone making serious allegations, implicating a head of a corporation in a bizarre scheme to intentionally create a pandemic, I should hope you would know more."

Richard Gains engaged his mike. "Is there a point to this badgering? Some civility is in order; otherwise, I'll advise my client to exercise her right to remain silent."

The Senator turned the joust to his advantage. "Very well. The point is – no such memo has been found on Malcolm Stowe's laptop."

A bombshell hit Janis. More shocked than enraged, she turned to Gains.

Gains held her back. "That claim is hearsay. You've never entered the laptop into evidence."

"We don't need to. The French supplied us with complete forensics."

"Precisely my point," snapped Gains.

"Computer hardware is not in question here. All pertinent data is in record."

"Have you properly vetted the French team that conducted the forensics?"

"Are you inferring the French are part of a conspiracy to deny us proper data?"

Gains sat square, prepared for battle. "Senator, I merely point out reasonable doubt. Given the seriousness of the crimes charged against Ms. Insworth, I suspect a jury might be persuaded to have similar doubts."

Delane reacted casually. "Such a jury will be quite busy no matter what was found on the laptop. Acting on intent to acquire secrets then trying to barter them to a terrorist group is more than enough to prosecute. And that's before we get to Title 18, interstate flight, and obstruction of justice."

The Chairman interrupted. "Let's try to stay with substance here. Mr. Gains, you've entered a request to challenge an entry in the record. This might be a good time for that."

"Thank you Mr. Chairman." Out of a coat pocket came talking points.

Turning to Gains, Janis shielded the microphone with a hand.

"What are you doing?"

"My job." For a few telling moments, Gains came out of character. Pressing closer to her, he whispered orders – both hers and his, "Now sit back. You've said enough. I need to get this into the record."

Gain's demeanor lay bare a sudden and disturbing impression. Janis sat back and absorbed what now seemed like a pageant play going on around her. The more she became aware of it, the more the situation felt strange. Certain things no longer were taken for granted. The proceedings abruptly felt staged.

Why was Senator Delane the only one engaging her? Who was Richard Gains? Why did their give-and-take seem forced? Weeks from now, when someone read back the printed testimony, exchanges between the two of them would appear combative, no doubt. But that wasn't the feeling in the room. She'd swear they knew each other. She'd bet somehow others on the panel knew they were expected to ease back and let Delane do the talking.

And then there was the memo – how could they have missed it? Even if it was accidentally deleted off the laptop, surely they had followed up by investigating the computer storage at GeLixCo. They could have found it there.

Nothing made sense. All of them knew too much about things that didn't matter – too little about things that did. Surrounded by unknown motivations, she sensed Gains was right about one thing – she had said enough. If nothing else was certain, the fact that her life was on the line came into focus.

Gains ignored Senator Delane and redirected his remarks to everyone else on the panel. "Mr. Chairman…Senators, the government can't have it both ways. On one hand, my client has been portrayed as nothing more than a distraction, an attention seeker needing help. On the other hand, she's being pursued with a litany of criminal charges as if she's public enemy number one. The inconsistency boggles the mind. The only thing Janis Insworth is guilty of is being a desperate, caring mother – and being gullible."

Janis felt her heart race. At no other moment since entering the room had she felt it so keenly – her fate was out of her hands. What was happening around her would play out as scripted. Her part now was to wait for the final act – to see if she appeared in it at all. If some kind of governmental collusion with Mass was going on, no way would they want the truth getting out. They needed her marginalized.

Gains continued to talk. Ears ringing with fear, Janis felt faint but heard enough to wish she was someplace else.

"…there's been a lot of talk about secrets. We're in closed-door hearings and I haven't seen evidence of any secrets yet. Anyone can claim there's something behind the curtain if they don't have to prove it. You expect a jury to take your word that somewhere there are secrets in jeopardy because of this woman. So far today, all you've established is the variety of things she *wasn't* aware of. Where are the redacted pages? What department of government takes claim to these secrets? Does this all-important project even have a name? Have we gotten to the point where accepting such things on faith passes as evidence of a capital crime?"

Senator Delane interrupted, "You know your suggestion is ludicrous."

"Why, because it suits you? Tell me, this secret storage that was broken into – where was it? At the NSA, the CIA, maybe the FBI? No, it was at a private biotech company in Puerto Rico. Let's stretch what's credible for the jury again; let's ask them to believe the United States keeps its most closely guarded secrets at one of GeLixCo's older research facilities offshore. Unless you're prepared to establish a reasonable explanation for this, I'd advise you to take it off the table."

Senator Delane sat back, making a show of frustrated fuming.

Gains didn't let up. "And what about all of the material you *did* manage to get into the record? What exactly is it? If someone not too clever extracts passages here and there, it sounds horrendous. There's talk of pandemics, billions of people dying, a fractured society in the aftermath. Who would think such things? Worse yet, who would formalize them in such great detail? If you've done your research, you know very well. Those documents on the laptop, the ones Malcolm showed Janis Insworth to prove that Eugene Mass was about to kill six billion people – those are actually from think tanks. They were hypothetical studies done years ago and only privately circulated. They're all about what-if scenarios, exercises to consider the full range of possibilities. The Pentagon does the same thing when they war game. There are no great secrets there, either."

Gains took a moment to refer to his notes. "Janis Insworth was taken in and used by Malcolm Stowe. You've established last week that he was a grieving, angry, and paranoid man. He got it in his head that Eugene Mass was responsible for the death of his lover, Riya Basu. The paranoia started when he saw the way NovoSenectus excluded him from sensitive operations. The truth was, they excluded him because they had just discovered his connection to British intelligence. He was right, they were watching him, but not for the reason he thought. So, what did he do? To get back at Mass, he fabricated 3rd Protocol out of old think tank documents. He wanted to cause trouble for Mass, as much as possible. What better place to plant his phony evidence than GeLixCo, the largest competition to NovoSenectus. Once they found it, they'd be sure to use it. But when the plot started to unravel, he scrambled to remove himself. He tried shifting everything onto Janis. He lied to her, made her believe population collapse would happen any day, suggested the U.S. government might even be helping Mass concoct the plan, even led her to believe NCO had her daughter. He went after anyone who opposed Mass, hoping to get them involved – all to give himself an escape and alibi."

Gains glanced over at Janis. "Janis Insworth is a victim. She was duped by Malcolm Stowe at a time when he found her vulnerable. Malcolm Stowe was driven to seek revenge on an innocent man. Both Janis and Malcolm acted from raw emotion – they both had watched a lover shot and killed. Janis had the added shock of seeing her daughter kidnapped. After two weeks of testimony, no other explanation makes sense. The Senator just admitted that the most damning memo in fact does not exist. Janis only breached GeLixCo's network because she was duped by Malcolm into believing the files she would find there belonged to Riya. If anything, my client was only attempting to retrieve files that properly belonged to her employer, NovoSenectus.

Gains was suddenly overdramatic. "Janis Insworth has been through enough. She had nothing to do with Oliver Ross. The real culprit behind her alleged crimes is dead. There's nothing to be gained by using her as a scapegoat. If anything, I would think the government would help her find her daughter. The facts suggest one thing – all charges against my client should be dropped. Janis Insworth should be released."

It didn't end there. For the next half hour, Senator Delane and Richard Gains had it out rhetorically. The Chairman interrupted at times, but only after each party in turn had a chance to make their points. Nothing was decided, but then nothing could be decided until the committee issued their report and said they were done.

By the time the special agents returned to the room to lead Janis away, she was numb to all of it. After being forced to sit through what felt like theater of the surreal, what came next was no longer on her mind. Whatever it was, it was sure to surprise.

Down a restricted hallway to a private elevator, Janis followed orders. The agents were wooden, said little, barely considered her at all. They led her to a private parking area where a dark, unmarked car waited. It was the same car that had brought her there. Only now, next to it was parked another car.

Janis was so intent upon processing what had just happened, she barely lifted her gaze from the ground. When she did, her anticipation of surprise wasn't disappointed. She halted and forced the agents to halt with her. Staring ahead, Janis looked upon the one person she never expected to see.

The one person she had never forgotten.

Faye Gardner.

CHAPTER 30

Private Capitol Parking
Washington, D.C.

A pale winter's sun broke through icy clouds. The added light was distant, without warmth. Janis couldn't move, her descent into surrealism complete. Shadows of a simulated truth appeared. This couldn't be the place she remembered from an hour before. She must be somewhere else, living someone else's dream.

Impaled behind a blank expression, she found herself unable to look away. Why Faye Gardner? Why now? Masqueraded emergencies must be at play just out of sight. All of them in the service of bad purposes with good reasons to stay hidden.

A familiar face in this setting was out of place.

In reflex, searing doubt and resistance ignited. Just then Janis looked at Faye and caught a flash of something else burning between them. In one terrible instant, all that was strange crystallized around an improbable certainty.

Faye Gardner was also a captive.

But of what? She wore no ankle bracelet, yet something in her demeanor hinted of being tracked. There were no special agents escorting her, yet the very air around her somehow was accounted for and approved.

Most disturbingly, Janis sensed something else in Faye – a *willing* captivity.

Was she in league with the masquerade or merely being forced onstage? Intervening years since their last meeting didn't matter. They'd known each other too long, too well to hide something so deep. With them as always before, the superficial was easily disguised; the truly personal transparent.

First impressions were strong. Faye stood in her own surreal space, captive of a raging dichotomy. Tellingly, Faye was not trying to mask it. In an unspoken instant, both knew their dilemmas were shared yet equally undefined.

Everything happening was too directed, too contrived. Willing or not, Faye Gardner was now part of it. Janis had to assume she'd been brought there to play her part, no less than Senator Delane and Richard Gains had fulfilled theirs. By a calculated but twisted necessity, Faye's dichotomy would be borne out in differences between how she felt and what she was expected to say.

Adding to the unexpected, both special agents flanking Janis left her standing alone. They walked forward to their car, got in, and sat waiting with the engine off. Janis was left rooted in place, positioned with only one thing to do but unwilling to do it. Too upset and uncertain to say anything, she made Faye come to her.

Faye was cautious, unsure how she'd be received. Intent to connect, she paced away the gap between them. When close enough, she forgot her prepared speech and said the only thing she could.

"I can't imagine what you're thinking."

"That's amazing; I'm agreeing with you already." The sarcasm was apparent.

"It's been a long time, hasn't it?"

Janis was matter-of-fact. "What are you doing here, Faye?"

"There's a lot going on you should know about."

"I don't need you to tell me that."

"Why don't we go someplace and talk."

Janis glanced over at the agents waiting in the car. "Just like that?"

"Yeah, just like that. They're giving you a choice. Go with them or me."

"That's sweet." Janis stood pat. "Either way, I don't know where I'm going."

"No, you don't. But one way has a future; the other doesn't."

"Is that an opportunity or a threat?"

"Listen, Janis – I know I'm the last person you expect to see. Confidence is *not high* – I get it. But you've got to trust me – as crazy as that sounds."

Janis couldn't help but laugh. "Oh, please…"

"You above all should realize not everything is as it seems. You just went through the funhouse. You know it, I know it – believe me, *they* know it. I'm offering you a chance to get off the ride. It doesn't end well if we don't work together."

"What guarantee do I have it'll end well if we do?"

"I'm not here to offer you guarantees. Would you believe them if I did?"

"Why you? What twisted psychology are they using? You don't want to be here any more than I do. You can't hide that. What are they holding over you?"

Startled by Janis' keen perception, Faye struggled to maintain composure.

"The future."

"What?"

"Get in the car and I'll tell you."

"I can't do that." Janis pointed to the agents. "At least I know what happens if I go with them."

"They want you to go with me! They want you to join The Project."

"You say that like it should mean something. To me it's clear what they want to do – shut down the truth. Co-opting me might help them do that. They're already adapting the facts so they can spin a rewritten history of what's going on."

"Sometimes, telling the public everything is not in the public interest."

"Oh, my – no chance for abuse there."

"It wouldn't be worth the panic."

"Same old story; give us the keys to everything and we'll save you from yourselves. Don't bother asking why we say one thing and do another."

"Damn it! This isn't about dual-use. After 14 years, don't get into that."

Janis tensed. "So what's it about? 8-Ball?"

"What?" The reference had no meaning for Faye.

"Or maybe BIOPONORE? Is that what they call the project?"

"How do you know about that?"

"I've heard all I need to hear. You said they want me to go with you…" Janis strutted towards the agent's car. "It was nice seeing you."

With rising helplessness Faye turned, flustered and frantic, and watched Janis walk away. The harshest truth was hard to say but only the truth might convince Janis to go with her. Desperate and out of time, Faye blurted it out.

"I have news about Alyssa!"

Janis was stopped cold. She was well aware Faye might say anything to get her to go with her. Janis spun around and glared back at her. If this was a trick, it was the cruelest device she could use.

Faye could stand no more. She started to shake. With determined strides she aimed back for her car. On the way, she had the strength for one more attempt.

"Come with me and I'll tell you everything! There's no other way to find out!"

Faye hurried behind the wheel and sat there blinking away tears.

Janis plopped down in the passenger seat next to her and slammed the door.

"What about Alyssa?"

Faye caught her breath. "I'll tell you but you have to hear me out."

"Where is she?"

"She's safe."

"And how in the hell would you know that?"

"Because the people who have her told me so!"

"Who are they? You trust them? Why would they tell you but not me?"

"Secrets! To protect the truth!"

"I don't believe you! Why does the truth need protection?"

As Faye started to cry, Janis' rage tempered back. She could see the tears were real. She could feel Faye's upwelling grief was overpowering.

Janis demanded, "What is it! Tell me!

Faye fought against the urge to withdraw. To hide her feelings would mean hiding the facts. Admitting them would leave her with no place to hide. Until that moment, she never expected telling Janis would be so difficult. There was no way to let Janis know everything she needed without exposing extreme and personal spaces.

Overwhelmed with thoughts of Alyssa, Janis couldn't hold back.

She grabbed Faye by the arm and cried out, "Who has Alyssa?"

Faye matched her in intensity. "The Project!"

"What Project? *Why* do they have her?"

"Because she's special!" Faye's shout emptied out from deep down.

Janis was taken aback. *Special* was the last thing expected; the incongruent way Faye had said it even more so. Waves of envy mixed with anguish washed over her.

Faye gripped the steering wheel, white-knuckling it with both hands.

Janis wouldn't let go of her arm. "Why are you crying?"

The words escaped on a whisper. "I'm pregnant."

The mind raced. Janis collected the pieces but didn't trust the way they fit. Faye, her pregnancy, a project named BIOPONORE, a lab in Kansas studying delayed fertility – Alyssa being special. So many pieces were left out; so much of the total picture still beyond her frame of reference. All she had was a picture without a frame. A puzzle without a border. Nothing left to go on but instinct and emotion.

Faye started the car.

Janis pulled on Faye's arm. "Hold on…where are we going?"

"Does it matter?"

The wrenching finality in Faye's words struck Janis sharply and gave her pause. A fleeting glimpse of Faye's hopelessness ran cold through her. Janis let go of Faye's arm and settled back, stunned by an intense impression of how serious matters truly were. If nothing else, the moment made her willing to go along for the ride. Whatever could it be, pent up behind such despair? She had to know.

Faye drove away from the Capitol heading northeast. As unlikely as it seemed, nothing was said between them. A winter's afternoon passed by outside. They hadn't gone far but in the tense and quiet time, left alone to share the same emotional space, they began to find a sense of all they had been to each other so many years before.

On impulse, Faye parked across from Stanton Park. A layer of snow from the night before blanketed the ground. Faye got out and walked off regretful energy, leaving Janis with no other choice but to follow.

The chill of the air both numbed and invigorated. A tangle of branches from bare trees stretched skyward. Like bones of massive carrion picked clean, the empty trees silhouetted over them a shroud of dread for all that must be said.

The drive had only marginally calmed them down. The vacant park only reinforced the isolation they shared. Each in her own way, they'd have to come to an understanding. Both sensed the best hope of salvation might rest in each other.

The thought of it was not comforting.

Side by side, they paced around the statue of Nathanael Greene. Permanently astride his battle horse with outstretched arm, the general of bygone struggles might as well have been pointing to their unknown fate. Faye realized she wouldn't have the inner strength for much more of this. Her goal in the moment was to get Janis to join The Project. The quicker she got there, the sooner the current ordeal would end.

Across the park, Faye caught sight of abandoned playground equipment. The image was unexpected and piercing. Where children should be playing, now there was only snow. Where laughter and young dreams should delight, an icy breeze blew silently to the west. Looking up, Faye caught sight of the general's outstretched arm. A ghostly premonition took hold. The general pointed toward the playground.

Taking it as a sign, Faye turned her steps. Maybe something beyond herself had meant them to be here. It was certainly the one place she never would have thought of going to willingly. She had stopped the car to take a walk, not to visit a playground. Of all places, why put herself through such a thing?

Now that she was here, the stark and definite necessity of it was clear.

A playground might be the only place that made sense.

Maybe there she'd have the force of will to bring Janis to an understanding.

Faye started with the most basic of observations. "They've put you in a difficult position. But they've put me in an impossible one."

Janis followed along, as yet barely willing to see where it all led.

"I'm limited by time and what I can say." Faye stopped and turn to Janis. "You have to decide now, today, what you're going to do. Unfortunately, so much within The Project is going on. I hope what I have time to say will convince you."

Janis stood firm. "From where I stand, you wouldn't believe any of that."

"You're going to have to believe something. Simply believing that's not possible won't be enough."

"I have every reason to think I'm being used. Why else get you to do this?"

"I know." Faye turned away and approached the border of the playground. "We both have a problem believing people. Maybe that's why we majored in science. In the lab, we're able to leave behind the hidden agendas for experimental fact."

"But you have no facts. Is that what you're telling me?"

"Wrong. I have no proof; none I can show you today."

"How did I know…"

"The facts speak for themselves."

"Go on…"

Faye clenched her fists around the top bar of a waist-high iron fence. "What I'm about to tell you, you must not repeat to anyone – ever."

Janis said nothing; her tacit approval was understood.

"I don't know how else to explain it except to say it flat out." Faye looked Janis in the eye. "Every child under the age of 14 is going to be sterile at puberty…"

The shock of it passed between them.

"…If this problem is not solved, the world is producing its last generation."

The playground came into focus. Janis' field of vision filled with it.

Faye leaned closer and moved a hand across herself below the navel.

"My child will be sterile. Anyone infected by Ghyvir-C will produce sterile children. Worst of all, I'm certain of it now – this whole thing was engineered."

A flash of memory and confusion came over Janis. "No…that's not right."

"I've checked the DNA. I've traced the markers. My God, I've seen it; there are millions of cases."

Janis shook her head. "It's not sterility."

"Of course it is! I didn't believe it at first. I know, it's too much to fathom."

"But that's not right…"

To Faye, it sounded like denial. "You wanted an explanation for the funhouse. This is it. They'll do anything to keep news of this from getting out. Can you imagine how people would react if they knew?"

"What if you're wrong?" Janis seized Faye by the shoulders. "I spoke with someone…he explained all of this. He also told me it was engineered. He said it's called 1st Protocol. It may look like sterility at first but it's not."

"Wait a minute; somebody already told you about this?" Faye was stunned.

"He worked with Malcolm…" Just then, Janis realized the trap she might have fallen into. Was talk of sterility just a ploy to get her to admit more about what he knew? She never told anyone about Knockout Mouse; it wasn't in her deposition. Were they using Faye to extract details of that from her any way they could?

Janis stepped back. "What's going on here? Are you setting me up?"

"Oh, come on, don't get paranoid on me again?"

Janis filled in the blanks as best she could. "You already know about delayed fertility. Of course, Manhattan, Kansas!"

"I don't know what you've heard, but I've proven sterility exists in the lab."

"I'll have to take that on faith, I suppose."

"Like I said, the facts speak for themselves. If you want proof, then you're going to have to join me in the lab. We can be there tomorrow. You'll have all the proof you need!"

Janis soaked in Faye's frankness and raw passion. She doubted it was an act.

Janis paced into the playground with Faye following.

"It doesn't line up. I was told people wanted to delay fertility until age 25."

"You're missing the point. This is about Ghyvir-C. That's the reason they need both of us in the lab."

"I know," said Janis. "I was told weeks ago that Ghyvir-C was engineered. The people behind it expected concern when teenage pregnancies started dropping to zero; that's why they prepared studies to release at just the right time to explain it."

"Like now..." Faye entertained a glimmer of her own doubt.

Janis marched back to Faye to confront her. "So what about Alyssa being special? What does she have to do with this?"

A snarl of what-ifs dashing away, Faye came back to the task at hand.

"The Project's been protecting Alyssa."

Janis didn't have to say anything. Faye could see she didn't believe her.

"Of all the children whose parents got infected with Ghyvir-C, she's the only one who isn't sterile. The DNA markers are different with Alyssa. They're unique."

Janis was interested but little impressed. If sterility didn't exist and delayed fertility was happening instead, then talk of Alyssa not being sterile only reaffirmed what Janis already supposed to be true. Janis changed the subject.

"What about Eugene Mass and 3rd Protocol?"

"I don't know. I've never heard of that."

"Why not? Why are they bending over backwards to make it seem like nothing is going on? They flat-out lied about evidence that proves the connection between Mass, Oliver Ross, and 3rd Protocol."

"What is 3rd Protocol?"

"A special agent to start a pandemic. He wants to collapse the population!"

"But why?" The insanity of it left Faye without a clue.

"He thinks it's going to save the planet. Who knows."

"You think there's evidence of this?"

"I saw the evidence! They have it on the laptop!"

"The Senate hearing is closed-door; all they told me was that you'd be having a rough time."

"I don't trust them. What if they're cooperating with Mass? We can't let them cover this up. Maybe they want him to release a plague."

"How can you believe that! Anyway, that's not what the hearings are about. What's that have to do with Oliver Ross? He had a poultry virus; that's confirmed."

"I'm not sure. It tied in somehow. They called it a trigger."

Faye contended with a swirl of thoughts. "The guy you said worked with Malcolm...what did you say he called Ghyvir-C?"

"1st Protocol."

"And you say Mass calls his pandemic 3rd Protocol."

Janis followed the line of thought. "You're right. The Group behind this is working on a 2nd Protocol too. This Group split with Mass years ago."

"According to this source of yours...what is 2nd Protocol supposed to do?"

"It puts a cap on lifespan – 70 years."

Faye had her own doubts. "Incredible. But that hasn't been done, has it?"

"No, not yet. But I was told they're getting it ready."

Faye shivered against the permeating cold but trembled at the thought of wilder possibilities. Her expectations about explaining The Project to Janis had given way to outrageous suggestions in return. Faye was unprepared to process what they might mean. As far as she could see, Janis had no reason to make all of this up. But if true, she could see how certain people in the government might want to conceal it. No matter how a panic might start – out of fear of global sterility or concern about a worldwide epidemic, it'd be better if something so major was handled in secret.

For Janis, the prospect of global sterility was the wild card of worry. Faye seemed so sure of it, even claimed to have worked in the lab to prove it. And yet Knockout Mouse was also convincing. The thought of someone engineering a delay to fertility made more sense than engineering the extinction of the human race. But that was assuming the mastermind wasn't a madman. Given what she knew about Mass' plans for 3rd Protocol, anything was possible.

Faye couldn't stand any more of the cold. Hugging herself, she approached Janis. "It comes down to this. I was told The Project's goal is finding a fix for the sterility problem. We think Alyssa is the key. No matter who's at fault, we know the sputnik inside Ghyvir-C did the damage. You might think it caused delayed fertility – we know we're dealing with permanent sterility. Either way, we need to get to the bottom of what's happening. Both you and I have worked with Ghyvir-C. I need your help going forward."

"You know me. I won't work without knowing the motives behind it."

"Then how about this – the motive is getting to the truth. I don't care who's proven right or wrong. I need to know for myself – and my baby."

A nagging doubt came over Janis. "You don't need me."

"Yes I do! If nothing else, I need to study you."

"Study me!"

"You were pregnant when you contracted Ghyvir-C. But the virus wasn't what we thought – the payload was taken out of the sputnik. That gave you a special type of immunity to pass onto Alyssa. That's why we think she's not sterile."

Janis thought back through a jumble of memories to make it all fit.

Faye added, "You were right all along! They didn't tell us the truth about what we were working on. They hid their own attempt to sabotage this 1st Protocol thing, whatever it was."

"They knew about 1st Protocol? I don't understand."

"You don't have to, not now. Just say you'll join me. I need your help."

"I don't know…doing what?" Suspicion fought an impulse to say yes.

"Help me find out what's really going on."

"You think they'll let you do that?"

"We can try! What if sterility is real? We have to do something!"

Janis shook her head. Fidgeting, she started for the car.

Faye had had enough. "For no other reason, do it for Alyssa! If you come with me, I promise you can see her, be with her."

Janis halted and looked back. An idea occurred to her. "Promise?"

Faye nodded and waited. The response she got was brusque.

"All right." Janis held her gaze. "But first I need to visit my mother."

CHAPTER 31

Bright Hope Farms
South Hero Island, Vermont

Clear skies and good omens were never farther apart. One could be seen, the other hardly felt. A day after leaving Stanton Park with a fragile understanding fashioned between them, Janis Insworth and Faye Gardner took a flight north, and then a drive back in time.

Nothing could come closer to bygone days of spring break and shared summer fun than being together again at Bright Hope Farms. While neither one believed a single visit would close the gap between them, a bright sky tested that belief with a late afternoon offering of pastel colors and positive wonder.

Assumptions about hardened hearts or clashes over personal histories aside, they couldn't help but question how much this trip might affect them. It was a question as unnerving as persistent, at the surface yet unspoken.

Once they drove onto the island, it didn't matter if they were old friends with new reasons to doubt each other or ex-friends with old reasons to resist getting close. Traveling the last mile to the house left them with very little to say. A leisurely cruise along sunny West Shore Road had a way of saying it all.

Tempering the mood was the ever-present reality of what they were facing. The tracking bracelet around Janis' ankle was gone but federal charges against her had only been suspended, not dropped. Their itinerary had been logged by nameless authorities who put a two-day time limit on their stay. Janis had been released into Faye's custody while Faye's every move was supervised to fit into a larger plan.

Both conceded there was far too much to catch up on, and not enough clarity on what was in store. If they were going to be able to work together, somehow they must reconcile an awareness of their bitter past with the looming prospect of a darkening future. Each wanted separate things but needed one another to get them.

They parked the car and climbed the weathered steps to the porch.

The welcome by Janis' mother was warm but self-conscious. The moment was a mosaic of sentiment, discovery, and awkwardness inlaid by all of them. Sara Rushton knew they were coming, had an early dinner ready, but first there had to be hugs and tears, then small talk about their trip up from D.C.

Sara busied herself in the kitchen while the girls meandered upstairs to settle in. Entering the bedroom, Janis paused to find that Sara had set up an extra bed; it was just the way they had always insisted on sharing the room during summers past.

Faye reserved comment as Janis found things to do. Her mother's action was transparent, a too-literal attempt to get the two of them together. If nothing else, it embarrassed them. Whether they'd become friends again was a question unspoken. Having it externalized in a way neither could avoid only made the adjustment to being back at the lake house that much more difficult. They commented here and there on remembered things in the room. Ignoring their shared discomfort, they mentioned nothing about the beds and retreated downstairs for dinner.

Far from the escape they thought dinner might be, Sara's conversation invariably settled on gilded times past. Neither Faye nor Janis needed to hear how good the old times had been, especially from someone prone to romanticize them. Knowing glances between them confirmed this fact. The only way to avoid any of it was to take over and steer the conversation themselves. Doing so became their first collaborated project. As such, it also became their test.

By the time dessert was served, all of them had loosened up. Even a bit of laughter came more easily, along with a relaxed willingness to share college stories.

"I thought about dropping out lots of times," confessed Janis.

"Oh, like when?" challenged Faye.

Janis chuckled, "Usually, the week before finals."

"That's what I thought. You like to make a big deal out of it but tell the truth; you breezed through most of your classes."

"I wouldn't say that." Janis' protest was hollow.

"For one thing, you had much more time to study."

"And whose fault was that? You didn't have to accept a lab internship while holding down a part-time job."

For Sara's sake, Faye held back from the answer on the tip of her tongue. Janis never had to work during college; her parents paid for everything. The story was different in Faye's case but putting too strong a point on that would do no good.

"The job paid for books and food. The internship was good on a resume."

"We *both* got into USAMRIID. Obviously, you didn't need it to get the job."

"Maybe not. It's easy to come to that conclusion now."

Sara watched mostly amused but sometimes concerned as the two of them bantered. The topic was casual but a rising undercurrent of tension was not.

Janis stuck to her point, smiling all the way. "It was overkill, admit it."

Faye felt pressured. Janis' unwillingness to let it go tested her reserve.

"I did what I could to be prepared. I wasn't like you; not everything came so *easily* to me."

"Just because I took things in stride and didn't sweat the small stuff, that doesn't mean everything was easy."

"Yeah, like senior project. Look how that turned out."

Janis threw back her head and laughed. "Oh, my, don't go there."

Sara was curious. "I don't think I heard about that."

"And you shouldn't!" laughed Janis.

"It's perfect," Faye shot back. "It's exactly what I'm talking about."

"Just because you spent sleepless nights coming up with some lame idea…"

"It wasn't lame!"

"You're the only one that says so. It got rejected, didn't it?"

Sara interrupted, "So what happened?"

"It's no big deal," started Janis.

"Let me tell it," Faye demanded; she turned to Sara. "Senior term paper was half of our grade; we had all semester to work on it. Miss Easy-Going, here, lollygags weeks away getting nothing done. Days before the paper's due, she saw me arguing with a visiting professor from another class and wanted to know what's going on. I told her I asked him to read my paper, you know, to get feedback on it before turning it in. To my surprise, he detested it, ripped the idea to shreds. Was Janis concerned? No. Instead, the whole episode came in handy for her. It was a reminder she needed to get started on her own paper. She had forgotten all about it."

"Not so!"

"Oh, yeah…I'm sure. The best part is the scandalous way she did her research."

"Don't exaggerate! You're just jealous."

"She shamelessly flirted with a TA, even plotted ways to bump into him. In return, he gave her detailed suggestions on topics, told her about high-scoring past papers; gave her tips."

Sara gasped in fun, "You didn't!"

"She led the poor guy on and got him to practically write the thing for her."

Janis protested, "He did no such thing!"

"So what happened?" asked Sara.

"What do you think? In four days she wrote her paper and got a top score. I turned in the paper I slaved over, something original and challenging. My score was barely a score at all. In fact, they suggested I rewrite it."

Janis shrugged. "You have to admit, no matter what grade it got, your paper was a classic." Her tone was derisive.

"What does that mean?" An old argument reopened.

Sara noted the friction and jumped into the conversation between them. "Sounds like a lot of thought went into it."

Janis was feeling her third glass of wine. She giggled, "Come on now… *Programmed Species Death*? Did you really expect them to buy *that* as your senior project?" Underneath the mockery was something else eating away.

"Why not?" Having avoided the wine, Faye's seriousness became defensive.

Janis was startled wide-eyed. "My God! You *still* think it was a good idea!"

"Don't act so surprised. I expected something condescending."

"I don't care how original it was. Maybe it was *too* original."

Sara tried to intervene. "What is it? *Programmed Species Death*?"

Faye preempted Janis from getting in a quick answer. "It was the topic of my paper, a theory I came up with."

"Admit it; it was science fiction; good science fiction, but fiction nonetheless."

Faye glanced at Janis but continued to answer Sara. "The premise was taken from a reasonable inference. In cellular biology, there's something called Programmed *Cell* Death. It's a known fact. At various times, certain cells in the body commit suicide."

"Suicide?" Sara sat back. "That sounds strange."

"Not at all," added Faye. "It's by design, other times it happens in reaction to disease; Programmed Cell Death is a natural fact. Either way, it's useful."

Smiling, Janis butted in. "Yeah, if it wasn't for PCD, humans would have webbed feet and fingers and much worse oddities."

"PCD is great at getting rid of unwanted or damaged cells. If this didn't happen, they'd reproduce and create defective tissue and organs."

"All true, very true," added Janis, "but where you took it was a big jump."

"Why? If a system like PCD operates in the body, why is it such a stretch to think something similar might operate in nature, regulating species?"

"It's a perfectly good idea – for science fiction, but there's absolutely no evidence that anything of the sort is going on."

"Maybe because no one's looking for it."

"They were teaching us *science;* it wasn't a speculation class."

"And how does science come about?"

"Observations and experiments on something *real*."

"Millions of species have come and gone. What if there's more to it than natural selection? When cells get old or damaged, or when they don't form right in utero, apoptosis is triggered. All I was suggesting is that the same thing could happen to whole genomes. There might be a natural process that genetically triggers the extinction of species – for the good of nature, in the same way."

Janis nodded, "And that's the leap of faith that makes it science fiction."

Sara gathered up the empty dessert plates. "There's no sense arguing about it."

Under breath, Janis muttered, "There's little sense to it at all."

Faye leaned across the table, getting in Janis' face. "Go on, sit there, you know so much."

"I know fact from fiction."

"What if *Programmed Species Death* is extremely rare?"

"Like unicorns?"

"What if nature has only used it once or twice in three billion years? You think there might be a chance we missed it?"

"Next you'll be claiming it killed off the dinosaurs."

"OK, even if you're right and there's no evidence it's ever happened. Maybe it's a natural process that's *never* been used before. It's always been there but Nature holds it in reserve, just in case it's needed for its own survival."

"Oh, I get it; you wanted your senior paper to be on the mysteries of Gaia."

"The human body has all kinds of autonomic systems. Are they mysterious to you? Why do white blood cells rush to defend the body? Who told them to? Why do some kinds of T-cells keep a memory of past diseases you've had? Is there a ghost in the machine? Why can't nature do the same thing? We already know that patterns in nature repeat."

"Anything's possible in the land of what-if."

"Don't look now but we're all living there." With so much flooding to mind, Faye was driven to a darker, harder edge to cut through Janis' dismissive attitude. "You think those things I told you in the park in D.C. were made up just to get you to do something. You've convinced yourself this whole thing was orchestrated to manipulate you – I know, because if you really believed it, you'd understand how close we are to a real *Programmed Species Death*."

"Why should I believe you? You're a tool of who knows what."

"Doesn't matter, doesn't change the facts. A billion kids are sterile. I've seen the evidence. I've been in the lab and studied the agent that did it. Whether that happened because we did it to ourselves or Nature did it, I don't know. One thing's for sure; when you finally come round to realize it's not about delayed fertility, it's about sterility, you'll think twice about what you call science fiction."

"You never change. Still trusting of anything official, forever wedded to your delusions."

"Am I?" Faye stood up. "You had Alyssa. She's healthy and whole. You can sit there and be smug. Everything comes easy for you, isn't that right."

Janis jumped up. "You'll never forgive me, will you! I took Colin. I had a baby. I moved on. It's my name on *GenLET*. I had a life! Well, so did you! Don't lecture me on what's happening to the fucking world. There's a madman out there about to kill six billion people. You're the one in denial. For some ungodly reason, you and your handlers are covering up for him."

Faye was too upset to yell back. "As usual, you've got it wrong. But I guess that's another thing that comes your way too easily."

Janis stormed out of the room, collected her coat and marched outside, slamming the front door behind her. Faye slumped back down, tears in her eyes.

Sara stood at the kitchen sink, her hands shaking, her hopes for the evening blown apart. "I don't know what's gotten into her."

Faye's eyes stayed downcast. "Nothing's normal any more."

"That thing you said – about all those children being sterile. Is that true?"

Faye nodded. "It's a nightmare. You mustn't tell anyone. I shouldn't have said anything. She just got me so worked up."

Sara came back to the table and took Faye's hand. "You have to go after her. You two need each other."

"What good would it do? She only agreed to come with me because I promised she'd see Alyssa."

"Did you mean that?"

Faye nodded. "Alyssa is being protected – for a special reason."

"Then go after Janis. She wants Alyssa more than anything."

"That doesn't mean she'll listen."

"That's ridiculous. You two are still having an argument that started long ago – and it isn't about your senior paper. If you can't get past that, then at least put it aside. Talk to her about what needs to happen now."

"She has to be open to it. She has to calm down first."

"No. That's the worst thing to do." Sara was emphatic. "I know her. If she calms down like this, her mind will be set. You'll never get through to her."

"Once I get her in the lab, she'll see the evidence."

"Evidence of what? Unless you can prove that Eugene Mass is not planning this thing she calls 3rd Protocol, she's going to resist. I would too. She already told you she thinks you and the government are probably involved with him."

Faye looked up. "Do you think that? Have I given that impression?"

Sara hesitated. "All I know is, Janis is convinced something's wrong. I don't believe you'd do such a thing. But I can't speak for the government or what they told you. If I were you, I'd make sure I wasn't being used."

Faye's own doubts resurfaced; a month of reluctant revelations from Colin came back to haunt her. Janis and she might have little but the past in common, but at least they could agree to go after the truth here and now.

"All right, I'll try." Faye stood and gave Sara a hug before getting a coat and heading out the front door. With weather so frosty, there was only one place to look for Janis. The boat house.

With hand buried deep in pockets, Faye set out at a healthy pace. Twilight was bright in the western sky and the settling air was calm and cold. The only sound was the crunch of snow underfoot or the errant call of a Pine Grosbeak in the far woods.

Along the footpath, the surroundings were familiar yet dreamlike. She knew the farm's extended grounds as if they were a favorite story told often but far too long ago; very little had changed. And yet, to come back in winter had her walking through a landscape out-of-sync with summer memories. Everywhere she saw reminders of something once enjoyed, something gone. All that was left was an ache, a regret. She wouldn't wake up from a reality that included Granite Peak Installation, the cursed mystery of Ghyvir-C, and the barren hopes of her unborn child.

At the boat house, Faye saw no light, only Janis' footprints leading onward in the snow. Faye followed the meandering path through light woods down to the frigid shoreline. There she found Janis, hugging herself for warmth and staring out across the frozen lake. She'd been crying but pretended she hadn't.

Faye pretended they hadn't argued but pulsed with the adrenaline of anger.

Shivering, she settled alongside Janis and took in the view.

"Now I know why we never came here in winter."

Janis gazed up through bare branches. "Were summers really that good?"

The question took Faye off-guard. To keep the conversation going, she was obliged to answer. "Yeah, they were good…"

"…but like anything out of reach, they seem even better now."

"We could say the same thing about ourselves. Are we really that different?"

Janis turned her head and looked at Faye. "Someone told me once that true success was having no regrets. I don't know about that anymore."

"I think most people have something they'd like to do over or make right."

"Perhaps, but most people aren't successful – not really."

"What do you regret?"

Janis took time to consider. "I regret the creation of *GenLET*. I should have known it would be put to no good."

"How so?"

"Oh, it's just a feeling I have, but it's just begun."

"If we only knew all the stuff going on."

"All of us can be such useful idiots. Useful for what we know but idiots for the way we keep expecting a different outcome."

Faye considered her own circumstances. "I know I didn't want to believe what I saw. I wouldn't have believed it if Ghyvir's sputnik wasn't right in front of me."

"So they lied to us. Why are we always surprised?"

"It's not just that. It's the idea of crafting something so elegant, so advanced, and yet so utterly malicious."

Janis sighed. "It's all a matter of degree. Create one bullet to kill one person, it's quite acceptable. Create one bullet that kills everybody, suddenly it seems evil."

"I guess if I was a pessimist, all of this would have been predictable."

"Yeah, think of that. If it was predicted, maybe it could have been prevented. But it takes a pessimist to see it."

"Or even believe it's possible." Faye prompted. "If we can't see what's coming, then let's reconstruct the past. It's the only way to find out what we're facing now."

"Easier said than done."

Faye couldn't help herself. She offered a conciliatory smile. "But things come so easily for you…"

Janis didn't smile. She met Faye halfway by letting all reflex anger drain away. "What are you after?"

Quick to be direct, Faye seized the opportunity. "The sputnik's payload contained a designer suicide gene so the sputnik died once the payload was delivered. What if we track the source of the payload? Was it something corporate, military, or rogue?"

Janis was two steps ahead. "You want me to contact Knockout Mouse. He stole the GAMA that got dumped in the Sargasso Sea…"

"Yes, as far as we know. That GAMA had a suicide gene in it. I'd be curious to see what kind of information you can get out of him."

"It's a touchy subject. I can give it a try."

"We have so little to go on. At least we can compare suicide genes."

"So you admit you don't trust what they've given you."

"I know I'm not being told the whole story."

Janis stepped away down the shore. "It's much more likely you're being told the *wrong* story."

"It doesn't make sense. Give me a good reason why and maybe I'll believe it."

"A good reason? There's nothing good about making one bullet that kills all people."

"You realize what you're suggesting. The government, as a matter of policy, wants to collapse the population. That's what you believe?"

"I don't know how things are being manipulated. Eugene Mass has worked on this for a long time. He's clever. I've met him, you know."

Faye followed Janis to a new spot. "All right. I'm not going to argue it. We'll get the information on the GAMA and take it from there. Agreed?"

Janis nodded and then pointed to the lake. "Remember this spot?"

Faye was caught mid-thought. She looked around. "Not really. Why?"

"Remember six of us in a boat?" Janis' mood lightened. "You and I went overboard to go for a swim…"

A memory jumped to mind. Faye knew the story and where Janis was going with it. "I remember. We got in the water…"

"I decided to take my suit off."

"Then you dared me to do the same."

"You didn't have to. You gave in to peer pressure."

Faye felt a flush of embarrassment return as if it was yesterday. "That wasn't enough for you, was it?"

Janis feigned innocence. "I didn't suggest we race…"

"Oh, no – but you encouraged it. Don't blame it all on the boys."

"It was all their idea – race to shore; the winner gets her swimsuit back."

Faye stared out at the frozen surface. "And what was the loser supposed to do?"

Janis laughed. "It was all in fun. You could have beaten me."

"Not likely. That water was cold. I wasn't used to it."

"No big deal. You survived."

"*You* didn't have to run up to the house *naked*."

"You could have stayed in the water until they went away."

"Yeah, like that was going to happen. With the way I was shivering? They knew they could outwait me."

Seeing the seriousness of Faye's reaction, Janis lost all humor. The cares of the present pressed in on her once again. "Look at it this way; compared to everything we know now, maybe it wasn't so bad."

Faye offered a weak smile. "Yeah…"

"If I could, I'd go back and trade places with you…if it would make any difference…if it would change things."

Faye stuffed a flood of feeling. "Like you said, true success is having no regrets. I guess we'll both have to work on that."

Janis nodded, hugged herself, then started up the path.

Faye took one more look at the cove where they swam the race. They were headed up the bank again, only this time there'd be no winners. For both of them, there was only a sense of being exposed and vulnerable.

Along the path, darkness had taken hold of the woods. Last light teased the sky. Without saying anything more, they made their way back to the main house. Sara had a fire going. There was time for a quiet evening, oolong tea and cookies, and plenty of fire-gazing. As it got later, Faye went upstairs to change clothes. Janis retreated to the den to use Sara's computer.

It didn't take long to write the email to Knockout Mouse.

It had been a long day. Too tired to make other arrangements, Janis and Faye prepared to sleep in the same room, in the matching beds. There was no sense disappointing Sara.

As Faye climbed between the sheets, Janis headed back to the den. In her hand was a small package, something that had come for her in the mail while she was away. It didn't take long to open it and do what she needed to do.

In no time at all, she was back upstairs, crawling under the covers.

It was so much like it had once been, but not in a way that made any difference.

Sleep at the lake house had always meant a deep rest. All three of them fully expected to sleep late the next morning. But that was before the helicopter hovered over the house at 6:00 a.m.

That was before the knock at the door and the shouts of authority.

That was before Janis and Faye were taken into custody by federal agents.

As they were being led outside to waiting SUVs, Faye saw it in Janis' face.

"What have you done?" Faye's question seemed almost rhetorical.

Janis knew it was anything but.

They drove off too quickly for proper goodbyes. Sara was left standing on the porch in shock. Janis said nothing and Faye was too worried to ask her any questions within earshot of an agent.

They were rushed to an open field just down the road where the helicopter had landed and waited with rotors spinning. Hustled aboard, they sat flanked by agents. As soon as they were buckled in, the chopper took to the air at top speed headed south. Faye couldn't stand it any more. She turned to Janis.

"Do you know what this is about?"

Janis saw no reason to be coy; Faye would find out soon enough. "After you went to bed, I posted something to the internet."

"You had something at the house?"

"Yes. I mailed myself something – from Marseille."

For Faye, the consequences were obvious. "You didn't!"

Janis was stoic. "Did you really think I was going to let them hide the truth?"

Faye was furious. "You used me!"

Janis stared her down. "You don't have access to Alyssa, do you? You were only told that to get me on The Project. You think I'm that naive?"

"Damn it! Everything you said at the park – it was all just to get loose so you could get up here and do this."

Janis was enthused. "It's out everywhere now…the memo, all the stuff about 3rd Protocol. There's no way they can pull it back."

"You have no idea what you've done!"

"Neither do you. You think they tell you anything?"

"There are good reasons not to upset things."

"Bad people with good reasons. Doesn't sound right to me."

"You don't think there's ever a valid reason to keep a secret?"

"Oh sure, just like there are good reasons for dual-use projects."

"It's not just about panicking the public – it's about panicking the *powerful*."

"Amazing how you know so much when you've been told so little."

"I've been told enough! What do you think is going to happen now?"

"If we're lucky, the end of 3rd Protocol. If the government isn't involved, then I guess they have nothing to worry about."

Just then, an agent from the front seat turned around and handed Faye a phone. She took it with hesitation then listened with interest and sudden concern.

"My God..." She began to tear up. "Are we going there now?"

Faye's emotion riveted Janis to her half of the conversation.

"…should I wait? I don't know. Are you sure? All right." She handed the phone back to the agent then turned to Janis. "That was my boss. There's another reason why they came for us so quickly."

"It's not about what I posted?"

Faye shook her head, tears running down her face. "Something's happened at The Nest…"

Janis was on edge. "Isn't that the place you said they had Alyssa?"

"They're taking us there now."

"What's wrong?"

Faye couldn't bring herself to repeat what she had heard.

She managed to say one thing. "…it's Alyssa."

Chapter 32

Frioul Archipelago
A mile off the coast of Marseille

Private boats dotted the harbor between the islands of Pomègues of Ratonneau. André Bolard moored the 26-foot cruiser and took a walk along the strand. His pace was casual and yet he aimed with steady determination for the blue umbrellas of a particular café. A man waiting there bought André a drink without a word spoken between them. Sitting among tourists, they relaxed and joined in, discussing nothing of importance.

Afterwards, the two of them strolled in the direction of the boat. Along the way, André stopped for a newlywed couple wanting their picture taken. Hugging and smiling, the pair asked if Château d'If could be included in the background.

André obliged then waved goodbye. He turned as the other man caught his eye. With nothing to say, André grinned. Patronizing clueless tourists cost nothing; if anything, it only demonstrated publically what a good guy he was.

Back on the boat, André and the man retreated to the shade and privacy of the inner cabin. André opened beers as the man tuned a radio to a music station and turned up the volume. They sat close.

"Did you see anyone?"

The man settled back, suddenly alert. "I never do."

André got comfortable. "It's just as well. Let them believe they're clever."

"I don't like it. After Rue Saint-Ferréol, I can do nothing."

"Don't worry; having you do nothing is working out just fine."

"Meanwhile, I'm on some fucking watch list."

"They let you go; that's all that matters." André shrugged; his humor was deadpan. "How were you supposed to know that crazy bitch didn't want a boat?"

"Meeting with her wasn't worth the risk."

Opening a laptop, André scanned a blog posting. "We can say that now."

The man gazed at the posting without reading. "You trust what she posted?"

"It's worth considering."

"As what? More smoke to hide the fire? Everyone is looking at it and seeing different things. There's no end to it."

"That's why there must be something to it. That much I'm certain of. Someone is going to an awful lot of trouble to confuse the issue, don't you think?"

"They can't confuse the facts."

"Facts? Let's not confuse the truth with the facts. No, this is something else. It's so...clumsy and mysterious all at once. Here we have twenty-year-old studies from think tanks offered alongside classified spreadsheets from Puerto Rico."

"If any of this crap really came out of GeLixCo, it raises all kinds of questions. Some are calling it a smear campaign against NovoSenectus."

"Strange, because the web post says the two of them worked together on a project for the U.S. government. Of course, the Americans are denying it. Their Senate says all of this is nothing but a vicious love triangle gone wrong."

The man sneered and laughed. "How did they ever get that idea? They should make a TV show out of it."

"If they did that, the Americans would believe it even more."

"There's too much to sort out. We're scattering our energies."

"No," snapped André. "We stay with the memo. That's where we have to focus. If the memo's real, then Mass intends on triggering *something*."

"How do we know this thing she calls 3rd Protocol isn't another diversion?"

"Of course it's a diversion! This is about *GenLET*. It's always been about life extension. The circus we're watching only proves whatever's being planned is much bigger than Mass. They were researching how to scan people's DNA with radiation – what the fuck is that about? This stuff about a UDIF/TZ Project is no joke."

"But *New World Harmony* is his idea."

"He can name it, but it's only his name for what other nameless powers have in mind. I've done some research too. A leaked report out of Washington claims *GenLET* was a secret U.S. project all along. NovoSenectus was contracted as part of the development cycle – that's all."

"What about the Nobel Prize?"

"They don't give a shit about trinkets."

"If that's right, we're seeing only a fraction of what we're up against."

"Even more reason to get serious about putting a boot into the gears."

"What should we do?"

André squinted in thought. "For now, we watch how Mass reacts."

"This morning he named a replacement for Riya Basu."

"To be expected. Janis is not his favorite person right now. Who is it?"

"Carlos somebody from Madrid; never heard of him."

"Do we know where he is now?"

"Vacationing in the Azores."

"Boating?"

The man nodded. "He just left Island Flora, headed for Pico."

"Good." André threw back a swig of brew. "Luckily, we know a thing or two about yachts. So what have we found out about the guy in the memo – Javier?"

"There's only one person named Javier connected to Mass. Open your email."

André switched over and opened the attachment. A front-page picture from a past issue of *Voici Magazine* opened up. In one corner was a grainy photo of two men on a sidewalk. The caption read, "*Gay Lover Follows Eugene Mass to Paris*."

"Javier Francisco – most certainly not his real name."

André groused, "You've got to be shitting me."

"They have a hideaway in Brussels. From what all the stories say, they don't need to be terribly discrete; apparently, Leah Mass doesn't care."

André stared at the grainy photo with suspicion. "I see product placement."

"What do you mean?"

"Either we believe this or we believe the memo."

"Most people already believe this."

"Then that's the way Mass must want it. Even more reason to stick with the memo."

"But if Javier's not the gay lover, who is he?"

"Couldn't he be the lover *and* something else?"

"He's been hiding in plain sight way too long."

"Unless we hear something else, we assume he's dirty. From the way Mass talked to him in the memo, he must be a fixer."

"I don't know…" The man finished his beer. "I don't like it."

"What's wrong?"

"How do we know we're not following crumbs they're leaving for us?"

"We don't." André was steely-eyed in his stare. "That's why we're going to start making some of them disappear."

"If we start that they'll come after us."

"They're coming after us anyway. We don't fit the new order of things."

The man stood. "What do you need me to do?"

André stepped closer. "Go to Stockholm and Brussels, then someplace unexpected…let's say Miami. Have a good time but go down a few side streets. Do your best *not* to act suspicious; that'll get them going."

The man stood in protest. "That's it? I play the wild goose again and let them chase me? Nothing more?"

"If you want, we can let the fuckers grind you up as foie gras. You want to give them something solid so they can shut us down? Would that make you happy?"

The man said nothing.

André grabbed him by the shoulder. "We all have something to do that sucks. Only yours gets to be a vacation. Quit complaining."

The man started to go.

André called out, "And keep up the research. Remember – unchartered waters dead ahead."

The man mumbled, "Got it," then left the boat.

André grabbed another beer, turned off the radio, and followed him up on deck. After downing half of the bottle, he pressed cell phone to ear. Staring at the peak of Notre-Dame de la Garde basilica in the distance, he waited for the ringing to stop. When it did, it went to voicemail.

"This is André. Call me when you get this. We have emergency maintenance to do. We'll need a specialist, someone who knows their way around a stuffing box."

André lowered the phone. The line went dead.

On a yacht, a stuffing box was used at the point were the propeller exited the boat's hull underwater. It prevented water from entering the hull while still allowing the propeller shaft to turn.

But his call wasn't about one of those.

André looked out to sea. He had hoped it wouldn't come to this.

But now that it had, he was going to go at it full throttle.

CHAPTER 33

GeLixCo Advanced Research Center
Aguadilla, Puerto Rico

All of it could have been a terrible misunderstanding. But then the private jet touched down with a shudder of rapid braking. For Janis, the past few weeks felt like a dream. Now the dream was having a nightmare.

The certainty of arrival rendered her numb.

Trying not to expect the worst only brought it to mind. She knew so little after so many hours. She was certain of nothing more than the one word Faye had managed to say. *Alyssa*. How telling when a single word could say so much.

Her tortured imagination ran wild.

As they hurried from jet to car, the tropical sun blasted away overhead. Dense, humid air enveloped her. A mother's heart had been ripped from ice and plunged in fire. The ride from Rafael Hernandez Airport down the coast was a blur. She was out of breath, powerless in the face of what should never be.

Faye was at her side but silent, respectful of her need to stay solid within herself and maintain. Being tense and overwhelmed left them both excited but exhausted. The agents escorting them were dutiful if not dispassionate. The lush scenery around them didn't matter. Neither of them had been on this road before.

Neither of them could get past the feeling that things were out of control.

On the northwest coast of the island, the GARC complex sprouted in the hills above the beach resort of Aguadilla. The winding road narrowed and views of the ocean became panoramic. After a brief stop at a gated guard station, their car was allowed passage behind the high walls of bricks and vegetation that hid the research center from street-level view.

Janis looked up to see three buildings farther up the hill. In the center was the larger, obvious main building. The smaller structure on the right was connected by a fifth-story sky bridge. But it was the smallest and newly renovated building, the one on the left that attracted Janis' attention. She had no reason to be so sure, but as soon as she laid eyes on it, she knew that's where they had Alyssa.

The car pulled up to the smaller building's side entrance. GeLixCo guards took over guiding them down a hallway and into an elevator. At the top floor, they were led to an office where a middle-aged woman stood looking out a window with her back to them. On the sound of their approach, the woman turned around.

"Welcome." Her smile was slight but genuine. "Please have a seat."

As Janis and Faye sat down, the woman sat nearer to Janis and mirrored her posture. She extended her hand. "And you are…"

"Janis Insworth."

The introduction passed on. "Faye Gardner."

"My name is Rebecca Yeats. I'm a scientist, but also a doctor. I was called in very recently. For the last couple of days, I've been caring for Alyssa."

Janis held back a thousand questions. She'd trust that the doctor would say what was necessary while respecting how fragile she was.

"First of all, let me assure you, Alyssa is stable and in no immediate danger. She's breathing on her own and shows no signs of distress."

Knowing that Janis might be unable to speak, Faye spoke for her.

"What exactly is wrong?"

Rebecca hesitated, not so much gathering thoughts as shifting through them for the right thing to say. "From what I hear, Alyssa has complained recently about certain symptoms: indigestion, diarrhea, bloating, some abdominal pain."

"I was told on the phone this came on suddenly."

Faye's statement was a question. The doctor would not be rushed.

"The last episode was sudden, yes. Before that there were chills and fever, nausea, all the signs of a flu or stomach infection."

"What exactly happened during this…last episode?"

Rebecca glanced at Janis but answered Faye.

"We're not quite sure. No one else was in the room. A care worker found Alyssa unconscious." She paused, dismayed at having to proceed. "She's been that way ever since."

The news struck Faye and Janis equally but the shock of it jolted Janis to speak.

"She's in a coma?"

Rebecca dropped her gaze, gave a nod, and eased back, at a loss for words.

Faye asked, "What's the diagnosis?"

"The blood work came back this morning. We found elevated levels of Urofollitropin, a purified form of FSH, follicle stimulating hormone. It's normally found in the brain, created by the pituitary gland."

"I know what it is," snapped Janis. "It works on the ovaries to stimulate ovulation."

Faye jumped in. "What's been going on down here?"

Grief became rage. Janis raised her voice. "Egg harvesting; that's what it sounds like."

Rebecca raised a hand to plead for calm and restraint. "I know nothing about that. I was told no such thing was ever authorized."

"And yet it happened – in a secured lab, under the care of top scientists?"

Janis' comment begged for explanation. Rebecca had none. "I don't know how it happened. I just got here. My priority is helping Alyssa now. There'll be time to find those responsible later."

Janis demanded, "What exactly is her condition?"

Rebecca opened a file folder to avoid Janis' withering stare. "The diagnosis is coma induced by a reaction to OHSS, ovarian hyper-stimulation syndrome. This is not my specialty but I've become quite an expert in the last 24 hours. I'm also in touch with top reproductive endocrinologists. From everything I've seen, I don't believe this was going on for long. That fact alone is cause for hope."

Janis broke down and sobbed. Faye put her arm around her.

"Can we see her?" asked Faye.

Rebecca stood. "Of course, whenever you want – for as long as you want."

Faye helped Janis down the hallway. They passed through secured doors into a separate wing, more hospital than office building. Rebecca led them to a corner room facing west. Heavy drapes shielded them from the afternoon sun. Rebecca stopped in the hallway. Faye paused in the doorway.

Janis took small steps inside. Stunned by finally seeing her daughter once again, she took in every detail without shedding a tear.

Alyssa looked asleep. But the peacefulness on her face was belied by the vital-sign monitors clustered around the head of the hospital bed. Janis was taken by the starkness of the room. It was such a contrast to the sweetness of her girl.

Janis approached the side of the bed. A dizzying wave of impressions swirled around one emotional focus. After everything of the past few weeks, they were together again. But after all her hopes, why did it have to be this way?

Janis searched for strength. She knew neither of their journeys was over. The hardest part might be yet to come. The power of intention must have its own, greater purpose coming to bear, something that aligned with things unseen but necessary nonetheless.

She took Alyssa's hand in hers and instantly knew something bigger than the both of them would come of this. It had too. The suffering of angels such as Alyssa couldn't be meaningless. Someway, somehow, Janis would make sure of it.

Faye drew near. Janis sensed her presence and a surge of anger returned.

"Take a good look at your project. And don't tell me you knew nothing about this."

"It's the only thing I can say…" whispered Faye.

"It doesn't matter. You agreed to what was going on behind the curtain. You didn't need to know what it was. But then, that's always been the difference between you and me. You believe what they tell you, no matter what else they're using us for."

Faye forced calm on her reaction. "I can't argue with you when you're right."

Janis looked over and saw conciliatory softness in Faye's eyes. "I guess next you're going to tell me – that's why we always argue."

The fact that Janis could manage even sarcastic humor and meet her halfway was more than Faye ever expected. She took hold of Janis' hand and squeezed. They stood side-by-side with their gazes trained on Alyssa.

With so much welling up, they couldn't help but turn to each other. Separated for so long but thrust together like never before, the two of them wavered before falling into each other's arms. They hugged and cried and held each other tight; they fully expected at any moment the world would fly off balance and fling them apart.

With nothing else left, they hung onto each other for dear life.

Rebecca gave them as much time as they needed. After respecting their privacy for awhile, she returned to the room ready to continue the business at hand.

"Sorry to interrupt, but I need Janis for a few minutes. There's a quick orientation; I'm told she should really get it done before settling in."

Janis and Faye both started for the door.

"Just Janis…" Rebecca didn't explain. Faye stepped back.

Janis followed Rebecca along the hallway past the elevator to a service stairwell. A single flight of stairs brought them to the roof. Rebecca opened the door but didn't go through. Her demeanor was all business but filled with compassion.

"I'll be in my office if you need me for anything afterward."

Walking onto the open roof made no sense. Janis held back, uncertain.

"It's all right," assured Rebecca. "It's something just for you."

With halting steps, Janis moved forward. Warm afternoon light hit her and ocean breezes swept back her hair. The view all around was expansive. The stairwell door closed behind her as the arc of her gaze brought a solitary form into focus.

She was not alone. A man walked towards her. Not just any man.

He said nothing at first. He didn't have to.

"You!" Coming from Janis, it was not so much a word as a yelp of pain.

Colin Insworth appeared before her.

"No! You can't be a part of this!"

"I'm the one who called Faye."

"You're her boss?"

Colin nodded.

Janis lunged forward. "Damn you!"

A swinging blow struck Colin in the side of the head.

A second and third blow was deflected by his upraised arms.

"How dare you touch my baby!" Janis was incensed and inconsolable.

Colin did nothing to try to stop the blows. Over and over he absorbed them until the last one broke through his defenses and caught him on the face. His head flung to one side as his hands grabbed Janis by the wrists.

Blood trickled from his nose.

"That's enough!" he yelled.

Janis jerked away and stormed back to the stairway door. When she got there, he found it locked. She spun around like a caged animal. "Open this door!"

Colin stood his ground. "I knew it would be this way. But I have to talk to you."

"Drop dead!"

"This is the only place where you can't run away. You have to hear me out."

Janis took determined strides to the edge and looked down. If there was anything down there to break her fall, she was furious enough to jump.

"There's no place to go. You might as well listen to me."

She rocketed away, checking the perimeter of the roof.

Colin followed. "I went to a lot of trouble to get you here. Everybody else wants to send you away for good. You pulled quite a stunt last night; created quite a shit-storm."

"Leave me alone!"

"You've made a lot of trouble for a lot of people."

"I've only gotten started!"

"It isn't what you think. Until two days ago, I knew nothing about what happened to Alyssa. I don't even work here. Ask Faye; she'll tell you where we've been working, if she hasn't already."

Janis stopped long enough to shout back. "You miserable piece of shit – don't lie to me! For once in your life, tell me the fucking truth. Man up to it – or can't you do that?"

Colin dragged the back of his hand across his bloody nose. "If you won't believe anything I say, then the truth is worthless."

"Then unlock the goddamn door and let me off this roof."

Colin took a step closer, his chest pumping with excited breaths. "I have to try. I don't want to but I know what's going to happen if I don't. Faye knows it too. She doesn't want to be here any more than you. She didn't join The Project because we're friends again. We're not. She joined because something bigger than all of us is happening. If we don't stop it, we have no future."

"That's right. Someone is trying to trigger a pandemic. For the good of the planet, they want to collapse the population. Would you happen to know who that might be?"

"You're jumping to conclusions."

"And you're a puppet. The people above you cherry-pick the facts for you."

"Like the thing in Kansas? The poultry virus? Is that the big pandemic you're talking about?"

Janis stomped off. "Why waste my time. You all hide behind a mask."

Colin ran after her, grabbed her arm and spun her around. She swung at him again. He caught and held her by the forearm. She struggled in his grip.

"I don't know if you're right or not. But let's say that you are. Is tipping your hand a good idea when the bet is so big?"

"Let me go!"

"All this 3rd Protocol bullshit is new to me. I've been locked in a hole, trying to figure out what sterilized a billion kids. You want the truth? OK, here it is. We kidnapped Alyssa to find out why she's the only one not affected. She's special, that's why she needed protection."

"Oh, really! Well, you manage to screw up everything, don't you. Protect her? She's lying in a coma!"

"I swear to you! Egg extraction is and never was part of The Project. Ask Faye, she'll tell you. She doesn't need to do that. You should know that. And even if we did, we've had Alyssa for over a month. We could have harvested an egg during her regular cycle. Think about it; we don't need dozens of eggs to study the DNA. Ask Rebecca; whoever did this took a lot of eggs."

"How do I know what you sick bastards are doing? As usual, they say The Project is one thing, but why waste an opportunity to do so much more."

"Why for God's sake would we risk the life of the one person in the world that might be the key to saving humanity? That's what we're talking about; because if we don't fix this, it's over in a generation." Colin let go of Janis.

"And what if it's all about delayed fertility? No one is really sterile; they just won't get fertile until age 25. It was designed that way, as you probably already know."

Colin stepped into her space. "You think The Project designed that? Is that the big 8-Ball conspiracy you like to talk about?"

"Or maybe it was designed 15 years ago by a secret group who wants to change the world. It's the same group Eugene Mass used to belong too, but he quit and bought NovoSenectus. Is that enough of a conspiracy for you?"

"Fifteen years ago?"

Janis yelled into his face. "Yeah, the group called it 1st Protocol. They used a suicide gene from a GAMA stolen from Naval Labs, a microbe that eats plastic. The same thing got dumped in the Sargasso Sea."

A flash of recognition hit Colin. "You know about that? You say a group engineered this 15 years ago."

"Don't look so surprised. It's the same group that's orchestrating these animal studies in Germany and Japan on animals – like the one in Kansas, all conveniently coming to the same conclusion – the explanation is delayed fertility."

"Did Knockout Mouse tell you this?"

Janis was startled. "How do you know that name?"

"After your stunt last night, we got permission to access everything, including your email. We checked the computer at Bright Hope Farms."

Janis turned and walked away. "It doesn't matter. Put me in jail. I'm not helping you."

"You won't work with Faye?"

"Faye works for you. What do you think?"

"Wait!" Colin ran after her. "There's something you have to know."

"Don't bother."

"It's something even Faye doesn't know."

"Just like you to keep secrets."

"It's about what happened 15 years ago."

"Let's not go there."

"It's not about us."

Janis halted and turned around. "It was never about us, was it?"

Colin ran a hand back through his hair in desperation. "I didn't want to do this. I wanted to stay in the background – let it be just you and Faye."

"Then why didn't you?"

Colin shouted, "Because it was the only way to get you down here to be with Alyssa! After what you did, they insisted I run everything directly. I didn't know if Alyssa was going to live. I owed it to you, at least to see her again."

Janis ignored the sentiment. "What didn't you tell Faye?"

"The reason why I didn't tell Faye is because I didn't think of it until a minute ago." Colin looked defeated. He stood in the middle of the roof with nowhere else to go but the truth. Surrendering to it, his body relaxed.

"So what is it?"

"I believe you." His statement contained all but said nothing.

"What?"

"I believe your conspiracy. I suppose Faye told you all about The Project…"

"Oh yeah, I know all about how you blackmailed Riya for *GenLET*. I've also heard about the master database you keep."

"You should also know that 15 years ago, I was part of a government project. It's not the project we argued about before the divorce. It's the one I couldn't tell you about. I had to help infiltrate a plot. Someone wanted to create a pandemic."

"Faye told me. She said you almost blew it. At the last minute, you had to scramble to sabotage the agent."

"That's right. We substituted a benign payload into the sputnik."

"I guess that explains why Faye and I argued so much at USAMRIID. We were given Ghyvir-C to study but something wasn't right with it. She preferred to ignore the signs. I didn't."

"It's worse than that."

Janis could see the color drain from Colin's face. He turned to face the western ocean. Limp with regret, he fought to bring himself to speak the words that had occurred to him only a minute before.

"You said something…you said the group called this thing 1st Protocol."

"So what?"

"I know what happened now. I know what went wrong."

"This just occurred to you?"

"Yeah. Stupid, huh?" Colin shook his head and looked to the sky. "No wonder we've all missed it for so long."

"What are you talking about?"

"The Group – the one Knockout Mouse told you about. I'll bet they're the same group my project was trying to uncover 15 years ago. The same group we sabotaged."

The realization hit Janis. "Oh my God – you sabotaged 1st Protocol."

"That was the plan. But now we know something went wrong."

"What could go wrong with a benign payload?"

"That's the billion dollar question – a dollar for every child now sterile."

"What are you saying?"

Colin turned to her. "I believe you. The Group wanted to release 1st Protocol. In secret, they wanted to delay fertility. My project went after their threat. We assumed they wanted to start a pandemic. We tried to sabotage it. But something went wrong. Something in the way we sabotaged it must have turned delayed fertility – into sterility."

The impact of it washed over them.

An added weight of remorse pressed down on Janis.

"You mean if you had just left it alone, all we'd be facing is delayed fertility."

Colin nodded acceptance of his confession.

Janis turned away, her gaze searching the ocean's horizon for clarity.

Colin explained. "No one knew the truth, neither The Group nor The Project. The Group thought everything was OK because delayed fertility wouldn't show up until the next generation came of age. The government project I was on concluded we had scored a big success. Obviously, the benign payload must have worked – there was no pandemic."

"That still doesn't explain what Eugene Mass is doing now."

Colin stepped up alongside her. "No, we don't know the answer to that. The Project was too busy swiping *GenLET* from him. Besides, it's hard to believe the unthinkable, especially when groups like New Class Order are shouting it."

Janis sighed. "It was all so unnecessary."

"It was an accident."

"An accident waiting to happen."

"It's not what we intended. I promise you, the payload was benign."

"If it was so benign, then how did it get changed?"

"I wish I knew."

"Does anybody know?"

"If they do, they're not telling me."

"We should be finding repressed fertility; instead, the children are sterile."

"I know, it doesn't make sense. We double checked the payload. We even gave it to primates to test it."

Janis flashed back to a memory. "So that's why at USAMRIID I found those requisitions for primate studies. One day they were on the computer, the next day they were gone."

"Yes. Someone forgot to lock down access rights. For a brief time, they were visible in your lab."

A puzzle piece dropped into place for Janis. She shook her head and gave a laugh. "Faye argued with me; told me I was being paranoid for thinking something else was going on. Why would primate studies be necessary for Ghyvir-C? Giant viruses infect amoebae, not humans."

Colin confessed, "We did test after test, before and after releasing the agent. We thought we were taking every precaution."

"Those primate studies – did they include a test to see if offspring of infected animals would be able to reproduce when they matured?"

"No."

"Of course not." Janis sighed away her frustration.

"Why of all things would we test for that; we didn't know."

"Unintended consequences from good intentions – that should be the last line written about human history."

"It's not over yet."

"Close enough. They're still out there."

"The Group?"

"The Group…and Mass. The Group has plans for a 2nd Protocol."

"To do what?"

"Put a cap on lifespan at age 70."

"That's insane!"

"Not if you believe extreme measures are necessary."

"Ridiculous. Some of them are probably older than that."

"Why should they care? In all likelihood, they have *GenLET* too."

For the longest while, the two of them stood side-by-side, staring out to sea.

Struck with a sense of completion and resignation, Colin reached into a pocket. He handed Janis a key.

"Here – to the stairwell. Do what you want."

Janis paused then took it. Holding it in hand, she didn't move. At first, the act of giving her the key seemed disjointed, but then she thought of all the follow-on messages he was sending her by offering her freedom. But freedom into what?

"If I walk down those stairs alone, what happens to me?"

"Every boss has a boss over him. That's the way it works."

"You can't guarantee a thing."

"Never could."

"I hate the way you manipulate people."

Colin shoved hands in pockets. "I don't make the rules and I don't control what others do. You made the wrong enemies by what you did last night. I have no power over that."

"Some choice – work with you or go away for life."

"You won't have to work with me. I'm not a lab rat. You'll hardly ever see me. But you'll see Alyssa. You'll get to work with Faye. More importantly, the two of you might come up with an answer."

"I'm not so sure the people above you would ever let us do that."

"Be realistic – they're all about power. If everyone's dead, where does that leave them?"

"I was told it's only a matter of time, one way or another – there *will* be a Phased Population Reduction. The government may not start it but if it happens, they'll damned well want to manage it for their own benefit. I can't be a part of that."

"Then don't. Concentrate on reversing sterility. Faye's convinced there are two keys to finding a fix – you and Alyssa."

"I'm not sure what to believe anymore."

"If it makes any difference to you, I read your email. Knockout Mouse sent you an answer earlier today. He wants to meet with you, says he has something for you."

Janis kept quiet. She thought back to her last email to him from Bright Hope Farms and the GAMA information Faye and her were interested in reviewing.

"Why not stay long enough to see what he's got? If you still want to walk out and take your chances afterwards, no one will stop you."

Janis thought about it. She had options but no real choice.

She handed back the key. "I expect no interference, no games."

"All right. Anything else?"

Janis started walking for the stairwell. "Yeah. You said I'd hardly ever see you. Keep your promise."

Colin unlocked the door and they returned to the top floor without another word said between them. Peeling off down a side hallway, he took the elevator down.

Janis headed straight away back to Alyssa's room. Faye and Rebecca were not around. That left Janis was alone with her thoughts, her feelings, and Alyssa.

She opened the drapes. Late afternoon sunlight filled the room.

Pulling up a chair, Janis sat down at Alyssa's bedside and held her hand.

They were on borrowed time but she resolved to make the best of it.

After all, it was borrowed time for everyone.

Chapter 34

Off the Coast of Madalena
Pico Island, Azores

Angelina Pena ran up from sleeping quarters to the fantail to check the wind. It was definitely blowing strong enough and best of all it was a headwind.

Delighted, she scampered to the pilot house.

"Papa! The wind is perfect!"

Carlos Pena knew what was coming but let silence be his first line of resistance.

Angelina's mother noted her daughter's new bikini.

"You put it on already?"

"Why not?" Angelina shrugged and smiled. She liked it when they put into port for refueling. It was the perfect excuse to go exploring and shopping. This time the precocious fifteen-year-old persuaded them to add a new swimsuit to her collection.

She hung onto the back of the pilot chair and persisted into Carlos' ear.

"We're going back tomorrow. This might be my last chance."

Knowing Carlos wouldn't want to disappoint, mother spoke up as the voice of reason. "I'm not sure that's a good idea; the boat's been acting up."

"No it hasn't," whined Angelina. "The man *said* it was OK."

"He saw black smoke."

Angelina appealed to her father. "What did he say, Papa?"

Carlos wouldn't lie to his daughter. "He said it could be a minor air restriction."

"But he checked it…"

"Yes, he did."

"And he said it's all right. There's no black smoke now."

Carlos glanced back at mother with the resignation of a father who could never say no to someone as sweet and determined as Angelina.

"All right…"

"Thank you, Papa!" She hugged him and kissed his cheek.

Carlos swung around in the pilot chair. "If mother will be so kind to be skipper and keep us in the wind…"

Mother grinned then nodded.

Angelina raced to get into harness as Carlos hooked up and positioned the apparatus on the swim platform at the fantail. The owners of the motor yacht had customized it with their very own parasailing gizmo. With enough speed and wind, an excitable fifteen-year-old could take flight off the stern and be towed along far up and behind the boat.

Carlos watched as his daughter donned a life vest. "Are you going to be warm enough up there? Remember last time; the breezes were quite chilly."

Angelina wavered. Carlos handed her one of his sweatshirts.

"Here…just in case."

Angelina put it on before the PFD. "You're probably right...."

Once in harness and securely clipped to the gizmo, Angelina was ready to launch.

She steadied herself in front of the parachute pack ready to deploy. Carlos signaled the pilot house and mother supplied more power to the engines.

Just like that, Angelina was swept backwards and up into the sky.

A squeal of delight could be heard as Carlos checked the tether lines feeding up and behind. With eyes upraised on his angel in flight, he watched cautiously over the controls and sea conditions. Above the furrowed wake, Angelina slipped higher and farther away. Carlos smiled. She was right; conditions were perfect.

Heart racing and grinning from ear-to-ear, Angelina took in the view and the rush of the parasailing glide. Before long, the motor yacht was small and distant, below and in front of her. All the ocean and the island of Pico were hers to see. In the distance, the looming prominence of Mount Pico pointed at the sky.

The wind was cool and invigorating and whipped through her legs and jostled her hair. She was thankful for the sweatshirt; the warmth of it would allow her to stay airborne so much longer in the chill.

In the worst way, she wanted this trip to last.

It had been so much fun but once it ended, she'd have to face a move to India. Would she like it there? It didn't seem to matter. That's where father was going to work. If she hated it, what would she do? Maybe they could put her in a boarding school back in Madrid. But would that be worse? There was so much to think about. She didn't want to have to be bothered with any of it.

She just wanted their vacation to go on forever.

A terrific explosion convulsed the air.

The impossible had happened.

She looked down but didn't believe it.

A fireball and smoke consumed the motor yacht below her.

Out of the burning cloud blasted shrapnel that once was her life.

She gasped wide-eyed and felt the tug of the boat no more.

Her tether was cut.

She was on her own.

CHAPTER 35

Sub-Basement of Building 3
GARC, Puerto Rico

"It's time."

"I know."

"You sure you want to go alone?"

"That's the only way he'll meet me."

Janis took off her lab coat and hung it to one side of her research station.

Faye snapped off rubber gloves and followed her into the airlock. "Did Colin back off?"

"You tell me. I don't talk to him."

They waited for bio-scans to complete. Faye was terse. "I can't see them passing up the opportunity for some surveillance."

Green-lighted clean, Janis stepped through. "I don't care if they watch from orbit; just as long as they stay out of sight."

They walked side-by-side into the freight elevator. "I still don't like it. Why does he have to meet in person? You asked for information, not a back rub."

Janis smirked as she glanced up at the RIDIS scan element in the ceiling. "I guess he doesn't trust technology; can you blame him?"

"He'd rather risk coming out in the open?"

"Maybe as far as he's concerned, anywhere is out in the open. There's no way left to hide – other than being inconsequential or irrelevant."

"Still, you can't be sure of his connections. Colin is right about one thing; you made enemies with what you posted. You're out there now; they know about you. They're not afraid to come after people."

"Don't you think I know that? I watched Riya die."

The elevator slowed to a stop. Faye wavered, having kept disturbing news to herself, fearful it might worry Janis. But the time had come. Faye could not hold it in any longer. This was her last chance to share it before Janis left. This was the last moment it might make a difference.

"Oliver Ross is dead. I heard it this morning. The news report says he hung himself in his cell while waiting for arraignment before the grand jury. Whatever he knew died with him."

The doors opened but Janis paused. "Don't worry; I have nothing more to post. Whatever I knew is already out there."

"What about revenge?"

"They're arrogant, not stupid."

"You think you're too high profile to be eliminated?"

"No. I think their plans are too far along for it to matter."

"How?"

"They're so close to the finish line, there's no point in looking back."

Faye held the doors from automatically closing. "Tell that to Oliver Ross."

"Why should they want revenge on me? Look at the way it's all been twisted. I thought posting everything would expose them; all it did was give them more conspiracy stories to hide behind. No one takes it seriously. The world is upside down. I should have known that exposing the villain would only make him a victim. Eugene Mass has gotten more sympathy than anything."

"Then why get rid of Ross? *Somebody's* taking it seriously."

Janis' lack of response was telling. She watched the concern on Faye's face until necessity drove her to stride forward. There was no time to second-guess vital things already in motion. It was time to see Knockout Mouse.

Her drive north alone was uneventful but the last part of the trip was tricky.

Janis slowed the car. The street narrowed as it bisected an airport from a golf course. To her right was the end of the runway; to her left a fairway. As instructed, she turned left onto a road that drove through the golf course.

Strangely, the path literally cut across several fairways until it curved into a tree line. Beyond the trees it became a dirt trail. The car crawled along over rocks and ruts until it neared the beach and her destination – the Borinquen Lighthouse Ruins.

The old Borinquen lighthouse was built in the late 1800s by the Spanish. In 1918 it was virtually destroyed by an earthquake and then tidal wave. All that was left standing were a couple stone walls and crumbles of foundation pieces in the sand. There were no other cars around. She appeared to be alone. It was an ominous sign. Had he not come or had someone intercepted him along the way?

Janis sat behind the wheel with the doors locked for several minutes. She waited for someone else to drive up or someone to show. At the first sign of trouble, she could start the car and at least attempt an escape. All of Faye's caution came back to her. Oliver Ross was dead. How many more would die? If someone was willing to kill six billion people for the good of the planet, it made no difference how many had to be killed to ensure the plan was successful.

With resolve waning, Janis reached for the key to start the car. Just then, motion caught her eye. Up from the beach, a man walked from behind the walls of the ruins. At a distance, she couldn't be sure who he was. She had only seen Knockout Mouse once, but the scrappy odd man was not someone she was likely to forget. His most distinctive feature was a rugged but cartoonish face but at this distance, all was a blur under a baseball cap.

She couldn't blink. She watched his every move. It wasn't until the man had entered the ruins and faced the car directly that she knew. It was him. He looked out of place wearing faded black jeans and dark sneakers in the tropics. Onshore gusts rippled a T-shirt. Just looking at him, he could have been stowaway from a merchant ship thrown overboard and washed up with nowhere to go.

Janis got out of the car and walked over to him. Content that they had made contact, he turned and strolled back to the sea side of the ruins.

Janis was curious. "Where did you come from?"

As usual, he couldn't repress his idiot savant. "I wasn't created, that's for sure. I think I emerged – from that airport over there."

"No car?"

"No need. I walked over. I'm not here you know. I'm nowhere."

"You had to fly in."

"I was unlisted cargo. I have a friend in FedEx." He stepped off into the sand. "Let's go down on the beach. Ruins are depressing."

"Then why did you want to meet here?"

He gave the old stones a long glance. "They remind me where we're heading."

Janis thought twice but followed.

Once on the beach, he stopped and looked out to sea. "Nice place for a vacation. But that's not what you're doing here, is it?"

Janis said nothing.

He added, "I didn't think so. You're not about to whip up a batch of plastic-eating microbes, are you?" He noted Janis' continual silence then reached into a pocket. "Oh, yeah, here…" He handed her a flash drive, "…that's everything I've got."

"Thanks." She took it but on impulse, sought clarity. "Why give to me in person? You could have sent it."

"I wanted to talk to you. I needed to get away."

"Really? I thought you were good at excuses. Why are you helping me?"

"Why? The one question we've never been able to answer. Why me? Why us? Why are we here? Why are you working for the U.S. government at GARC?"

Janis' gaze raced to his.

He smiled. "Yes, I know. Why else would you be on this side of the island?"

The intensity of the situation surged up in a need to reveal. "They have my daughter."

All humor dropped from his face. "And now they have you."

"You don't understand. I've seen what they're working on."

"You've seen what they've shown you."

The thought of it crushed down on Janis' heart. "All of you think you're so clever. You crazy bastards have fucked it up for everybody!"

"Which bastards are you talking about? There are so many."

"The Group, the government, 8-Ball, whatever you call it, Eugene Mass…"

"We're not all doing the same thing…"

"Yes, you are! You all think you know better than everyone else."

"Well, you're right about that."

Janis stepped close. "You told me The Group released 1st Protocol to delay fertility. That's why they needed the GAMA, for the suicide gene."

"Yes. Those same crazy bastards have 2nd Protocol about ready."

"It won't matter."

"It won't matter how?"

"All the children are sterile! It's not delayed fertility that's happening."

"That can't be…" He saw the tears in her eyes.

"Fifteen years ago, a government team sabotaged 1st Protocol by substituting in a payload they thought would do nothing. But something went wrong. I've seen the evidence. My ex-husband was on that team. Remember codename SENEX?"

Knockout Mouse looked back at the restless sea. He laughed.

"If that's true, that makes 3rd Protocol redundant! Mass is about to collapse a population that's coming to an end anyway."

"Yeah, hilarious isn't it?"

"Who knows, maybe it's a good thing – puts humanity out of its misery. Imagine having life extension but knowing you can't reproduce. That's a fucking long time to wait for nothing but the bitter end."

"How dare you say anything of this could be a good thing!"

His mind raced. "That would also explain why the government used GARC for their operation to steal *GenLET*. It seems all along the sly bastards were also using the *GenLET* operation as a cover for getting close to the 1st Protocol lab."

"What lab?"

"The basement of Building Three."

"That's where I'm working now."

"Final synthesis of 1st Protocol was done there. We knew the government was running RIDIS out of GARC. We also knew they were using RIDIS as an excuse to frame Riya. The government wanted *GenLET*. But they weren't the only ones. We let them use GARC to get *GenLET* so we could steal it from them."

"Who are you talking about? The Group?"

"Yes."

"They have *GenLET* too? My god, who *doesn't* have *GenLET*?"

"Just those without the money, power, or resources to take it – I'd say that's about six billion people."

"How did The Group have access to GARC?"

"Oh, that's right. I never told you."

"Told me what?"

"A member of The Group holds a controlling interest in GeLixCo; he owns it."

Janis was rooted to the spot. "Who is it?"

Knockout Mouse considered his options.

"In over twenty years, I've never betrayed The Group, not really. I've kept their secrets and did what they asked. But it's gone too far. I can't do it any more." He stepped closer to the waves. "That's why I had to come here in person."

Janis followed after him, persistent. "Who is it?"

"Who? Curtis Labon, of course."

"The same Labon mentioned in Mass' memo? The one behind Oliver Ross at the lab in Kansas?"

He nodded. "The same one behind delayed fertility studies in animals. Labon was supposed to produce one of three studies to explain what was happening."

"But if Labon knows what's going on at GARC, he must know about sterility."

"He might or might not; it all depends on what kind of security the government has wrapped around it. He certainly knows you're here. He may not know why."

"But he must know my daughter is here."

"People are harder to hide than project secrets. Especially if she's been the focus of any attention, he has to know."

Janis felt rage rise up in her again. "He must be the one who did it."

"What?"

"Alyssa's in a coma from accelerated egg extractions."

For a moment, surprise replaced all swagger. "How is she?"

"They don't know. They say she's stable. There's only so much they can do."

Knockout Mouse took a moment to consider those in play. "Whoever would do such a thing knew they'd have cover. There are too many hands in the fire. If you make the wrong assumption, you'll get burned."

A drifting cloud unveiled the sun. Janis squinted into the glare. "I'm beyond the need to trust. It's down to things very basic for me now."

Knockout Mouse followed her line of sight. He watched the cloud begin to dissipate in the air currents. "I know what you mean."

"In your business, I can't see there being any trust."

"What exactly is my business? All these years, I don't think I've had any."

"You did whatever The Group told you to do."

"Not any more."

"You're not afraid of them?"

"I think I'm finally more afraid of what I've become."

"Malcolm Stowe blackmailed you for most of your life. That only worked because you were so loyal to them. You wanted to protect them."

"I was also afraid of what they would do. If he had exposed me as the one who gave LALO the GAMA, I would have been worse than an embarrassment to them. They don't want liabilities on their balance sheet. I was young; I wanted a life."

"And now?"

"I've seen everything from life extension to killer plagues up close. I know better."

"What changed?"

"I realize I'd rather live one meaningful day than have a long life living a lie."

"It's getting harder to do that any more."

"It has to start somewhere." Knockout Mouse turned to her. "I told you up in Vermont that I was going to try to get a hold of 2nd Protocol. That's why I had to come here in person – to tell you. I got it and not just the base. I got the whole thing. I had to face you and see if you were willing to take it and work on it."

"I told you in the boathouse – there's nothing I can do with 2nd Protocol."

"Find a way to stop it! Use it to do some good."

"Easier said than done. Even if I wanted to, I'm not in the position to do anything. You want me to give it to the government?"

"Fuck no! Why give it to nameless people without faces. I didn't steal it from monsters just to give it to the beast."

"I don't have my own lab. What would I do with it?"

"How you use it is up to you. We need to try something, to set things right."

"What about exposing The Group? Go to the authorities with it; give them names and the evidence to put them away."

"Like you, I'm beyond trust. You forget, I've been on the inside with them for many years. I've seen the way they own the authorities."

"Then give *me* the names and the evidence."

"Oh yeah, maybe we should post it all on the web for everyone to see. We know how well that turns out."

The reference to Mass' memo was succinct. Janis felt the sting of sarcasm. "2nd Protocol caps lifespan. I don't know what to do with that."

He challenged her. "Oh, but you know what to do with sterility?"

Janis was taken aback. To be accused of a double standard was missing the main distinction. Working on the fix for sterility involved extinction, and Alyssa. She would not leave her daughter.

Knockout Mouse paced the sand. "What the hell are you working on in the lab? If you don't want to play god then why did you come willingly to Mount Olympus?"

"It was the only way to be with Alyssa."

"Excuse me for saying so, but there's a hell of a lot more at stake and you know it. If you didn't think so, then why risk everything, dragging around Malcolm's laptop? Why take the heat testifying before Congress?"

"That was about Mass, about collapsing the population."

"So what are you working on here? A vaccine for 3rd Protocol? A way to stop the population collapse? No! If that's what matters to you, then why do you work for them on something else?"

Janis turned away. "They brought me here. They thought she was dying."

"Excuse me once again, but join the club."

"There's only so much I can do!"

Knockout Mouse raced around in front of her and grabbed her by the shoulders. "Then look me in the eye and tell me you're not staying here for any other reason than Alyssa. You're not playing god in the lab. You're not trying to reverse sterility. Is that what they told you?"

Janis turned to turn away. Knockout Mouse wasn't about to let up.

"What kind of conviction do you have? What does it take to convince you; serious shit is about to happen if someone doesn't take a chance to stop it? How can you walk away from 2nd Protocol when you might be the only one who can help? Does a clear conscience come that easily to you? I guess everything comes too easily for you!"

His last words hit her hard – everything comes too easily for you.

She jerked from his grasp and pushed him back.

"How dare you berate me! You've been a mouse all your life, running the maze just the way The Group wanted you to. Don't lecture me about what needs to be done. Where were you the last twenty years while these assholes were making their plans?"

The words were harsh. Knockout Mouse backed away and stared at her.

"Do whatever the fuck you think you have to. You got what you wanted on the GAMA. Go play god with it. If you change your mind about 2nd Protocol, let me know." He turned and walked away.

Janis stood a long while and watched him go. She never expected his abrupt departure. With an ache in her chest she wanted to call out after him but couldn't. Something held her back. He had made her feel like a hypocrite and a coward. Worse of all, he had echoed what Faye had said.

Everything comes too easily for you.

The anger and hurt was too raw. She wouldn't give him the satisfaction.

She also couldn't fathom what she would ever do if given a BSL4 agent that capped lifespan. The offer was immense, if overwhelming.

The only way she would ever be able to work on such a thing was in a proper lab. To do that now meant taking it to Faye and the government Project. But that didn't guarantee anything. That didn't mean they'd let her work on it and devise a way to combat it.

Chances are, they'd thank her and then take it away to be handled in secret by others. If that were the case, neither she nor Knockout Mouse could ever be sure what was being done with it. What might The Project learn from 2nd Protocol that could be used in a different way?

Once again, the specter of dual-use deception gave Janis pause.

Knockout Mouse didn't trust the beast. And neither did she. The last time The Project tried to set things right by sabotaging 1st Protocol, sterility resulted.

She'd be damned before she'd give them 2nd Protocol.

After a few minutes, she walked up the beach to the ruins.

She strolled through the crumbled foundation and rested a hand on one of the remaining walls. The cracked and weathered stone was beautiful but abrasive.

The day had turned to debris, her confidence in shambles.

All around was devastation.

CHAPTER 36

Comme Chez Soi Restaurant
Place Rouppe 23, Brussels

The limousine pulled up in front of the restaurant on time for 8 p.m. reservations. Eugene Mass considered the golden light from the familiar windows with fading fascination. An extended meeting near The Grand Place had left him reflective and tired. He wanted nothing more than to settle in for some good food and wine. Whether out on the town or at home, it didn't matter.

Leah wanted to go out for the evening and so here he was.

As he prepared to exit the car, he wondered if she had been seated already.

In the moment it took to wait for the driver to open up the rear door, the phone rang. Mass considered ignoring it but decided to check caller-id.

It was Samuels from the lab. A call this late in the evening was unexpected. The limo door opened but Mass held up a hand. Seeing that Mass needed a minute, the driver closed the door and waited outside.

Mass accepted the call. "Samuels, working late?"

"Sorry to bother you sir but it was necessary."

"According to whom?"

"It's about the tests your wife wanted."

Mass settled back with a bit more curiosity. "Yes…?"

"I thought you should know, the results are identical to Jayden's."

"Are you talking about sterility?" Astonished, Mass failed to mask his alarm.

"Yes. All three cases came back the same."

"And what about their parents?"

"Same as before. Unaffected."

Mass took a disquieted moment to absorb all it might mean. The timing of the news couldn't have been worse. He sighed with aggravation. "Does Leah know?"

"Yes, sir. She checked in with us this afternoon."

"What a coincidence."

"Not really, sir. She's been following test milestones all along. She was well aware we might be getting results today."

Mass closed his eyes to let them rest. "All three children…were they given the same therapy regimen as their parents?"

"Yes, they all got the same *GenLET*."

"From the same facility?"

"No, one child came to the lab. The other two went to a clinic."

"Of course, you've kept all of this to yourself."

"Yes, sir. The subjects believe it was a routine follow-up exam."

Mass opened his eyes. "Good. We wouldn't want them alarming the others."

"No, sir."

Focused on pressing but grim necessity, Mass switched to damage control. "This is only one test so let's not jump to conclusions. We'll need to find another way to verify this. You should get started with that right away."

"If I may suggest, I believe we might want to broaden the next round of tests to include many more subjects. Looking at three children from the same city is a token effort if we want to nail this down."

It was not the suggestion Mass wanted to hear; in fact, it sounded like something Leah herself might have suggested to the lab earlier in the day. Mass was infuriated that Samuels would try to offer it up as his own idea.

"If you think it was such a token effort, then why are you wasting my time calling me this late with results?"

"I just meant…"

"You have results that don't prove anything? Is that what you're saying?"

"Ah, no sir. I didn't mean to imply…"

Mass cut him off. "Token efforts are made to placate people. Is that what you think we're doing?" By getting Samuels to deny the truth, Mass laid down a plausible cover for the little support he had given to the tests. If anything, he looked upon them as little more than fallout from Leah's psychosomatic troubles.

"No, sir."

"Has it occurred to you that the more people we involve in these tests, the greater suspicion we'll generate in the overall population of *GenLET* recipients? We can't afford a culture of doubt developing within the *GenLET* community."

"I agree."

"Then you must also agree that your findings, while interesting, only raise more questions. The prime question I see concerns the parents of the subjects. If *GenLET* therapy caused the sterility, then why aren't the parents affected? Do you know?"

"Not yet."

"And that's the problem. These children were born before their parents received *GenLET*, weren't they?"

"Why yes, of course."

"Are you the only one missing the logic of this? If *GenLET* caused the sterility, then you need to find out why it hasn't made the parents sterile."

"It's a much more difficult proposition but plans for that are underway."

"Good."

"One more thing, sir. Until we get final answers, I recommend we restrict *GenLET* therapy to adults only."

"Sounds reasonable. The children will have lots of time to get it later. There's no sense causing unwarranted alarm. We risk less suspicion if we shut down only part of the program instead of all of it."

"My thoughts exactly. And we do have confidentiality agreements in place."

"Is that all?"

"Yes, sir."

"Then you know what to do…." Mass added a false smile to his voice. "By the way, Samuels, thanks for the heads-up. I'd rather hear such things from you first."

Mass ended the call before Samuels could answer.

The impertinence of hired scientists irritated Mass to no end. But he needed them and in this case; wanted them on his side. Leah was campaigning behind the scenes for a moratorium on *GenLET* and 3rd Protocol. He couldn't let her jeopardize either program needlessly. If there was a problem, fix it, but do so in a way that preserved the overall plan. If that meant token studies to placate a worried wife, so be it. Of course the tests were limited in scope; just as Mass wanted. The very least should be done, whatever would calm Leah and put the issue to rest.

The problem was – he never expected any of it to find a real cause for concern.

He stepped out of the car suddenly burdened, in no way ready for the drama of having to argue what must be done now. Entering the restaurant, he was recognized at once by the receptionist and promptly shown to the private dining room.

Leah sat amidst hardwoods and china and inspected a menu.

Mass was abrupt. "I hope you ordered for us."

"I did." Leah didn't look up.

Mass took his seat. "What are we having?"

"Sole stuffed with crab, shrimp in tarragon sauce, the usual trimmings."

"And the wine?"

"Something appropriate."

The casual banter was awkward but welcomed by both. Neither wanted to argue, especially in public. The dining room was private but the venue was public. Wait staff would be coming and going. It could never be certain what someone might overhear. Both had so much to say yet felt constrained. On the other hand, the limits imposed by such a setting might help them avoid what otherwise could be heated and ugly. They settled in to their meal knowing full well that the rhythm to their civility was artificial, the structured peace between them fragile.

Leah spoke to Eugene's tension. "You seem preoccupied."

"Do I?" Mass gave his appetizer his undivided attention.

"I take it you got a call from Samuels." Leah held her fork up, suspended mid-motion, and awaited a response.

Mass looked up. He hoped to short-circuit an unpleasant scene by summing up, straight to the point. "I know all about it. I agreed to his recommendation to restrict ongoing therapy to adults. I instructed him to verify the results with additional tests."

Leah finished taking a bite of food. Her gaze dropped in disappointment. "You don't seem surprised."

Mass reached for his wine. "Of course I am."

"How could you be? You're still allowing adult therapy go ahead."

"They found no problem with the adults."

"But you've asked for more tests. Obviously, you don't think they know enough. If that's so, then all therapy should stop until we know for sure."

"Likewise, we shouldn't panic anybody. A sudden stoppage might do just that."

"You're worried about how it might look? At a time like this?"

"A time like what?"

Leah pressed her napkin to her lips to hold back emotion. "Think about what this means. Hundreds of children have gotten the therapy. We don't even know what it might be doing to the parents. Anything else you've created with the same research can't be trusted."

The veiled reference to 3rd Protocol hit home but Mass was fatigued by the day.

The weight of the news conspired with Leah and the wine to disarm him. Left defenseless, he could only plead his case.

"What would you have me do? Stop everything? Give up on *everything*?"

Leah straightened her posture. "Would it be so terrible?"

"You really mean everything. You'd let the population spiral into the perfect storm. How can you abandon New World Harmony?"

"Simple. I've gotten a good look at the means to the ends."

"You see it as so unthinkable but you're only looking at one side. What if we *don't* go through with this? You want to trade the unthinkable for the horrific?"

"You don't know that."

"I most certainly do. How do you want to spend the next fifty thousand days of extended life? What kind of life will it be if we let the planet go down in flames?"

Leah shook her head. "What you're suggesting is too big to control. There's no way you can know for sure how it would all turn out."

"No one ever does, with anything."

"Nothing goes as planned. Why is your plan any different?"

"I refuse to be a defeatist. If everyone thought your way, nothing would get accomplished. I try because someone has to. You know what's going on. You know where it's headed. Not so long ago you were with me; you wanted to do it."

"I can't even think about it now. How could I do it?"

"It's the lesser of two evils."

Leah stared at him. "So you admit it's evil."

"No more evil than amputating arms and legs to save the body."

"You are so good at using ethics to justify mayhem. If only you could be sure. But you can't. No one can."

"Stopping things in motion can be just a difficult as getting something going."

Leah saw an opening. "It doesn't have to be. You have plenty of excuses. Carlos Pena is dead. You can say you have to stop the program while you find another geneticist for the top spot."

"That could take a while. Recruiting isn't what it used to be. People are afraid of being the next target."

"What about the quick-therapy modalities? Janis was working on those but didn't finish. You know she's not coming back. You can say we need time for someone else to get up to speed and finish her work. Tell people we're switching to the quick-therapy method and we'll resume therapy as soon as it's done."

"And never finish it. Is that your idea?"

"No." Leah waited until a waiter came and went. "I'm not for stopping *GenLET*. I'm for fixing it. I only want to stop the other thing."

"The other thing."

"Yes."

In public, neither of them were about to mention 3rd Protocol by name.

"Even if we solve the problem? Even if we rule out its involvement?"

Leah nodded. "Fix *GenLET*. Stop everything else."

"You're not thinking it through."

"And you're assuming too much."

Mass considered his choices. If test results had been different, their conversation would have been so easy. As it was, an unease tempered his brashness.

"All right. I'm willing to put everything on hold pending the outcome of tests. I agree with you; we have to find out what's going on with sterility. But once we work that out and have an explanation or fix, then everything's back on the table. We both have to take a hard look at what kind of future we want. Is it a deal?"

Leah accepted his concern as genuine. Finally, she was sensing an effort to compromise. No doubt the shock of the test results had brought him to the table. No longer dismissing her apprehension, if anything he seemed shaken that a wider problem, beyond Jayden, had been discovered. She wondered; was there more to it?

"Yes, but I'm curious. Why be so conciliatory?"

Mass set down his fork. "I guess I'm tired. Overly tired."

"There's something else. You're worried about something. What is it?"

He thought twice about sharing. "It may be nothing."

"Maybe…" Leah held her gaze on him.

"It's just that we might not be the only ones willing to do something."

"Do something how? You mean social reordering?"

"Yes. Along the lines we were planning."

"What makes you say that?"

Mass leaned back. "Oliver Ross is dead."

"But that's old news."

He rocked forward and whispered. "I spoke with Javier. It wasn't him."

The full meaning hit Leah and set her on edge. If Javier had not succeeded with the hit on Ross, then what should they conclude about his death?

She opted to deny snap judgments. "The official report says it was suicide."

"I think someone else is in the game – and they're not afraid to go all the way."

"In what way?"

"I imagine in every way."

"Is it The Group?"

"Who else?"

"Why now? Why would they change and act this way."

"Don't forget; Curtis' name was on the memo. And it's now public. He has to have seen it. How would The Group react to that? Especially when we had the media spin it to say the leaked material was nothing but a smear campaign against me."

For Leah, the dominoes started falling. "Orchestrated by GeLixCo."

"Yes, with a little help, it didn't take long for the press to connect a name like Labon with GeLixCo."

"My God, I never thought The Group would react this way to the exposure. Still, having Labon's name out there draws attention to them."

Mass added, "The one, absolute thing that must never happen."

For Leah, the implications filled her with unsettling dread. Eugene had narrowly avoided one assassination attempt in India. Then Carlos Pena's boat had blown up. Now Oliver Ross' suicide might have been planned by others.

If The Group had abandoned their long-held reservations on aggressive behavior and tactics, what else might they be planning? Had The Group finally come to the same conclusion that caused Mass to split with them so many years ago?

"Too bad Malcolm is dead. He could have leveraged the Mouse to find out so much more from the inside. Aren't you curious how the kid might be reacting to changes in The Group?" Leah couldn't help broaching a sore subject between them.

Mass resented the injection of Malcolm and the information gained from blackmail. He ignored it and returned to his food.

"It might not matter if I put our projects on hold. The need to do something probably has occurred to someone else. Someone with the means to see it through."

The suggestion dismayed Leah. After convincing Eugene to a moratorium on 3rd Protocol, the specter of a rising menace from The Group was disturbing. Worst of all, what if they now agreed with him? Were they ready to take desperate action to save a planet in peril – even at the cost of something horrific? If so, containing what might happen next was no longer up to Leah and Eugene Mass.

Unable to accept it, Leah fought to find logic to diffuse the threat. "There's no way of knowing how much of the violence is being done by New Class Order. André Bolard is much bolder and more militant."

"Yes, but NCO can't be behind all of it. They had no reason to go after Ross."

Leah was done with dinner. She was done with so many things. "All the more reason to stop this. It's time to step back from the edge."

"And what if you're wrong? What if we fail to seize the one moment we could have made a difference? Think about the legacy we're building."

"We'll be all right," insisted Leah. "Look how easily everything that Janis posted was disregarded. People don't believe you could do such a thing. Let that work to our advantage."

Mass sneered. "It took a lot of work behind the scenes to get people to realize that easy conclusion."

"Perception is what we say it is. Opinion becomes reality. Use that to buy us time so we can finish the testing. Regardless what The Group may be doing, we have to find out what's going on with the children."

Mass finished his wine. "If the problem's real, there's only one thing I think it could be – but I hesitate to even say it." His mood sunk somber and grave.

"What are you talking about?"

"It just occurred to me – the cause of the sterility."

Leah was wide-eyed. She never expected Eugene to admit he took the subject seriously, let alone offer up an explanation for why it was happening.

"Tell me," she demanded.

Mass let the moment ride on the weight of what he was about to say. "What if sterility results from a bad interaction – *GenLET* and 1st Protocol."

Leah was stunned. "But The Group couldn't have planned it that way; 1st Protocol was complete long before *GenLET* was developed."

"Even worse. Somehow, maybe it affects only the offspring…"

Leah gasped, "If that's true, then *GenLET* is a dead end – it can only be used on people over fourteen years old. What will we do?"

Mass finished his wine. "Disturbing isn't it. A plan can be defeated. But chaos knows no bounds. The future might get away from us no matter what we try."

CHAPTER 37

Spa Club
Financial District, New York

Curtis Labon got up off the massage table, put on a robe, and stepped into slippers. After an hour of bodywork he was relaxed but remained agitated. So far, the evening diversion at the spa wasn't helping his mood. The body was willing but the mind wouldn't release all it held onto.

A steam-infused sauna was the last thing to try. The spa closed in less than an hour; more than enough time to sweat away the remnants of the day. Curtis returned to his locker and traded the robe for a wraparound towel. He found the sauna hot and deserted, just as he had hoped.

Lounging back on the hot tiles, he let the steam's intensity become a sweltering meditation. Silence and seclusion settled around him and purified the moment. The heat could not be ignored. In demanding his attention, it added quiet to his mind.

A timeless passage of silent warmth flowed through and around him. In reality, only a few minutes had passed. The door opened and the sanctuary was no longer solitary. Curtis opened his eyes on the sound and sized up the man coming towards him. Annoyance became surprise when he realized the man was Hasuru Tamasu.

Curtis was in no mood for greetings. "Where did you come from?"

Hasuru sat down on opposite tiles and adjusted his towel. "I was hoping to talk to you after the benefit tonight. You left early so I asked around and found you here."

Curtis used both hands to wipe sweat from his face. "Remind me to better cover my tracks next time."

"Any reason you're keeping to yourself?"

"Am I?"

"You missed the last Group meeting."

"No I didn't. Which one?"

"The one right after the Senate hearings."

Curtis closed his eyes. "Oh, that. Wasn't that optional? It was all discussion. Nothing needed to be voted on."

"You've never passed up a chance to discuss things before."

"I've never had so much to contend with before."

Hasuru got to the point. "You mean the memo."

"As I remember, your name wasn't on it."

"I never took you for one who worried about conspiracy theories."

Curtis rolled his head on the tile so he could look straight at Hasuru. "I'm concerned about the publicity, as you should be. The memo connected me with Ross. And the other material that got posted was mostly old think tank studies that Group members commissioned years ago. Don't you see? Mass let this stuff leak out hoping to expose us or if that didn't work, at least disrupt what we're doing."

"I'd be more concerned if there was more reaction. So far, people don't know what to believe. They have a short attention span anyway."

"You think that's good? We don't need them so curious this close to us."

"What are you afraid of – blowback against GeLixCo?"

Curtis leaned forward and raised his voice. "Didn't you read the memo? Do you think it's fake? I don't. Everything it talks about checks out. We know how Mass uses Javier. He obviously bought off Ross. The last time I checked, a poultry virus was not part of delayed fertility studies. He flat-out talks about 3rd Protocol."

"Yeah, and the government stopped him before he could trigger it. They have the virus now. They can study it. Mass can't release the same virus; he wouldn't be sure if the government was waiting with a vaccine."

"And that's it? It's over? Why a poultry virus? It doesn't make sense. What went on in Kansas couldn't have been 3rd Protocol."

Hasuru gave his head a shake. "You know very well what Mass was doing. He wanted 3P to be blamed on a U.S. biodefense lab. And what better lab to pick than the one where you are running a project. To him, it sweetens the pot."

"So Mass just walks away. Game over."

"No, but you're talking about two different things. What Mass is up to with 3P is one thing. Whether or not the memo and the crap that got posted on the Internet is a threat to us is something else."

"Aren't you worried about either one of them?"

"Sure! What do you think? Mass is not going to give up. He'll regroup. But it'll take time; I imagine quite a bit of time. He has to come up with a variant, something new he can be sure they haven't prepared for."

"There's no relief in that." Curtis sat back. "We have confirmation that he got close to doing it for real. The idea of population collapse is no longer hypothetical. It almost happened. Why do you think all the media are saying the memo was fabricated by GeLixCo as part of a smear campaign against its major competitor?

Hasuru shrugged. "The government probably needs to set up GeLixCo to take the fall in case the U.S. theft of *GenLET* gets discovered."

Curtis paused. The idea hadn't occurred to him before but it was plausible.

Hasuru prompted, "So why the smear campaign?"

"Because it hides the fact that the memo is real. That keeps the field of play open for Mass. Mass needs that memo to be fake to keep the heat off of him."

"To be expected if he wants to regroup. But the heat isn't off. He knows it. You made sure of that when you convinced Oliver Ross to commit suicide." Hasuru waved off Curtis' impulse to explain. "Don't bother denying it. The Group knows you were behind it."

"Who said I was going to deny it? Ross had to go; he was the only one at the lab in Kansas who could connect me with the delayed fertility studies. The Group was adamant about that, remember? The three reports shouldn't be traceable back to us. I wasn't covering only for myself. I was protecting The Group."

"That's not the only heat you've supplied. We know about the assassination attempt in India. By now you have Mass worried and confused. He needs to figure out who's after him. That's even more of a problem, one that makes him a greater danger. Without a certain target, he might be forced to shatter-shot at all of us."

Curtis tried to read Hasuru's expression but it was impenetrable.

"So why have you followed me here? To tell me The Group is displeased?"

"They're displeased about being kept in the dark. You're now operating on your own, no discussion, no voting. And the actions you're taking are not minor."

"The Group has never shown interest nor the will to make the hard decisions."

Hasuru sneered. "Excuse me, but that sounds like Mass talking."

"No one is all good or bad. Mass has his strengths. To deny that is to underestimate him. If you have something to say, say it. I think I've had enough of the heat in here."

"Very well. The Group would like to know what you're hiding in Puerto Rico, at the research center."

"Wow, just like that. Am I under surveillance?"

"You weren't – until your personal couriers started visiting GARC."

"I see. And since when were our personal couriers on The Group's agenda?"

"They weren't – until they started carrying materials labeled as biohazard."

Curtis grinned. "Amazing how you knew that without surveillance."

For Curtis, provocation met irritation. He stood and headed to the door.

Hasuru braced himself. "They need to know. What are you going to do next?"

"I'm going to take a shower." Curtis paused in the doorway. "If you want to know more, you'll have to follow me. This place closes in twenty minutes."

The two of them walked into the shower room. Curtis dropped his towel and stepped into the cooling spray.

Intent on getting an answer, Hasuru joined him under the next nozzle.

Curtis closed his eyes. Jets of water cascaded onto his head and down his back. "First of all, you have to realize. The Group is no longer viable. It's useless, passé. Events have overtaken it. We have to be realistic about what's going on."

Hasuru didn't respond. It was more important to listen.

Curtis rubbed his face awake and spat out a mouthful of water. "I'll tell you the truth because I consider you a friend. But if you can't keep what I tell you a secret, then dry off and leave me alone. It's your choice."

Hasuru stood motionless, oblivious to the shower hitting his back. "No matter what you tell me, it stays between us? How can I do that? Why would I do that? Why won't you share what you know with The Group?"

"I told you. They don't matter. They can only get in the way."

"Under those conditions, why tell me? You don't want a partner."

Curtis turned and stepped out of the spray. The two men stood face to face. "I'm not alone on this because I walked away. I'm alone because the rest of them stopped walking with me. I have no reason to exclude you."

"All right. Then tell me. Between you and me."

Curtis looked around to make sure they were alone. "A United States biodefense team has Alyssa Insworth at GARC. They're studying her. They're the same ones who kidnapped her."

"What for?"

"I've been trying to find out. The secrecy around the project is like nowhere else. You would think the owner of GeLixCo could find out what's happening in his own research lab but all I get are cover stories. I've had to piece it together."

"But you did find something?"

"Some of the team down there are the same ones who worked on swiping *GenLET* from NovoSenectus. It makes sense it has something to do with *GenLET*."

"But why Alyssa?"

"She's Janis' daughter. Janis co-created *GenLET* with Riya Basu. You know whatever advances Mass developed for *GenLET*, Janis has to know about them."

"What advances? You mean quick-therapy approaches Janis was working on?"

"Possibly, but I don't think so. It has to be something to warrant all the rushing around and trouble they've gone to in setting things up and maintaining secrecy."

Hasuru stepped closer. "Then what?"

"I've narrowed it down. It can only be one thing. It has to be the solution to Mass' greatest problem."

"What the hell is that?"

Curtis held up his hands in revelation.

"How to protect *GenLET* people from the plague of 3rd Protocol."

"Immunity?"

"Yes. Janis must have devised a way to build in 3P immunity inside *GenLET*."

"Inside?" Hasuru had to process the idea.

"Sure, why not? They don't have to be two separate things. We always suspected Mass would develop an immunity agent for 3P if he decided to go that far; it only makes sense if he wanted to release an agent of that magnitude in the wild. Why not package them together. One therapy does both?"

"I see that but what's that got to do with the daughter?"

"Janis and Riya were Mass' top scientists. They gave him the fountain of youth. Of course he let them drink from it. If for no other reason, he would want their experience and talents with him for as long as possible in the future. And you know Janis didn't get extended life without also giving it to her daughter."

"Then the U.S. should have kidnapped Janis. She'd be more valuable to them."

"Who said they didn't try? We'll never know what really happened in the park in Hyderabad. Was it a busted operation? Janis testified to the Indian police that she saw three men in the getaway car. Three men to grab one girl? No, they wanted both of them but something went wrong. They had to settle for Alyssa – until recently."

Hasuru showed surprise. "They have both of them now?"

"Yes, Janis is there. Now you know it has to be something critical if they were willing to step on Indian authorities to get her."

Hasuru took a moment to patch things together.

"That might explain the increased activity around GARC. The same surveillance we had on your couriers picked up a surge of other activity."

"Makes sense. After Kansas, they know they'll need to reverse-engineer immunity quickly, before Mass regroups."

"If that's true, then the government must know the memo is real."

"Of course they know but they're not going to admit it. The point is – imagine if we could get our hands on the new *GenLET* – the one with 3P immunity."

Hasuru mused, "No wonder Mass never came after the people who stole *GenLET*."

"Why should he care? Basic *GenLET* gives no protection from 3rd Protocol. In fact, I wouldn't put it past him to have devised a strain of basic *GenLET* to be susceptible to the plague. What better way to get rid of those who would challenge his future New World Harmony."

"Like us." Hasuru stood, captive of a thousand-yard stare. "Extended life doesn't matter if a plague takes you out."

"Sure. He must know that The Group has *GenLET*. But so what? He knows it's the basic kind, the one without protection."

Hasuru prompted. "So what about the couriers…"

"Ah, yes, the couriers. My couriers did manage to get something. It's not the final answer, not yet, but it's the next best way to get there."

"You didn't get the new *GenLET*?"

"No, but I managed to get a dozen eggs extracted from Alyssa."

"Eggs?" Hasuru gaped.

"I have a lab working on them now. The unique genetics and stem cellular properties give us our best hope of reproducing the immunity. We may not get the new version of *GenLET*, but we should at least be able to figure out the 3P vaccine."

"But will it work if it's not integrated into *GenLET*?"

"One of many questions they're working on."

Hasuru turned off the water. "There's amazing potential there."

"But we have to watch ourselves. The egg extraction didn't go unnoticed. In fact, there were complications."

"Did something happen to the girl?"

Curtis shut off his water. "By necessity, it was an aggressive procedure. My access to her was extremely limited. She had a reaction. She's still unconscious."

"Damn it!" Hasuru turned to the tiles. "You should have let them finish working with her. Stealing it from them would have been easier than trying to reproduce it by guesswork."

"It may be just as well. If we get the vaccine and the government doesn't, what's the downside? The fewer *GenLET* people we have to deal with when this is over the better."

Hasuru was shocked. "What are you talking about? You'd keep the vaccine to yourself and let the population collapse?"

Curtis ran his hand back through his dripping hair. "The meek will not inherit the Earth. Even The Group knows this. I can't imagine them handing out *GenLET* at every free clinic."

"What's gotten into you? You're more concerned about positioning yourself for the future than making sure we have one!"

Curtis stuck an index finger at Hasuru's face. "You think the government is going to hand out immunity to everyone? Ask The Group; would they do it? Think again. Just announcing that everyone has to get a shot would start a panic. No way. A few industrialized countries will get it but other than that, everyone will be quite content to let nature take its course everywhere else."

"You can't mean that."

"It's the way they think. What's the downside to less competition for resources?

The stakes are high. Why not trade a level playing field for a better strategic position? You seriously think they're going to give up their advantage? Like they say, it's better to seek forgiveness than permission."

"This isn't what we talked about. The humanity, the Earth we fought for all these years. How can you piss that all away? It's become nothing but a power grab."

"No, it's *exactly* what we talked about. Look at the equation for global CO2. P x S x E x C equals total CO2. To get global CO2 down, we have to reduce those four factors. P is population. S – the services they use. E – the energy those services take. And C – the CO2 put out to make that energy. It all comes back to people. We even have an equation that *proves* we need fewer people! You know as well as I do; you can't make that equation work unless you lower the population – dramatically."

Hasuru shouted back. "But not like this!"

"Face it. The ship is sinking. There aren't enough life boats. I don't want to live my extended life headed for the bottom."

Hasuru took a step towards the exit then halted. "Chances are, Mass will beat you to the punch. He'll regroup 3P long before you ever figure out immunity."

Curtis laughed. "He should live that long."

Hasuru stood, astonished. "You're really going all the way with this?"

"You can come join me, anytime you want." Curtis turned to face a floor drain.

Taking penis in hand, he urinated into the drain.

Disgusted, Hasuru stormed out of the shower room.

Curtis stared at the arc of urine headed for the floor. There was something so raw, so freeing and powerful about standing naked in a public place.

Pissing it all away.

CHAPTER 38

Sub-Basement of Building 3
GARC, Puerto Rico

Dinner, half-eaten and cold, waited in a takeout clamshell to be reheated. Ventilation fans cycled on overhead and pushed the smell of food across the cluttered desk. It was enough to break one's concentration.

Janis rose up from work and caught sight of the date/time display – 2:30 a.m.

The windowless lab hid the passage of time. Surrounded on three sides by consoles displaying data, Janis hunched forward and reread an entry from her log.

Something didn't fit. Had she entered a variable incorrectly or was she right to assume something in the data was off? How long would it take to track it down? She had found many references to the variance but what she really needed was the source. The anomaly could be from lab work she had done or in the GAMA material given to her by Knockout Mouse. Determining which was the first order of business.

Millions of bits of genetic data meshed precisely and yet one out of place could change the results for everything. Was she looking for a needle in a haystack or a single grain of sand on an endless beach? Perhaps it was the smallest star in the visible universe or just possibly, the final number to be included in an infinite set.

After a full day, the search for answers remained enormous and elusive.

Janis was well aware that difficulty in genetic research was measured by orders of magnitude which were daunting at any level chosen. It all came down to rigor and perseverance over invisible minutiae. While she was used to being meticulous and relentless at any scale, she had yet to adjust to the level of consequence if they failed.

Faye sat across the way, cloistered in another collection of consoles and lab equipment. The two of them were close enough to talk but far enough away to do individual work. While Faye labored to unlock the mystery of how to reverse sterility, Janis attempted to reconstruct why the sabotage of 1st Protocol had gone horribly wrong. For days, progress on both fronts had been slow but both of them were determined to keep it steady.

Janis swiveled in her chair and called out to Faye. "How are you doing over there?"

Dropping reading glasses to a mouse pad, Faye rubbed the bridge of her nose. "Ask me again in an hour; I'm too tired to answer right now."

Janis could only manage a grin in response. Digging into a pocket, she pulled out a small object and dangled it in front of her. "Why don't we go see the stars?"

Faye looked over. "What is that?"

"The key to the roof."

"I thought you gave that back."

"I did, but later I found it in his office."

"You went to see him?" Faye didn't try to hide her surprise.

"I went to sign papers – immunity from prosecution if I complete Project work. I wanted it in writing."

"I don't suppose they defined the limits of Project work. They could have you on the hook forever."

Janis clutched the key in a closed fist. "Yeah, but like you said, if we don't figure this out forever's not that far away."

Faye rocked back and motioned to the fist. "Does security know you have that?"

"They're on a need-to-know basis. Come on, let's get some fresh air."

Janis stood and stretched as Faye grabbed her jacket from the back of the chair. Their elevator ride to the top floor passed without comment. The deserted complex was lit by security night lights. From silent hallway into a quiet stairwell they strolled, dragging the weight of their fatigue.

Once on the roof, Janis lifted her eyes to the sky and took in a deep breath. "It's different being someplace where you can see the stars."

Faye looked down on the lights of Aguadilla in the distance but was distracted by the blackness of ocean beyond. "If they ever move us to Granite Peak Installation, you'll really see some stars. That place is in the middle of nowhere. The closest light is twenty miles away."

"After what happened to Alyssa, I thought we'd be there already."

"It's hard to say what's holding up the transfer. Then again, I'm not sure Dugway Proving Ground would be the best place for Alyssa right now either. They may be having security clearance issues rounding up medical support for her."

"That should be easy; just bring Rebecca and her team with us."

"You would think so but nothing's that simple with The Project."

Janis dropped her gaze back to Earth. "If we stay here, I worry if something else might happen to Alyssa."

"I think it's OK. They've got things pretty well locked down. No more use of GeLixCo personnel for anything. We can't get more insulated."

"You're right, it seems I wound up a prisoner anyway. It'd be nice if we were allowed some time in town or on the beaches. We can't go anywhere."

Faye stepped along the roofline. "What are you talking about? We have the whole roof to explore."

Janis followed her. "It's hard to think out of the box if I'm kept in one."

"Speaking of out of the box, I've been thinking about the offer you got from Knockout Mouse."

"What about it?"

Faye stopped and turned back to Janis. "The more I consider it, the more it sounds like a good idea."

"Don't we have our hands full enough already? What would we do with the 2nd Protocol virus?"

"You know it's going to take something new to get us out of this mess. Anything we can learn from 2nd Protocol can only help us. Who knows what improvements The Group made over their 1st Protocol base?"

Janis sauntered away. "Capping lifespan has nothing to do with our problem."

"But how they did it might tell us something. You never know."

Janis folded her arms against a sudden chill. "And what would The Project do with it? I'm not giving them a new agent they can use for something else."

"Something else might be something good, something we need. It's too late to hold back on anything. We don't have the time."

"I don't know..." Janis continued to stroll with Faye at her side.

Faye persisted, tantalized by an emerging idea. "Think about it. The Group made 1st Protocol to delay fertility. Now 2nd Protocol is supposed to cap lifespan at what age?"

"Seventy."

"OK, seventy. And what's the basic functionality, what happens? 1st Protocol doesn't allow a process to start and 2nd Protocol doesn't allow a process to finish. The Group engineered the two protocols to be genetic flipsides of each other."

"So?" Relaxing into her tiredness, Janis fought to concentrate.

"So what if we could exploit the differences? What if somehow we were able to use elements within 2nd Protocol to flip the completion of sterility in utero?"

"Even so, what about the children already here?"

"Sure, it wouldn't cure sterility for those already affected, but children not yet born might have a chance. We know that epigenetic changes that take place in the fetus between the fourth and sixth weeks of pregnancy result in sterility. If we can isolate what that process does and use 2nd Protocol techniques to make sure it never gets a chance to finish, we might be able to turn off fertility's shutdown."

"That's pure conjecture. We don't know how 2nd Protocol works. And even if we did, it's specialized to cap lifespan. It's not a generic process we can use interchangeably."

"We know its purpose. There can only be so many reasonable ways to the end state. The point is, we also have no idea how 2nd Protocol might help us."

Janis stood at the edge of the roof. She was ready to take a leap of faith.

"All right. I'll contact Knockout Mouse and ask him for it – but under one condition. For the time being, we keep this to ourselves. If we get 2nd Protocol and we find it can help us, only then do we tell The Project about it."

"I'm fine with that."

A long silence passed between them.

Faye drew closer, encouraged by the added trust shown by Janis' decision.

"All that GAMA stuff you got from KM – how's it working out?"

Janis shrugged. "Nine million base pairs. Eight thousand protein-encoding genes. The suicide gene is just one of them."

"You're not talking about the GAMA, are you?" Faye was confused.

Janis shook her head to chase away the weariness. "Oh, no, of course not. I was talking about the original bacterium. The one with the suicide gene the Army experimented with."

"I thought the plastic-eating microbe was developed by the Navy."

"That's right, but they used a suicide gene from Army research."

Faye was still confused. "But aren't you studying the Navy's GAMA?"

"That's right, but the key problem leads back to the suicide gene. Both the original 1st Protocol payload and the benign payload created by The Project as sabotage agent share one thing – the suicide gene. I thought it might be good to go back to the source of that gene, back to Army research on the source bacterium,

Streptomyces Avidinii. As a control group, I wanted to see how the suicide gene operates in its natural state, how it's triggered, how the cascade of effects is expressed genetically."

Faye reached out to touch Janis' arm. "What bacterium did you say?"

"Streptomyces Avidinii."

"You sure about that?"

Janis chuckled, "I've been staring at it all day."

"You sure it wasn't Streptomyces Avermitilis?"

"Positive. I read the Army's patent on the suicide gene just the other day. They used a suicide gene from Streptomyces Avidinii. Why? Is something wrong?"

Faye circled around to Janis' other side; the movement helped her think it through. "I've got to double-check but I could swear an abstract on the sabotage agent mentioned Streptomyces Avermitilis. Come on – I've got it in the lab."

Faye bolted in the direction of the stairwell door with Janis in quick pursuit. They scurried down the stairs and suffered the wait in the elevator.

Back in the sub-basement lab, Faye raced to her desk and grabbed her reading glasses. Before she was in her chair she was typing.

Janis hung by and watched the display screen over Faye's shoulder. "Could it be a clerical error? Would it even make a difference? They're both Streptomyces, both Actinobacteria, both gram-positive; their genomes would both have high guanine and cytosine content."

"That doesn't mean they share identical suicide genes." Faye's forefinger shot to the screen and swept across a passage of text. "Here it is!"

Janis pulled up a chair alongside. "This is from where?"

Faye toggled another window forward to double-check. "As far as we're concerned, this doesn't exist. It's from the operation that sabotaged 1st Protocol. All of this is TS-4 Sensitive Compartmented Information. The operation was part of The Project, which is an *Unacknowledged Special Access Program.* Remember, most of the government doesn't know about this. If you're asked about it, deny it."

Janis steadied herself. "Sounds about right – take an oath, promising you'll lie."

Faye scanned then read the text. "It is believed that the original source of Ghyvir-C was discovered growing in seawater amoeba and was exploited as a 1st Protocol agent because its double-stranded linear chromosome carries great coding capacity. As one of the largest known viruses, Ghyvir-C gave genetic engineers the opportunity of dual leverage, in that the virus was found to contain a sputnik."

Janis couldn't help reading ahead, then reading aloud.

"The Ghyvir-C sputnik is a small icosahedral virus, 50 nanometers in size. The sputnik cannot multiply in Ghyvir-C but grows rapidly after an eclipse phase. The sputnik's aggressive growth is deleterious to Ghyvir-C, resulting in abortive forms and abnormal capsid assembly of the host virus."

Faye zeroed in on the pertinent section. "The Ghyvir-C sputnik is functionally analogous with bacteriophages and can be classified as a virophage. As such, it could be a vehicle mediating lateral gene transfer between giant viruses. This gene transfer could include a suicide gene. Testing conducted with the GAMA-supplied suicide gene (sourced from Streptomyces Avermitilis) has completed successfully."

Janis reeled back. “My God! They used the wrong suicide gene!”

As Faye drilled farther into the text, Janis rolled backwards in her chair to get to her own workstation across the way. Waking her console from hibernation, she set about finding her own references in the material from Knockout Mouse.

She called out to Faye. “Natick Laboratories…”

“The one near Boston?”

“Yeah, they’re a division of the Army’s Solider and Biological Chemical Command – SBCCOM. It says here that the Army’s terminator systems were developed by Boston University working with a biotechnology research unit at Natick. The anti-material Pseudomonas species engineered by the Navy uses a lethal gene from the bacteria Streptomyces Avidinii.”

Stunned, Faye leaned back in her chair. “How did they get the wrong one?”

Janis continued to search the Knockout Mouse material. “Here it is…”

“What?” Faye got up and joined Janis at her console.

Janis sat back. “When 1st Protocol was engineered by The Group, the Army was doing its research with one suicide gene – the one from Streptomyces Avidinii. At that time, they only had one suicide gene.”

Faye looked at the console and saw what Janis saw.

“By the time The Project scrambled to finish the sabotage agent, the Army had expanded their research. They were testing a different suicide gene from another Streptomyces bacterium. The Project must have grabbed the wrong one. Could it be as simple as that?”

Janis grimaced in perverse amazement. “Up to that point, there had only been one. So why check? The one you pick must be the one, right?”

“Remember what The Project abstract said – the sputnik’s aggressive growth is deleterious to Ghyvir-C, resulting in abortive forms and abnormal capsid assembly of the host virus. The Group had to know this. They had to make sure those abnormalities wouldn’t affect the payload.”

Janis closed her eyes. “But with a different suicide gene, there would be different capsid abnormalities. Ghyvir-C wasn’t engineered to deal with those.”

Faye returned to her station and sat down. “That’s how it happened.”

“That explains the crazy variance I’ve been chasing down all day.” Janis ran her hands back through her hair. “A clerical error; a stupid accident.”

“It’s like your Mom used to tell us,” mused Faye, her eyes tearing up. “Don’t play rough with anything you can’t repair or can’t do without.”

“Shit!” Janis stood and paced away her aggravation. “How do we repair it?”

Faye stood, preparing to go. “I wish we were trying to reverse delayed fertility. At least we could fail at that. I’ve had enough for one night. I’m going to bed.”

Janis joined her in the freight elevator headed up. For half the ride they said nothing to each other. Then Faye turned to Janis.

“This may be as good a time as any to tell you. I got a call from my doctor today.”

Janis came alert with concern. “About the baby?”

“About me – and the baby. It seems I have a risky pregnancy. It’s too soon to be alarmed but she tells me I should prepare to stay in bed if I want to keep it.”

"When did you find out?"

"Late this afternoon. She didn't want to alarm me but needed to warn me, get me thinking about it in case I needed to shift things with the work I'm doing."

Janis took her hand. "There's no way you should be working 18-hour days. That's got to stop."

Faye started to cry. "I don't know what to do. I can't leave the work…but I want the baby."

Janis hugged her. The elevators doors opened at the ground floor.

"Don't worry about the work. You do what you need to do."

"That's just it! I can't give up on the work. If a fix isn't found, what good is it having a baby?"

Janis smoothed back her hair. "Don't talk that way. There's lots of time to do both – have the baby, then we'll fix sterility."

Faye buried her face into Janis' shoulder. "I don't know anymore. I don't know what to do."

"Whatever it is, you don't need to decide right now. Let's get some sleep. It's not certain. The doctor said maybe. Let's take it a day at a time. Come on…"

Janis led her out of the elevator, through the lobby, then outside. With arms around each other they walked back to Building 2 where their temporary apartments had been set up. Janis stayed until Faye was in bed and the lights were off.

Then Janis walked back to Building 3.

She walked the deserted hallways until she came to a corner room on the top floor. She paused at the door and watched as hallway security cameras pivoted on their mounts, following her every move.

She pushed on the door and stepped through darkness.

The blinds were open.

As she approached the windows, the lights of Aguadilla blazed up from below.

Clustered around the bed, vital sign monitors blinked and glowed with tiny indicator lights. The hum from watchful electronics filled the room.

Janis stepped to the side of the bed and looked down on her sleeping daughter.

She brushed back her hair with the tips of her fingers.

She watched the rise and fall of her breathing.

Then she sat down in a chair, bedside.

For the longest while she sat. She thought. She cried.

An hour before light returned in the east, she fell asleep.

Chapter 39

Off the coast of the Frioul Archipelago
Marseille, France

Awareness returned with disorientation and pain. Javier Francisco regained consciousness with the world swaying around him. Dizziness alone didn't explain it. A splitting headache throbbed at the back of his skull. With great effort he opened his eyes. Lying on his back with hands tied behind him, he wondered where he was.

The night sky was overhead. Stars were in motion from side to side. All around was the smell of the sea. What was the last thing remembered?

Javier had come to Marseille to visit an informant, a man with a price for sharing the inside strategies of radical group New Class Order. The day had gone well. The meeting in the afternoon had been brief but helpful. His evening was open to enjoy. He gravitated to a club. At the bar he struck up a conversation with a young man. There was obvious attraction. All the signals were right. The young man invited him back to his place for some quick man-on-man love.

But they never got there.

The last thing Javier remembered was leaving the club and walking down the sidewalk. It was right after midnight when everything went dark.

Into the void went missing time.

A face appeared overhead. The stranger called out, "He's awake."

The sound of a zipper and a yank to the side jolted Javier. He raised his head long enough to look around. He could see he was zipped up in a body bag on the aft deck of a boat. Two men stood nearby; a third came out of the cabin. The cabin light caught the man's face and Javier recognized him. It was André Bolard.

The leader of New Class Order stood over Javier and considered his fate.

"You have a choice to make," announced André. "To be helpful or to be dead."

"It doesn't help you to kill me."

André squatted down and grabbed Javier's jaw with one hand while playing with the body bag's zipper with the other.

"My friends don't believe you're going to be helpful so they put you in this weighted bag. They want to get back to shore and have some fun. The sooner they drop you overboard, the sooner the fun begins. I convinced them to wait. I thought I should check with you first."

Javier fought vertigo and pain. "What do you want?"

André stood back up. "I like a good conspiracy theory. Unlike most people, I believe that memo between Eugene Mass and you was real. I think the two of you do all sorts of things together. I mean, besides being lovers."

"I don't know anything."

"Famous last words. Stick with that and they certainly will be."

Javier could hear the ocean nearby. The thought of being zipped up alive in the body bag and shoved overboard was hitting home.

"I'm small time, a fixer, nothing big, nothing that would interest you."

"That's for me to decide." André stepped closer to the fantail. "Tell me something I don't know. Something about Eugene Mass. Surprise me."

Javier tried to concentrate but struggled to find something to say. "We have a place together in Brussels, in Marie-Louise Square…"

André paced. "I can read about that in any scandal magazine."

Javier stammered through the pain. "…when we're there, he likes to meet in the top floor bedroom, the one that faces the street."

Dissatisfied, André jerked his head to signal the others.

One of the men zipped the body bag closed. The other pushed it overboard.

From inside the bag, Javier's shouts could be heard.

"…no wait! Don't do this! I'll tell you whatever you want…!"

The body bag slid into blackness. It dropped off the fantail and splashed into the water. The weighted watertight bag headed for the bottom.

The men stood by and watched as a fifty foot tether uncurled and shot into the ocean after the bag. The other end of the line was secured to a deck cleat. After the full length of the line had uncoiled overboard, André stepped to a bench seat and sat down to wait a tantalizing few seconds.

"All right," he ordered. "Haul him up."

The two men pulled fist over fist on the rope until the body bag emerged from the sea. Hefting the weight of it back onboard, they watched with satisfaction as the man inside the bag struggled and shouted in panic.

André stood and approached the bag. He unzipped it enough to reveal Javier's head, then gazed down on a man back from the dead.

"I think we should try that again."

Javier heaved terrified breaths in and out.

Relaxed and casual, André asked again, "Tell me something I don't know."

"What do you want?" gasped Javier in terror.

André squatted down alongside him once again. "The memo says *3P will be a fait accompli.* Is 3P referring to 3rd Protocol?"

Javier was eager to comply. "Yes, yes it is."

"What exactly is 3rd Protocol? Is it really a method to collapse the population?"

"That's right. Yes, it's a virus."

For André, it was one thing to have suspicions; quite another to face confirmation. Every implication of what it all meant drove home and infuriated him.

"You're going to tell me the plan. You're going to tell me everything you know about 3rd Protocol. At any time, if I'm not satisfied with what I'm getting, I'll let these gentlemen throw you away. And next time, they'll disconnect the rope. Understand?"

Javier answered with a vigorous nod. He raised his head up and watched as one of the men disconnected the tether from the foot end of the body bag. If he was ever going to get out of this alive, he would have to give André Bolard something he didn't know, something that was reasonable, but something that was explosive enough to warrant keeping Javier as a valuable resource, at least for the time being.

All Javier needed was to buy time. If he could get through this night, any way he could, maybe tomorrow would present opportunities for escape. But he had to think quickly. André was sharp. He'd see through a blatant attempt to lie his way out of this. It had to be something that André would accept. But most of all, it had to be something that, if possible, would protect Mass if not help him.

But how? How could Javier shift the situation, use it and hopefully live?

Javier thought back to the memo. André had quoted the memo. That was the place to start. If he could use something else from the memo, spin it in a way that fed into the drama André expected, but what?

André had said he liked a good conspiracy theory, so why not give him one.

Javier shivered away the feel of deep water coldness. He raised his head up off the deck and directed all his energy into his story, straight at André.

"There's only one thing you need to know about 3rd Protocol..." Javier's teeth chattered. "It's the one thing everybody's missed, even the intelligence services."

André held his skepticism in reserve. "One thing...?"

Javier nodded. "The New World Harmony is more harmonious than people think. You have to watch for misdirection. The thing you believe the strongest is probably the thing they want you to believe. But it's not the truth."

André was restless. "What are you talking about?"

"NovoSenectus and GeLixCo. They're made out to be such big competitors, rivals. But it's all a sham. Eugene Mass and Curtis Labon are best of friends. They're really partners."

André was shocked. "Partners? How?"

"Mass takes the heat and gets all the attention so Labon is free to work silently in the background. But make no mistake; they both want the New World Harmony."

"Are you talking about *GenLET* or 3rd Protocol?"

"All of it!" Javier put all his remaining energy into it. "They want the focus to be on Mass. That lets Labon develop 3rd Protocol without interference and without fear of being exposed."

André drew near. "GeLixCo is creating 3rd Protocol?"

"Of course," snapped Javier. "Mass is the perfect cover for him. But they're all in it together. They all want the new class order – *GenLET* for the elite few and a population collapsed to a sustainable size in harmony with the planet. 3rd Protocol is real and they're getting ready to release it. The masquerade in Kansas was the final sign. Every time you demonstrate or riot against Mass or NovoSenectus, you're doing just what they want. They're using you to draw attention away from the real action."

André was neither believing nor disbelieving it. He stared down at Javier but could only read exhaustion and pain on his face.

"If GeLixCo is getting 3rd Protocol ready, where are they doing it?"

Javier thought back to days past working with Malcolm Stowe. "That's the big secret now, isn't it? No one's told me for sure, but it could only be one place – their Advanced Research Center. It's somewhere in the Caribbean."

André stood and stared down at Javier a long while. Finally, he turned away.

"Take him below. Lock him up. We may need him again."

As the two men dragged Javier into the boat, André stayed out on deck.

A dark ocean surrounded him. But an even darker plot needed to be stopped.

CHAPTER 40

Le Monnaie
The Royal Opera House, Brussels

The house lights came up, the curtain closed, and lingering applause died away. Seated in a prime box near the stage, Leah Mass lifted her gaze and took in the view across the great hall. Crimson balconies lined in gold sprung full of movement. Patrons everywhere stood and murmured while edging their way to intermission.

Eugene Mass lowered opera glasses. "You want to go down?"

Leah watched the private boxes on the far side empty of people. "I should make an appearance."

"One of the small prices of stewardship…" Eugene frowned.

Leah stood. "It's a benefit, not a concert. At a thousand Euros a seat, they expect to see us."

"Nonsense." Eugene struck a sarcastic tone. "They're here for the Wildlife Fund. Knowing they did their part to help save Sumatran tiger cubs or boost rhino populations should be more than enough satisfaction for them."

"It won't take long. I'm a bit hungry anyway."

Eugene followed her out of the box. "Ah, yes…canapés and champagne; typical fare to fuel the Green Movement."

Outside their box, Leah nodded hello to the bodyguard but couldn't repress annoyance at Eugene. "What's gotten into you tonight?"

"I wish I knew. Maybe the music is making me melancholy."

"That's strange. Music usually has the opposite effect on you."

"Yes, but it's intermission; we're closer to the end than the beginning."

"You're not making any sense." Leah headed down the small flight of stairs to the lobby. Everywhere one looked, people dressed in their finest were standing, talking, drinking, and eating. Waitstaff worked the crowd armed with trays of specialty bites. Bartenders were fast and efficient keeping all the crystal flutes full.

Leah smiled and said hello here and there. Eugene shook an occasional hand and remained pleasantly casual but quiet at her side. He passed on the food but accepted something to drink. As Leah talked away at his side, he looked around and enjoyed people watching.

One man in particular caught his attention. Although dressed well, the man appeared out of place. Something about his temperament didn't fit the occasion. Locking eyes with Eugene, the man abruptly parted company with a couple he was speaking to and worked his way through the throng to approach Eugene.

"Mr. Mass…" The man extended a hand in greeting. "It's a privilege meeting you. Graham Fry from the London Times."

Eugene endured the handshake. "I didn't know they let your sort in here."

"If you pay the price, I imagine they let anybody in."

"Apparently. I presume your paper picked up the tab."

"Why yes, they love wildlife just like me."

Eugene sipped and smiled. "Don't we all."

"I was curious to get your opinion..."

"Ever inquisitive. What a surprise."

"NovoSenectus has never officially released *GenLET* for use, isn't that right?"

"You're absolutely right."

"That's what I thought. What do you think of the peculiar rumors going around that say *GenLET* has become an underground business servicing the world's elites?"

"Is that a quote from André Bolard?" Eugene chuckled.

"Hardly. It's one thing to whisper behind closed doors but when people shout in celebration, someone's bound to hear."

"I don't quite understand what you're getting at." Mass gazed beyond Fry at no one in particular. Mass' bodyguard started to move in but Mass raised a hand to keep any disruption at bay.

The reporter hurried his point. "No one will go on record but plenty are talking – they're excited about having extended life. News like that is hard to contain."

Mass took a step closer to Fry. "The fact that they won't go on record should be your first clue. Beyond that, you don't need many others."

"No one's accusing you of running such a business, of course."

"How generous of you..."

Graham Fry was tenacious. "If the rumors were true, perhaps it's more likely that someone else is profiting off your creation. If someone had stolen *GenLET* secrets from you, the resulting black market trade in life extension could soon be out of control. Spending billions in investment without retaining proprietary management would be a disaster for NovoSenectus. I can see how your managers might want to keep news of such a theft under wraps."

Mass' eyes widened in mock surprise. "You have some imagination but as I'm sure you know, plenty of hucksters and scam artists around the world claim to have *GenLET* for sale. What they offer is not even good snake oil. Every day police arrest another fraud injecting people with sterile saline solution and calling it *GenLET*."

"But if the secret had been stolen, it would help NovoSenectus to have everyone believe that all the other *GenLETs* are frauds, wouldn't it? It might be the only way to try to put the genie back in the bottle."

Eugene tired of the exchange. "What exactly is your question?"

Graham saw Leah approaching and the window of opportunity for his interview was closing. "Do you have a secret program to sell *GenLET* to the wealthy or has someone stolen the secret and is doing it without your permission?"

Eugene smiled. "You violated the first rule of interviewing..." He put his arm around Leah's shoulder. "Never ask a question you already know the answer to."

Just then a chime sounded marking the ten-minute warning to end of intermission. Eugene led Leah through the crowd back towards the stairs.

"Whatever was that about?" asked Leah.

In passing, Eugene set his half-empty flute on a waitstaff's tray.

"Nothing, just a desperate man on a fishing expedition."

They headed up the stairs side by side. Securing the way in front of them, their suited bodyguard cleared a path with polite motions for others to step aside.

Eugene changed the subject. "Sorry, I missed your conversation, but at least I heard your laughter."

Leah flipped her hand to one side. "Don't even ask. It never fails to surprise me what some people think is important."

She stepped into their private box to find a champagne bucket in front of and between their seats. Taped to the chilled bottle was a small card.

"Oh, my, look at this." Leah opened the card and scanned it. "A thank-you from the Wildlife Fund for organizing the benefit."

Eugene pulled the bottle from the ice and checked the vintage.

"Indeed! Only a non-profit could afford this label." He popped the cork.

Leah sat down, exasperated. "Why do you insist on denigrating any attempt to make things better?"

"Why?" He found a glass nearby and poured. "Because all the good intentions are a drop in the bucket and you know it." He motioned out at the audience. "None of this is going to save wildlife. Since yesterday, another 200,000 people have been added to the planet. Every day, 200,000 more."

"You don't have to remind me."

He handed her the glass of champagne but she refused it. Satisfied that his chivalrous duty was complete, he sat down and drank half the glass in one draft.

"We all have to be reminded. It's far too easy to turn away from what we don't want to face."

Leah sank back in her chair. "I'm not turning away."

"But you want me to stop everything."

"I want us to step back from the edge of doing something horrible."

"And after that, how are you going to stop everything else? You know as well as I do, if the population doesn't collapse, civilization surely will. Not one indicator says it won't. Forty years from now, global energy demand will double. Billions of more people will need water, food, housing, sanitation, education. The climate will de-stabilize and all bets are off."

Leah reached over and grabbed his hand. "Let's not argue about it. At least tonight, can we do that?" She looked into his eyes and the two of them held silent and still for a moment.

Eugene nodded. "I can do that." He reached down and refilled his glass.

"We should get away." Leah's suggestion was out of the blue but the need to say it was strong. "We haven't had a real vacation in years. Maybe we should take some time to decompress, clear our minds, rest our hearts. The stress of all of this has been rough on both of us."

"But we've gained so much."

Leah leaned close. "Yes, we have so much life ahead of us; more than we ever dreamt possible. But adding years to life is not the same as adding life to years. I want to feel the way we used to. I want to feel good when a new day begins, not worried sick about a world with no future."

The orchestra began to play an overture. In minutes, the curtain would open.

Eugene listened and stared down at the stage.

"When we were first dating we came to the opera. Remember?"

Leah nodded.

Filled with champagne and reflection, he sat back. "I want to feel that way too. Only not much of what we hoped for back then has come true – only *GenLET*. But what good is *GenLET* in a world on fire?"

"We now have extra time to work on things, to see things through."

"To see *what* through?" Eugene shook his head. "Every movement for change went off track. It's all gone crazy. Celebrities travel in private jets to fancy benefits to raise awareness about rising CO2 levels. People who predict rising sea levels turn around and buy oceanfront mansions. Sustainability has been turned into a codeword used by politicians to regulate, control, and tax. The very people who champion the cause have been co-opted or seduced by short-term interests wanting nothing more than power and wealth. None of it's going to end well."

Leah couldn't hide her vulnerability. The part of her that reasoned agreed with him but the part of her that knew love wouldn't accept that all hope was gone.

"All I want is to be happy with you. Maybe it's selfish to say, but I don't care about anything else."

Eugene's smile was weak. "I want that too. I wish the world was different and would let us have it that way."

The lights dimmed and the curtain pulled open. With a flourish, dramatic music filled the hall. Eugene and Leah squeezed hands together in solidarity. Finishing his champagne, Eugene eased to one side and turned his attention to the stage.

Leah felt the weight of the drama and the music upon her. The soaring libretto was in a language not her native tongue. And yet, the ache and pathos of the performance spoke to her of all the loss and hope for what might still be possible.

The spirit of it was triumphant even as the misunderstandings between characters on stage played out as bitterly tragic. It was all there for her to feel. It was all too real. In so many ways it resembled the heartbreak of the greater world outside.

As she watched and listened, she became aware of Eugene slumping to one side. She turned and touched him, only to have his body droop off balance and collapse out of his seat and onto the floor. He landed awkwardly contorted with face buried in the carpet and arms twisted under him.

Leah bolted out of her seat and let out a scream.

The performance on stage sputtered then stopped.

"No!" she yelled, rushing to his side. She shook him and turned him over. Her trembling hands felt his face and lifted his head. His mouth hung slack, his eyes were closed, no breath was evident.

Their bodyguard rushed into the private box and knelt at Eugene's side. He checked for pulse at the side of the neck then put ear to chest to listen for a heartbeat.

Leah crumbled back, sitting on the floor next to Eugene. Her cries of shock and grief reverberated throughout the hall. Some in the audience were on their feet. All eyes turned to the box location near the stage. The performers stood stunned, frozen between the drama they were pretending and the drama unfolding.

The bodyguard pulled out his phone and called for help. Ushers from the Royal Theater arrived to assist. A doctor from the audience ran up the short flight of stairs and entered the booth. He loosened Eugene's tie and opened his shirt. He checked for vital signs but found none. Eugene Mass was dead.

Leah was helped up from the floor and into her seat by the bodyguard. She sat silent and shivering and stared down at the motionless form that was her husband.

The doctor lifted Mass' eyelids and then opened his mouth wider before glancing back at the bodyguard. "This man may have been poisoned. Proper toxicology should be done. Finding the source would be helpful. Look around."

Leah overheard. Her eyes shifted to the champagne bucket at her side. She reached forward and grabbed the open bottle from the ice.

"Check this," she ordered. "It was the last thing he had."

A razor chill of realization shot through her – the champagne was meant for both of them. If not for her momentary aggravation at Eugene, she might have accepted a glass of the rare vintage when he offered it to her. The difference between living and dying was so thin and chancy. Experiencing it close up was terrifying.

A commotion out in the hallway announced the arrival of paramedics. As the bodyguard took possession of the open bottle, Leah stood and watched as Eugene was lifted by two men and carried away. She stepped after them.

"I'm going with you."

A uniformed attendant was polite but direct. "We are taking him to Clinique Saint-Jean. You can meet us there."

Leah's shout echoed into the lobby. "Damn it! No! I'm going with you!" Leah followed on their heels. As she walked, she turned to her bodyguard. "Have that bottle analyzed immediately. Find out who put it here. Do whatever it takes. If this was poison, I'll do anything to find the one responsible."

"Yes, ma'am." The bodyguard stayed at her side as a path cleared in the lobby's commotion to let them pass.

The paramedics placed Eugene on a rolling stretcher, covered him with a sheet and blanket and secured him with straps, then hurried him outside to the open rear doors of a waiting ambulance.

Leah watched as the gurney supports folded away and Eugene's stretcher was pushed onboard. She started up the step into the back of the ambulance but paused to snap at the bodyguard one last time.

"Call me as soon as you know. Remember – whatever it takes."

For the next hour, Leah endured an agonizing wait at the hospital.

When the preliminary toxicology report came back, she felt a change in her heart. The diagnosis was poisoning, ingested with the champagne. She wanted to cry but found she was too angry for that. A short time later, the bodyguard called to confirm what she already knew. Someone had injected poison through the cork into the bottle given to them in thanks, as celebration.

A nurse escorted her to an office so she could have a private moment to sit and grieve alone. The certainty collapsed around her; life would never be the same.

Eugene and she were just starting their extended life together. Now it would never be. She was isolated and tired and deeply hurt. The crime of it would haunt her for the rest of her many years. In that instant, she wished she had never been given *GenLET*. She wished there was a way to go back to simpler, happier days.

But most of all, she wished for vengeance.

CHAPTER 41

Sub-Basement of Building 3
GARC, Puerto Rico

"Your package has been cleared. It's arrived in containment."

Janis stuffed the phone back in pocket and looked up from her work. The message from Project security was both ominous and exciting. The FedEx Express box had no return address. Security suspected the worst and had delayed its receipt until additional scans for hazardous or explosive materials were completed.

Janis knew the package would be transported through an isolated hallway that was sectioned off from other areas of the facility. It would be taken under guard to a special BSL2 unpackaging room adjacent to the basement BSL3 and BSL4 suites. Each area was accessible only by computer-controlled biometric and RIDIS scans.

Janis hurried to a wall-mounted intercom. Through a window she could see Faye at work in a clean suit in BSL3 confinement.

"Faye, the package has arrived. I'm going to unpack it and prep it for Level 4."

Faye raised a double-gloved hand and nodded in her helmet.

Janis hurried instructions to two assistants while on her way out into the hall. A dozen steps later she stood for a RIDIS scan and gained access to the special confinement hallway. Halfway down that hall another scan was required before she could enter the unpackaging room.

She quickly donned protective coat, mask and gloves. The mask was a basic surgical style unreliable for viral filtration but as standard procedure it serviced as a reminder not to touch gloves to face at any time.

Following Project requirements, Janis activated video capture and prepared for the annoyance of talking her way through the unpacking process to provide a verbal record of her method and what was found as it happened.

The brown box awaited her on a clear high table. She approached the box and found its top flap already slit open by security. She removed packing material until a metal cylinder was uncovered. Speaking loudly for the overhead microphones, she made her motions clear and systematic.

"The Primary container is a standard screw-top canister…"

She lifted it from the box and inspected what little markings it had. The standard agent label with biohazard symbol was just below the screw cap. Below that was the customary label for shipper information.

"Hand-printing on the agent label says *2nd Protocol.* Normal shipper information is absent; in its place are two letters – *KM.*"

She turned the canister over and found tape on the bottom. She pulled it back.

"One computer flash drive has been taped to the bottom of the canister…" She pulled the flash drive off and set it aside.

Then she unscrewed the canister cap over a metal tray.

"There's dry ice and shock absorbent material between the Primary and Secondary containers..."

Gingerly, she removed the Secondary Container, which was a smaller canister also secured by a screw top.

"The Secondary container's specimen record label is blank. The only other marking is a red biohazard symbol..."

Janis unscrewed the cap from the Secondary container.

"Absorbent packing material is wrapped around the Primary Culture Container..." Janis slid the final package out and into her hands. Carefully, she removed the packing material until a long tube appeared.

She examined the long clear tube. It was capped at the top and stuffed with white sponge at the bottom. The tube was internally divided into compartments with a single thin wire traversing through all levels.

"The agent is confined by a standard flexible twisted-wire transport swab..."

Behind her, the door opened and in rushed Faye and one of the assistants Janis had given instructions to. Faye quickly suited up in coat, mask and gloves and joined Janis at the table.

"How's it going?" asked Faye.

Janis held the tube up. "Here it is..."

"Any instructions?"

Janis reached over, grabbed the flash drive and handed it to Faye. "We've got our work cut out for us."

Faye turned to the assistant. "Until we know what we've got, we'd better use the cabinet lab. Go shower and suit up. We'll need you to stage it for analysis."

The BSL4 environment was divided between suit and cabinet labs. The suit lab allowed the greatest freedom of movement but the cabinet lab provided the highest level of safety and containment. Unfortunately, it was also the most challenging and fatiguing to work in.

The containment cabinet stretched long with space for six researchers at a time. Thick stainless steel provided a formidable barrier to the pathogen but researchers could only access their work through large and cumbersome glove ports. Anyone working in either of the BSL4 suites would have to shower before entering and exiting as well as change clothes on the way in and out. Required garb consisted of a bulky containment suit kept at positive air pressure.

Janis set the clear tube down on its packing material and turned to Faye. "Let's go see what kind of information he gave us."

The two of them shed the protective gear and left the assistant alone to work.

The walk back to their workstations was quick but long enough for Janis to get an update on Faye's work on sterility. The exchange was fast and technical.

"Any luck with the immunoassay?"

"Not yet."

"Do we know any more about ubiquitin?"

"It's a complex mixture, that's for sure."

"What about trying a multi-variant regression analysis?"

"The problem is: ubiquitin is used in all kinds of cellular processes. Labeling proteins for degradation and apoptosis is just one of them. Without time-consuming tests, there's no way to tell if the effect we're seeing is from interaction with the payload or a natural process. Whoever designed 1st Protocol hid their tracks well."

Janis arrived at her desk and sat down.

"What if we concentrated on the E1 enzyme? That's where the ubiquitin cascade starts. We could check out anything that influences E1."

"We may have to go there to lock it down but I was trying to avoid indirect indicators. In the long run, they'll be just as time-consuming for other reasons."

Faye handed back the flash drive and pulled up a chair while Janis loaded it.

"Let's see what the Mouse gave us…"

Janis opened the file folder to find a treasure trove of sub-directories; half of them in German and half in English. At root level she found a single video file named appropriately enough – *Play Me First*. She clicked on it and the screen filled with a complex menu. She moused over one labeled *Overview* and selected it.

For the next five minutes, voice-over narration guided them through a series of animations, graphics, and charts describing the structure and function of the 2nd Protocol agent.

Faye couldn't pull her eyes from the screen. "My God, this is everything!"

Janis hurried back to the main menu to review other options. "We're going to need more assistants…"

Faye wondered, "Why would they put all this together? This is more elaborate than any documentation I've ever seen."

Janis shrugged. "I guess they want a private historical record. They see themselves as the saviors of mankind. Future generations will need to know all about them."

"If that's so, their egotism has given us all we need."

Janis clicked on a menu item at random and advanced the video to sample it. The animation picked up in the middle of an explanation of how 2nd Protocol researchers overcame the problems of capping lifespan at age 70.

"*…while the constraint appears arbitrary and is little understood, it is a fact that human cells have a built-in limitation on the number of times they are able to divide. This is hardwired into each human by nature and is called replicative cell senescence. Baring all negative influences of environment or lifestyle, this limitation puts a maximum value on possible human lifespan. While aging in most organisms depends in part on progressive oxidative damage to macromolecules, aging in humans also progresses in proportion to changes in the structure of telomeres located at the ends of chromosomes. As the end caps degrade, telomeres shorten. After no more than 50 cell divisions, a human cell enters a nondividing state from which it never recovers. It was assumed that an increase in CKI proteins played a role in these stopping mechanisms…*"

As they listened, the lab door opened and in walked Colin Insworth.

Janis turned and noticed him with visible irritation then turned back. She stopped the video as Faye stood to intercede. She met Colin halfway.

"What is it?" asked Faye

Colin was somber. "Something's come up. Eugene Mass is dead."

Janis overheard and stood to join the discussion. "Mass?"

Colin held a newspaper folded in his hands. "Yes. He collapsed at the opera in

Brussels. The police say he was poisoned but most of the media are talking about *GenLET*."

Janis stepped closer. "What about *GenLET*?"

"There's speculation that Mass died after trying *GenLET* on himself."

Faye laughed. "Last week they were all saying he was selling it underground. If he was passing it around, why haven't other people died?"

Colin looked from Faye to Janis to read reactions. "Maybe they have."

Janis paced. "That's ridiculous. *GenLET* is safe."

"Safe for many but not for all? Have there been any human trials?"

Janis grew defensive. "The primates we tested carry 98% of the same DNA as humans. Computer models mapped the differences every which way…"

Faye interrupted, "The police should know from the toxicology report. If they find a known poison in his system, then *GenLET* is cleared."

"It won't matter," added Janis. "They'll put the doubt out there anyway. It's probably what they want."

"What do you mean?" asked Colin.

"What's the best way to get the common people to not want *GenLET*?"

"Make them fear it; make them think it's unsafe," answered Faye.

"Exactly."

Colin asked, "Wouldn't that make the rich fear it too?"

Janis leaned back on a desk. "The rich probably already have it."

"One thing we know for sure. What happens to it next is up to Leah, his wife. She inherits NovoSenectus."

Faye asked, "How much do we know about her?"

"Not much other than she's the typical socialite," answered Colin.

Janis asked, "I wonder how she feels about 3rd Protocol."

Faye folded her arms in thought. "I remember seeing her at Oxford when Mass gave his lecture. I can't imagine the two of them so close without also being like-minded."

Colin frowned. "You have to wonder how much she knows. I wouldn't put it past Mass to keep her in the dark."

Janis saw his concern. "Why do you say that?"

He unfolded the newspaper. "Intelligence services picked up some unusual behavior. It started around the time the news of Mass' death hit the newswires."

"What kind of behavior?"

"Financial transactions from numbered accounts, securities passed between shell corporations, all tied to a rather peculiar name – *Goodwin Godspeed Diye III*."

"Any record of this person?" asked Faye.

"Only that he appears to be owner of an enterprise incorporated as GGD3. We assume it's no coincidence – there's a rash of advertisements appearing all over the world – in newspapers, on billboards, in fifteen-second spot commercials, on the web."

"What do they say?" asked Janis.

"They all say the same thing." Colin opened the newspaper to show them a full page display ad. The lettering was black; the symbol was green.

Goodwin Godspeed Diye III

Janis pushed off from the desk and grabbed the paper out of Colin's hand. She had to hold it for a closer look.

"Green, green, green….wait for my signal."

The reference to the posted memo flared in Faye's awareness.

"GGD3 – could that somehow mean 3rd Protocol?"

Colin was grave and still. "You tell me. It looks like Eugene Mass prepared a surprise for anyone who wanted him out of the way. Nothing was going to stop his plan for a New World Harmony – even his death."

Janis' thoughts raced. "Has anything else happened? Have there been any outbreaks of disease?"

"Nothing major – there's a few new cases of flu in Asia we're watching."

"Why are they on the radar?"

"The buzz from local doctors in Asia claims the sickness has something to do with chickens. They have no proof but people are killing chickens anyway."

"That doesn't make sense," noted Faye.

"Of course it does – they heard the stories about Oliver Ross and what he tried to do at the *Agro-Defense Facility* in Kansas."

"The poultry virus…," gasped Janis.

Colin explained. "In Asia some don't believe we stopped Ross in time."

"How can they say that?" asked Faye. "There's no poultry-related influenza in the U.S. If Ross had succeeded in releasing the virus, it would have hit here first."

Janis added, "I thought his virus only affected poultry…"

"That's right," confirmed Colin. "We checked it out. It was non-reactive around humans."

"Unless…," started Janis. She held the newspaper up again. Below the triple-green recycling symbol was the only text on the page – *Goodwin Godspeed Diye III.*

"GGD3 – if the 3 refers to 3rd Protocol, then what is GGD?"

Colin snapped, "It has to be a bogus name for some dummy corporation that controls Mass' post-death trigger."

"Yes, but is that all? What if Mass used a zoonotic agent, one that transfers genes from poultry. What if he used it as a base for the 3rd Protocol payload? It would make sense if Ross had done what he was supposed to do."

Faye followed Janis' line of thought. "Ross releases his virus and poultry start to die. As the virus spreads, Mass releases 3rd Protocol. When researches look at it, what do they suspect? Horizontal gene transfer between poultry and humans."

"Causal chain of evidence. Blame gets transferred…for as long as it matters."

Colin shoved hands in pockets. "But GGD3 was triggered on Mass' death. That doesn't make sense if he took *GenLET*. He had extended life. Why set it up so 3rd Protocol is released on his death?"

Janis threw the newspaper aside. "As backup, in case someone got to him."

Faye took a breath. "I imagine the CDC and World Health Organization are all over the Asian outbreak or they're about to be?" Colin nodded.

Hit by a realization, Janis closed her eyes. The deception was complete.

"He's laughing at us…it's all right here. It's so obvious; he wanted us to know. GGD – Gallus Gallus Domesticus. It's the subspecies name for chicken."

CHAPTER 42

Lugano-Agno Airport
Switzerland

Knockout Mouse paused for security inspection with coat collar up and the brim of his driving cap low over his eyes. The guard's OK-to-pass was efficient and polite yet Mouse said nothing in return. Papers in order, he pushed out the door and made brisk strides across the snow covered asphalt.

At his side swung a metal briefcase secured to a wrist. In front of him waited a private jet whose door swung open upon his approach. He squinted at the bright blue sky before scurrying up the steps. Once aboard, the crew secured the door behind him. A few steps down the aisle, Hasuru Tamasu waited for him.

"Where's Heinrich?" Hasuru checked behind him.

Mouse unlocked the suitcase from his wrist.

"Still in Milan; he got delayed. He sent me along with this."

Hasuru reached for the case. "How long is he going to make us wait?"

Mouse dug hands in coat pockets and sat in a leather chair across the aisle. "Last I heard he's on the road."

"I knew his little side trip would wind up in a delay." Hasuru turned and gazed out a porthole window. "I envy you. The weather's finally cleared; it's gotten quite beautiful and you get to stay here a couple more days."

Mouse snorted. "I've had enough of winter. I'd rather come back in spring."

"Ah, yes, when the camellias and magnolias are in bloom and all the tourists are trying their hand at *dolce far niente*. The world is coming apart and everyone's aspiring to be carefree and idle."

"It's better than spending all day in a clinic being worked over."

"A minor annoyance considering all the lifetime you're gaining."

"As if it matters."

Hasuru turned back from the window. "Of course it matters."

"What good is extended life when 3rd Protocol is loose? Face it – Mass won."

"The battle but not the war." Hasuru eased back and patted the metal case with a gentle hand. "Have any idea what's in here?"

Mouse sat expressionless. "That's not my job."

"Correct, but it should be your curiosity."

Mouse resented Hasuru's coyness. "What I'm supposed to know, I know."

"You know that Eugene Mass is dead. What you don't know is how much Leah Mass wanted to find his assassin. The same night he died she put the word out – she'd do whatever it took to get to the bottom of it."

"And the briefcase?"

"Leah was willing to make a trade."

"Of what?"

"We had proof that Curtis Labon was behind the assassination. She had the immunity vaccine."

Mouse eyed the case. “A vaccine for 3rd Protocol? Is that what I’ve been carrying around?”

Hasuru nodded. “Remarkable, isn’t it? So as you see, the battle may be over but the world is ours to win.”

“I can’t believe you contacted her – and she listened.”

“Actually, Heinrich made the arrangements through an intermediary. I doubt she even knew it was us she was dealing with. It’s amazing how grief and anger can motivate some people to bargain with their devil.”

“We’ve never spoken to her…”

“But we always knew Mass must be developing a vaccine in parallel. We never could get close to it. It was his most guarded prize. Why *not* do business with Leah.”

“Why?” Mouse snapped. “They triggered Triple-Green. Why would she give it to you?”

“Apparently, with Eugene gone, Leah had no intention of releasing 3rd Protocol. If there’s no plague – then there’s no need for an immunity agent. She thought she was trading something she had rendered worthless.”

“This must have gone down before all the advertisements came out. Before Goodwin Godspeed Diye III.”

Hasuru smiled. “Fortunately for us.”

“And what does she think about the trade now?”

“Who knows; who cares? She can’t be happy but that’s business.”

“So Mass did it on his own – without her.”

“Mass had an insurance policy; something he hid in reserve, even from her. You’ve got to hand it to him; he was determined to help the planet no matter what. Even assassination wouldn’t stop it.”

“What about Labon?” asked Mouse.

Hasuru dismissed the topic with a wave of the hand. “He’s on his own. Mass left The Group as a rogue and now The Group is leaving Labon to his fate for similar behavior. None of us are to have any contact with him whatsoever.”

“You’ll let Leah take care of him so everyone keeps their hands clean.”

“Actions have consequences. He’s a big boy; he should have known that.”

Mouse stared at the case. The weight of what was possible rooted him in place.

“It’s hard to believe. Immunity is right there; the key to six billion lives.”

Hasuru looked away. “Why yes, it’ll save many lives.”

Mouse detected a hedge. With rising concern, he struggled to keep casual. “You’re going to hand this over…make it available to the world?”

The pause was expectant. “We’re considering all factors…several options.”

“What’s to decide? Doesn’t it need to be mass-produced as soon as possible?”

“That’s right but it’s more complicated than that. Something like this is too important to turn over to governments or some other collection of bureaucrats. For twenty years we’ve had to deal with their incompetence and corruption. You know that; you’ve seen what we’ve had to go through. Over and over again the people in charge have proven incapable of coming to grips with long-range problems.”

Mouse moderated his tone; he wanted information not an argument. “The Group is going to distribute it?”

"Don't worry. We'll do the right thing."

"What *is* the right thing?" Mouse meant the question literally even as Hasuru considered the matter with philosophical detachment.

"Precisely, it's the age-old question. Differing vantage points yield different conclusions. Any answer may need adjustment given a change in circumstance."

"But the facts won't change. Billions of people will die…"

"Yes, yes," interrupted Hasuru. "It's a crisis, to be sure. It's nothing that The Group would have sanctioned. We rejected Mass years ago when he first suggested it; that's why he left us. But now that it's begun, now that the unthinkable is happening, we have no choice but to take into consideration what it means. We can't deny that circumstances have changed."

"What are you saying? Never let a good crisis go to waste…"

Hasuru squinted and shook his head. "It's not as crude as that but it's true – the reality of things can't be denied. We can go forward, we *will* go forward, but we can't pretend it didn't happen. Even if we raced to get the vaccine out to people today, the toll would still be enormous. As with anything, we need to step back and look at the positive side of things."

"Having the vaccine available is the only thing positive," asserted Mouse.

"Of course, but we have to think beyond that. What possible good can come out of this? If there is something of value, we should help it along."

Mouse felt Hasuru's growing distrust of the line of questioning and eased back. "So what now?"

Hasuru checked his wristwatch. "Well, if Heinrich ever gets here, we'll take this case to his lab in Basel."

"That's not the 2nd Protocol lab…"

"No, but the city of Basel is German-speaking and it's still in Switzerland. The Swiss penchant for privacy will come in handy and being so near to the borders of France and Germany will be convenient."

"You're keeping it at that one location?"

"For a while. The first order of business is getting key people immunized."

Mouse wavered. "Does that include me?"

"Certainly."

"This is the first I've heard of it."

"Arrangements were made for your stopover in Basel on the way back, after you finish up here in a couple of days. When you got here with the case I planned on telling you."

For Mouse, a game plan took shape. "I'd rather go with you now and be immunized."

"But that's so unnecessary. You have *GenLET* therapy to complete."

"I can still do that afterwards can't I?"

"I suppose so but it's a lot of back-and-forth extra travel."

Mouse pressed. "*GenLET* won't do me any good if I catch the plague."

"But a couple of days shouldn't matter – the reports of sickness are in Asia."

"And Africa. I just heard the news today of another outbreak."

"Really? Well, if you want, I don't care. Ride with us to Basel. If it'll ease your mind, so be it. Just let the *GenLET* people know what you're doing."

"Oh, yeah," remarked Mouse. "I'll give them a call." He lifted his phone from a coat pocket and held it in hand for a moment while deep in thought.

Hasuru pressed a call button intercom and ordered some food from the galley.

Mouse stood. "I'm going to the restroom. I'll be right back."

Hasuru barely gave notice as Mouse stepped down the aisle towards the back of the plane. On the way Mouse passed another Group member engaged in a video conference on his laptop. The Group member was too absorbed to acknowledge him.

The lavatory door shut behind Mouse and he locked it in place. Turning in the cramped space, he faced the washbasin mirror. For a full minute he stood and stared into the glass, at his face, into his eyes. He gripped the basin and leaned forward, on edge and with racing thoughts.

It took all the effort he had to keep under control and not shout his anger and frustration. The obscenity of Hasuru's cool calculation, given the magnitude of human suffering underway, was alarming. Never had he heard The Group cater so callously to what was expedient over what was just.

The interchange with Hasuru was disturbing in so many ways.

For Mouse, it seemed certain now – the group would sit on what they had and let the plague ravish Asia and India, the most populace regions of the world. Then they'd stand by while Africa, the poorest continent with a soaring birth rate, got decimated. Only then would they make their discovery public.

They had chosen the middle ground. They wouldn't stop 3rd Protocol as soon as possible yet neither would they allow the population collapse to continue unabated.

They would work the crisis for all it's worth.

Afterwards their conscience would be clear, just the same as if Leah killed Curtis Labon. For both, they weren't to blame. After all, it was Curtis who had gone rogue. It was Mass who had triggered wholesale death. They shared no guilt if 3rd Protocol should happen to run its course for awhile. Instead of six billion dead, a more acceptable compromise of three billion might do the planet some good.

In the end, the world would be better off and they would have no reason for self-reproach. If anything, they'd be left standing to reap the benefits of a humanity no longer stressed to the point of no return, but they'd be free of all responsibility for doing the unthinkable to get there.

Only one question remained – what would Leah Mass do?

Now that 3rd Protocol was taking lives, now that the engineered contagion was sweeping through continents, would she publically come forward with the vaccine? The CDC and WHO were at a loss on how to combat the virulent disease.

So far, the mortality rate was 90% for those infected.

There had been no word, nothing in the news of any vaccine even possible, let alone planned. Leah and Eugene had shared much over the years, including rising concerns about the critical state of the planet. Hasuru said she traded the vaccine because she decided not to go ahead with 3rd Protocol. Had she changed her mind? Now that it was out there, had she adjusted her answer to the circumstances too?

What was she waiting for?

Mouse took phone in hand and furiously started to send a text message.

Chapter 43

Near the Forest of Soignes
South of Brussels, Belgium

The Mass estate was warm and inviting. Dining and living room fireplaces danced with welcoming light. In the kitchen, house staff cleaned up after serving family favorites. Music played and vases were stuffed with exotic flowers to brighten the mood. Everyone was sated with good food, conversation, and the comforts of overstuffed couches. Everything had been arranged as normal was possible.

Despite the travails of a beleaguered outside world, Leah was determined that inside her home she'd maintain a refuge where the act of family coming together was honored. She enjoyed the visit; she needed it, even though she knew it might turn out as heartbreaking as it was endearing.

Her daughter and son-in-law were attentive and consoling, considerate and respectful, but it was little Jayden that tugged the most at her heart. To watch him was to witness the lost innocence of a world gone wrong. For her to be the only one in the room aware of his sterility only intensified the anguish she felt.

Jayden idolized his grandfather and Eugene had responded in kind with a tender side of himself rarely evoked by anyone else. The absence of Eugene's strong and animated presence in the house was palpable.

But it was no less felt than in the way Jayden reacted.

Gone were the games, the funny banter, the private time in Mass' upstairs study between the two of them. The billiards table sat unused in the basement game room. Story time from pirates to Pinocchio had gone silent.

The boy had lost his mentor, playmate, and buddy.

As Leah helped Jayden put on his coat and hugged him, tears she had held back the entire evening came silent but strong. Daughter and son-in-law kissed her and smiled, wished her well and said goodnight. They thought they understood her grief. She knew they were only aware of half of it. An extended future with Eugene had been swept away but Jayden's future was also barren. Within the weight of that knowledge was a struggle to overcome the pointlessness of it all.

The guests were gone and soon the vast estate was empty again, empty in a way Leah had never felt before. Not only was Eugene no longer at her side, now she had an immeasurable extended life to go along with the hollowness. Isolated with so long to live, she now had more than she ever wanted to feel.

She thought of going to bed but she wasn't tired. She thanked the house staff for their wonderful care then headed upstairs. She found herself drawn to Eugene's study and paused in the hallway outside the double doors.

A part of her wanted to back away, not put herself through the misery of remembrance. But the evening had drained any resistance left. She felt impelled and needy and told herself if nothing else, being around Eugene's things, just as he had left them, might quiet the desolation closing in on her.

She opened the door as if unlocking a chamber of her heart. On her movement the lights came on and everything appeared in place, except Eugene.

She closed the door softly behind her and strolled into the study. At once the dark woods of the surrounding bookcases and the mosaic of stone in the fireplace imprinted a sense of something so solid and sturdy. A favorite chair, a wet bar at the ready, all of it remained so much like the husband she had known. In the silence she stood and took it in. To no one present she spoke in a whisper.

"What now, Eugene?"

It was as much a prayer as a cry for help. She closed her eyes. As tears fell she felt the room embrace her. The smell of coffee and brandy and Eugene's cologne enveloped her with memories of his presence. To anyone else, the aromatics of Jamaican Blue Mountain Peaberry and 30-year-old Armagnac mixed with a hint of musk held no special essence other than what they were. But to her in the moment it became so easy to believe Eugene might appear any second to comfort her.

Along with the warmth of the sense memory, a rising anger arose in her. Yes, this was the man she loved but he was also the man who had engineered Goodwin Godspeed Diye III to trigger upon his death. What kind of world had he left her?

Had Eugene lied to her when he promised to put everything on hold until more tests were done? Her heart grappled with finding excuses for him. He'd simply never expected to be assassinated. Perhaps he had put everything on hold, only he excluded plans for what would happen if anyone tried to defeat him by taking his life.

Maybe he had felt too insulated to die. She knew all too well what he'd thought about the demands of fate. It had been easy for him to see himself as the one destined to make the hard choices, to save humanity from overrunning itself into extinction.

If he had only told her this kind of predicament was a possibility. If he had at least warned her that his untimely death would mean severe consequences, she could have prepared. But why should he? He knew she had no intention of collapsing the population if left to do it on her own. She had made that clear in so many ways. And maybe that was enough for him to keep the secret.

Only now, as a result, others had the vaccine to do with as they may.

The predicament she was left with was stifling. She didn't want anyone to die and yet coming out with the vaccine herself would only convict her and Eugene as the ones responsible. As it was, she could live with speculation and conspiracy stories. But confirmation of her culpability she could not.

If she hurried the vaccine to the authorities, she knew what would happen. All the conspiracy theories about 3rd Protocol would be proven. Suddenly appearing with the antidote for a custom poison was highly suspicious. Helping the world would mean admitting guilt for creating the plague. How could she do that? Her life would be over. On the other hand, not helping would mean the end of so many lives.

She had to think, find a way to help the world without going down in history as the one responsible for the greatest act of mass murder, an act so horrendous that calling it mass murder was not doing it justice. Killing six billion people was an apocalyptic act beyond compare. She refused to take the fall for Eugene's crime.

She only hoped that The Group would release the vaccine she had given them in her ignorance. So far they hadn't and it worried her. What were they waiting for? If they released it, the pressure would be off of her to do the same. But with every passing day, the likelihood of their involvement waned and the need for her to act grew stronger. One thing was certain – she had to find a way to give the world the vaccine while keeping all connection to any of it far away from her.

She looked down at Eugene's desk and suffered a slashing ache. Resting there was the plastic hospital bag holding Eugene's personal effects. It was right where she had placed it that terrible night. Emergency medical staff had emptied Eugene's pockets and given her the contents. Unable to look at any of it once she got it home, she had placed the bag on his desk and forgotten it.

Seeing it brought her back to the opera and the last words she spoke to Eugene.

"*All I want is to be happy with you…*" The sentiment now seemed so naïve.

She stepped closer and took notice – inside the plastic bag was Eugene's phone. A single indicator light meant a saved message was not yet heard. The light hadn't been on when she placed the bag on the desk. The message must be new.

Hesitating but knowing full well that she must, she reached for the bag and took hold of the phone. In moments she was listening to voicemail.

A vaguely familiar voice spoke on the recording.

"Eugene, it's Javier. We've got to talk. I had a run-in with André Bolard. NCO is planning to shift focus onto GeLixCo. I think we can flip this if we get to him right away. I'm going to be in the European Quarter on Tuesday. If you can, meet me at Marie-Louise Square as usual, lunchtime date. I'm going there either way so if you can't make it, no problem; no need to get back to me."

The message ended. Perplexed, Leah stood holding the phone. What did Javier mean – *shift focus onto GeLixCo*? Why would NCO do that? And even if they did, why would Javier and Eugene be interested in flipping that situation? It didn't make sense unless they wanted NCO to continue its focus on NovoSenectus instead. But Eugene had always complained about the constant demonstrations by NCO against *GenLET*. If anything, shifting focus onto GeLixCo should be a good thing.

On impulse, Leah dialed Javier's number back. She would ask him straight away. The problem was – he didn't answer. Her call went to voicemail and she hung up before the recording started.

Leah never had any dealings with Javier although she'd heard quite a bit about him from Eugene. She knew how valuable a resource he could be. He knew people and got things done. More to the point, Eugene had trusted him for years. If Leah needed something covert carried out, who better to turn to? The arrangement for a meeting was on Tuesday. That was tomorrow. If Javier wasn't answering his phone, maybe she should go meet him at the time arranged for Eugene. Javier said he'd be going there whether or not Mass could make it.

Obviously, Mass wouldn't be attending – at least Eugene Mass.

Leah had to get ideas and make critical plans. There was work to do. She had a vaccine that needed a way out into public use. And final justice had to be done regarding Curtis Labon. Javier was the one to ask. She'd start with him first.

She put the phone in pocket and walked out of the study. Standing in the doorway before she left, she looked back and remembered Eugene's last words. They were as true for her as they ever were for him.

"*I wish the world was different…*"

CHAPTER 44

Apartment Level, Building 2
GARC, Puerto Rico

The flow of water over skin became a morning meditation to start the day.

Janis stood beneath a warm shower with eyes closed and let residue sleepiness drain away. Work from the night before lingered in mind. In a fog of drowsiness her late-night session in the lab seem closer than the day ahead. And yet disturbingly, the day ahead seemed farther away than the consequences of an on-rushing future.

She had stayed late by herself deciphering 2nd Protocol. Afterwards, as usual, she had gone upstairs to be with Alyssa. By the time Janis crawled into bed, she knew she'd be sleeping in late. Morning would come quickly. She hated disrupting her sleep routine but was determined to do whatever it took to find answers.

Faye had left two hours ago. Janis had the apartment level to herself.

She shut off the water and grabbed a towel but froze on a sound in the distance. Oddly, it was the sound of water. Drying herself, she strolled into the bedroom and caught sight through the window. A squall of heavy rain was passing over the island. It beat on the roof and against the glass with primal force. The insistence of it was dispassionate. Its resolve, arbitrary. It was going to come down regardless of anyone's opinion. For Janis, it added stress and a powerful reminder of how nature considered humanity. So soon from the shower, it only extended her meditation.

She finished drying off while heating coffee and starting toast. She dressed in laboratory scrubs and went to the living room to check the computer. There were no messages from Faye but world news was nonstop. Janis watched a report.

Panicked regions in southwest Asia and sub-Saharan Africa in desperation were using any vaccine stocks on hand to try to combat the GGD3 plague. Nothing was working; if anything, the situation was getting worse.

The combined death toll on both continents now topped 10,000. Travel to and from impacted areas was restricted. Teams of experts in the field had collected samples and were trending on how the infection was spreading. The virus had been identified and blood tests were being done in outlying populations to see if others had been exposed. Some researchers disputed the value of such tests since the incubation period for the virus was so short. If you were exposed, you soon knew it.

Janis retreated into the kitchen to collect her toast and coffee. The news was overwhelming but she couldn't let it sap her energy for doing work. She simply had to concentrate on problems with an attitude that anything could be solved.

Foremost on her mind were all the sterile children. If the population collapsed and the world also faced a generation who couldn't reproduce, what hope was left for humanity? Now more than ever it was critical to find a cure for sterility.

The goal of Eugene Mass was a human population of 500 million in harmony with nature. He knew the survivors of his tough love would go through a rough adjustment period; that's why he'd planned on a core group of *GenLET* recipients to guide the world back from the brink. Such was his New World Harmony. But he had never expected that survivors would have to face being the last people on Earth.

Janis returned to the computer and sat to have breakfast. She brought up a video feed from the sub-basement lab in Building 3 and switched the display into multi-view mode. Six different lab rooms were shown in separate windows; two of the views alternated between prep and lab areas. In one of the windows, Faye worked in BSL3 containment. Hidden in a safety suit, gloves, and helmet, no one else would have been able to tell. But Janis knew Faye, knew the way she worked. It hadn't taken long for the two of them to fall into sync as lab partners. Whether or not they would ever achieve such harmony outside the lab was as yet unresolved.

Flitting her gaze from window to window, Janis watched as more than a dozen technicians in eight different rooms concentrated on their research. She hoped that measures Faye and her were working out would prove viable enough so the results could be sent to Granite Peak Installation for animal trials. She wanted to have hope. Then again, she didn't realistically expect their first or second attempt to find a fix would turn out to be the magic bullet. Even more reason for work into the late hours.

Janis eased back with coffee in hand and changed the surveillance feed. This time, Alyssa's room appeared on the screen. The camera's vantage point was from a corner at the ceiling. A wide-angled lens added some distortion but the scene was unmistakable. Entranced, Janis watched the live action as Rebecca Yeats, the supervising care provider, checked monitors and gave instructions to a nurse. The audio was off and Janis left it that way. It would only interrupt her reverie.

Rebecca left the room; the nurse soon after. Janis at last had an unobstructed view of Alyssa lying in the hospital bed. She looked just the same as when Janis last left her in the middle of the night only now the light of day shined on her face. On her window, the rain's mottled pattern ran in freckled shadows down the walls and across the bed. It was as if nature herself was tapping on Alyssa with a thousand silent calls to come to life.

Janis wanted to be there with her but, as with the rain, her wishes didn't matter.

She also wanted a solution. For that she was needed in the lab.

She pushed up from the chair and got a lab coat from the entryway closet. While slipping on the coat she headed out the door. Her natural habit was to thrust hands in pockets. There she found her phone. On it was a waiting text message.

Standing on the threshold with door still open, she checked the sender.

Knockout Mouse.

Interesting. Her thumb tapped through panels for access. When the message came up, she gave it a quick scan but it went through awareness and didn't register. She needed to read it again. Was this real?

411 \\\ vac 4 3P exists! me 2 get & give 2 u asap 1 way or other ///

Janis slammed the front door shut and took off in a dead run down the hall. She reread the message as least ten more times during the elevator ride to the lobby. Running through RIDIS scan to check out, she burst outside, oblivious to the rain.

The distance between building 2 and 3 wasn't huge but it was enough to get drenched, even after running the whole way. Security agents in building 3 at first were alarmed when she tore into the lobby. Two of them reached for their holsters.

"Everything's all right, it's all right," she yelped. "I've got to get to the lab."

Dripping wet, she endured check-in and scan with no patience but rising hope. Once through, there was only the freight elevator ride to the bottom. A minute later she was on the intercom to Faye in BSL3 containment.

"Faye, get over here! You've got to see this!"

Faye reacted with concern until she saw Janis' smile. Dragging her positive air tube with her, Faye sidled to the thick glass.

Janis held up the phone and pressed it to the window.

"It's from Knockout Mouse. He says a vaccine for 3rd Protocol exists! He's going to get it for us!"

Overjoyed, Faye squinted to read the message for herself.

"That's incredible. Wait there, I'm coming out."

It took several minutes to shed the layers of BSL3 confinement and follow proper egress procedures. Faye hurried but completed each one. Once outside, she had to see the message again for herself.

"This came in early this morning. Anything else since then? Any email?"

Janis took the phone back. "No, this is it. This is enough! If he manages to come through, just think what that means!"

"It's hard to believe. I've gotten so used to bad news."

"We knew something like this had to exist. Mass wasn't about to hand out extended life only to have it wiped out by 3rd Protocol. He had to protect his friends."

"Never mind his friends. Once 3P got out there – he had to protect himself. Besides, it's standard procedure – never a measure without a counter-measure."

"Especially with viral agents. They can come back on you too easily."

"Yeah, if you're mad enough to release them into the wild."

Janis floated an idea that came to her in the elevator. "Knockout Mouse must be getting this from The Group. I wonder how *they* got it?"

"Ask him. And while you're at it, ask him what he means – *one way or other*."

"I saw that too. You have to think about the position he's in. The Group is probably inoculating all their people, Mouse included. That puts him near it but might not give him access. If he can't swipe a dose of vaccine to bring us…"

"He can bring himself." Faye finished Janis' point.

"Sure. He'll have the vaccine in his system. He'll make antibodies. Like he said, we'll get it one way or another."

Faye sat down. "I'm afraid I'm not going to be able to concentrate until we get this in hand. This is huge."

"Oh, I know. Working against the generational time limit set by sterility is one thing. Trying to find a fix before a plague takes out 90% of the population was impossible."

"Imagine that nightmare." Faye's voice dropped to a whisper.

"With so many people gone, support structures will implode. Power generation, basic services might be interrupted. We'd be lucky to get needed supplies for the lab to continue our work."

Until the promise of a 3P vaccine seemed assured, such things had gone unspoken between them. Hearing them said, even with a vaccine on the way, proved to be no less disquieting. Faye hugged herself and rocked in the chair.

"I thought sterility was impossible enough."

Janis detected a tinge of disappointment. "But we don't think that anymore. We're making progress."

"I just wonder sometimes if our so-called progress is sending us in circles."

"Why do you say that?"

"I've had to redo some of the viability assays. One of our assumptions was not quite right."

Some of the cheer dropped from Janis' face. "But you've adjusted?"

"Yes, after a frustrating morning."

"We told Granite Peak we'd have something for them to test this week."

"We will." She grinned. "We didn't say what day this week. It might be on the eighth day."

Just then, the lab's general phone line rang. Faye answered it.

"Faye Gardner, may I help you?" As she listened she rocked forward in her chair. Her mouth dropped open. "Thank you! Sure, right away."

Faye bolted from her seat and clutched Janis by the hands.

"It's Alyssa! She's awake!"

Janis was stunned. "What?"

"That was Rebecca. A nurse heard a noise on the monitor. When she went into check, Alyssa talked to her!"

Janis burst into tears and ran for the elevator with Faye right behind.

On the ride up they hugged and shared the joy. Neither one could stop talking.

As the doors opened, Faye held Janis back a second.

"Good things happen in threes. This makes two. I wonder what's next."

Janis smiled but couldn't bring herself to say what was on her mind.

She rushed on. She didn't want to jinx it.

Chapter 45

Alyssa's Care Room
Building 3, GARC

Janis burst into the room intent on seeing her daughter's eyes and hearing her voice and yet the deep disappointments of the past few weeks prompted restraint and reservation. In a world careening off balance, believing good news on face value had become harder to accept than trying to deny that terrible things could happen. Only confirmation would give her heart reprieve from doubt and solace for her quest.

"Is it true?" The whispered wish was barely a sigh but it filled the room.

Rebecca and the dayshift nurse huddled bedside blocking the view. Excitedly they turned and an opening parted between them for Janis to approach.

Rebecca smiled. "Come see for yourself!"

Janis drew near to witness the awe and splendor of renewal. The essence that was Alyssa inhabited the body again. Her eyes were tired but bright, her smile weak but exquisitely sweet. A more glorious sight could not be described or imagined for a mother to see. The stubborn veil of grief that had become a dullness from which Janis feared she'd never escape suddenly lifted to reveal elation.

Alyssa didn't move her body, only lifted her eyes. "Hi, Mom…"

For Janis, no greater sound could be heard.

She rushed the bed on the wings of joy through a shower of tears.

"Ah, baby, you're so beautiful!" She kissed Alyssa on the forehead, smoothed back her hair, and took her hand in hers.

"How do you feel?"

Alyssa blinked in a slow, labored attempt to respond. Her lips parted then paused as wisps of disorientation cleared. Her voice was weak, a word or two slurred, but the message was unmistakable.

"Tired but I'm OK."

Holding fast to Alyssa's hand, Janis looked to Rebecca. "How did you find out?"

Rebecca smiled and looked down on her patient. "She said she was thirsty."

"I heard her through the monitor," added the nurse.

Standing behind the bedside trio, Faye beamed as she watched. At first she was speechless, overcome. Such an event was a triumph, a shared revitalization, not only for Alyssa but for the hopes of everyone that things could work out no matter how discouraging they appeared at times.

Faye felt consideration for what Janis, as mother, would want. She spoke to the caretakers. "Maybe we should give the two of them a little time together…"

Rebecca responded by tapping the nurse's arm. "Of course…"

They retreated out the door. On the way out the nurse added, "I'll be right by in case you need anything."

Faye stepped up alongside Janis and touched Alyssa's arm in hello. "It's good to see you doing so well." She turned to Janis. "I'll be outside."

Janis gave Faye a hug. "Thank you."

As Faye exited and closed the door behind her, Janis scooted up onto the bed and sat next to Alyssa. Looking back on her daughter to marvel, she saw a change of expression that signaled confusion.

"Why is everyone so excited?" asked Alyssa.

Janis stroked Alyssa's cheek with the back of her hand. "You've been very sick. But you're better now."

"What happened?"

"I'll explain it later if you want; it doesn't matter right now."

"Why are you here with that woman?"

"That's Faye Gardner. Remember, I used to work with her a long time ago."

"But you don't like her."

Janis paused to ensure tact. "We had some problems in the past…"

"I saw her once when I was little. She was nice to me."

"Yes she was."

"You went to college together but you said you couldn't work with her…"

"None of that matters now. We all need each other."

Alyssa started to cry. "Why did they bring me here? What have they been doing to me? I want to go home…"

The smile faded from Janis' face. There was so much to tell and so little time. "A lot has been going on. Some very serious things are happening. I didn't understand it fully myself until just recently."

"Why do I have to stay here? Who are these people? What do they want?"

The quiet tears became open sobs. Alyssa's whispers became cries for help.

Janis struggled to organize her thoughts as she cradled Alyssa to comfort her. How could she explain it all in a way that would satisfy her daughter's curiosity without overwhelming her with fear?

There was no easy way, no half-answer that would do. The only thing Alyssa knew was that strangers had kidnapped her and taken her to a strange facility and kept her there against her will, away from family, in order to carry out medical procedures which were unexplained and seriously invasive. Now her mother appeared with these same people and a colleague from the past she didn't like.

The juxtaposition had to be baffling if not frightening. Was it any wonder Alyssa wasn't making sense of the world she found upon waking?

Janis rocked Alyssa in her arms and hoped her presence and physical connection would explain more than words could ever hope to. At a loss for excuses to offer in the moment, Janis was left with only the bare truth to tell.

"You're here…because you're special, very special."

"I don't understand…"

Janis looked up and realized the rain had stopped. Through the windows, sunlight returned as fast-moving clouds raced inland. The sudden brightness in the room gave her courage to let the hard truth find a form that Alyssa might accept.

"The people here found out that the world's children have a serious problem."

"What kind of problem?"

"When they grow up they won't be able to have children."

"Me too?" The alarm was apparent. "I can't have babies?"

"That's just it. You don't have the problem. That's why you're special. And the people here need to find out why. If they can figure out why you're special, then maybe the rest of the children can be helped."

"But if I don't have the problem, why am I sick?"

"That wasn't supposed to happen. They didn't plan on that."

"So can we go home?"

"It's not that simple."

"Why not?"

"Well, they explained the problem to me...and they explained it to Faye...and both of us decided to stay to help them find a cure. It's very important."

For Alyssa, bewilderment persisted. "But they grabbed me in the park; they took me away without telling you."

"They had to do that to protect you."

The incongruity strained for explanation. "Protect me?"

"There are all kinds of people in the world. Not all of them want what's right."

Alyssa shivered. "I don't care. I don't like it here. I want to go home."

"We're together, that all that matters. This is the safest place for both of us."

From shivers to sobs, Alyssa sank into herself. "I don't want to be special! I want to be like I was..."

A knock on the door intruded but Janis ignored it.

"Alyssa, don't cry. Don't you see? You were always special. Nothing about that has changed..."

The door opened and Rebecca took a step into the room.

"Excuse me; she needs to get some rest."

Just then, Janis realized the monitors were still on. All that had been said had been picked up by microphones. Just who had overheard was left for her to wonder.

"Maybe just a little more time?" Janis didn't want to go. Not like this. There was so much more to say, so much more for Alyssa to understand. To leave her frightened and confused was wrenching.

Janis never expected such a reunion would take a bitter turn.

Rebecca persisted. "I'm really going to have to insist. She's been through a lot. It's still very early in her recovery."

Janis dipped her head to signal compliance. She kissed Alyssa on the forehead and hugged her. She knew no other parting words to give than the ones that had been in her heart all during the many weeks of searching for her.

"I love you..."

As Alyssa settled and rested, Rebecca hurried forward to attend to her.

Janis' steps into the hallway were halting. She was leaving with a full heart but emptied of the energy to muster any more strength and composure in the face of such emotion. The experience drained her even as she felt relieved. Her daughter was back; she'd pull through. The terrible question of her survival was no longer holding Janis hostage. The affirmation held true – life was in no way perfect and yet the many problems of life were preferable to the alternative void.

Janis looked both ways in the hallway. She discovered Faye leaning against the wall with a phone to her ear. The conversation was obviously intense. Janis couldn't tell if Faye was excited or aggravated. Whatever the topic of conversation, it had Faye's undivided attention. As such, it sparked interest in Janis.

"Who was that?" asked Janis.

Faye pocketed her phone. "Colin."

"Oh…" Janis turned away with intent to return to the lab.

Faye stayed in place. "He just got a field report from OpSec."

Janis intended her curious pause to be brief. "OpSec?"

"Operation Security. The Project has made a move against The Group."

Janis stepped back. "When did they decide to do this?"

"I don't know. We'll have to ask Colin. He's in his office. Wanna come?"

Janis wavered. The need to know firsthand outweighed anything else.

"Why not…"

The two of them hurried downstairs to Colin's office.

They found him at his desk intensely focused on computer screens.

Faye led the way. "We came to get the details."

Colin's gaze stayed riveted to a report. "I haven't gone through all of it myself. Like I said, most of this just came in."

Knowing Janis' reluctance around Colin, Faye asked the question.

"When did they decide to launch an operation?"

Colin's concentration broke. He glanced over at them. "It's been brewing one way or another ever since that guy Knockout Mouse came to the island to visit."

Janis asserted, "So you *did* have us under surveillance…"

"With good reason. We weren't going to pass up a chance to follow him."

Janis stepped near the desk. "Off the island?"

The tone of the question was accusatory. Colin bristled.

"What do you think? He works for The Group. They masterminded 1st Protocol and you said they were about to let loose with 2nd Protocol. The Project won't let that happen. After what Mass did, they won't take any more chances."

"Don't you think it's a little late for that?" Janis' sarcasm struck home.

"Do you think it's too late for the children?" He glared through her silence then added, "Preemptive action is authorized to get things under control. As soon as the 2nd Protocol shipment arrived for you, that cinched it. Once The Project knew 2nd Protocol was real, a response was certain."

Stepping between the two of them, Faye asked, "So where did Knockout Mouse go when you followed him?"

Colin shifted to one side. "He led us to some interesting people. The first one is a man you might know. Hasuru Tamasu."

Faye sat down. "The Japanese industrialist?"

"Same one. Hasuru led us to a spa club in New York. Coincidentally, Curtis Labon was at the club at the same time. They were seen together."

Faye looked to Janis. "That would verify what Knockout Mouse told you about Labon being part of The Group."

"There's more." Colin tapped his computer screen. "Soon after the spa meeting, Hasuru took off to Switzerland where a few Group members showed up for a rather odd conference."

"What was odd about it?" asked Faye.

Colin's eyebrows rose. "They never met together at any one time. For some reason it was important for all of them to be there but from the outside it looks like nothing got done. We know that can't be the case."

Faye stood and stepped around the desk to look over Colin's shoulder.

"Where was this?"

"A place called Lugano. It's a resort town near the border with Italy but it also does quite a bit conference and banking business."

Janis joined Faye behind the desk so she could see the report onscreen.

Colin clicked on a graphic and a map of Switzerland zoomed into a street map of Lugano. Color-coded markers had been interspersed across the grid of the city.

Colin explained. "These are locations where individual Group members spent time. Four colors – four Group members."

Faye singled out a particular point of interest. "This one place was visited by all four of them. I don't see any other location getting equal attention."

Janis asked, "What's there?"

Colin drilled down to finer detail. "It says here it's a clinic specializing in homeopathic treatments."

"How odd?" commented Faye.

Janis pointed to color-coded dots across the border in Italy. "What are these?"

"It looks like two of them went on separate trips to Milan. I don't see any explanation for it."

"I don't get it." Faye straightened up. "On the phone you said The Project made a move against The Group."

"That's right," Colin confirmed. "This map is hours old. The latest news just came in." Colin toggled another window forward on the screen. Janis and Faye leaned in to take a look.

On the screen, a field report was clear and terse.

After reading a line or two, Janis reacted. "You took out their jet?"

Faye read an excerpt. "...subject jet destroyed over Aletsch Glacier in the eastern Bernese Alps."

Colin added, "The flight plan had them headed for Basel-Stadt."

Janis was incredulous. "You killed them?"

Colin set his jaw firm. "The Project arranged an accident."

"My God," gasped Faye. "Are you just assassinating people now?"

"The time for delicate surgery is over; only amputation is going to save us."

"So what's the plan?" asked Janis. "Find all eight members of The Group and just kill them?"

Colin avoided a direct answer. "We have no way of knowing what these madmen are up to next. We can't let it get any worse. There's no time to be delicate."

Faye took control of the mouse and navigated the report to the jet's manifest. "Besides Hasuru, who got targeted?"

Colin watched the report scroll by. "I haven't gotten that far."

Faye paused on an entry and stiffened. "Two pilots and a service attendant – I guess they're acceptable collateral losses."

No explanation was necessary but Colin felt impelled to make a case.

"If this was an accident, that's exactly what would happen. Janis said there were eight members in The Group. This operation got half of them. The other half must believe this was an accident."

"Why not wait until they're all together?"

"We have no way of knowing how often that happens, if at all. For security reasons, they might avoid that and videoconference their combined meetings."

Faye moved down the manifest. Onscreen, a thumbnail photo aligned beside a short bio of each passenger. The next entry caught her eye.

"...Heinrich Jaeger. I've heard of him. He's big in European biotech."

"According to the map he took a side trip to Milan," added Colin. "He also owns a research lab in Basel-Stadt. It was no fluke they were headed there."

Faye scrolled down the page. The next name caught her eye like none other. At first she didn't believe it. Too stunned to speak, she pointed at it on the screen.

Colin leaned forward to make sure what he thought he saw was correct.

When he finally spoke, the room went cold.

"...Kevin Mass."

Frozen in place, Janis repeated what all were thinking.

"...Mass?"

Faye rushed to click on the thumbnail photo.

Janis jerked across the desk to see it. The look on her face told Faye everything she needed to know. It was a photo of Knockout Mouse.

"...KM..." whispered Janis. Tears welled up in her eyes and behind it surged a rage and frustration that launched her into a fit across the room. "No! You bastards! What have you done?"

Faye slumped, stunned. She sat back on the edge of the desk. "It can't be..."

Taken aback by their emotional reaction, Colin tried summing up their shock. "So Kevin Mass is Knockout Mouse..."

Across the room Janis stood shaking with eyes closed.

Faye glanced at her then stared at Colin before dropping her gaze to the floor. "You don't understand..."

Colin waited but both Faye and Janis were too distraught to explain.

Taking control of the keyboard, he expanded the bio and scanned details. "Kevin Mass...son of Eugene Mass."

Janis looked to Faye. She wanted to shout but could only whisper. "He told me he was just a kid in college when his father got him a job doing research for a new think tank."

Colin read on. "...his mother was Eugene's first wife. They split up when Kevin was in his early twenties..."

Janis added, "That would be right around the time when Mass left The Group."

Faye considered all that Janis had told her since they first got back together. The line of evidence was falling into place but pieces of it were not yet evident.

"But all these years, Kevin stayed with The Group."

"He must have taken sides with them against his father."

"Or the divorce split the family three ways," reasoned Colin.

Janis thought back to her last days in India.

"And Malcolm Stowe blackmailed him. Malcolm worked for Eugene."

Faye drew the conclusion. "A father's revenge – plus that would give Mass an inside way to keep track of what The Group was doing."

The distress was too much for Janis. She began to pace.

The day had just started and yet the highs and lows coming at her were more than she could bear. Sadness vied with anger to overpower her. She felt crushed. The misery she had seen in Alyssa's eyes only compounded with the news that Knockout Mouse was dead. The fact that such news originated with Colin only served to feed simmering resentments. She became indignant.

"When will you people stop screwing with things…?"

The non sequitur drew both Colin's and Faye's attention.

Janis stared Colin down. "You've probably killed all of us."

The wretchedness and fury in Janis' tone set the room on edge.

Considering the soaring emotion, Colin tried holding back but he couldn't help reacting defensively. He knew Janis had become somewhat friendly with Kevin Mass but this level of despondency out of her seemed out of place.

"Hold on. I'm sorry he was on that flight – but let's not overreact."

Janis turned to confront him. "I don't believe you."

"You don't believe what?"

"I think The Project had this manifest long before that jet ever took off. They knew *exactly* who'd be on that flight. They let it happen anyway."

Colin grimaced. "Why do that?"

Faye interjected, "Why not? To you he's more collateral damage; accidents are like that."

"No!" Janis shouted. "It was because of the surveillance – you knew Kevin was about to go public with all he knew. He'd decided to turn against The Group. He told me he was going to expose it all and you couldn't let that happen, could you? If the truth about 1st Protocol ever got out, the secret of your fuckup trying to sabotage it might see the light of day. Everyone would find out who really caused sterility. He wasn't collateral damage – he was a bonus kill!"

"Come on…" started Colin. "I think we all need to take a step back from this."

"All of you are so fucking pathetic. We were so close!"

Bursting into tears, Janis ran from the room.

Faye examined Colin's suddenly perplexed reaction.

"…So close? What the fuck – was she in love with the guy?"

Faye scowled. In the moment it was more important to comfort Janis than stay and make sense of it with Colin. Faye jumped up and rushed out the door.

Janis had already caught an elevator going down. Faye noticed the lit-up down arrow and took the companion elevator to catch up. At the first floor security station she asked the guards about Janis. They motioned she had run outside.

Faye tore through the lobby and out the front door. Outside everything was wet and bright with shimmers of reflected sun. Looking both ways, Faye caught a glimpse of Janis heading up the service road along a perimeter fence. Faye's first impulse was to take after her in a sprint but then she remembered the warning from her obstetrician. A long and thoughtful walk would be all she'd be able to manage.

It was better that way. It gave them both time for the intensity to settle down.

At the back of the property, at the highest point, Faye finally caught up with Janis. She stood alone in a small field looking out to sea. On approach, she ignored she had company. For a while, Faye stood silently by and shared the view.

The ocean was a sight to behold. The greenery of the hills around them was resplendent. Everywhere the majesty of planet Earth was on display. And yet for all its inspiration, the glories of the surrounding world seemed other worldly compared to the civilization that ran rampant across it so recklessly and self-absorbed.

The day's events only highlighted the poignancy of how true that was.

Janis stood her ground, enclosed within herself, silent but obviously hurting.

For Faye there was no point mentioning anything more about what had happened. Some things were too raw and understood, too close to the surface to need comment. Purely reactive, she let impulse take flight.

"We should get out of here."

The suggestion didn't faze Janis. She said nothing.

"This would be a perfect day to go to the beach," added Faye

Janis took the bait. "And what would you tell security?"

"At this point?" Faye took a moment to let the proposal peculate. "What does it matter? I'll tell them I'm going. If they don't like it they can shoot me."

Janis was expressionless. "Some would call that a win-win proposition."

The dark humor was depressing but at this point it relieved some of the stress.

Faye turned and tried to catch Janis' eye. "I'm serious."

"You usually are."

"Wanna come?"

Janis paused. She glanced down on the cluster of buildings that was GARC. "I can't stay here right now."

Faye perked up. "So where should be go? Any ideas?"

Janis thought a long while. She scanned the distance from south to north.

"Yeah," she said finally. "I know a place. A lighthouse used to be there."

Faye reflected on the Borinquen Lighthouse Ruins, the island place where Janis had gotten together with Knockout Mouse.

Going there would be Janis' way of paying last respects but it also might be a shared way to come to peace about all that was lost.

Faye turned to go. "All right, let's go."

Janis started after her but got an idea and paused.

"Just a minute." She clutched her phone from lab coat pocket.

"I want to send Colin something. Maybe that asshole will figure it out."

She gave the text one last look, selected message forwarding, and pressed send.

411 \\\ vac 4 3P exists! me 2 get & give 2 u asap 1 way or other ///

Chapter 46

Curtis Labon's Estate
Quebec Province, Canada

The crunch of snow was underfoot but unheard beneath the noise of machinery. Curtis walked beside the job foreman and listened to a progress report. Around them stretched ten thousand acres of wilderness that encircled Labon's private lake. His home property was a special refuge from the clamor and craziness of the world.

No more than today.

A skip loader carried dirt from a leveled-off area cleared of brush. Not far away, a newly-in-place pre-fabricated building received finishing touches. The impressive structure would soon function as a small warehouse. Its twin roll-up doors were open and forklifts shuttled in and out with goods being unloaded from the back of a semi-truck.

"Tomorrow we start on the fuel tanks." The foreman motioned to a plot of land behind the building. "First the gasoline tank gets buried then the propane tank will be set up on that clearing. We widened the drive-up access like you said."

"What about the perimeter fence?" asked Curtis.

"We got the one you wanted." The foreman lifted a clipboard. "One other thing; it's about this stock order. Are you sure these figures are right?"

Curtis gave a glance and walked on. "What's the problem?"

"Oh, no problem. It's just a hell of a lot of stuff. When it first got called in I thought someone in my office heard wrong. I mean, it'd take a couple of years and one hungry group to eat through all of this."

Stopping at the door of his SUV, Curtis obliged with a condescending smile. "I like to have enough on hand. It cuts down on trips into town for supplies."

The foreman backed away. "I guess it would. All right, I'll get back at it."

"You do that. Good job. Thank you."

Curtis got behind the steering wheel and started the engine. A blast of air shot from heater vents and the center console television lit up with a CBC sports report. Despite the reporter's impassioned account of last night's game between the Vancouver Canucks and the San Jose Sharks, Curtis failed to take notice.

He sat as the car idled and watched the transformation – his idyllic estate was becoming a survivalist compound. To think that such a thing might be necessary was one thing. To watch it happen for real was sobering and put things in perspective. A world losing most of its people was horrendous enough. But not having the means to self-protect against what was killing them was unbearable.

And center to his thoughts.

He put the car in gear and started up the gravel path headed for the main house. The sports report ended and a recap of hourly headlines took its place. He half-listened until news of a jet crash in the Swiss Alps caught his attention. The mention of two names in particular caused him to step on the brake and watch intently.

"…Hasuru Tamasu, Heinrich Jaeger…"

He reached for his phone and dialed a number only recently put on speed dial.

"Hannah…it's Labon. Have you seen the news?"

The woman's voice was rushed and distracted.

"Ah, no, I'm in the middle of something."

Curtis ignored her clear indication of being interrupted.

"Aren't we all. I have another job for you."

Reserved, Hannah's tone became more focused with marginal interest.

"You have something else that needs to disappear?"

"No, at least not yet." Forming a plan, Curtis watched the CBC broadcast showing brief bios of wealthy crash victims. "A private jet went down in the Alps. It left Lugano headed for Basel. Several important people were onboard. I need to know if it really was an accident."

Hannah filled the pause on the line with a quizzical moan.

"…I don't know. Where does one start with that?"

"That's up to you. You can have whatever resources you need."

"Oh, OK," huffed Hannah. "Would that includes MI-6, the CIA and Mossad?"

"What are you saying? You can't do it?"

"I'm saying it's a tall order. If the crash was an accident, there's nothing to find. How will I know when to stop looking? If it wasn't an accident, it's a sure bet someone's working hard to make scarce any facts you want."

Curtis hadn't expected this resistance. It only highlighted his vulnerability. Forays into covert work had become necessary only in the past couple of years. What started with private investigations ultimately had led to Hannah's operation to silence Oliver Ross. Her questions now pointed out how much his approach suffered from a lack of cohesiveness and sophistication.

"You'll have all the intelligence at my disposal."

"Can I hire other operatives?"

"Why? Can't you go at this full time?"

"It's not that. The scope of what you're asking is beyond one person."

A work truck came up the single-lane road behind the SUV.

Curtis glanced into the rear-view mirror and let the truck wait.

"As usual, I prefer those involved kept to a bare minimum."

Hannah hardened with the prospect of taking on business set up to fail.

"And you need an answer as soon as possible…"

Curtis held back his angered impatience. He simply expected too much of a limited tool. Faced with that fact set him uneasy but the pressure of events demonstrated how ill-prepared he was in critical ways. He had called Hannah on impulse expecting to order up an answer as easily as he had ordered food for his survival stores. He saw the folly of that now and yet, the threat to his security was obvious. Options for a timely response were few.

He had no choice but to press her to take the case.

"I need an answer as soon as you get one. Give it whatever effort you can spare. I really need eyes on this. Are you willing to look into it or not?"

Hannah relented. "I'll do what I can. I can't promise anything."

"Keep me posted, even if nothing's happening."

As the line went dead, Curtis tossed the phone onto the passenger seat in frustration. He gunned the engine and spun wheels in the compacted snow and gravel. Shifting into four-wheel drive, he got the SUV moving up the road with the waiting truck tagging along behind.

The phone rang. He leaned over and grabbed it, expecting to hear Hannah with a question. Instead, it was a member of the household staff.

"Sir, just a reminder, your son Noah is expected to arrive in a few minutes."

"Yes, of course. Don't bother sending the car. I'll pick him up."

Curtis steered for the helipad weighed down with unexpected restlessness and anxiety. On the heels of disturbing news from Switzerland and Hannah's reluctance to assist, the prospect of a reunion with his estranged son now seemed taxing. He never expected such a meeting to be easy but the way he felt promised to make it even more difficult.

At the helipad, Curtis waited as the helicopter flew in from the south, hovered to get orientated, then landed. As he watched, he reflected. Noah would graduate from college this year. The last time they saw each other, Noah had just become a teenager. The divorce came soon after. It was brutal in many ways but none crueler for Curtis than the loss of connection between father and son.

The intervening years had not been kind and the estrangement had only grown, not softened. Noah's emotional resentments had found intellectual support when the lures of class warfare and environmental causes took hold of his idealism. Noah rejected family position and wealth. Instead, he embraced militant expressions of a rebellion that Curtis believed had roots far more personal than political.

The helicopter door opened and a young man hustled out from under the spinning blades. He hopped into the SUV's passenger seat and avoided prolonged eye contact with the driver.

"I'm glad you could make it," offered Curtis.

Properly antagonistic, Noah mumbled back, "Mom said it was important."

Curtis was put on notice; Noah had only agreed to come because of his mother's suggestion. That was quite all right with Curtis. He had worked long and hard to get her to intercede. It was unfortunate that it took dire innuendoes about global changes to persuade her to help.

The drive back to the house was short but long enough to establish how tense and awkward father and son felt in each other's presence. Curtis noticed that Noah arrived without suitcase of any kind. No doubt it signaled he didn't intend on staying. Curtis forged ahead anyway, requesting house staff to show him to his room.

Noah protested. "No one said anything about sleeping over. I'd rather get to the point of why I'm here."

"Very well…" Curtis waved off the staff member with a forced smile. "We'll be in the family room. We'll need privacy."

Curtis led Noah from the entrance hallway to the back of the house. They entered the expansive family room where on three sides windows looked out over the lake and wilderness beyond.

Noah stepped to a window. "How much of that out there is yours?"

"As much as you can see." Curtis was in no mood to be apologetic about all his life's labor had gotten him.

"I guess the helicopter too."

Curtis fixed himself a drink. "It belongs to a company I own."

Noah turned and stepped around the room inspecting the furnishings. "Why should any one person have so much when so many go without?"

"As a matter of fact, natural resources *are* limited but wealth isn't. There's no limit to how far the money supply can expand. One simply prints more dollars as new value is added to the marketplace."

Noah chuckled. "The marketplace…nothing but a rigged game."

"The problem with your way of thinking, you think wealth is a zero-sum pie with only so many pieces to go around. If that were true, then tell me – who had all the collective wealth that exists now a hundred years ago? The truth is, there's more millionaires today than ever."

"And they got that way by exploiting people."

"I guess that includes your favorite music groups, sports stars, the princes of social networking, and the purveyors of *the inconvenient truth.* Wealth is all right in some hands but not others?"

"Some people don't have to cheat, steal, and lie to get it."

Curtis tired of the expected exchange. "I can hardly argue with someone who is only willing to parrot slogans and sound bites heard at the last rally they attended."

"A slogan is more precise and relevant than the same old excuses…"

"So how much should one have? Where would *you* draw the line?"

Noah flopped down on a couch. "Equity."

"You mean equally rich or equally poor?"

"You *would* put it that way, wouldn't you."

"I've thought it through." Curtis sat at the wet bar. "You see, by the time you are my age there will be nine billion people on the planet requiring equity. I wonder if you're really prepared to accept the standard of living true equity would entail."

"Here we go. The same old scare tactics…"

Curtis drew a steady gaze on his boy. "As much as it may disappoint, I didn't ask you to come here to debate macroeconomic theory."

"That's a relief."

Curtis downed the rest of his drink. "Yes, well, there's only so much either of us can bear when it comes to that."

"What's your point? You want to debate family history instead?"

Determined to get through this, Curtis set his mind on the task at hand.

"I know we haven't been close the past few years. It's obvious you disapprove of my work and lifestyle."

Mention of it prompted Noah's anger. "Yeah, are you still raping a whole province to get rich off oil sands?"

Curtis snapped back, "And are you still driving a car? Have you been using any one of millions of products produced with oil? Have you even bothered to find out which ones those are? Where's your commitment to act locally, think globally?"

"This is a waste of time…"

Curtis forced composure. "Nonetheless, as much as you might discount it, I care about you. Naturally, I don't expect you to believe it; not yet. But as a gesture of reconciliation, I'd like to make you an offer."

Noah laughed. "What possibly could you offer me that I would want?"

Curtis stared at Noah until he caught his eye. "How about *GenLET*?"

"Oh yeah, like *you* have *GenLET*…"

The disbelieving reaction was kneejerk but insincere. Curtis could see surprise and wonder on Noah's face even as he shook his head and sniggered.

"And why not? Because it belongs to NovoSenectus? You already believe I run an evil empire. Why should that stop me? There's no reason to be surprised."

"Next you're going to say *you've* had the treatment…"

Curtis could tell the boy was fishing. "What's the point of having it otherwise?"

A serious recognition came over Noah. Curtis could see it was sinking in.

The offer was real. All humor left Noah's face.

"Something's going on. What do you want from me?"

"I told you. I want you to take the treatment just like I did. I'm offering you extended life."

There was a long pause. "Why would you do that?"

"Your lack of an attention span makes me repeat myself – I care about you."

"No shit," snapped Noah. "Out of the blue you care about me."

"A lot of things have gone wrong. That doesn't mean we can't make some things right."

A rising bitterness showed up in Noah. "You can't buy me with this."

"That's not my intention. If you want, receive the treatment, go on your way; afterwards, you never have to see me again."

"Really, you'd do that for me. How big of you."

Curtis refilled his drink. "It's a one-time offer. No strings attached. Considering the delicacy of the matter, you can see why I needed to present it to you in person."

Curtis could see wheels of interest as well as rebellion spinning in Noah's reaction. For the first time it was hard to tell whether the boy was genuinely attracted to the idea or merely confused how best to refuse in a way to annoy his father.

Noah got up and stepped to the window.

"If this is a one-time offer, then everything needs to be worked out between us right now, right?"

"Yes. There should be no misunderstandings going forward."

Noah stared across the distant lake. "So what about my girlfriend? We're planning on getting married. Can she have *GenLET* too?"

The suggestion caught Curtis off-guard. It was either a clever way of negotiating or a test of a father's resolve. To win his son back, Curtis was willing to bend a long way.

"I don't see why not," answered Curtis. "Naturally, you both would be bound by confidentiality agreements not to tell anyone else about what you received."

"Oh, is that the way it works..." Noah glanced back, "And what happens to those who break the agreement?"

Curtis hedged around what could be a fatal flaw. "There's no reason to worry about that if you keep it to yourself."

Noah nodded and turned back to the view. "I have a couple of best friends; I've known them since I was a kid. How about them?"

Curtis could see where this was going but it was too late. He had opened the door to others and now he was too far into the game to pull back.

"To a limited extent, some others, close friends could be added."

Noah turned to face his father. "But wait a minute. If I'm going to have this extra long life, I'm going to meet all kinds of people. I might get remarried or have a son. I'll make other friends. I'd want them to have it too. There's no way I can give you a complete list of people right now. I'd have to be able to pick and choose when the time came. Is that doable?"

By this point, Curtis was beyond playing the game. He was prepared to promise the boy anything to get him to take the initial treatment.

"I see your point. I think something can be worked out."

"Great! One last thing; no way would I want to do any of this unless *Mom* was on the list."

The look in Noah's eye told all. The whole thing was a ruse. The boy was playing with him, pushing him, trying to force him to his limit.

And he had just found it. Curtis set his glass down and prepared for battle.

"People who waste my time usually regret it."

"Oh, yeah? Well, new world elitists like you who think they can hand out life to a select few are going to regret it."

"What are you going to do? Firebomb me like the man in D.C.?"

Noah froze, guilt sweeping his face. "What are you talking about?"

Curtis was livid. "You know damned well what I'm talking about. Washington, D.C. Franklin Park. The lobbyist on K Street."

"What do you know about that?"

"I know you fucked up royally. The federal prosecutor had you and your merry band of NCO assholes lined up for hard time. How stupid can you be?"

"Why is that any of your business?"

Curtis yelled, "I *made* it my business! Like hell was I going to see a son of mine rot in jail for twenty years. You're not brainless; you're just too fucking young to know you have brains. You certainly have never been taught how to use them."

Noah stood stunned. "You got involved with that? You did something?"

"Damned right I did something. You needed to be saved from yourself. You have a chance, now don't screw it up."

"I never asked for your help; I didn't want your help."

"Maybe not but you needed it."

"Stay out of my business."

"Wake up. New Class Order doesn't care about you."

"And neither do you!" shouted Noah. "You think you can bribe me to make nice so you can feel better about yourself. It isn't going to work."

Noah headed for the hallway intent on a return trip helicopter ride.

The moment was pivotal. Curtis knew if he didn't somehow stop his son from walking out, he might never be seen again.

"There's something else you should know. It's critically important."

Noah halted, expecting only to take a second to be dismissive.

"That's just it; we have differing opinions about what's important."

Curtis slid off the bar stool and stepped slowly towards his son.

"The whole planet is about to change. Billions of people are going to die. Whatever life you and your girlfriend thought you were going to have is over."

Stunned into interest, Noah wavered. "What kind of crazy shit is this?"

"It certainly is crazy but I assure you it's going to happen. The government won't tell you; most aren't aware of the scope of what they're facing. Those in power don't want a panic. They've made sure that news of this gets sanitized."

"News of what?"

"A plague – one that will decimate populations everywhere. You might have seen the advertisements for it – the recycle symbol…Goodwin Godspeed Diye III."

A smile creased Noah's face. "That shit? That was just some crazy media hoax by some old, eccentric billionaire."

"I wish it were…" Curtis was deadly serious. He drew nearer to the boy.

Attempting to diffuse any hint of peril, Noah clung to denial. "Are you really that desperate? You're going to try to *frighten* me into going along with you?"

"It's already begun. Tens of thousands are dead in Africa and Asia."

"There's always something like that going on..."

"Not like this," Curtis interrupted. "There are people in Bangkok, Hong Kong, Shanghai, all over Asia, starting to stay indoors. They're worried about rumors they've heard. Many people in places like New Delhi and Mumbai have started to wear surgical masks when they go out on the street."

"Yeah, so what? Things like that happened with the Swine Flu."

Curtis became impassioned. "Just this once listen to me! You want proof? I'll show you results from one of my biopharma labs. Field researchers got samples from the bodies of early victims. They isolated the pathogen and got a good look at it. The damned thing was engineered to be insidious. No one's going to stop it."

"Engineered?" The key word kept Noah in the room.

"That's right. Goodwin Godspeed Diye III. What's about to happen has been years in the making. It's not by accident."

"Why on Earth would anyone do that?"

"You said it – Earth. Don't you want to save the planet – lower CO2, save the whales, stop the destruction of the rainforests? Eugene Mass believed fewer people was the only way."

"Mass? That geezer's dead." Noah took a step towards the hallway.

"Thankfully, but I'm afraid his legacy lives on. You need a microscope to see it but it's more potent and clever than anything the world ever had to contend with."

"OK, say this is real. Then what are you doing about it?"

"There's only one thing to do. Prepare. Until a vaccine is found, no one's safe. Like any storm, you're only as secure as the refuge you take. Mine will be here. Those close to me, if they choose, can ride out the worst of it here on the estate. The chance of infection will be greatly minimized by staying away from population centers."

"You expect me to come live here?"

Curtis arrived at the central reason for the visit. Everything came down to how his son reacted to the final offer.

"Yes. I'm pleading with you to do just that. Bring your girlfriend if you want. I won't get in the way. As you see the place is big enough we can avoid each other."

Noah shook his head, laughed, and looked at the floor.

"Wow. You're fucking serious."

"I know, it's a lot to absorb. You don't have to answer right now. Take your time. You may think there's no reason to trust me but trust your gut. This is critical."

Noah held a hand to his forehead and avoided eye contact.

"I don't know. I can't do this right now. I'm going to take a look around."

Unsure of his own feelings, Noah fled the room.

Curtis let him go. The boy hadn't asked for a return flight home and for now that was progress enough. Maybe at least he'd consider the offer. It was all Curtis could hope for. But it left him feeling drained. Having everything finally out between the two of them gave no sense of relief. So much that was vital remained unsettled.

Curtis returned to the wet bar but thought better of having another drink. His phone rang. He answered it while strolling to the window. A top researcher was on the line with a daily status report.

Curtis was in no mood for long-winded explanations.

"Never mind all that; what's the bottom line?"

The researcher shifted gears and responded as abruptly.

"There's no evidence of *GenLET* or a 3rd Protocol vaccine in the subject DNA. We've run every possible test from the eggs you sent us. Except for a few variations that don't apply, what we found matches any normal, untreated person."

Curtis paced. "I can't believe there's nothing else to try…"

"Maybe if we had more eggs. We're limited by what little embryonic stem cell production is possible. Can you get us more eggs?"

"The research center in Puerto Rico is wrapped tight. You'll have to find some other way to keep working. You must keep at it."

"But like I said, we've reached the point where there's nothing else to find."

"Somehow I find that incongruous with being a researcher. There has to be."

"If you want, we can redo tests or ask around, possibly think of new ones – but all that does is bring us back to the eggs. Without more eggs, there's no way to test."

Curtis halted. "That means GARC is the key."

"That's what I'm saying."

"All right. I'll see what I can do. In the meantime, double-check what you have. What we've started we have to finish."

The call ended. Out in the hallway, hidden around a wall, Noah stood listening. He had only heard one side of the conversation but it was enough to solidify his resolve. He didn't trust his father, now more than ever, but he'd stay and see what else he could learn. So far he knew *GARC was the key.*

Curtis's last words echoed back. "*…what we've started we have to finish.*"

Those were Noah's sentiments exactly.

CHAPTER 47

Two Weeks Later
Sub-Basement Conference Room, GARC

The room's silence matched its starkness. Small spotlights highlighted the table's blank surface as if nothing beyond the narrow halos of brightness mattered. Empty chairs hugged the table's perimeter. A whiteboard stood by blank and in shadow. There was room for twenty at the conference table.

Janis and Faye walked in to find only one.

Colin Insworth sat relaxed, leaning back, ignoring the tablet computer before him. An active screensaver gave measure of how long he'd been quiet, still, and lost in thought. His eyes flicked focus from a vanishing point across the room to watch the women walk in and take a seat.

"Thank you for coming," he began, a marked gravitas all too apparent. He glanced at Janis. "I realize after a long day this is the last thing you want to do, but bear with me. I have news both of you should hear together. It's from Granite Peak."

Neither Janis nor Faye reacted openly but they'd been expecting to hear test results of their trial sterility fix for days. If anything, such news was overdue. The first trial was their best effort so far to find a way to reverse sterility. Preventing it from happening in utero was to be their next project. To be able to move forward and develop trial two, they needed positive results on their work so far.

Colin's relaxed posture belied the severity of the news. "They had no success."

For a moment, the certainty of it smothered every sound and hope in the room.

Colin added, "They ran every test you suggested and a few of their own."

Deflated, Faye quizzed, "They saw nothing? No change?"

"No, none that meant anything. They tried variations, noted some effects on secondary characteristics but nothing that reversed sterility."

Janis prompted, "Don't hold back on the data. We need to review exactly what they did. Something might have gotten overlooked."

"You'll have the data on the servers within the hour. But they're confident with the results. Nothing was overlooked."

Janis' frustration edged into defensiveness. "If it was overlooked, I hardly think they'd know it. That's just the point."

"I get it," snapped Colin. "I'm disappointed too, but we can't spinoff rehashing what doesn't work. We don't have time."

"What delayed them getting back to us?" asked Faye.

"Sequencing the animals against their control group took longer than planned."

Colin had hit on a sore point with Janis. She folded arms and sat back. "Are these conclusions based on the animal tests?"

"Primarily."

Janis tried to keep calm. "What about the computer models I recommended?"

Colin paused, knowing full well his answer would not be liked.

"Project management decided models would take much longer to develop than conducting animal trials. Even if they found a model that worked, they'd still have to conduct real world testing on what the model suggested."

"But in this case, I think a model would be more precise."

Colin's face twisted, bewildered. "I'm not a scientist; so explain that – what's more precise than a test on a live animal? It's not theoretical; it's a live subject."

"And what about the 2% variation in DNA between chimpanzees and us? The Project can't be certain with these results; there is a distinct margin of error."

"They know that but in this case they believe it's negligible."

Janis was confrontational. "You don't understand. We're dealing with a level of precision where if just *one* base pair is off the whole thing might not work. How can they simply write off a 2% variation across the whole genome?"

Colin's patience was short. He responded in kind. "They didn't. That's why they did other tests. Like I said, they came up with a few of their own."

"What kind of tests?" The concern on Janis' face drew Faye's attention.

Faye turned back to Colin. "You don't mean human trials…"

"Yes…" Colin was firm. "It was always the last option if animal tests failed."

"Who would volunteer for such a thing? What about maintaining secrecy?"

Faye's question was intentionally naïve. But the implied answer wasn't the worst of it. Janis rocked forward and leaned on the table.

"A valid human test could only be done on someone sterile. Are you telling me they experimented on children?"

Colin nodded. "It was the last resort…"

"Last resort?" shouted Janis. "This was our *first* trial…"

"What children did they use?" demanded Faye.

Colin was subdued in manner but his posture held firm and defiant.

"There was one criterion; they had to be terminally ill."

"Did the families know?"

Colin looked Faye in the eye. "What difference would it have made?"

Janis bolted from her chair and paced to the whiteboard and back.

"What else is this Project doing and not telling us about?"

"It's no secret. I just told you," asserted Colin.

"After the fact!" yelled Janis.

"Did any of them die?" asked Faye.

Colin watched as Janis stopped her pacing to turn and watch him answer.

"There was one. An inoperable brain cancer patient."

Janis steamed. "As if that makes it any better."

Colin shifted forward, his patience at an end. "What do you think is going on here, huh? Realistically, how much time do you think we have? You know what's happening; the situation is deteriorating by the hour. We have to do some difficult things but it's gotten to that point – we have no choice."

Janis stood her ground. "There are other ways…"

"That take more time!" Colin interrupted. "If Mass' virus keeps spreading like it has without any way to fight it, most of the world's population will die this year."

Colin's statement filled the room. The terror of hearing such words said in earnest gave all of them reason to pause. Faye was the first to seek some hope.

"There's still a chance the vaccine will be found…"

"Will it matter?" asked Colin. "People are afraid to take vaccines – Mass made sure of that. His MIOVAC vaccines are on every continent. Everywhere they've been tried, the spread of disease gets worse – not just his disease, *every* disease. As best as we can tell, the latest batch of MIOVAC turns off the immune system. Healthcare workers are facing impossible triage situations. It's hard to know how to treat when multiple symptoms overlap and look the same. If The Project had a 3P vaccine right now, I doubt we could get people in many parts of the world to take it. They've seen too much; they've lost trust."

"So what are you saying?" asked Faye. "It's too late?"

Colin had to choose; answer with his head or his heart. Unwilling to give up but unable to rally much enthusiasm, he dodged the question.

"No one can answer that. But we know the game has changed."

Faye looked to Janis. "It's strange; before Mass died, all we had to worry about was sterility. Who would have thought we'd ever see that as the better alternative?"

"At least sterility gives us one generation to find an answer."

Faye answered her, "And we thought *that* was pressure."

Colin added, "That schedule doesn't work any more. At best we have twelve to fifteen months. After that, chances are, it will be impossible to continue our work. Supplies, utilities, infrastructure, personnel…it's all about to change. After the collapse, none of it will be reliable – if it exists at all."

"So what do we work on now?" asked Janis.

Faye leaned on the table and bowed her head. "If 3rd Protocol isn't stopped, what good will it do?"

"Then we have to work on that."

Colin pressed Janis, "You'd want governments to mandate vaccination?"

"If the vaccine worked. The success rate using it would develop its own momentum. At least with 3P under control, we'd have a whole generation to complete our work on sterility. We'd have a chance."

Colin took the tablet computer in hand and stood, preparing to leave.

"Labs around the world are studying 3P – there are enough people on it. You two need to stay focused. No one but The Project is working on the sterility problem; no one else even knows about it."

Faye sighed. "But we need a fix before the population collapses – a solution to give the survivors."

"That's for damned sure," remarked Colin. "It's a reasonable bet that survivors won't be able to develop one themselves. They'll have more immediate problems. Besides, they won't even know about the problem until it's too late."

"We need to get more researchers involved…" suggested Faye.

"Things are too far along; that's not going to happen."

Janis stood at the opposite end of the table. Her eyes filled with tears.

"If you're right…if our first trials have failed, that puts us back at the beginning. We won't have time. There's no way we can devise, analyze, test, and deploy a sterility treatment in time. Even if we did, if people are afraid of vaccines, do we really think they're going to hand over their children for some mysterious treatment we can't explain just because Project secrets need to stay secret?"

Colin headed for the door. "With some things it's better people don't know…"

"What do you mean?" asked Janis.

Faye answered for him. "The Project never intended on telling people they were getting the treatment for sterility. Deploying the fix means coming up with a way to release it into the wild – the same way Ghyvir-C infected them in the first place."

Janis nodded. "Of course…I forgot. Solve the problem in the riskiest way."

Colin paused in the doorway. "The greatest risk at this point is in believing an answer is going to be conventional or without sacrifice."

"Maybe I'd feel better if a secret Project wasn't the arbiter of sacrifice."

Colin threw up his hands. "None of that matters. You don't have a solution anyway. And now you say there won't be time for one. What's riskier than that? You two have a name for that don't you? What's it called? BIOPONORE?"

Colin turned and was gone but his last word resonated between the women left behind. They looked to each other in recognition and dismay.

…BIOlogical POint of NO REturn…

For Faye, hearing Colin choose that word in context was even more unsettling. She and Colin had talked about it briefly at Granite Peak, but Faye had never explained its meaning. The fact that he now knew it gave implicit proof that Project managers were using all covert means possible to find out whatever they wanted.

For Janis, despite all efforts, the worst case scenario suddenly seemed more probable. Overcome with emotion, she rushed from the room.

"Janis…" Faye stood and called after her but she was gone.

Faye found her minutes later, in the lab, standing at the glass that looked in on the BSL3 containment box. She was silent and still, dazed and preoccupied.

Janis ached to turn her thousand-yard stare into a thousand-year gaze.

Faye stepped up alongside her but said nothing.

"It's incredible," started Janis. "Human history stretches so far back. It's so easy to assume it'll go on forever. We might be able to deal with sterility or the plague, one or the other, but not both of them, not at the same time."

"I thought for sure the test trial would work," whispered Faye.

Janis turned her back to the glass and leaned against cold stainless steel.

"What did we miss? We had everything at our disposal to look at – Ghyvir-C, the RIDIS data, 2nd Protocol, the gene mapping from Alyssa…"

"We didn't miss it," asserted Faye. "We simply haven't found it yet. If we had more time, we'd find it."

"Huh!" Janis pushed away from the wall and paced. "Mass took care of that. Now we don't know what to do."

"There's nothing else *to do*. We have to push on. If we discover something, even if we don't get to deploy it in time, at least we'll be able to give the survivors something to go on."

Janis lingered on the thought, unable to agree. "But what if we spend the little time we have left trying to find a fix and we don't succeed? That's highly likely given the time we have. In that case we leave the survivors nothing."

"Yeah…" Faye shrugged. "But what else can we do?"

Janis picked up a mug of tea, sat down, and thought. Sipping at the edge of the mug, she let her eyes roam the room as her mind explored the possibilities.

"What are we saying?" she started. "Given enough time, we believe we'd find an answer. That's what you said; we didn't miss it, we just haven't found it yet."

"That's right. I believe that wholeheartedly. If we didn't think it was a solvable problem, we couldn't go at it like we do."

Janis stood and paced with the mug in her hand. "Then time is the key."

"It has to be," agreed Faye. "If Colin had said we had 24 or 36 months, something, anything more would make finding a fix much more certain."

Janis turned, the light of an idea on her face.

"So why don't we give the survivors more time?"

The idea hung between them crystalline and expanding as Faye took it in.

Janis hurried to add, "Let's give the survivors *GenLET*."

"*GenLET…?*" gasped Faye. She sat down and followed Janis' movements.

"If there's only one generation left, then they'll need as much time as possible."

Faye thought it through. "…but, life extension for everyone?"

"Why not? What other way can survivors have the time and continuity of experience to find an answer? They'd have 200 to 300 years instead of 70 or 80."

"You're talking about changing the entire species…"

"Only for a generation," countered Janis. "The trait wouldn't be inheritable."

"I don't know…how would that work?"

"Colin said the greatest risk is in believing an answer is going to be conventional. Let's take him at his word."

"I know, but even if we decided to do it, wouldn't time still be a problem?"

Janis waved it off. "It's a whole different issue. There's nothing to find or create. *GenLET* already exists. It simply needs to be packaged and deployed."

"But we don't have it."

"The Project does. They can get it for us."

"And what do we do with it? How do you make sure the survivors get the treatment before the population collapses?"

Janis halted her pacing then raced through the possibilities for an answer.

"Why not do it the same way they planned on releasing the sterility fix?"

"A virus in the wild, released secretly? In the conference room, you called that *the riskiest way*."

"It is, but they'll do it anyway. Why not use it for something like this?"

"I didn't think *GenLET* could be administered so easily."

"Yes and no. Riya Basu got a Nobel Prize for *GenLET*. In her acceptance speech she mentioned me. She said when the full story was told, I'd be standing where she was. She knew my contribution on delivery modalities. NovoSenectus was keeping that development secret."

"So what's possible with it?" asked Faye.

"It all depends on which generation of *GenLET* you're talking about – 1GenGEN or 2GenGEN. 1GenGEN requires a treatment schedule over several visits. They're long and arduous. The breakthrough I worked on was 2GenGEN – *GenLET* administered in a single dose."

"Is that complete?"

"All the pieces are. I just never got a chance to synthesize them. I was about to do that when all of this started."

"I don't know..." wavered Faye. "You're going to a whole different place. Talk about making global changes! That would be huge."

Janis was adamant. "But it's going to take something huge. We're out of time. After the collapse, the world won't be able to rely on one project, one group, one government to be stable enough to do what's necessary. All survivors will need a chance to do what's necessary. Somebody among them will have to step up and carry this forward. There's no way of telling who's going to survive..."

Faye continued the thought. "...but whoever does will need as much time as possible before the last generation dies out."

Janis drew nearer. "What's Colin's attitude? He says we have to accept the facts. All right, we're out of time, the population's collapsing, and child survivors are going to be sterile. It's no time for Plan B. Let's go to Plan A-Plus. Let's at least give the survivors time; that has to give them more of a chance."

"Yeah, it would...but..."

"But what? There's no coming back from extinction. Colin said survivors are going to be too busy adjusting to fundamental change after the collapse. It's going to be a new world. This will give them plenty of time beyond that critical adjustment period, time to regroup and do the work that's needed."

Faye wasn't convinced. "I'm not sure. It's too bad we can't just give ourselves *GenLET*? Then we'd have all the time we need to work on sterility."

"We could but there's no guarantee we're going to survive the plague. Even if we beat the odds and live, we might not be able to work. You heard what Colin said – supplies, utilities, infrastructure, they all rely on people. With six billion gone, running a lab might be impossible for a while. But how long is *a while*? A lifetime? Humanity only has one of those left. Why not make it as long as possible?"

"I see your point," relented Faye.

"So what do you think? You want to ask Colin to get us *GenLET*?"

Faye hesitated before committing. "I guess I can do that."

"Great. While you're at it, maybe he can get his Project friends to snag some of my work files from NovoSenectus. It would help if I didn't have to work completely from memory."

"Sure thing," agreed Faye.

Janis paused to dwell on a thought before pulling up a chair and sitting close. "There's one other thing we need to talk about."

Faye saw the concern on Janis' face. "What is it?"

Janis held a comforting hand over Faye's stomach. "...it's about bed rest for the baby."

Faye drew tense. "What about that?"

Janis' other hand took hold of Faye's hand. "Last week, in the apartment...I overheard your conversation with the doctor."

Faye shuddered. "I thought you were in the other room..."

"Why haven't you been staying in bed?"

Faye was on edge. "There's been so much going on…"

"So?"

"There's work to do."

"Never mind that." Janis squeezed Faye's hand. "What about what the doctor said?"

"I'll be all right…"

Janis toughened. "And what about the baby?"

Faye lowered her gaze. "The baby will be all right too. I'm taking it easy where I can."

"That's not good enough and you know it. You've worked the same as always, right alongside me ever since that call. You can't keep doing that."

"I'll manage…it'll work out."

"No it won't! You have to do what the doctor said."

"But the baby will be sterile, just like millions of others. I don't want to stop work on finding the fix. It's not just me but everything that's at stake, don't you understand?"

"I understand you have to do what's right for you. You know what you want."

"I want both!" wept Faye.

"So let's find a way to have both."

"Why did this have to happen now? I don't want to be selfish…"

"Selfish? Who said anything like that?"

Faye held silent.

For Janis, the implication was clear. "Does Colin know about this? Did he say anything?"

Faye avoided a direct answer. "It's an impossible choice; keep the baby or keep working on something that means so much."

"Maybe you could do some remote work by computer; we'll get a laptop you can use sitting up in bed. There's ways to do this!"

Faye despaired. "What can I do to help sitting in bed?"

"The work will go on," asserted Janis.

"But what's more important? Like you said, there's no coming back from extinction. What good is bringing a sterile baby into the world the way it is?"

Janis stiffened. "This doesn't sound like you. Who else knows about this?"

Faye hesitated. "…Colin."

"I thought so," snapped Janis. "I don't know what he told you. I don't want to know; I think I can guess. But you can't listen to any of that. You hear me?" Janis moved in and held Faye by the shoulders.

Faye answered with a weak nod.

Janis leaned in, took Faye in her arms and hugged her.

"We'll get through this," whispered Janis. "You're going to do what the doctor said. Don't listen to Colin. The baby will be fine. The work will go on. It doesn't have to be one or the other. We won't let it. You're not being selfish."

Faye leaned into Janis shoulder, releasing into the consoling embrace.

Janis tried lightening the mood. "I'm surprised you put any stock into what Colin says at all. It was strange hearing him use the word BIOPONORE like that. Did you also tell him about our other word?"

Faye wiped her tears. "What word?"

"You know, the one you used to tease me with all the time?"

"Teased you? You're the one who liked to tease unmercifully."

"Don't tell me you don't remember."

"I remember BIOPONORE." Faye tried to chuckle, "How can I forget? I remember you wouldn't let me forget my biological clock was ticking…"

"Yeah, and to get even, you had your own special word for me. Maybe you didn't use it as much but when you did you made it count."

Faye's interest was piqued. "So what is it? Tell me…"

"You really don't remember? I'm surprised…"

"It must have been good if it bothered you," remarked Faye.

"It made its point."

Faye sat up. "So are you going to tell me?"

Janis grinned. "I don't know…"

"Why not? What's the big deal?" Faye sighed. "You're acting just like you did in college, being a little shit."

Janis looked past the tears and wonder on Faye's face. In the instant, she saw the girlfriend she'd once shared classes and dorm rooms with. The feeling took her back and suddenly she was that mischievous classmate once again.

"I'll make you a deal…," offered Janis. "You get Colin to get us *GenLET* and my files from NovoSenectus. When I finish synthesizing 2GenGen and everything's done, I'll tell you the word."

"Promise?" demanded Faye.

"I promise. It'll be our codeword for success."

Chapter 48

Marie-Louise Square
European Quarter, Brussels

Javier Francisco stood at the upstairs window looking down on an anxious world. An occasional snowflake fluttered by, headed for the busy street. Thoughts of other days standing in the same place, waiting for Eugene Mass, were inescapable.

To protect the necessary work that had to be hidden, Mass never hesitated to sacrifice the artifice of propriety. In return, the rabid press never failed to provide a plausible but scandalous cover for what was really going on. It was the perfect partnership between adversaries who seemed to be forever at odds with one another. The tabloids profited off the salacious innuendo about Mass' occasional rendezvous in Marie-Louise Square with Javier, his suspected lover.

And Mass got his dirty work done in broad daylight.

Javier watched as the black Bentley Mulsanne pulled to the curb and parked. It was a familiar sight but the circumstances made all the difference. Stepping from the car was not Eugene Mass, but his wife Leah. She was accompanied by one guard, a well-heeled and suited veteran of Marie-Louise Square, today in topcoat and cap.

There was nothing Javier could do. He watched as they crossed the sidewalk and ascended the short flight of stairs to the front door. They turned the key in the lock and made their entrance four flights below. The moment of truth was about to arrive. At the mercy of fate, Javier kept his gaze fixed and downcast on the snowy park across the street. The scent of fresh-brewed espresso tormented him with visions of better times.

There was no commotion downstairs. None was expected. No doubt, the way it would all work out had been too well planned to let such a thing happen. Whatever was about to occur could only be guessed. He only hoped it included his survival.

Muffled voices and hurried steps on the staircase preceded a burst through the door. A gloved man led the way brandishing a gun equipped with silencer. Behind him was Leah Mass followed by another man who guarded the doorway.

Javier turned to catch the terror in Leah's eyes. At the same moment, both of them turned their attention to a third man lounging on the sofa. He had been in the room with Javier for quite some time, waiting.

"Well, well, look who it is…Leah Mass. I'm so glad you could join us."

The man on the sofa set down his cup of Jamaican Peaberry.

Leah turned to Javier. "Javier, what's going on?"

Javier's embittered expression told all even before he spoke.

"There was nothing I could do. They took me in Marseille…"

Leah demanded of the man on the sofa, "What's the meaning of this?"

The man leveled a steely glare at his guest. "You took the words right out of my mouth? What's the meaning of this? Why are *you* here?"

"Why shouldn't I be here? I own this place and I don't remember inviting you. What do you want? Is this a robbery?"

The man stood. “Hardly. One might call it an intervention. I call it justice. You’re the one who’s guilty of robbery.”

“What are you talking about?”

“The *future.*” He strolled closer and let the word hang. “You and your husband have robbed humanity of its future. That in my eyes is a capital offense.”

Fear shot through Leah’s face. “Who are you?”

“You don’t recognize me?”

Leah glanced back at the other armed accomplices. “No…”

“I’m surprised…” He sauntered around her. “Eugene and I go way back. In fact, I didn’t realize how far back until I had a chance to talk with our friend here. It’s been over ten years…back when I was helping out the *Friends of the Ocean* in the North Atlantic; Eugene had Javier track my efforts to form a new group. But you knew that already, didn’t you?”

Recognition widened Leah’s eyes.

“New Class Order…?” gasped Leah. “You’re André Bolard!”

Snow began to fall on the slanted windows in the vaulted ceiling.

André stepped to the window next to Javier and looked out at passing flakes.

“I remember back then…the thought of life extension was a dream. Reducing the population to save the planet was offered as a noble but lofty goal. Eugene wanted to help. He bought NovoSenectus. He made himself beloved by spending a fortune distributing free vaccines to the world…”

André turned back to glare at Leah. “But I saw through it. Even back then, I knew if he had his way it wouldn’t end well, at least for people like me. When your husband first started lecturing on the utopia of his New World Harmony, I knew it was a sham, a cover for a new class order. Eugene Mass wanted two kinds of people; the elite class who would live hundreds of years in positions of power and privilege, and the rest of us, the second-class survivors he’d manage under an all-encompassing net of global governance.”

Leah saw the fear in Javier’s face. Desperate, she tried to speak up.

“You’ve got it wrong…”

“No!” shouted André. “You got it *right,* didn’t you? Everything is happening just as Eugene planned. And now that he’s gone, you think you’re going to finish what he started. You’re dead wrong!”

The reference sent chills through Leah. She realized the next few minutes would mean her life one way or another. The invitation from Javier to meet had been a ruse, a desperate attempt to entrap whoever showed up. Javier had obviously been kidnapped and forced to send the message. Having her show up was nothing less than the grand prize for New Class Order. There was low probability she could talk her way out of this and yet with no other option she had to try.

“You’re a smart man; you’re quite aware that things are not always as they seem. I would be surprised if you’d accept conspiracy theories on face value.”

André leaned back on the window. “I don’t have to see the spider to know it’s there; all I have to see is the web.”

“A web of lies,” asserted Leah. “You must admit there are other parties at play. The media exaggerates and fabricates; business competitors smear and conspire.

Some are merely envious, others deranged by greed. Do you really think in the swirl of all of that you could possibly know what's really going on?"

André stared back. "*GenLET* is a fact. So is GGD3. What people say about them is one thing. Regardless they exist, all according to plan, your husband's plan. Don't try denying it. I didn't come here to debate it with you."

"All right, then what do you want? Eugene is gone. I am heiress to his estate, not his way of thinking."

"Then why are you here?" snapped André. "Why did you show up expecting to meet with Eugene's underworld lapdog?"

Leah hesitated as Javier traded glances. She stood stern and defiant.

"I came here to arrange justice for the man who poisoned my husband."

André jerked away from the window and lit up with sarcasm.

"Arranging justice are we? How decent and gallant of you. One man dies and you are compelled to deliver justice." André's tone soured. "Well then, tell me… what would be justice when *billions* of people are murdered?"

Leah felt a surge of panic. André was only toying with her. Any idea of talking him out of whatever he planned faded. She rushed to his side.

"I also came here to arrange the release of a vaccine…"

Blurted out, the statement was as much a confession as a plea for leniency.

"Vaccine for what?" snapped André. His skepticism showed.

"GGD3."

"Amazing! The smartest minds are frantic in their search for such a thing. How could you have it so quickly? Are you admitting you and your husband are the ones who started the plague?"

"No. I'm telling you I have a vaccine for it."

"If that was true, why not simply give it to the world? News like that would be momentous; you'd be the savior of mankind. But no, you sneak around and come here."

Leah's attempt to use the truth had trapped her. If her story of a vaccine was true, then André was right; giving it to the world openly would be the thing to do. That is unless she needed to hide her complicity in creating GGD3. If André believed a vaccine didn't exist, her excuse failed. But if she tried any harder to convince him, she'd only be admitting her attempt for an anonymous release of the vaccine was necessary to avoid the presumptive guilt for GGD3 that would surely follow.

She couldn't defend her excuse without incriminating herself.

She tried to stall. "There're reasons for everything. Don't presume you know the way things work."

"Admit it; you'll say anything to save yourself." André stepped closer to her. "No doubt you've already received *GenLET*. Look at you – you stand there smug, thinking you're going to outlive me by a hundred years."

Her desperation turned frantic.

"We don't have to be enemies; I am not Eugene," offered Leah.

"After twenty years of supporting him? I saw the two of you standing side-by-side at Oxford when he gave his speech. What did he say? '*Necessary actions might seem severe. But without them and our resolve to see them through, none of us will reach the distant shore.*' You said nothing against his call for 'severe action.' Now, I'm afraid, I have to take mine."

André signaled the man with the gun with a jerk of his head.

The man grabbed Leah by the shoulders and pulled her back.

"What are you going to do?" wailed Leah.

The doorway guard left his post and shoved Javier onto the sofa.

André stepped to the open doorway.

"What did you say earlier? The media exaggerates and fabricates…"

Javier tensed, preparing to bolt, but the guard held a gun on him.

"This makes no sense, André. This won't stop anything…"

"Maybe not," answered André. "But it will be justice."

"Tell me what you want, anything," pleaded Leah. "You have to listen to me – the vaccine is real. Let me give it to you!"

"As they say, the cat is out of the bag. You can't give me what I want. I want all of what you've done taken back. I want it undone. Can you give me that?"

"I can give you extended life. I'll give you the vaccine," yelped Leah. "It's real. Take it. You can be the savior of humanity."

André was unyielding. "I have no reason to believe you. Besides, this isn't about what you can do for me. This is about what you've already done."

"You won't get away with this," shouted Javier. "How do you think this is going to look?"

André put on his winter coat. "A love triangle is a sad thing. No matter how good it is or how long it lasts – someone always gets hurt."

Javier became frenzied. "Wait, think about it. I'm just a mercenary. I did what they paid me to do. I can do the same for you…"

André ignored the plea. "I can see the headlines now…" He stepped to a table and picked up his cup of Jamaican Peaberry. After downing the last sip, he put the cup in his coat pocket and took his fingerprints with him.

"Grieving Billionaire Heiress Shoots Dead Husband's Gay Lover then Herself. Read all about the Love Triangle Murder/Suicide."

Leah was frozen in fear. Javier wanted to run but knew his slightest move would trigger the gunman. André gave one more look around the room. His eyes lifted and considered the snow now covering the vaulted ceiling's slanted windows.

"Javier…what did you say this room used to be?"

"Eugene told me – it was a children's bedroom."

André took a moment before settling, subdued. "Hmm…what a shame."

He turned and walked out. On his way out he closed the door.

On the way downstairs he heard the silencer go off. A few moments later, it went off again. He knew the gloved one would place the gun in Leah's dead hand.

Downstairs, the body of Leah's suffocated guard awaited removal. It would be incinerated and the ashes scattered at sea, probably near the Frioul Archipelago.

The plan was working. New Class Order was fighting back.

A serious blow had been landed against the New World Harmony.

Not since the windswept decks of the research ship PaxTerra years before had André felt such a surge of satisfaction. If he had his way, it wouldn't be the last.

CHAPTER 49

Turnberry Tower
Rosslyn, Virginia

Colin left the Metro Station five stops from National Airport and set out on foot. The early evening air was brisk but it felt good to exercise his legs after the flight in from Puerto Rico. The neighborhood was new to him but he stepped confidently, guided by classified instructions given to him back at GARC.

He was on time, reporting to an address he was warned to keep to himself.

It didn't take long before the lights of the porte-cochere came into view. The building's front entrance was resplendent and bright. Passing gleaming pillars and a lit fountain, his steps slowed on cobbled stones. He'd expected something else.

It seemed unlikely that The Project would schedule an important meeting at a luxury residential high-rise. He glanced up and followed the span of twenty-six floors reaching for an overcast sky before pulling out his phone.

He dialed a private number. A quick call as a heads up that he'd arrived would give him a chance to verify the location.

"This is Colin. I'm at the address. It's Turnberry Tower."

A woman's voice answered. "Go on in. I'll meet you in the lobby."

The call ended. Colin stepped through the entrance to find a woman approaching him from an opulent side seating area. She acted like she knew him but in fact he had never seen her before.

Dressed in silk floral lounge pants and matching top, her casual elegance and upscale beauty took him by surprise. She hooked his arm with hers and led him past the concierge and security desks. The suited attendants gave her a glance and the polite wave deserving of a well-known tenant.

"How was your flight?" She smiled without introduction.

"Smooth as silk," mused Colin, falling into character.

She led him past the main elevators to a more private access area. Only after they had stepped into their unit-numbered elevator car and the doors had closed did she card-key the ride to begin.

With the car in motion, she turned to look Colin up and down.

"You seem surprised…" She traded her hostess smile for a cunning smirk.

Colin admitted, "It's not what I expected."

"Good. That's the idea."

Taken with her charm, Colin added. "It's a long way from Stark Road."

She had already turned away. She turned back, "Ah…Stark Road?"

"The dirt road leading to Granite Peak," explained Colin.

"Oh…yes," she turned away and waited for the elevator car to stop.

When the doors parted, they opened directly into a top floor luxury suite.

Stepping forward, the woman caught Colin's eyes watching her walk.

She gave him a knowing glance that stung. "Don't let the trappings fool you; we all have a part to play, no matter where we find ourselves. Even here…"

Colin accepted her rebuke as a polite business reminder. Any familiarity she was showing him was part of the illusion. He'd be wise not to read anything more into it. But as illusions went, this one was worth entertaining.

From the entrance hallway, Colin followed her through the living room. The suite's luxurious furnishings were only surpassed by the view beyond the floor to ceiling windows. Subdued lighting allowed a clear panorama across the Potomac River with the Lincoln and Washington Monuments and Capitol Dome lit up in the distance. Storm candles glowed on the balcony but sounds of a television came from another direction. In the family room they found a middle-aged man in jogging sweats stretched out on a couch with a cell phone to his ear.

"Pardon me…Mr. Insworth is here." The woman halted and let Colin pass.

The man on the couch waved Colin forward but continued the phone conversation while keeping an eye on an interview program playing on the wall-mounted flat screen TV. The woman turned back to Colin.

"This is Mr. Mann. He's the one you want to talk to."

As she pivoted and strutted her exit, Colin offered a "Thank you."

Left to wait while the phone conversation continued, Colin took a seat and got comfortable. If he had to wait, he couldn't have been delivered to a more perfect place to do it.

"Sorry about that…" The phone call ended and the phone got tossed aside.

Colin leaned over to accept the man's handshake.

"Alexander Mann…and you're Colin."

"Yes," confirmed Colin. "We spoke on the phone a few days ago…"

Alexander muted the TV and lounged back in place. "Yes, you had a proposal."

"That's right; you should have received a detailed whitepaper on it."

"As a matter of fact I did. That's why you're here. I showed it to The Project Board. It ginned up quite a bit of interest but, unfortunately, just as much concern."

"Over what?" asked Colin.

Alexander stretched out his legs on an ottoman. "C2. Command and control. They're not convinced proper controls can be maintained."

"By the facility or by me?"

"Both. They would rather keep critical things locked down, in one place. Taking something like this offshore and including so many others into the know-circle creates issues. There are many elements of your proposal that compound risk."

Colin thought on his feet. "What if we did it at Dugway? It can't get safer than being buried under Granite Peak."

Alexander played with the TV remote. "No, under no circumstances can there be any chance this might be found on a government installation. That connection can never exist."

Colin hunched forward. "Given the severity of what's going on, some risks have to be taken."

"Not unacceptable risk."

"What's more unacceptable than knowing we've run out of time on this?"

Alexander held a firm gaze. "You're convinced of that?"

"Yes, we're at that point." Colin stared back. "Sterility fix trials have failed. All calculations say there won't be time for another round. If a vaccine isn't discovered or created right away, we're out of options – except for the proposal I sent you."

The grim news was reinforced by silence. Alexander drew a breath.

"The Project has mandates. One of them is to preserve and maintain life as we know it – not to usher in blanket modifications to the species, the consequences of which no one can be certain."

"Agreed. A determination when to release the new *GenLET* would have to be made at a later date depending on how quickly world conditions deteriorate..."

"...or what kind of progress we have in the lab," added Alexander.

Colin shook his head. "Again, I have to emphasize – there isn't time."

"But you claim there's time to complete your proposal..."

"Janis only needs her files from NovoSenectus and a sample of 1st Generation *GenLET*. She doesn't have to discover 2GenGEN, only put it together. The time involved is not open-ended like the other research."

"But the other research is on the problem we need fixed..."

"But it won't be completed in time!" Colin energized his pitch. "We wouldn't even have this option if Janis hadn't come forward. Single-dose *GenLET* packaged in a Ghyvir-C sputnik could give survivors all over the world the one thing they're going to need most – time. Time to recover, time to discover the fixes we haven't been able to find. With only one generation left, survivors of GGD3 will need time."

Alexander hesitated. "What about C2? After that fiasco with the egg extractions, The Board is not so confident."

Colin stood to make his point. "That didn't happen on my watch! I was at Granite Peak. You have nothing to worry about. You'll have your C2."

Alexander sat and stared at Colin a long while. Then he stood and used the remote to shut off the TV.

"Want a drink?" asked Alexander.

Colin stood, puffed up with unused anger. He nodded. "Sure..."

Alexander fixed drinks at a wet bar and then led the way back into the suite.

"Come along, I'll show you around..."

Colin was caught off-guard. He didn't expect the sudden familiarity or a tour.

"This is quite a place..." noted Colin.

"It's many things," admitted Alexander. "...living quarters, project office, safe house, command center, or meeting place, like tonight."

"You live here?"

"At times," Alexander hedged. Stepping down a hallway, he guided the tour so one by one the three bedrooms were revealed.

The master bedroom was as Colin expected, lush and inviting. To his surprise, the other two rooms were not bedrooms at all. They were outfitted with high-tech intelligence gear and computers, RIDIS scanners and receivers, and devices even Colin didn't recognize. The rooms were solid evidence that the luxury suite was in fact the D.C. office of The Project.

Colin stood in the doorway. "Why are you showing me this?"

Alexander nursed his drink. "We thought it was time. The Project has plans for an expanded role for you in the future. Getting acquainted with Turnberry is necessary; it will probably figure in on your future assignments."

Surprised, Colin spoke his thoughts. "With all that's happening, whatever could they be planning?" He knew better than to think it warranted an answer.

He was right. Alexander responded with a knowing grin then led the way back to the family room. Standing tall, he addressed Colin in summation.

"At the airport, there's a squad of Project operatives waiting at your plane. On my word, they'll accompany you back to GARC with a *GenLET* sample. I will give them a call provided you promise me two things – the work on 2GenGEN will complete as quickly as possible, and you'll personally guarantee command and control over the work."

Colin was taken aback but delighted by the abrupt agreement to go ahead.

"Done!"

Alexander refilled his drink. "Good. Now get out of here and make it happen."

Colin nodded and stepped away.

"Oh, and Colin," Alexander called out. "Remember, The Project is watching."

Colin read the intensity on Alexander's face and retreated back to the private elevator. He would let himself out. There was no time to lose.

Back in the family room, drink in hand, Alexander Mann turned to the window. His face reflected in the glass but beyond it, the lights of D.C. and cars crossing the Teddy Roosevelt Bridge drew his attention into a studied meditation. He lingered a few moment before stepping off to the kitchen.

Alexander strolled in knowing right where to look.

Pamela Mann sat at the granite island, a laptop to one side, a glass of Chenin Blanc nearby. She busied herself spreading Camembert on toast points.

"All done?"

"He's on his way back to National."

"Is he motivated?"

Alexander chuckled. "What do you think? He's gotten a glimpse of his future."

Pamela sipped her wine. "Good. We need him to see this through."

"I hope you're right about the risk…"

"Of course I'm right. The prize is too great to pass up. We know the problems with 1st Generation treatments. Single-dose is the only stable way to go. Anything else was premature. She's going to give it to us on a fucking platter. The Project will be the only ones to have it. You can't buy that kind of position."

Alexander gave a nod. "Everything's gotten so P.C."

Pamela crossed her legs and bounced a toe up and down. "P.C.?"

"Yeah," remarked Alexander. "Post Collapse. It's all about positioning now."

"Damn right," asserted Pamela. "You heard the man; we're out of time."

"They're going to be pissed. They think they're preparing the last option."

"Let them think whatever they need to just as long as they get it done. As soon as GARC produces 2GenGEN, we shut it down and lock it up. The Board was emphatic about that. We want the single dose method. That's all that matters."

"No last option?"

"There always has to be a last option…" Pamela lifted a toast point.

Alexander downed his drink. "It just won't be theirs."

CHAPTER 50

Seven Weeks Later
GARC's Sub-Basement BSL4 Lab

It could have been midnight or noon. Without windows to tell and absorbed by the work at hand, Janis was mentally in a place out of time. The narrow workspace around her was sterile and confining. She stared into a microscope then glanced to one side to correlate what she was seeing with readouts from the controlled atmosphere glove box behind her. The stainless steel and safety-glass behemoth had twelve glove ports, enough for six researchers to work side-by-side.

Tonight, only she and one other technician had survived until the late hour.

The Advance Research Center's Biosafety Level-4 Suit Lab demanded the highest concentration and precision. As the maximum biological confinement area, work and safety procedures were rigorous. There was no room for error when the slightest mistake could be the difference between life and death.

Even more reason to fear work exhaustion.

Moving around in a ten-pound pressure suit connected to the ceiling by a spiral air hose was fatiguing. Being confined behind a helmet and face-shield that added six inches to one's height took some time getting used to. Everything from the smallest instruments to computer keyboards had to be handled through doubled neoprene gloves. It was easy to feel separated from the world. Work too long in such a space and a technician could feel separated from themselves.

A voice squawked through the headset built into the pressurized helmet.

"Hey, Janis, isn't it about time to knock off?"

Janis turned reflexively, at first thinking it was lab assistant Karen who had spoken. Then she recognized the voice as Faye's and turned the other way. On a computer screen, a video window displayed Faye sitting up in her apartment.

"What time is it?" asked Janis, too tired to look for herself. Absentmindedly, she lifted a hand to scratch her nose only to find her face shield in the way.

Noticing the gaffe, Faye answered, "It's time to come out of there."

Janis looked over to Karen who gave an approving nod.

"I think you're right," agreed Janis. She turned to Karen, "Why don't you go ahead. I'll catch up in a minute."

"Sounds good." Karen stood from her work stool, stretched then disconnected her air-hose umbilicus. "I'm out of here. Good night."

"Good night." Janis watched for a second as Karen stepped off headed for the chemical shower room. Turning back to the video screen, Janis found a second head next to Faye in the picture.

Faye smiled. "Someone else is here that you might know…"

"Hi Mom!" chirped Alyssa. "I decided to wait up for you."

"I see that," remarked Janis. "You two having fun?"

"Oh, yeah…" Alyssa was quick to answer.

"As much as can be expected in Building Two," smirked Faye.

"Yeah, I know," added Janis. "All the fun happens in Building Three."

"How did it go tonight?" asked Faye.

Janis leaned back from her microscope. "I may look beat but actually I'm feeling good. We replayed the interaction tests for the last time. Once again, they came out negative."

"That's great news. That was the last hurdle. I think you've done it!"

"Done what?" asked Alyssa. "Didn't you finish 2GenGEN last week?"

Faye interrupted. "Maybe it's a bit too late for long explanations; your mother's tired..."

"That's all right," Janis interjected. "I need a few minutes to decompress anyway." She looked to Alyssa on the screen. "You're right, Alyssa. I finished synthesizing 2GenGEN last week. But we can't just release it into the wild without testing how it might interact with other things already out there."

"Why not?"

"Because we wouldn't want it to get together with something else and create a hybrid we didn't plan and couldn't control."

"Get together with what? What did you test it with?"

Janis hesitated. Her daughter's questions were perceptive. "It's called 3rd Protocol."

Alyssa's eyes lit up. "Isn't that another name for the GGD3 virus, the one that's killing all those people in Asia and Africa?"

"Where did you hear that?" Janis noted how inquisitive and resourceful Alyssa had gotten over the past few weeks. She had become much more interested in what was going on in the lab. Her precociousness was to be commended but restrained.

Faye chimed in. "I'm afraid I'm the culprit. We got talking about all the news reports about how the disease is spreading; Europe had its first case just today."

"Oh..." Janis paused, wondering if Alyssa was being given too much information. The news of late had her daughter rattled, especially given everything going on in the labs around her. Janis had thought she could get away with the 3rd Protocol reference without Alyssa knowing the tie-in.

Alyssa leaned closer to the screen. "You have GGD3 in Building 3?"

Janis did her best to make light of it. "In a modified form. It's not contagious."

"How can you be sure?" Fear swept across Alyssa's face.

Faye saw no end to this. For the sake of Janis' need to sleep, Faye butted in and tried to preempt Alyssa's line of questioning. "That's much too complicated to go into right now..."

"I don't know," countered Alyssa. "I'm getting pretty good at this stuff. I sit over in the lab with Mom lots of times and she explains things to me."

Janis cut in. "Alyssa, we talked about the virus within the virus...remember the parasite virus called a sputnik?"

"Yeah..."

"Well, GGD3 or 3rd Protocol, whatever you want to call it, it's built like that too. The giant virus on the outside is just a nasty cold virus. The sputnik on the inside is what contains the deadly payload. All I did was take the sputnik out of the giant virus. We've been studying the deadly part without it being loaded in the contagious part. The sputnik is actually a fragile virus that doesn't live long outside the body. Even if someone in the lab accidentally got sick from the sputnik, they couldn't infect someone else unless they shared bodily fluids…"

Alyssa made a face. "Eeww…"

Faye added. "The version in the lab is now more like HIV."

"Oh, HIV/AIDS?" Alyssa responded. "We learned about that in class."

Janis summed up. "I need to make sure that the new 2GenGEN will not mix adversely in the wild with the deadly part of 3rd Protocol. We wouldn't want to release something that might make the plague any worse than it already is."

Enthused with the answers and attention she was getting, Alyssa carried on. "So the giant virus makes it contagious. But how does it do that?"

Steeped in her work from hours in the lab, Janis found it reflexive to answer in spite Faye's attempt to end the questioning for the night.

"The giant virus acts like a rhinovirus, a cold virus," answered Janis. "Ghyvir-C is highly contagious. The sputnik goes along for the ride as Ghyvir-C is passed from person to person."

"Oh, I see," announced Alyssa. "So you're going to make 2GenGEN contagious the same way."

"That's right."

Alyssa's brow furrowed. "But didn't you say everyone caught Ghyvir-C back when I was a baby?"

"Yes, it's one of the reasons why you're special…"

"But in biology class we learned that the body builds up antibodies to stuff it's already been sick with. You can't use Ghyvir-C again can you? Everybody's already got antibodies to it."

"Smart girl," remarked Janis. "You're thinking like a scientist. And you're right. But I'm not using the same Ghyvir-C from thirteen years ago. I'm using a variant that was created for something called 2nd Protocol. The variant was specifically engineered to get around that problem."

Proud of being called a scientist, Alyssa pressed her logic further. "Do you think the same thing happened with 3rd Protocol?"

Janis sighed and glanced towards the glove box. "I'm certain of it."

"OK, that's enough," snapped Faye. "There'll be plenty of time tomorrow for questions and answers. Right now, why don't you let your mother get some rest?"

Alyssa smiled then mugged into the screen. "I'm coming over. I want to walk home with you."

"All right," relaxed Janis. "I'll meet you in the outer work area. Faye, if you could warn the guards she's coming…"

"Sure thing," answered Faye. "And stop by…I've got midnight snacks."

"I'm on my way."

Janis smiled but slicing behind her smile was an edge of melancholy. Alyssa's reference to *walking home* had struck a nerve. To hear her daughter refer to confinement at a corporate blockhouse as being *home* was unnerving. Beyond that, to think of a clandestine Project controlling them and the terrible fate befalling the greater world only expanded the sadness at hearing mention of *home*.

Even if The Project released them, nowhere in the world was ever going to be the same. What kind of home would be possible again? In retrospect, day-to-day troubles and cares of life before any of this happened now appeared idyllic.

Janis looked up to find Faye repositioning the webcam in front of her.

"You still there?" asked Faye.

Jarred out of a reverie, Janis turned back to the video screen but said nothing.

"Alyssa's taken off," reported Faye. "She's excited to see you. She missed meeting you for lunch."

"I know," admitted Janis. "I couldn't break away."

"Before you go," prompted Faye. "There's just one thing…"

"What is it?"

Faye vacillated. "It's about seeing Colin."

"Not that again," snapped Janis. "I told you, Colin and I have an agreement. I do my work and he stays out of my way."

"He wants to see both of us. He says he has important information but prefers to tell us in person. I think we should meet with him."

"I don't see why he can't tell you and then you can tell me."

Faye became grave. "There must be a reason. Janis, really, I've never seen him this serious before. It must be something major."

Janis followed the concern in Faye's face and tone of voice. "…major."

"I really think we should meet with him. We need to know what's going on."

"All right," Janis relented. "Anything so I can get out of here. Signing off…"

The video connection ended. Karen, the lab assistant, was long gone. Except for the transfer of pressurized air inside the bulky suit and a weary pull and release of her own breath, Janis suddenly found the lab tomblike in silence and confinement. Being alone in the late hour only amplified the effect.

Janis stood and paced to the glove box for one last look inside for the night. Through thick safety glass on the near side she stared at samples of 2GenGEN and 3rd Protocol brought together in various containers and Petri dishes to see if they'd interact. Looking down to the far end, Janis could barely see the sectioned-off area of the box where final synthesized versions of 2GenGEN had been inserted into a sputnik and then the sputnik was inserted into the 2nd Protocol version of Ghyvir-C.

The finality of the accomplishment settled over her. At last she had finished work that was a decade in the making. Not so strangely, there was little joy. Janis thought back. If only Riya Basu were here to see it.

And then there was 2nd Protocol, the newly crafted select agent that had greatly aided making 2GenGEN contagious. Janis dropped her gaze on thoughts of Knockout Mouse. For obvious reasons, she preferred not to remember him as Kevin Mass.

She turned away, tired but determined to not allow thoughts to wander into an emotional down spiral. She had to believe that what they were doing was important and would make a difference. In the most ultimate terms, they were simply trying to make the best of a horrific situation. They might not be able to solve the problems in time but maybe it would be possible to engineer some hope from their lab work.

With a pop and a whoosh, Janis disconnected the air hose feeding her suit and turned towards the door leading to the way out. Now all that remained between her and a good night's sleep was the required gauntlet of windowless rooms and procedures that all technicians had to endure to enter or exit a BSL4 lab.

On the way back out, a decontamination shower came first. Janis extended arms and turned around as a spray of chemicals pelted her pressure suit and helmet.

After drip-drying and walking through an air blast, she stepped through into the Suit Room. There she took off the bulky pressure suit and double gloves and exposed the green scrubs worn underneath. Now she could pass into the Inner Work and Interaction Area, a mid-range confinement and security area that also shared a pressured door into the BSL3 lab space. After that came the changing room, a cramped space where every technician was required to shed their scrubs and walk naked into the second shower room for a less caustic spray.

After dropping her scrubs into a receptacle for soiled clothes, Janis welcomed the vigorous spray of water against her skin. After the required time, the spray ended and Janis passed through into the locker room. There she put her street clothes back on and headed out into the Outer Work and Interaction Area. Immediately upon stepping out, Janis was greeted by Alyssa running up and giving her a hug.

"There you are!" yelped Alyssa. "I thought you'd never come out."

Janis smoothed back her daughter's hair. "It takes a while to get in and out."

Alyssa peaked into the locker room as the door automatically closed. "What's it like in there?"

Janis smirked. "It's like being inside a tiny submarine locked in a bank vault."

Alyssa giggled. "That's bizarre…"

"You're telling me!" Janis headed off to her computer console.

"You have more to do?" asked Alyssa.

"I need to backup a couple things; that's all. Don't worry; it'll take two shakes of a lamb's tail."

Alyssa grinned. "Or two twitches of a bunny's nose?"

"Exactly," chuckled Janis. Her fingers sped over the keyboard and shifted the mouse. "Sorry about missing lunch today…"

Alyssa plopped on a chair and rolled over closer. "I know. It's OK. I got to stay in and bug Faye."

The first backup started and Janis shifted attention to a second monitor. "You two have been spending quite a bit of time together. I bet you're learning a lot. Faye is a good teacher. I've seen her instruct newbies in the lab…"

"Oh, yeah," agreed Alyssa. "The only problem is, she won't answer all my questions."

Janis furrowed her brow. "Really? Well, I'm sure there's a good reason…"

Alyssa was direct. "She says when she's done with her work, you'll tell me about it."

Janis was all too aware of the topic and Faye's reason for being reserved about it. Faye's research from bed was concentrating on the sterility issue. In particular, what about Alyssa had prevented her from becoming sterile and how might her genetic uniqueness be leveraged to find a cure for the rest of the world's children. Given some of the subject matter, Faye believed it would be best if Janis was the one to explain the particulars to her daughter.

The second backup started and they could go. But Janis hesitated. Maybe it was time to let Alyssa in on the theory Faye had come up with. Perhaps an overview of what was being researched would be best; it might placate Alyssa's curiosity while maturing for her the concepts of what the future might have in store for her.

Janis swiveled round to face Alyssa. "You know that for the past couple of months, Faye and I have been working on different things..."

"Yeah," affirmed Alyssa. "You've been doing 2GenGEN..."

"A single-dose version of *GenLET* that's spread by a cold virus..."

"And Faye's been looking at the sterility thing."

"That's right. More importantly, she's been looking into your role in solving the problem."

"Me?" Alyssa stopped her fidgeting.

"I told you; you are special."

"Yeah, I know. I can have children. Other kids when they grow up won't be able to."

"And why is that?" asked Janis but Alyssa could only shrug. "I was pregnant with you when I caught the Ghyvir-C cold. That Ghyvir-C didn't have a sputnik in it so I didn't get inflected with the damaging payload. Because of that, a special immunity got passed to you while you were still inside of me."

"I know, you told me that before. But that's not what Faye won't tell me."

"No," agreed Janis. "Faye's been working on some very complex computer models. No one knows about it but the three of us. For now, let's keep it that way."

"Your big boss doesn't even know?"

"No, The Project hasn't been using our computer models so we haven't told them yet. Faye's been putting gobs of data into her computer and defining lots of rules and constants and variables...and out the other end comes what-if answers."

Alyssa screwed up her face. "What's a what-if answer?"

Janis smiled. "What if you sit on your left leg until it falls asleep and gets all tingly then a bee comes after and you try to run. What will happen?"

Alyssa grunted. "I'd probably fall over."

Janis nodded. "You just gave me a what-if answer. You're able to answer that because you blended the facts of what you know with realistic rules governing a possible situation. Faye has done the same thing...*only about your children.*"

Alyssa's eyes widened. "My children! I don't have any kids!"

"Of course you don't. But someday you might. And when you do, you'll pass your genetic code to the next generation."

"So why is that special?" asked Alyssa.

"That's special because *you're* special." Janis leaned forward and took hold of Alyssa's hands. "If a fix for sterility isn't found, you are going to be the last woman who can bear children." Janis couldn't help but tearing up. "Faye and I tried to find a fix but our first trial failed. Faye believes her computer model might have discovered why."

Seeing the emotion and seriousness on her mother's face, Alyssa struggled to concentrate. "She got a what-if answer..."

"That's right, but not about you – about your children. The computer model told her the reason why the first trial failed is because you are only half of the specialness we need. When you have children, your children's germ cells will have that completeness. Using those cells, the computer model says the fix might work."

"Germ cells?" Alyssa glowered.

"Not that kind of germ cells. The germ cells I'm talking about are special sex cells; they're the kind of cells that allow us to reproduce."

"So what are you saying?" asked Alyssa, suddenly concerned. "You can't come up with a fix until I have children?"

Janis paused. "Unless we can figure out a way to simulate the same chain of interactions in the lab – no, we can't. Even if we found a way in the lab, so much can go wrong. That's why the best, the most certain way might be to derive the fix from your children's germ cells."

"But I don't want any kids…" Alyssa pulled back.

"Of course you don't; not right now. That's why Faye's working up new models to plan what it would take to do the same thing in the lab."

Alyssa shifted nervously. "Is that everything Faye wouldn't tell me?"

Details of the topic flooded Janis' mind. So many of them were overly technical but one in particular had yet to be spoken. It probably would have little significance to Alyssa now, but the thought of what it might mean in years to come gave Janis pause. She tried to not let her inner anxiety show.

"There's one last thing. To have a child, an egg and a sperm must come together. You have the egg, a special egg. For your children to have the right kind of germ cells, the kind of cells we can use to make the fix work, Faye's model predicts the sperm must be equally special."

The two of them had had the birds and bees conversation years before. Janis knew a lot of detail in this area wasn't required.

Alyssa rolled her eyes and chuckled timidly. "How do you find special sperm?"

"It has to be from someone who produced the sperm before they were ever infected with Ghyvir-C. That part is critical."

Alyssa huffed. "Well that rules out everybody!"

"No, it doesn't," countered Janis. "If the sperm was donated and frozen over thirteen years ago, before Ghyvir-C started infecting people, that kind of sperm would be special."

The topic was turning sour for Alyssa. "That's like weird. I have to get pregnant with old frozen sperm?"

Janis stood. "You don't have to do anything. It's a theory and like I said, Faye is trying to come up with a way to do the same thing in the lab. Besides, what are we still doing here? Didn't Faye say she had snacks?" Janis forced a lighter mood.

Alyssa grinned. "They're good ones too!"

Just then, a massive concussion buffeted the building above them.

A roar came from the ceiling.

The lights flickered and went out.

The two of them stood in pitch darkness.

Alyssa screamed as Janis rushed to hug her close.

Moments later, auxiliary lighting flickered on, then off, then on again.

All BSL4 labs have redundant, dedicated systems for just about everything. In the moment, Janis was thankful they were close to dedicated BLS4 power and fresh air exchange. She rushed to the phone and punched in the three-digit extension for the security desk.

She thought she heard a connection but couldn't be sure.

"This is Janis Insworth in the sub-basement lab. What's going on up there?"

Janis waited. Hearing no response, her heart accelerated. She listened to clicks and dead air before the line got redirected. After one ring, a frantic voice was heard.

"GPAX Mobile One. Over."

"This is Janis Insworth. I'm in the sub-basement lab…"

"Building Three?"

"Yes," blurted Janis. "Who is this?"

The voice was out of breath. "Shit! Are you alone?"

"No, my daughter's with me."

"Stay where you are! Right now, you're in the safest place!"

"What are you talking about? What just happened?"

"Listen! Don't attempt to come to the surface! I repeat – stay where you are!"

Janis watched the lights dim then flicker. "We're on auxiliary power but it's been going on and off."

"If the lights go out, you should still have emergency power for air exchange."

"Who am I talking to? What's GPAX?"

"Locate a fire extinguisher and get to a safe place away from heavy equipment..." The line went dead.

Again and again the concussions returned. The last blast shook ceiling panels down around them. Janis grabbed her cell phone off the desk and tugged Alyssa towards the entrance to the BSL4 lab.

"Come on!" shouted Janis. "Follow me."

Cowering, Alyssa scurried alongside.

Janis yanked the heavy door open leading into the locker room. Scurrying inside, she closed the door then jerked a fire extinguisher from the wall and set it on the floor in between their feet.

Huddled together, the two of them listened as peals of thunder passed overhead. Behind the windowless room, they could hear debris falling.

Janis felt Alyssa shivering next to her in panic. To hide her own fear, Janis considered a hopeful irony – a lab designed to keep deadly things on the inside might also keep a perilous unknown on the outside.

"Remember what I said about a submarine in a bank vault?"

Too afraid to speak, Alyssa could only nod.

"We'll be OK. We're in the submarine."

A moment later, auxiliary lighting failed.

Alyssa squealed and clung tighter in the dark.

In pitch blackness, Janis closed her eyes

It was all she could do to fight off terror and intense dread.

But far worse than the fear – was not knowing.

CHAPTER 51

Grounds Perimeter
GeLixCo Advanced Research Center

Under a moonless sky the flicker of roaring flame drew the eye to a patch of land in the distance. Sirens and small arms fire distressed the midnight hour. The narrow service road paralleling the perimeter fence led downhill into blackness. At the fence line a GeLixCo security vehicle sat pockmarked with bullet holes, the left side of its windows blown out. Inside, a pair of security agents manned what was left of their mobile command post.

Colin Insworth holstered his .45 pistol and hurried across the conquered high ground. Wincing, he grabbed his left bicep as blood soaked through the strip of cloth ripped from his shirt and used to tie off the flesh wound.

Nearby, a GeLixCo guard rummaged through the pockets of three dead men dressed in black. The bodies were strewn alongside weapons in a small field at the highest point of the GeLixCo property. Unzipping a satchel, the guard discovered a cache of rocket-propelled grenades. The guard brandished one for Colin to see.

"We got here just in time," remarked the guard.

Colin reached out a bloodied hand. "Give me your binoculars."

The guard complied and Colin adjusted the night vision lenses. Stepping to a rocky prominence, he took aim with a viewfinder tinged in surreal green. Zooming in, he had to squint. The fires consuming what was left of Building 3 flared white hot in the night vision field of view. Colin jerked away from the intensity and scanned the darkness. A warm engine flare from another GeLixCo security vehicle swept into view. Farther on, infrared outlines of two guards, sprinting with rifles at the ready, rushed past.

One of the security agents from the nearby mobile command post ran up to Colin. "Sir, we haven't been able to secure all access roads..."

Colin held firm holding the binoculars before his eyes. "Have first responders been notified?"

"We've gotten through to central dispatch but we can't be sure all field units have gotten the word."

"Damn!" snapped Colin. Shifting binoculars farther afield, he searched the dim vastness on the edge of city lights where he knew city streets intersected. As he feared, the flashing red strobes of a fire truck dispatched from the city of Aguadilla came into view. As the truck snaked up into the hills from the city below, Colin searched the blackness around it for heat signatures.

"There's one coming up the hill. Keep trying with dispatch!" ordered Colin.

"Yes, sir." The agent hustled back to the security vehicle.

Colin adjusted the zoom and night vision resolution. As he did, a wisp of a heat trace was detected. His eyes were drawn to it even as it streaked across his field of vision. The arc of heat traced a deadly path through the darkness. It only took a second for it to intercept the fire truck's flashing strobes. A moment later, Colin's green screen erupted with a fireball of destruction. A moment after that, the distant roar of what he had just witnessed arrived at his ears.

Colin jerked the binoculars down. He was too angry to yell, too determined to stay put. Ignoring the pain in his arm, he jogged back to the bullet-riddled security vehicle where two agents operated separate radios. Colin jerked open the driver side door and motioned to the agent.

"Stay here with the guard. Secure and hold this point."

The agent hustled out of the way. "Yes, sir."

Colin jumped behind the wheel and revved the engine. He spoke to the remaining agent in the passenger seat. "We've got to get down there. We need those roads open."

The agent held a satellite phone to his ear. "There's a Medevac chopper standing by, ETA ten minutes as soon as we give the word."

Colin stomped on the accelerator and spun them around headed downhill.

"There are too many places in these hills to hide. We've pushed them back but now we have to go beyond the perimeter and finish them off."

The tattered vehicle rumbled on one flat tire. The agent reloaded his sidearm. "They knew right where to hit us."

Colin increased their rate of speed. "What's the latest damage assessment?"

The agent braced himself with one hand holding onto the dashboard. "Municipal and onsite backup power generation was hit first along with key security substations. Next, a barrage of RPGs slammed Building 3 and its support sub-plant. None of the hits appear random. Strike locations were chosen surgically. At a minimum, somebody had access to plant schematics and floor plans."

Nearing the main campus, Colin's gaze gravitated to the burning and blown-away sections of Building 3. "They ignored the other buildings…"

"Luckily, the lab's in the basement."

Colin's grip on the wheel tightened. "Any word from there?"

"Not since the initial call."

"And no one's been able to get downstairs?"

"Not yet. They're still fighting a first-floor fire blocking the stairwell."

"Is sub-basement air exchange still working?"

"On backup power. We've had to move a generator into position from building 2. The primary backup for building 3 was damaged."

"What about communications?"

"We haven't been able to reestablish the landline. We're rerouting any incoming calls to Building 3 security to GPAX Mobile One."

Colin paused to clear anxious thoughts. "Keep dialing the private line for Janis Insworth. We have to get through."

"If she's taken cover in the BSL4 lab, cell phone signals won't work in there."

"Do it anyway!"

"Yes, sir."

Stopping the vehicle, Colin jumped out and motioned the agent into the driver seat. As the agent slid across, Colin held up the binoculars. "Where's the RIDIS coupler for these?"

The agent lifted a flap on a shoulder bag and handed over a dark object.

Colin took it and made quick work of snapping it in place over the eyepiece. He gestured to the agent's rifle. "Give me that too."

"Where are you going?"

"Outside the line."

The agent hesitated to close the door. "By yourself?"

Colin shouldered the assault rifle. "I know; it's not standard procedure. I'm hoping that's exactly why they won't expect it."

"Don't you think most of them have already scattered? They'll want to get off the island quick. It's typical hit-and-run."

"If these were professionals, I'd agree with you. But somebody just took out a fire truck. I think some of them want to stick around long enough to enjoy their handiwork."

The agent wasn't convinced. "If they're out there, they're risking a lot just to watch something burn. They have to know the hit was clean and surgical."

Colin closed the door. "It shows you what inside information can do. Keep a GPS track on my phone. I'll signal if I need support."

The agent put the vehicle in gear. "Roger that."

Colin watched for a moment as the agent drove off towards the flaming wreck of Building 3. It took all the discipline Colin had not to rush to the building and fight his way to the sub-basement. Not knowing the fate of Janis and Alyssa was both torture and impetus to fight on. There was only one hope to cling to. Everything hinged upon the unique protective features and redundancies of a BSL4 lab.

Turning into drifting embers and dust, Colin scampered off down the road and into the brush. Navigating by the position of city lights twinkling at the base of the hills, he headed into the area where he had watched the RPG arc into the fire truck. Most of the time, he crept with night vision binoculars before his eyes. Analyzing the slope of the hillsides, he estimated the best observation and launch-point for the projectile and angled his advance for a position upslope above it.

After several minutes of stealthy approach, Colin crouched down and trained his eyes on the green display in the viewfinder. No heat signatures displayed. Sweeping the area, all was clear. Patiently, he waited. Lying on his stomach, he kept a steady gaze on the key area of interest.

After ten minutes, the beat of helicopter blades approached from the north. Colin tensed. The Project must have ordered the Medevac despite the risks. As the chopper made its descent towards the GeLixCo campus, Colin drew extra alert on his field of vision. Off to one side, two specks flashed on the infrared. Angling over and zooming in, two bodies could be seen rising up from behind a rocky outcrop. On the shoulder of one of them was poised a RPG.

Colin noted the range to target in the binoculars' viewfinder. He then shifted to the assault rifle, knowing full well that it lacked night vision or scope. It would be a shot in the dark but hopefully enough to prevent them from firing.

Taking aim as best he could, he squeezed off several shots.

Shifting back to the binoculars, he watched as the two forms scurried away down the hillside. He hadn't hit them but the near approach of a sniper had changed their plans.

Colin stood and activated the RIDIS coupler. With viewfinder pressed to his eyes, his fingers deftly manipulated the controls. Just as the calibration was complete, the fleeing pair disappeared on the other side of a ridgeline.

Colin took off in a sprint down the hillside. Brush and brambles snared his legs and scratched at his arms. By the time he reached a better viewpoint, the escaping pair had reached a motorcycle hidden off road. In the distance, Colin could hear the bike's engine throttle up. The white front light and red taillight flared into view.

Colin drew a steady bead on the light source with the binoculars. With fingers poised at the coupler controls, he tracked the bike's movement as it sped away. The bike's driver hunched over the controls. His passenger held on from behind. Before the two of them could zip out of view, Colin activated the RIDIS beam. Locking on, pulsating green crosshairs divided over the subjects and snapped back together. On snap, the crosshairs turned red, signaling RIDIS capture was complete.

A second later, the bike sped out of range and was gone.

Looking back over his shoulder, Colin watched the helicopter settle down for a landing in GeLixCo's parking lot before shifting his attention back to the coupler in hand. Thumb-pressing the controls, he activated a request for transmission and analysis. The command was picked up by satellite and relayed to Granite Peak.

Drawing his sidearm, Colin raced back up the hill to the spot where, in his hurry, he had left his rifle. Shouldering the weapon, he noted a blinking receive indicator on the coupler. He pressed activation of the heads-up overlay and a drop-down readout appeared in the night vision eyepiece. Crouching on the ridgeline, he watched as RIDIS database confirmation returned from Granite Peak.

DPG/GPI RIDIS IDREPORT / 11:09:49PM MT
Field scan data received via NVCD/64/1-2M
[18.4274454 -67.1540698]
Subject-1..........................André Bolard
Subject-2..........................Noah Labon
Match%-99.99999

Colin didn't have time to react. In his pocket, his phone vibrated. "This is Colin…"

"Sir, you wanted to be informed of any transmissions with Turnberry Tower…"

"That's correct."

"In the last half hour there's been one call out and one call returned."

Colin lowered the binoculars to his side and turned back towards GeLixCo. "Who made the call out?"

"One of the three new security agents you instructed us to monitor."

"Can you sum up the exchange?"

"Yes sir. The outcall informed Turnberry of tonight's attack."

"And what was the response?"

"It just came in," stressed the caller. "It was brief…"

Colin started walking back to the campus.

The caller finished. "…All it said was: *Decision Point Self-Destruct*."

Colin halted, letting the phrase find context. As possibilities coalesced around all he knew, he stepped forward. With every step, a slow burn of anxiety caught fire.

"Has a security team gotten to the basement of Building 3 yet?"

"I'm not sure. Last I heard, they were still fighting the fires."

"Damn it! Get somebody down there! Do whatever it takes!"

Colin broke out in a dead run.

CHAPTER 52

BSL4 Locker Room
Sub-Basement Lab

Emergency lights had come back on minutes before but Janis and Alyssa remained huddled together in the windowless locker room. The smell of acrid smoke and caustic chemicals seeped in from cracks the room had suffered during a series of thunderous concussions. The explosions had stopped and yet there was no way to know what was on the other side of the door. Janis realized that opening it might release the last bit of fresh-air exchange provided by the isolated BSL4 systems.

Even as she found it difficult to move, she knew staying in place was equally untenable. The building's landlines were dead and private cell phones didn't operate within the shielded confines of the inner lab. If no one showed up to rescue them, there was only one way she could try to make a call to the outside world.

She'd have to leave the relative security of the locker room and step back into the Outer Work and Interaction Area. That area had suffered untold damage. She considered trying to venture out alone to attempt a call but up until now terrified Alyssa refused to leave her side. One thing was for sure: if no one was showing up to help them, they'd have to risk venturing beyond the locker room to help themselves.

Janis shifted in place, causing Alyssa to startle and clutch tighter.

"I'm going to have to try to make a call," announced Janis.

"Can't you do it here?" asked Alyssa.

"There's no signal in here…"

"But we can't go out there!"

"Shh-shh," quieted Janis. "It'll be all right. I'm just going to take one step outside the door. You'll still be able to see me."

"But what about the fire?"

"I'll open the door a crack. If it's too hot, I'll close it right away." Janis steadied Alyssa by grabbing her by the shoulder. "Listen, I've got to do this. We may be OK in here right now, but we don't know how long that'll last. Now stay put; I'll be right back."

Alyssa had no choice but watch her mother move away.

Janis drew near the locker room door and felt it. There was no heat so she turned the handle and gave a slight push. Through the open crack came darkness and the stench of fiery destruction. It appeared emergency power was only on in the BSL4 lab environments. There was no fire in the Outer Work and Interaction Area but the smoke level was dangerous for prolonged exposure. Janis poked her head out, finding conditions acceptable for the time it would take to make one call.

Janis swung the door wider and took a step into black. Mindful to keep Alyssa in sight, she activated her cell phone and redialed the security desk number from before. A series of crackles and line exchanges transferred her call.

To her great relief, a voice answered as before. "GPAX Mobile One…"

"Oh, thank God!" she sighed.

"Who is this?"

"Janis Insworth…I'm in the lab…"

On mention of the name, the voice interrupted. "Ms. Insworth, please stay on the line. We're trying to get to you. We need to know your situation."

Janis coughed away a lungful of smoke. "We have emergency power in the BSL4 lab. The rest of the floor is without power and heavy with smoke and debris."

"We're trying to get to you by way of the western stairwell. A chemical fire from the auxiliary plant has been blocking our way."

"What the hell happened up there?" asked Janis.

"There was an attack. That's all I can say right now. Please stay on the line. I was ordered to transfer your call in case we heard from you. Just a moment. Whatever you do, stay on the line. This is critically important."

Janis ducked her head back into the locker room for a draft of fresh air before returning to the phone. "You don't understand…I can't stay on the line…there's too much smoke…"

The call was already in the process of being transferred. For an instant, Janis considered ending the call and diving back into the more survivable environment of the locker room. She watched the fear in Alyssa's eyes grow more serious as a stinging waft of chemical smoke triggered more coughing. Janis held the phone at arm's length into the smoke while leaning back into the fresh air. In the silence of the smoky darkness, she heard a voice squawking through the phone's small speaker.

She pulled herself back into the smoke and pressed phone to ear.

"…Janis…Janis…are you there?"

It was Colin's voice, frantic and more serious than she had ever heard it.

"I'm here!"

He spoke as he ran. "We're trying to get down to you…"

"You have to make this quick…"

"Then understand I don't have time to explain. You have to trust me…"

"Trust you about what?"

"I've intercepted a call from The Project. You must act right away. They're going to self-destruct the lab."

Janis closed her eyes to prevent the sting of the smoke. "What are you talking about? Is the attack over?"

"We've secured the perimeter."

"Who did it? Do you know?"

"New Class Order."

"Are you sure?"

"Positive but listen; what NCO didn't destroy The Project intends on finishing."

"I don't understand. If the fire's out, the lab is stabilized. Why would they want to destroy it?"

"You have to listen to me," ordered Colin. "I was going to tell you and Faye together…"

"Tell me what?" Janis thought back to Faye's plea to meet with Colin.

"Your plans for 2GenGEN…the last option for survivors...," started Colin.

"What about it?"

"I found out The Project has no intention of following through on their promise. They only agreed to it to get you to synthesize 2GenGEN for them."

Janis struggled to speak. "They're not going to release it for plague survivors?"

"No – and now that your process for making it has been transferred on the mirrored servers to Granite Peak, they don't need your sample. They can recreate 2GenGEN any time they want."

Janis struggled to comprehend and maintain her position in the smoky darkness. "But why destroy what we've already created?"

"The attack tonight was a surprise but they've decided to use it, to give them a way out, an opportunity to accelerate their schedule. It's what they always intended."

"What do you mean?" gasped Janis.

"They want sole control of single-dose *GenLET*. With your sample gone, they can be certain your final option won't take place. It's just as you suspected; they plan on distributing 2GenGEN according to a select plan. Not everyone will get it…and Janis…from what I've overheard this past week – it's clear the same holds true for the sterility fix. They plan a phased and selective application of the sterility fix."

"You can't be serious!" Through the smoke, The Project deception became clear. Janis jerked around and stared back into the locker room but saw beyond it. "Then we have to save what we have. The rest of the world will need time to discover the problem and solution on its own – independent of The Project."

"There may not be enough time. We have no way of knowing what kind of self-destruct device they've planted or when it'll go off. We need to get you two out of there right away!"

Janis only had a second to consider her options. "Get down here and evacuate Alyssa. I'm going back in and save 2GenGEN."

"No! It's too risky. We'll find some other way…"

"From what you're saying, The Project won't let that happen," snapped Janis. "When will they ever allow me to have *GenLET*, 2nd Protocol, and 3rd Protocol all together again to work with? What are we working for? What good is coming up with a sterility fix if they're not going to give it to everyone!"

Colin knew a direct and true answer would only feed Janis' resolve. "If you die in that lab, there's no chance of recovering anything you planned."

"If I don't recover the sample of 2GenGEN, everyone may die before humanity finds an answer to sterility. If The Project is the only one with answers, we can't trust them to do the right thing. We all agreed – the survivors need more time!"

"Stay where you are! We're coming down to you. The fire by the stairwell is out. There's debris blocking the way but we're removing that now. It won't be long; we can have you out – just hang on."

The smoke was becoming too much. Interspersed with coughs, Janis strained to say enough to end the call. "Hurry up….you need to get Alyssa out of here…she's in the BSL4 locker room…I'm going in."

Janis didn't wait for a response. She ended the call and rushed back into the fresher air of the locker room. Intent on a single purpose, she flung open a locker door and crouched down. Rummaging through emergency supplies, she found a flashlight then turned to face Alyssa.

"Stay right where you are," ordered Janis. "They're coming down for you."

"What about you?"

Janis leaned down and held her daughter's face. "There's something I have to do. It's very important."

"I want to stay with you..." Alyssa started to get up.

"Listen," snapped Janis. "I don't have time. Where I'm going you can't go. They're coming for you. They expect to find you here." She bent forward and kissed Alyssa on the forehead one last time and hugged her close. "...I love you."

Alyssa made the most of their parting hug. "...I love you too."

Energized with purpose, Janis stood and stripped all her street clothes off as Alyssa watched with renewed apprehension. In her eyes were questions Janis had no time to answer. Quickly naked, Janis hurried the door open to the shower room and lunged forward.

With the door shut behind her, the sudden isolation of her task weighed heavily upon her. The gauntlet of BSL4 intake procedures were now a deadly obstacle course. Running them on a time limit would have been bad enough. But having to rush in and out without knowing which moment might be her last made every second critical, every breath a gift that might become her legacy.

Janis looked up at nozzles. Shower water never came on. An ominous sign.

Gripping the flashlight, she raced forward. Beyond the first shower room was the changing area where normally she'd put on scrubs. To save time, she ran right through it. The only thing she really needed to wear was the pressure suit at the end of the line. As strange as it seemed to be passing through various lab sections naked, the thought of a self-destruct device about to go off gave single focus to her advance.

Inside the Inner Work and Interaction Area she found intense heat coming off the door that connected to the BSL3 lab space. Emergency lights were dimmer here and trace smells of smoke scented the air. Dodging around furniture, she sped on.

Next, she entered the pressured suit room where a row of light blue body sacks with attached helmets hung on hooks in a row. Grabbing one of them, she rushed to put it on but found the fatigue of the day fighting against the adrenaline driving her task. The bulk of the suit was cumbersome as never before. Worst of all, the feel of it against her body's bare skin was cold and peculiar.

She stretched her fingers into place. The double layer of neoprene gloves was so familiar and yet, under these conditions, they seemed better meant for some alien world. By the time everything was on and she had passed through the chemical shower, she wound up charging into the final lab out of breath and sweating.

Adding to her nervous sweat, lab conditions gave her pause. It was darker and warmer than any of the other compartments. She had hoped that the progression of dimming lights and rising temperature she had found on her way back in would not lead to such circumstances. Not only would the dim emergency lights make her task harder, the rising temperature was a certain threat to kill the live virus she was trying to save.

She lumbered across the room in her deflated pressure suit and grabbed one of the coiled air hoses dangling from the ceiling. Quickly connecting it to her suit, she expected the whoosh of intake and inflation that normally occurred.

This time air flow was minimal. Something was wrong.

The weak stream of air was never going to fully pressurize the suit. The little bit of air that did manage to flow in was tainted with a burnt metallic odor. In reaction, she instinctively jerked her head from side to side to get away from the stench but she knew the reflex was futile.

Inside the helmet there was one way to breathe and one air source.

She shifted her focus on the task at hand – live specimen retrieval of 2GenGEN composited in a single contagious agent. Such a sample was at the opposite end of the glove box on the far end of the room. Light levels were weakest in that section. She switched on her flashlight and shuffled forward. Halfway down the glove box the rising heat became oppressive. She jerked the flashlight's beam from ceiling corners to floor. In both places, streams of smoke were oozing into the space. The sight of it left her no doubt – a fire would soon consume the room. Starting from this most important location, it would undoubtedly destroy the entire BSL4 environment. But long before actual flame broke through the walls, soaring temperatures would render glove box specimens useless. Already, one side of the room was too far gone.

Janis felt nailed to the floor, wrapped in layers of terror, dread, and indecision.

There was no point trying to retrieve the specimen from the far end of the case. From the heat she felt where she stood, she knew that sample was dead.

Only one other sample might be alive.

The thought of it sent chills through her sweat.

She only had seconds to decide. The advancing fire was most probably the self-destruct sequence that had already started. Using an incendiary device would make sense instead of a bomb. A fire in a genetic lab would be more easily explained and accepted than a dramatic explosion that would leave telling blast patterns and residue.

Janis turned and faced the near end of the glove box. At first, only the rising heat at her back drove her towards it. Dragging the clammy pressure suit with her, she scuffled back to the first glove port and drew close to the safety glass. The lack of full pressure in her suit, along with the mixture of heat and sweat, was starting to fog up the inside of her face shield. If it fogged up completely, she'd be blinded with no way of wiping it clear. Whatever she was going to do, she needed to decide fast.

Everything came down to the next few seconds.

It was hardly any time at all.

And yet, what might still be possible in those few seconds could provide a pivotal difference. What was it worth to give all of surviving humanity enough time to avoid extinction? After the GGD3 plague ravished world populations, the survivors would be in no condition to tackle the task of solving what the present world couldn't even answer. It might take an entire generation or more for the world to recover from the trauma of population collapse. But few people knew the truth and it was now clear, even if a sterility fix was found, The Project had turned as complicit as Eugene Mass in thinking it could arbitrate who would and would not be worthy of survival. Faye's new model gave a glimmer of hope but not a fix.

If nothing was done, the surviving generation was destined to be the last.

Unable to reproduce, they would need more time. Time to find the solution.

Janis' heart and thoughts leapt back to the locker room.

Alyssa would also be a part of that world. Her specialness needed enough of a chance to be recognized and leveraged. Between possible worlds available in the next few seconds, what kind of world did she want to leave her daughter?

The Project and others might have plans on doling out extended life to the privileged, the well-connected, the sanctioned few – but power and position had blinded them to the darker possibilities of the savaged world about to be. A humanity on the edge of the abyss needed whatever the present world had left to pass on.

Janis flashed back to what Colin had said.

...the last option...they have no intention of following through on their promise.

The will to make a difference overruled everything else.

Janis flung the flashlight onto a nearby table and thrust her gloved hands into the glove ports. Leaning her face shield against the safety glass, she struggled to poke fingers into proper place.

Before her, the remaining viable specimens waited in solutions and Petri dishes.

Every vessel held cultures of composite, single-dose 2GenGEN.

But all of them also contained payloads of 3rd Protocol.

Her quivering chills turned to passionate ice locked solid on the target.

These were the specimens she had tested for interactions between 2GenGEN and 3rd Protocol. There was no way to separate the viral strains. Saving one would mean exposing herself to the other. Although this version of 3rd Protocol was not contagious, it remained equally lethal to anything wrecking havoc in the wild.

Frenzied in her motions, Janis paid no respect to lab procedures. Everything around her was about to be destroyed anyway. There was only one way, in the time allotted, to possibly get herself and the target virus out of the lab alive.

Seizing upon the sharpest instrument she could find, she set about slashing through the pressure suit above the elbow. When a sizeable gash opened up, she dropped the instrument and used her fingers to rip the fabric wider.

Immediately, what little air she had in the pressurized suit escaped into the glove box. The weak stream of replacement air leaking in from the air tube wouldn't be enough to sustain her for long. She would have seconds to do what she needed to do and flee the lab. Glancing to her left through a patch of fog in her face shield, she could see the first licks of flame entering the room at the base of the far wall.

Satisfied that a bare left bicep was exposed inside the glove box, Janis wasted no time snatching the sharp instrument back into her gloved right hand and slashing a wound across her flesh. With the sting of the cut she tensed but kept moving.

Dropping the instrument, she manipulated the glove box arm ports and seized hold of a Petri dish known to have the most abundant viral colonies. Lifting the clear lid off the dish, she soaked an absorbent material into it and watched as infected solution was drawn up into the fibers. Without hesitation she lifted it and slapped the wet fabric onto her bleeding wound. For an eternity that took two labored breaths to endure, she held it there. It wasn't hard to tell if chemical smoke or something else brought tears to her eyes.

Her fate was sealed.

But it only mattered if she could survive the gauntlet back out of there.

Dropping everything, she yanked her arms out of the glove ports and disconnected her air hose. The suit was completely depressurized now and breathing was near impossible. She held her breath to avoid caustic smoke fumes. On the way back to the door that led to the chemical shower, she felt faint. Exhaustion and fumes along with searing heat threatened to become the perfect storm aiming to defeat her.

She fought for a second wind she couldn't take in.

Collapsing into the chemical shower on her knees, she raced to hold a protective hand over her wounded bicep as a spray of decontaminating chemicals washed down over her.

When the shower stopped, she crawled into the suit room to face the agonizing chore of climbing back out of the pressure suit. As she struggled to get it off, she could hear thuds and pops as structures in the lab behind her were consumed by fire.

Kicking free of the pressure suit, she stumbled to her feet and raced into the Inner Work and Interaction Area. Immediately, she wished she had remembered to pick up the flashlight tossed aside back in the lab. The work area was dark except for a red glow coming from the edges of the door that connected to the BSL3 lab. No doubt the advancing fire had already overtaken the adjoining space.

Crawling on the floor, she took breaths in measured gasps and tried to stay as far below the smoke level as possible. Following the arrangement of minimal furniture as she remembered it, she managed to find her way to the opposite door and into the changing room where weak emergency lights were still on.

Normally she shed the underlayer of scrubs in this room. Instead, she headed for a first-aid kit and made quick work of sealing a protective patch over her left bicep. It was a minimal barrier to keep the viruses localized in her wound but in the moment it would have to do.

Soot-covered, sweaty, and naked, she stepped into the final shower room and turned to close the door behind her. Just then, an explosion rocked the compartment beyond and jarred the door on its hinges. Somewhere, flames had reached chemicals or a pressurized tank. The concussion had hit the Inner Work and Interaction Area hardest and busted open the BSL3 doorway. Open flame now entered the area.

Janis heaved and pulled to shut the inner shower room door to no avail.

She managed the door closed most of the way but it would not shut tight. A quick inspection of the frame showed why. The door had been rocked just enough off alignment to make a proper seal impossible.

For the first time, fatal panic surged through Janis. She knew right away the heart-stopping predicament she faced. As a last line of defense against an escaping biohazard, safety engineering of the shower compartment mandated that the outer door could not be opened until the inner door was closed. No exceptions. If she couldn't get a good seal on the inner door, safety systems would prevent any escape through the outer door.

On the other side of that outer door was the locker room.

Beyond that was the Outer Work and Interaction Room.

To make it so far, to be so close – and then be trapped.

This couldn't be happening. She wouldn't let it end this way.

Janis grunted and screamed and pulled with all her might.

A wave of terror and sudden claustrophobia coursed through her quivering body and rooted her to the spot. The terrible fear of confinement she had experienced so long ago under USAMRIID quarantine came back with a vengeance. To do her work in labs all these years, she had forced herself to work through the idea of being in confined spaces. But being trapped in one was far different. She had never faced or dealt with the feeling of terror of being imprisoned in a windowless box after the experience at USAMRIID.

Now was not the time to be overtaken and incapacitated by it.

She had to fight against the paralyzing fear.

Turning from the misaligned door, she struggled to focus on what was still possible. There was no sense using wasted effort on something she would never be able to do. She had only one hope left. She reached in and dragged a metal chair from the Inner Work and Interaction Room into the shower. Already the chair was hot to the touch. Wielding it as a club, she lashed it against the outer door. Again and again, the metal chair impacted the barrier. All the while she screamed for someone, anyone to hear her cries. Maybe Alyssa was still on the other side. Maybe she'd hear.

Panicked thoughts ran wild. Even if Alyssa heard, what could she do? Maybe Colin had already gotten down to her and taken her out. Then rescuers should be on the other side; certainly they'd hear her cries. Unless the self-destruct fires were all around. If that were the case, her fight to escape would lead to oblivion.

Behind her, rising heat and smoke flowed through the remaining crack opening in the outer door. If there was any consolation, Janis knew one way or another it wouldn't take long under worsening conditions to suffer her fate. The end would not be slow but it certainly would be agonizing. She tried pushing fatal thoughts out of mind. She still had some fight left in her. One more crack at the door could be the sound someone would hear. She had to keep trying.

In time, her strength waned. The chair strikes against the door weakened. Her desperate shouts for help grew softer. As smoke filled the compartment, she finally found it impossible to mount any practical attack to open the door.

Staggered, she tossed the chair aside. Slumping down at the base of the outer door, she pressed her naked body against the relative coolness of its metal. She tried not to breathe too deeply. She closed her eyes to try to keep them from burning.

Utterly spent but clinging to fading hope, she pressed her ear to the door and listened for signs of rescue. All she heard was her own labored breathing. Suddenly dizzy, she felt she was about to pass out. As consciousness tunneled away from her, she released into the peace that only comes when there's nothing left to do.

She had tried her best.

CHAPTER 53

Outer Work and Interaction Area
Sub-Basement Lab

Across the smoky gloom, shafts of shaky light from a pair of flashlights broke through the yawning blackness of the outer corridor. Wearing gas masks, Colin and a uniformed security agent rushed forward and materialized out of the smoke and drifting ash. Kicking aside slanted projectiles of newly fallen debris, Colin fought his way back to the locker room door and flung it open in frantic anticipation.

"She's not here!"

Behind Colin, the security agent navigated the devastation then halted at the locker room void. The news was not unexpected. As Colin rushed across the room to try the handle on the shower room door, the security agent stood back in the outer doorway and maintained radio contact with an outside command post.

"We know the lab is gone," confessed the guard. "Sensors indicate the fire is headed this way. It's in between floors. There's no way we can get to it. It's going to have to burn itself out."

Colin looked the shower room door up and down. "We have to get this door open right away. We've got to find a way."

The guard pulled back. "We've been advised against it."

"I don't care!" shouted Colin.

"The whole room might go up. Giving it oxygen might cause a back draft."

Colin swung around to face the guard. "I'm not asking you to stay. But I'm telling you – we need this door open. Do it!"

The guard gave his head a shake. "So far we haven't had any luck. Sensors indicate the inner door is not sealed. The doors are interlocked. This one won't open until the inner door closes."

Colin yelled, "What about an emergency bypass?"

"It didn't work the first time. By now the relays are probably fried…"

"Try them again!"

"The interlock may be controlled electronically, but it's held fast mechanically. It's also under pressure."

Colin inspected the unusually wide frame around the door. "You're talking about the pressure bladders…don't worry about those. I'll take care of them. You just get the interlock released."

The guard paused as he considered all that would entail.

"Go!" shouted Colin.

Jerking away into darkness, the guard rushed to obey orders.

Colin retreated through the Work and Interaction area to the outer corridor to retrieve a fire ax from the wall. Returning straight away to the locker room, he set about chopping away at the frame of the shower room door's pressure bladder. Compromising the inner seal, he recoiled as a jet of air rocketed from the breach.

Ripping at the rent sections of the bladder with his hands, Colin could see into the door frame and parts of the armature that held the interlock in place.

As he inspected the framework, repeated clicks of relays and motorized hinges engaged along the inner frame from ceiling to floor. As he watched, all but one of the interlocks disengaged. The errant relay buzzed and clicked again as its corresponding servo attempted to activate but the stubborn hinge wouldn't budge.

Incensed at the mechanical delay, Colin turned his ax around and leveled the blunt end against the defective part. With all his might, again and again, he struck blows against the stressing metal until the powerful impacts bent and snapped the troubled connection to pieces.

Dropping the fire ax at his feet, Colin grabbed the door handle with both hands and gave a yank. His effort was with such force that when the door gave way, both the door and he flew backwards onto the floor.

A wave of heat coursed over him. He kicked the door aside and jumped up.

There, draped over the threshold laid Janis' naked body. She was unconscious and streaked with sweat and ash. He stooped down and scooped her up into his arms. On the way out of the locker room, he dodged aside to grab hold of her street clothes from the work table. There was no time to waste. Even as he crossed the darkness leading to the outer corridor, he could hear the advance of flame behind him.

From outer corridor to the base of the stairwell, Colin raced with Janis cradled in his arms. In the stairwell, fresh air fed from above was a welcomed relief.

Colin carefully set Janis down on the concrete then attached an oxygen canister to an intake hose leading to his gas mask. He slipped the gas mask over her face and switched on a forced air feed. He checked her neck for a pulse. He found one but wished it was stronger. He dare not risk the time it would take to carry her up and outside. She needed oxygen now. He cradled her up over his lap in his arms and called to her.

"Janis…it's all right…Janis…!" He tapped her cheek and rubbed her hands in his. Luckily, by collapsing, it appeared she had spent the worst time near the floor, under the heaviest smoke layer. Within minutes, she was blinking.

When her eyes opened and looked up at him, she was disoriented.

"Where am I…?"

Colin held her steady. "You're safe."

She rolled her eyes to gaze up into the stairwell. "Where's Alyssa?"

"We got her out. She's fine."

"You came back for me…" The statement established the sequence of events as much as it did a tacit surprise.

Colin stared into her eyes. "I had no choice."

Becoming more alert, Janis raised her head. "I'm naked."

Colin swept his gaze over her body then quickly returned to the patch on her arm. "What happened in there?"

"I tried to outrun the fire…the self-destruct."

"You made it." Colin considered they were still on sub-basement level. "You need to get your clothes on. We have to get out of here. Come on, I'll help you…"

He leaned her up. She leaned back against the wall.

Colin retrieved the wads of clothes he had dropped nearby. In proper order, he started helping her slip things on. After underwear and socks, he helped her to stand.

Holding onto the wall, she let a wave of vertigo pass.

"I have to get out of here…" she mumbled.

Colin supported her while she slipped into blouse and pants.

"I'll feel better when I finally get you outside."

"No, that's not what I mean," countered Janis. "I have to get away."

"You need medical attention, then rest."

She leaned on his shoulder. "You don't understand…"

"You did your best," offered Colin. "There's no point beating yourself up about it. We both knew it was going to be a long shot. It was foolish even to try – we could have lost you."

Janis turned into him. Her face was inches from his. "I didn't fail…"

The words didn't register. Colin stared back. "What do you mean? You brought nothing out with you. I found you collapsed on the floor."

Janis lifted her blouse's left sleeve to expose the bicep patch.

"You brought me out – that was enough."

The impact of what she was implying knocked Colin back. "You didn't…"

"Now do you understand? I have to get away before they find out."

"You infected yourself? You gave yourself 2GenGEN…?"

Janis teared up. "There was only one way left when I got there…"

Colin read her face. Concern mixed with sadness. "The interaction sample…"

Janis gave a nod.

"No!" Colin's shout echoed up the stairwell. "Why the hell did you do that!"

"It was the only way…"

"And now what?" yelped Colin.

Janis buttoned her blouse. "What do you think?"

"I can't imagine…" Pangs of grief took away his breath.

Stepping over to her shoes to slip them on, Janis turned back. "…the final option."

"You mean now?"

Janis started up the stairs but found herself too weak to continue. "I must get away. You can't let them find me." As Colin hesitated, Janis stepped back to him. "What did you think was going to happen when I came out of the lab with the specimen? You must have planned an escape…"

Colin knew what was coming but couldn't resist it. "There's a private plane waiting at the airport. You can tell it where you want to go."

"Fine," snapped Janis. "I have to take Alyssa along with me."

Colin stiffened. "You know what The Project thinks of her…"

"This is non-negotiable. Make it happen."

Colin wavered. "All right. I'll think of something."

"You always do…"

"Where will you go?"

"It's best if you don't know." She held a hand to her head.

"You're right." Colin eyed the arm patch. "How long do you have?"

Janis grew somber. "You've followed the news. You know the incubation period.

3rd Protocol comes on quick but 2GenGEN is even quicker. I'd say I have no more than 48 hours." She paused. "The last few…will be spent incapacitated."

"You're sure you want to do this? There are medical things we can try."

Janis' smile was weak. "There's nothing worse than a hopeful lie…"

"You never know." The sadness overtook Colin. "We could have found another way…"

Janis remained resolute. "I'm afraid I don't trust any of you to do what's right. This is my one chance to make sure it's done. There's no other way. I have to try…"

Colin saw the strength in her eyes. He took a deep breath. "Then let's get going."

Janis smiled. "You're going to have to carry me up these steps."

"It's the least I can do…"

Her smile faded. "I know."

He paused, absorbing her intent.

Regretting her snap sarcasm, she drew near to him. "Thank you for saving my life..." She hugged him. "Let's hope it means we can now save so much more."

They held their embrace for as long as they could. When they finally pulled back, their eyes met with a tenderness not seen for each other for fifteen years.

The feeling was strong; much was lost but something was gained.

Once again, Colin scooped Janis up into his arm, this time to carry her to the surface. Emerging into the night air, Janis was thankful to see the stars again. Even more so, she was overjoyed to be reunited with Alyssa. The two of them hugged even as Janis dodged all questions about what had gone on in the lab.

As Janis delighted in Alyssa's hug, she couldn't help but take in the aftermath of destruction around her. The devastation to Building 3 was beyond surprising. To imagine she'd survived such an attack from below was even more miraculous. Then again, to survive the onslaught only to emerge with only 48 hours to live seemed a cruel twist of fate. All of it made more bittersweet by the reunion with Alyssa.

Shunning attempts by security personnel to route her to a medical aid station, Janis collected Alyssa and followed Colin's lead to the far side of Building 2. There she found a parked car waiting for her. Colin handed her the keys, passports, and instructions to give the airport guard. He gave both of them a kiss on the forehead.

"We're crossing into unchartered territory…" he warned. "Once we do this, so much is out of our control."

Janis drew Alyssa close to her side. "If there was any other way, don't you think I would have taken it? This is everything I hoped for – and the last thing I wanted."

"It's not over. I won't give up on the hope that we still have other options…"

Janis got behind the steering wheel as Alyssa took the front passenger seat. Janis gave Colin one last look. There was nothing more to say. She drove off.

Rooted in place, Colin watched them go. His phone buzzed. It was Faye.

CHAPTER 54

Apartment Level
GARC Building 2

Faye swung open her apartment door and Colin rushed in.

"What the hell is going on?" demanded Faye.

From the text message he had received, Colin expected a confrontation. If it had to be, he wanted to set the pace. "When did they let you back in the apartment? I thought everyone got herded into the basement shelter."

"I just got back." Faye followed him across the room. His bandaged arm drew her concern. "What happened to you?"

"I'm all right…"

Faye drew near. "What's going on with Janis and Alyssa? Did they get out of the sub-basement or not?"

From the elevated window, Colin peered through darkness to find a campus in disarray. "They both got out."

"Then where are they?"

Colin paused. "They're gone. They had to get away."

"Gone! Where?"

"She didn't want to say…"

Faye paced and rubbed her temple. "You're not making any sense. They wouldn't just leave and you wouldn't just let them."

"It was necessary to keep them away from The Project…"

"Were they hurt? Are they going for medical care?"

"No…." Colin turned from the window to face Faye. "I told you days ago – I needed to talk with both of you…"

"Janis didn't want to meet; you know that. I kept after her to make it happen. It was only earlier tonight I finally got her to agree to meet you."

"Really…," noted Colin. "Well, I spoke with her. I'll tell you the same thing I told her. This business about a final option, giving plague survivors extended life…The Project never intended to make good on that."

"Why not?"

"All they want is sole control of 2GenGEN. They only agreed to Janis' plan to get her to synthesize what no one else in the world possesses. Once they got her process documented and they knew they could duplicate it…well, tonight they saw a way to make sure she'd never get a chance to use it."

"They're behind the attack tonight?" Confusion mixed with surprise.

"No," answered Colin. "NCO and André Bolard was behind the attack. But as usual, The Project never lets a good emergency go to waste. When they found out the attack was on, they ordered the lab destroyed."

Faye took it in. "How do you know this?"

"I placed a tap on any secured calls in and out of here that connected to the agents that came back with me from D.C."

"You've never talked about that trip. Why?"

"At first I wasn't sure. I suspected something wasn't right. I took a chance in D.C. and planted a bug. After I left the meeting, I monitored conversations for days. It took about a week to catch them speaking their truth."

"But that's two months ago. Why wait so long to tell us?"

"I didn't want to bring you two in on it until I had a grip on what to do. When Janis refused to meet, it gave me time to think."

"What's to decide? Janis could have stopped work on 2GenGEN."

"It didn't matter. She had already drafted her process. Key concepts were already in place and backed up. You don't understand the kind of people you're dealing with. Believe me, if we get cut out of the game, there's no chance to win."

Faye folded her arms. "That's the difference between Janis and you. She never looked upon it as a game."

Laden with the weight of all that had happened, Colin sat down. "There's something else you must know. It's not easy to say…"

Seeing his face taut with dismay, Faye drew near and sat across from him. "It's about Janis, isn't it?"

Colin swallowed on a dry throat. "I told her about The Project…how they were going to destroy the lab. I told her what I overheard The Project talking about…"

"What else did you hear?"

"Even if we come up with a vaccine for 3rd Protocol or a sterility fix, they plan on a distribution that's phased and selective. They have no intention on giving it to everyone."

"What happened in the lab?" Faye filled with dread.

"She said there was only one way to defeat them. She had to go in and save it."

"2GenGEN? She went back in?"

Colin nodded.

"…but you said she was all right…" Faye's anxiety rocketed.

Colin lowered his gaze. "I said she got out. I never said she was all right."

"I asked you if they were hurt…," snapped Faye, her dread venting as anger.

He raised his eyes and leveled with her. "The fire was about to take the lab. There was only one specimen left. There was no time to do anything else…"

Colin paused, hoping Faye would realize what he was about to say so he wouldn't have to say it. But Faye stayed silent, stunned by unthinkable anticipation.

"…she infected herself." Colin's words split the air between them. Into the gaping space once reserved for hope poured sadness one could drown in.

Faye gasped and raised a hand to her mouth. "The interaction test…"

Colin nodded. "She told me she believes she has 48 hours."

Faye slumped back, buried her face in her hand, and wept. Through her tears, she managed to vent an aching rage. "Why on Earth did you let her go!"

"It's her time. It's what she wants to do with it."

Faye lurched to her feet. "What she wants to do with it! And what exactly do you think that is?"

Colin kept calm. "My guess? She wants to spread single-dose *GenLET*."

"That's right. She has it in her blood. She'll catch the cold and spread it from person to person. Aren't you missing something?"

"What?"

Faye paced away her agitation. "She obviously wasn't in her right mind. She was probably in shock. Of course she can walk around spreading the 2GenGEN virus but my God, there's a better way!"

"She had to get away. She couldn't take the risk of The Project finding out what she had done and putting her in a locked-down quarantine."

Faye stopped before Colin and lectured him. "Don't you understand! We need to take and preserve samples of her blood. You shouldn't have let her out of your sight! If she dies before we get those samples, her sacrifice could be all in vain. There's no guarantee she'll pass 2GenGEN to enough people to make a difference. She sacrificed all to get it out of the lab for us. Now we need to preserve it in a way that makes sense – a way that The Project doesn't know about."

"What good is her blood? It's also loaded with 3rd Protocol."

"The non-contagious kind. One can be extracted from the other in the lab."

"What lab?"

"You'll have to find me one. But first you'll need to find Janis."

"I got a report from the private pilot I hired. She told him to fly her to Atlanta."

Faye backed off and sped to her computer. "And why not – it has the busiest airport in the world. Lots of people to mingle with…"

Colin caught on. "People flying everywhere."

After a quick Internet search, Faye scanned the statistics. "Hartsfield-Jackson serves 151 U.S. destinations and more than 80 international destinations in 52 countries…more than 240,000 passengers a day." Faye turned back to Colin. "When The Project discovers her gone, you know they'll be going after her…"

The facts were harsh but Colin had to say them. "There's no treatment for 3rd Protocol plague. With every passing hour she becomes less valuable to them."

"Regardless, they still won't want her spreading 2GenGEN. Are you saying they won't go after her?"

"No, they will. They won't want to take the chance of letting her spread it."

"Then we need to get to her first." Across the room, Faye's phone buzzed. Rushing to it, she noted an incoming text message.

"Who is it?" asked Colin.

Faye's eyes lit up. "It's from Janis!"

Colin jumped up and hurried to her side.

Faye punched keys to retrieve the message. When it appeared, she stood surprised, saddened, and overwhelmed. A past conversation and a flash of memory conjoined upon an insight. At first it made no sense – and then it meant everything.

LIBIPONOCO

Colin sounded out the word. "Libi-Po-No-Co…what does it mean?"

Faye had to sit down. Through her tears, she smiled. "It means success."

"In what language?"

Faye thought back to college days with Janis. "Our language."

Colin sat down next to her. “You lost me.”
Faye had to smile. “It was my answer to BIOPONORE.”
Colin answered, “...biological point of no return.”
“Yes...”
“And LIBIPONOCO?”
For Faye, the college memory was now clear.
“*...Libido's Point of No Control.*”

CHAPTER 55

Fourteen Hours Later, Concourse D
Hartsfield-Jackson Atlanta International Airport

Delta Flight 422 from San Juan, Puerto Rico disembarked at 3:46 p.m. into a concourse cluttered with activity. A throng of passengers waiting to board the next flight sat or milled about the gate area. Threading their way through them, a stream of arriving passengers emerged from the breezeway and headed for baggage claim.

Faye Gardner stood aside a support column, out of view of the main hallway. She kept a watchful eye, her attention split between arrivals at the gate and suspicious faces in the crowd.

A woman traveling by herself with a shoulder bag caught her eye. Deliberate and serious, the woman stepped out of the flow of disembarking passengers and paused by the ticket desk. Her eye roamed the crowd until they met Faye's.

Contact had been made.

The woman set off straight away in Faye's direction. In reaction, Faye stepped forward on an intercept path ever mindful of her surroundings.

"Thank you for coming, Doctor Yeats."

Faye directed their steps back towards the main hallway.

Rebecca Yeats fell right in step beside her. "I'm glad to help."

As Alyssa's doctor back at GARC, Rebecca had acquired unusual access to Project personnel and workspace all due to her availability and medical specialty. Although not part of The Project, she had come to know certain members quite well over the past many weeks. Faye was one such person who had confided much to her about Project goals and issues. From Faye's first hand testimony and what both had witnessed at GARC, Rebecca had grown suspicious of The Project and its motives.

"Did Colin have a chance to see you before you took off?"

"Yes," confirmed Rebecca. "He briefed me on the situation – as much as he was willing to tell."

"Then you know the urgency of getting this blood sample."

"Yes. Have you located Janis?"

Faye directed their steps out of Concourse D towards Concourse E.

"It took a while. The RIDIS scanner helped…"

"RIDIS scanner?"

Faye needed Rebecca's implicit trust and cooperation. This was no time to keep her in the dark. "It's a device Colin let me borrow. Apparently, all Project personnel are given something during their intake physical that shows up on this scanner. It makes quick work of picking Project members out of a crowd."

Since Faye was so forthcoming, Rebecca followed up with something else she was wondering. "How did you get here so fast?"

"I was at Rafael Hernandez Airport before the sun came up. Colin had a private plane waiting. You were closer to San Juan. There was no sense you driving to the west side of the island. A commercial carrier made more sense. This is your layover time isn't it?"

"I have an hour and a half before my flight boards for Europe."

"At least you'll have lots of time to rest on the flight. You won't get to India until tomorrow. You all set for Hyderabad?"

"I think so," offered Rebecca. "I'll be at Janis' house in Jubilee Hills. Colin said to stay there until his people escort me to NovoSenectus. Apparently, he knows somebody on the inside who will take the blood samples."

"Yes..." confirmed Faye. "He made several contacts there many years ago. It was on the RIDIS project – just like the scanner I used today."

"That remind me," hurried Rebecca. "Colin told me to tell you – he got word that The Project has activated something called ORIDIS. He seemed quite concerned."

Faye kept their pace steady. Thoughts from past conversations with Colin came to mind. He knew just the mention of that name would tell her all she needed to know.

"Do you know what he means?" asked Rebecca.

"Orbital RIDIS," announced Faye. "It means The Project is using everything they have to track down Janis. We may have less time than we think."

"Orbital...?" quizzed Rebecca. "Whatever could they do from orbit?"

"They could scan buildings looking for Project personnel signatures inside."

"They can do that?"

"I suspect they can do even more. Colin told me certain groups or classes of people have been given different markers. From orbit, members of any one group can be targeted for identification."

"That's incredible!" gasped Faye.

"I wouldn't worry. Colin wouldn't have asked you to do this if he knew you had the mark."

"The mark?" Rebecca recoiled. "It sounds like the mark of the beast."

Faye sneered. "It very well may be. But you were brought in quickly, during Alyssa' emergency – you didn't have a Project medical intake, did you?"

"No," sighed Rebecca. "There was no time; they thought she was going to die."

Faye turned down Concourse E. "If ORIDIS scans the airport, it'll pick up three signatures – Janis, Alyssa, and me. As long as we get the blood sample and you get to your next gate before Project agents get here, we'll be fine." Faye caught sight of her target in the distance. "Come on....there they are."

Rebecca followed her line of sight. Milling among departing passengers waiting at a crowded gate were Janis and Alyssa.

Faye held out a hand. "Give me the sample pack."

Rebecca handed over her shoulder bag.

"Hang back here for a minute," ordered Faye. "Let me make contact first. If they're under surveillance, we don't want you compromised."

Rebecca slowed her pace then veered off the walkway towards windows behind an empty ticket counter. Faye stepped on. As she did, Janis then Alyssa caught her eye. When Faye came close, she couldn't resist giving each of them a hug.

The last hug was reserved for Janis. She held it as she spoke in Janis' ear.

"What have you done?"

"You once said good things happen in threes….I finally found the third."

"You've broken my heart."

Janis looked haggard and weak. She hugged back. "No lectures, please."

Faye fought back tears. "I know what you're trying to do. Let me help you."

Janis pulled back. "You're here to take samples, aren't you?"

The surprise of Janis' insight struck Faye and lit up her face.

Janis smiled. "I'm not stupid, I'm just dying. After wandering the gates for a few hours, the same thing occurred to me. I'm just a little slow…"

Faye stayed close. "You should be in the hospital. It's any wonder you can stand at all. You were dead tired last night before any of this started…"

"Poor choice of words…but yes, I'm dead tired…" Janis reached out and smoothed back Alyssa's hair. "But I'm with Alyssa…and we've been meeting lots and lots of people."

Faye glanced back to locate Rebecca. "I don't have much time. The Project is on its way. I need to draw blood."

Janis noted Faye's glance and followed her line of sight to recognize Rebecca across the Concourse. "I see you have help…"

"Don't worry about the details; it's been all arranged."

"Where's Colin?" asked Janis.

"He's been coordinating everything. He couldn't come. For as long as he can, he needs to make The Project believe he's still one of them."

"How can he ever do that now?"

"He won't for long," admitted Faye. "He only needs to hang on until we can get a sample of your blood to an independent lab. Once we separate the viruses, we can mass-produce and release 2GenGEN – just the way you planned." Faye saw satisfaction sweep across Janis' face. Faye added, "…the final option."

Faye leaned close to whisper, "Colin told me about Project plans…"

Janis steeled herself against the thought. "*…phased and selective…*we can't let them get away with that."

"You're right. With enough time, some among the survivors will break through. We'll give them time to do it. The Project…no one will be able to contain it."

The prospect of such support buoyed Janis' energy. "All right…let's do this. We can go in one of the restrooms."

Faye bent down to Alyssa's level. "Doctor Yeats is right over there. Go visit with her. We'll be right back."

As Alyssa scuttled off, Faye grabbed Janis by the right arm and supported her walk to the nearest restroom. Once inside, they locked themselves in a handicap stall.

As Faye dug into Rebecca's shoulder bag for a cotton ball and sterilizing fluid, Janis took a seat on the commode.

"Did you get my message," asked Janis.

Faye doused the cotton ball and rubbed it on the inside of Janis' right elbow. "Yes, I did," grinned Faye. "It brought back memories."

Janis' eye blinks dropped heavy until she left them closed. "Good ones I hope."

Faye reached back into the bag for a syringe and collection vials. "It was a different time, wasn't it?" Faye's voice trailed off.

Janis' head wobbled and jerked alert. "We didn't know what we didn't know."

Faye brought a needle to Janis' right arm. "Now we know too much."

Janis opened her eyes. "If you could go back, would you?"

Faye stuck the needle in. "Only if none of this had to repeat."

Janis winced at the pinprick. "Would it make any difference?"

"It would have to." Pulling back on the stopper, Faye watched a trickle of crimson become a gush and fill the first vial. In seconds the length of it was full.

"It depends..." countered Janis. She closed her eyes again. "What if some things are meant to be? Maybe all we're doing is interfering with it."

"With what?" Swapping collection vials, Faye started drawing blood again.

"What if your college paper was right? Maybe there *is* such a thing as *Programmed Species Death*. Why can't there be a natural process that triggers the extinction of species – for the good of nature?"

"You don't believe that," asserted Faye. "Neither do I any more."

"I'm not so sure." Janis bowed her head. Her chin fell into her chest.

Faye rushed to grab Janis shoulders to keep her from toppling over. "Stay with me...I'm almost done." Faye fought back tears.

Janis planted the palms on her hands on her knees and held on. "I didn't know how tired I was until I sat down..."

Faye plugged in the last collection vial into the back of the syringe. She needed to keep Janis alert and talking. If possible, she hoped to convince Janis to leave the airport with her right away. The last thing she wanted for Janis was to spend her last hours in Project hands. No telling what lab tests they had planned for her.

"What kind of symptoms are you having?"

Janis paused to answer. "It's hard to describe. I feel like I'm slipping away."

"Hold on a minute more and we'll be out of here..." Faye pulled out the syringe then pressed a cotton ball on the puncture. She directed Janis' other hand to hold the spot of cotton in place.

"I've had some time to think while wandering around..." Janis reflected.

Faye turned and began packaging away everything into Rebecca's shoulder bag. "You've worn yourself out. I bet you've been all over this place."

Janis was lost in her own line of thought. "...I got thinking about all that's special about Alyssa. Of all the children her age and younger...she'll be the only one who can have children."

"That's right." Faye slung the bag over her shoulder. "And Alyssa's children might be the key to finding a fix for sterility."

"Except, I was thinking..." added Janis. She looked up with heavy eyes ready to weep. "She and I share genetic changes and antibodies that are unique..."

"What about it?" asked Faye.

Janis reached forward and had Faye help her to her feet. She stood holding on to Faye. "I don't think my synthesis of 2GenGEN will take effect in her – not if she catches it from me. Promise me....If you duplicate it in the lab...you'll give it to her again. Otherwise, she might be the only survivor without extended life."

Faye tried to process the news but didn't have time. "I promise...but right now, we need to get out of here. I have to get these samples to Rebecca."

Janis took a deep steadying breath then stepped towards the exit.

Back onto the concourse they hurried. They found Rebecca and Alyssa waiting across the way in a sundry shop. Faye wasted no time transferring the shoulder bag back to Rebecca.

"These samples are critical," stressed Faye. "Take good care of them."

"I will," answered Rebecca.

Faye whispered, "I put the RIDIS scanner in there too. I don't want it found on me. When you can, return it to Colin. Now get to your gate. Good luck."

Rebecca gave a nod then turned to offer Janis a brief yet heartfelt smile.

Janis caught her eye and mouthed a thank you before Rebecca strode off.

Faye and Alyssa flanked Janis and led her from the shop. As the three of them passed a coffee shop, Janis halted, distracted by a TV mounted up and away. The sound could not be heard but the images told all. Body bags were being loaded into the back of a flatbed truck somewhere in India. The ordered rows of victims lined the truck as far back as one could see.

Janis whispered to no one, "…So many people!"

Faye glanced up but couldn't hold the same gaze that held Janis in place. "Come on, let's go…" She pulled gently on Janis' arm.

Janis turned, sensing Faye's intention. "I'm not leaving,"

Faye didn't want an argument. "We have the sample now. You've been here all day. You've done enough."

Janis looked around at the crisscrossing movement of people headed for their destinations. "Where else should I be?"

"There are people in other places. The Project is looking for you here. We can go to a shopping mall, anyplace you want. I'd rather not stay here."

Janis looked down the concourse at the many gates. "But these people are going all over the world. It only takes one of them to spread it to another city."

Faye heaved away a tortured frustration. "If they come for you, you won't be able to spread it anywhere."

Janis held steady. "Then I'll do it as long as I can. It'll work out; remember, everything comes so easily to me…" She walked on noting the sunlight low in the west. To no one in particular she whispered, "Come to think of it…next week is the first day of Spring…"

Faye and Alyssa hurried after her, flanking her once again. There was no use arguing with Janis. As Colin had said, it was her time; she was going to do with it what she wanted.

Over the next half hour, the three of them strolled into Concourse C and then B. Alyssa held her mother's hand and Faye supported Janis when she felt dazed and weak. The vertigo episodes came more often as time passed. Faye wondered how long Janis would be able to continue.

It was a question she never had answered.

At the far end of Concourse C, Faye was the one to see them first. Suited men accompanied by airport security and paramedics were racing along the wide hallway in electric vehicles. Amber lights spun above the carts in warning. Insistent beeping cleared a path through the pedestrian traffic.

The suited men took the three of them into custody as if it were a medical emergency. Which it was.

The Project agents didn't identify themselves. They didn't have to.

Alyssa sat next to Janis on the cart. They held hands the whole way.

Riding back through the concourses, Janis watched the curious faces of strangers as they stared at her and watched her pass by. There were so many faces, some of them interested, some annoyed. Most were oblivious to her passage.

Everyone had places to go, lives to live.

Janis tried to make eye contact with as many as she could.

She and they had so much in common.

Most of them, like her, would soon be ghosts.

Later that evening, in a television studio high above the streets of New York, a news broadcaster stared into the camera's eye and read what was written for him on the moving teleprompter.

> "*...earlier today there was a brief scare at Hartsfield-Jackson International Airport in Atlanta after an anonymous caller dialed 911 to report a plague-infected woman walking airport concourses. First responders arrived at the scene soon after and took two women and a teenager into protective custody for medical quarantine until tests could be conducted.*
>
> *The identities of the trio have not been released but only minutes ago preliminary reports were issued from a government lab indicating there is no cause for alarm. I repeat; no cause for alarm. No traces of contagious plague have been found either in the woman or her two companions.*
>
> *A government spokesperson repeated his estimation from earlier today that this incident was nothing but a disturbing hoax. He added it would be a shame if the irresponsible actions of one person should disrupt the lives of so many.*
>
> *He reiterated:*
> *...There is no need to panic.*"

2050

The leaf is jealous of the tree
  whose life extends beyond the cycle of seasons.

In turn the tree is jealous of the forest
  whose life extends beyond that of a single tree.

But it's the forest that's jealous of the ephemeral leaf
  whose life never need buttress
  against the sting of the Age of endless winter.

For some the way will be made straight.
For most there's no escape from fate.

Some dare not see the forest for the trees.
Some would rather burn than freeze.

The coming storm shows no compassion.
What once was green soon turns ashen.

Nature abhors a vacuum.
But even more,
She abhors the unnatural.

What have we become?
How long do we have?

**Who will ever know
if all of us go?**

THE 21ST CENTURY AS THRILLER NOVEL

Reprinted from M.C. Miller's blog, *Prefetching Self.*

One word sums up both the promise and predicament of humanity in the 21st century – that word is *sustainability*. What started as a buzzword for the enlightened sourcing and handling of food ingredients is rapidly expanding to become the critical barometer of overall survival regarding everything from food to fuel, pollution to population, animal and ocean habitat to entitlement cultures depending on debt-based banking systems for financial stability.

As farm soils erode, ocean life plummets, fresh water grows scarce, energy demands skyrocket, and the tides of restless, burgeoning populations seek equity in a global standard of living, a creeping sense of unsustainability haunts the future.

The prospect that advancing science will rescue us with wondrous new technologies yet undreamt is tempting but illusory. Most projections of current trends foresee a convergence of a perfect storm by mid-century. For a world that hasn't been able or willing to even find and implement a suitable replacement for the internal combustion engine based on fossil fuels – after 150 years, chances are science alone will not save us in time.

It's never been just about the science. The worn-out cry, "*If we could put a man of the moon, then why can't we...* {fill in the blank}" has long since been repudiated. The moon shot was a technical problem. Humanity's issues back on Earth are so much more complicated by social, political, religious, and ideological morasses.

Before the Titanic struck the iceberg, social conventions and civility prevailed. After the strike, denial and distress by necessity quickly switched to expedient actions aimed at certain survival. Left with only so many options at a time of crisis, it's all too easy for the veil of civil morality and accepted convention to give way during the icy scramble on tilting decks.

It makes one wonder, when the time draw nears for humanity's own perfect storm, what will the captains of industry, power, and political position decide to do? Surely in their elite certainty of knowing better than the rest of us, they will not hesitate to act. Given a choice between the certain collapse of civilization headed for extinction…or a severe but structured social reorganization that produces a manageable and properly governed social order…what will they choose?

After a quick Internet browse, one can find real world quotes like the following.

They're not from a doomsday thriller novel.

They only sound like it.

Real World Quotes

"A total population of 250-300 million people, a 95% decline from present levels, would be ideal."

Ted Turner
CNN founder, UN donor, Member Club of Rome
Interview with Audubon Magazine

"World population needs to be decreased by 50%."

Henry Kissinger
Former National Security Advisor, Former Secretary of State
Nobel Peace Prize Recipient, Member Club of Rome

"If I were reincarnated I would wish to be returned to earth as a killer virus to lower human population levels."

Prince Phillip
Duke of Edinburgh, Member Club of Rome,
Quoted in Are You Ready For Our New Age Future?
Insiders Report, American Policy Center, December 1995

"The world has a cancer, and that cancer is man."

Merton Lambert
Former spokesman for the Rockefeller Foundation
Harpeth Journal, December 18, 1962

"There are many ways to make the death rate increase."

Robert McNamara
Former Secretary of Defense
From *New Solidarity*, March 30, 1981

"We are on the verge of a global transformation. All we need is the right major crisis and the nations will accept the New World Order."

David Rockefeller
Club of Rome Executive Manager

"... the resultant ideal sustainable population is hence more than 500 million but less than one billion."

Club of Rome
From Goals for Mankind

"The extinction of the human species may not only be inevitable but a good thing."

Christopher Manes
Earth First!

"Global Sustainability requires the deliberate quest of poverty, reduced resource consumption and set levels of mortality control."

Maurice King
Professor at Makerere College and Leeds University

"We need to continue to decrease the growth rate of the global population; the planet can't support many more people."

Nina Fedoroff
Penn State Professor, Bush appointee to National Science Board, adviser to Hilary Clinton

"The only way to get our society to truly change is to frighten people with the possibility of a catastrophe."

Daniel Botkin
Professor Emeritus, Department of Ecology, Evolution, and Marine Biology, University of California

"The Technetronic era involves the gradual appearance of a more controlled society. Such a society would be dominated by elite, unrestrained by traditional values."

Zbigniew Brezhinsky
Advisor to 5 U.S. Presidents
From Between Two Ages

"Mankind is the most dangerous, destructive, selfish and unethical animal on the earth."

Michael Fox
Vice President of The Humane Society

"I suspect that eradicating small pox was wrong. It played an important part in balancing ecosystems."

John Davis
Editor of Earth First! Journal

"Unless we announce disasters no one will listen."

Sir John Houghton
First Chairman of Intergovernmental Panel on Climate Change

"It doesn't matter what is true, it only matters what people believe is true."

Paul Watson
Co-founder of Greenpeace

"...Advanced forms of biological warfare that can 'target' specific genotypes may transform biological warfare from the realm of terror to a politically useful tool."

Rebuilding America's Defenses
The Project for a New American Century

"The most merciful thing that a family does to one of its infant members is to kill it."

Margaret Sanger
Planned Parenthood Founder

"A reasonable estimate for an industrialized world society at the present North American material standard of living would be 1 billion. At the more frugal European standard of living, 2 to 3 billion would be possible."

United Nations
Global Biodiversity Assessment

"We put out a lot of carbon dioxide every year. Over 26 billion tons. For each American it's about 20 tons. For people in poor countries, it's less than 1 ton. It's about an average of 5 tons for everyone on the planet. And somehow we have to make changes that will bring that down to zero. It's been constantly going up; it's only various economic changes that have even flattened it at all. So we have to go from rapidly rising to falling, and falling all the way to zero. [CO2 = P x S x E x C] This equation has four factors, a little bit of multiplication, so you've got a thing on the left, CO2, that you want to get to zero – and that's going to be based on the number of people, the services each per person is using on average, the energy on average for each service, and the CO2 being put out per unit of energy. So let's look at each one of these and see how we can get this down to zero. Probably one of these numbers is going to have to get pretty near to zero. Now that's a fact from high school algebra, but let's take a look. First we've got population. The world today has 6.8 billion people. That's headed up to about 9 billion. Now, if we do a really good job on new vaccines, healthcare, reproductive services, we could perhaps lower that by 10 to 15 percent. But there we see an increase of about 1.3."

Bill Gates
Founder of Microsoft and The Gates Foundation, TED Lecture

"The United Nation's goal is to reduce population selectively by encouraging abortion, forced sterilization, and control of human reproduction, and regards two-thirds of the human population as excess baggage, with 350,000 people to be eliminated per day."

Jacques Cousteau, UNESCO Courier, Nov. 1991
French naval officer and explorer, member Club of Rome

"We must speak more clearly about sexuality, contraception, about abortion, about values that control population, because the ecological crisis, in short, is the population crisis. Cut the population by 90% and there aren't enough people left to do a great deal of ecological damage."

Mikhail Gorbachev
Former President of the Soviet Union, member Club of Rome

"The present vast overpopulation, now far beyond the world carrying capacity, cannot be answered by future reductions in the birth rate due to contraception, sterilization and abortion, but must be met in the present by the reduction of numbers presently existing. This must be done by whatever means necessary."

Initiative for Eco-92 Earth Charter

"Childbearing should be a punishable crime against society, unless the parents hold a government license. All potential parents should be required to use contraceptive chemicals, the government issuing antidotes to citizens chosen for childbearing."

David Brower
First Executive Director of the Sierra Club

"In searching for a new enemy to unite us, we came up with the idea that pollution, the threat of global warming, water shortages, famine and the like would fit the bill ... All these dangers are caused by human intervention and it is only through changed attitudes and behaviour that they can be overcome. The real enemy, then, is humanity itself."

Alexander King, Bertrand Schneider
Founder and Secretary, respectively, of the Club of Rome
The First Global Revolution, pp.104-105

"The hungry world cannot be fed until and unless the growth of its resources and the growth of its population come into balance. Each man and woman-and each nation -- must make decisions of conscience and policy in the face of this great problem."

Lyndon B. Johnson
Former U.S. Vice President and President

"The first task is population control at home. How do we go about it? Many of my colleagues feel that some sort of compulsory birth regulation would be necessary to achieve such control. One plan often mentioned involves the addition of temporary sterilants to water supplies or staple food. Doses of the antidote would be carefully rationed by the government to produce the desired population size."

Paul Ehrlich
Professor of Population Studies, from The Population Bomb, p.135

"The state of Colorado could seize antibiotics, cremate disease-ridden corpses and, under extreme circumstances, dig mass graves under executive orders...Infected corpses might have to be isolated at temporary morgues to prevent the spread of disease, Estock said. In certain situations, mass cremations or burials might be required. 'I don't want to come across as saying the state's going to make this decision to do mass cremations and ruin the lives of families. That's certainly not the intent,' Estock said. 'But it (the executive order) just gives us maximum flexibility.' "

Rocky Mountain News
"State prepares for bioterrorism / Executive orders give governor additional powers", February 8, 2003

"At present the population of the world is increasing at about 58,000 per diem. War, so far, has had no very great effect on this increase, which continued throughout each of the world wars.. War has hitherto been disappointing in this respect, but perhaps bacteriological war may prove effective. If a Black Death could spread throughout the world once in every generation, survivors could procreate freely without making the world too full. The state of affairs might be unpleasant, but what of it?"

Bertrand Russell
Author and Philosopher
From The Impact of Science On Society (1953)

"Gradually, by selective breeding, the congenital differences between rulers and ruled will increase until they become almost different species. A revolt of the plebs would become as unthinkable as an organized insurrection of sheep against the practice of eating mutton."

Bertrand Russell
From The Impact of Science on Society (1953)

"...while great wars cannot be avoided until there is a World Government, a World Government cannot be stable until every important country has nearly stationary population."

Bertram Russell

"Those least fit to carry on the race are increasing most rapidly...Funds that should be used to raise the standard of our civilization are diverted to maintenance of those who should never have been born."

Margaret Sanger
Founder of Planned Parenthood
Quoted by Elsah Droghin in *The Pivot of Civilization*

"Effective execution of Agenda 21 will require a profound reorientation of all human society, unlike anything the world has ever experienced - a major shift in the priorities of both governments and individuals and an unprecedented redeployment of human and financial resources. This shift will demand that a concern for the environmental consequences of every human action be integrated into individual and collective decision-making at every level."

UN Agenda 21

"In my view, after fifty years of service in the United National system, I perceive the utmost urgency and absolute necessity for proper Earth government. There is no shadow of a doubt that the present political and economic systems are no longer appropriate and will lead to the end of life evolution on this planet. We must therefore absolutely and urgently look for new ways."

Dr. Robert Muller
UN Assistant Secretary General

"Democracy is not a panacea. It cannot organize everything and it is unaware of its own limits. These facts must be faced squarely. Sacrilegious though this may sound, democracy is no longer well suited for the tasks ahead. The complexity and the technical nature of many of today's problems do not always allow elected representatives to make competent decisions at the right time."

Club of Rome
The First Global Revolution

"We need to get some broad based support, to capture the public's imagination... So we have to offer up scary scenarios, make simplified, dramatic statements and make little mention of any doubts... Each of us has to decide what the right balance is between being effective and being honest."

Stephen Schneider
Stanford Professor of Climatology, Lead author of many IPCC reports

"Humans on the Earth behave in some ways like a pathogenic micro-organism, or like the cells of a tumor."

Sir James Lovelock
From Healing Gaia

"Public health measures for child survival don't necessarily have to be put into practice, merely because they are possible."

Professor Maurice King
Compiled and edited the bible of the primary health care movement, Medical Care in Developing Countries From 1990 article in the Lancet

"No matter if the science of global warming is all phony, climate change provides the greatest opportunity to bring about justice and equality in the world."

Christine Stewart
Fmr Canadian Minister of the Environment

"We've got to ride this global warming issue. Even if the theory of global warming is wrong, we will be doing the right thing in terms of economic and environmental policy."

Timothy Wirth
President of the UN Foundation

"Isn't the only hope for the planet that the industrialized civilizations collapse? Isn't it our responsibility to bring that about?"

Maurice Strong
Founder of the UN Environment Program

"If we do not voluntarily bring population growth under control in the next one or two decades, then nature will do it for us in the most brutal way, whether we like it or not."

Henry W. Kendall
Nobel Prize recipient, a founding member of the Union of Concerned Scientists

"A cancer is an uncontrolled multiplication of cells, the population explosion is an uncontrolled multiplication of people. We must shift our efforts from the treatment of the symptoms to the cutting out of the cancer. The operation will demand many apparently brutal and heartless decisions."

Paul Ehrlich
Professor of Population Studies
From The Population Bomb

"Current lifestyles and consumption patterns of the affluent middle class - involving high meat intake, use of fossil fuels, appliances, air-conditioning, and suburban housing - are not sustainable."

Maurice Strong
Rio Earth Summit

"My three main goals would be to reduce human population to about 100 million worldwide, destroy the industrial infrastructure and see wilderness, with it's full complement of species, returning throughout the world."

Dave Foreman
Co-founder of Earth First!

"The big threat to the planet is people: there are too many, doing too well economically and burning too much oil."

Sir James Lovelock
Scientist, environmentalist, futurologist; proposed Gaia hypothesis, from BBC Interview

"Giving society cheap, abundant energy would be the equivalent of giving an idiot child a machine gun."

Prof Paul Ehrlich
Stanford University

"The optimum human population of earth is zero."

Dave Foreman
Co-Founder of Earth First!

"We must make this an insecure and inhospitable place for capitalists and their projects. We must reclaim the roads and plowed land, halt dam construction, tear down existing dams, free shackled rivers and return to wilderness millions of acres of presently settled land."

David Foreman
Co-founder of Earth First!

"Complex technology of any sort is an assault on human dignity. It would be little short of disastrous for us to discover a source of clean, cheap, abundant energy, because of what we might do with it."

Amory Lovins
Rocky Mountain Institute

"Which is the greater danger - nuclear warfare or the population explosion? The latter absolutely! To bring about nuclear war, someone has to DO something; someone has to press a button. To bring about destruction by overcrowding, mass starvation, anarchy, the destruction of our most cherished values-there is no need to do anything. We need only do nothing except what comes naturally - and breed. And how easy it is to do nothing."

Isaac Asimov
Author

"There are only two possible ways in which a world of 10 billion people can be averted. Either the current birth rates must come down more quickly or the current death rates must go up. There is no other way...to put it simply: excessive population growth is the greatest single obstacle to the economic and social advancement of most of the societies in the developing world."

Robert McNamara, Former U.S. Secretary of Defense

"The only hope for the world is to make sure there is not another United States. We can't let other countries have the same number of cars, the amount of industrialization, we have in the US. We have to stop these Third World countries right where they are."

Michael Oppenheimer
Environmental Defense Fund

"A massive campaign must be launched to de-develop the United States. De-development means bringing our economic system into line with the realities of ecology and the world resource situation."

Paul Ehrlich

"One American burdens the earth much more than twenty Bangladeshes. This is a terrible thing to say in order to stabilize world population, we must eliminate 350,000 people per day. It is a horrible thing to say, but it's just as bad not to say it."

Jacques Yves Cousteau
UNESCO Courier

"Frankly, I had thought that at the time Roe was decided, there was concern about population growth and particularly growth in populations that we don't want to have too many of."

Ruth Bader Ginsburg
Supreme Court Justice

"Each person we add now disproportionately impacts on the environment and life-support systems of the planet."

Paul Ehrlich

"We should all be obliged to appear before a board every five years and justify our existence...on pain of liquidation."

George Bernard Shaw
Author, co-founder of the London School of Economics

"A finite world can support only a finite population; therefore, population growth must eventually equal zero."

Garrett Hardin
Author, ecologist, coined the concept of The Tragedy of the Commons

"Still, whether we like it or not, the task of speeding up the decrease of the human population becomes increasingly urgent."

Havelock Ellis
British physician, psychologist, author, and social reformer

> "Instead of controlling the environment for the benefit of the population, maybe we should control the population to ensure the survival of our environment."
>
> Sir David Attenborough
> Author, broadcaster, naturalist

> "Once it was necessary that the people should multiply and be fruitful if the race was to survive. But now to preserve the race it is necessary that people hold back the power of propagation."
>
> Helen Keller
> Author, Blind/Deaf Advocate

> "Either a species learns to control its own population, or something like disease, famine, war, will take care of the issue."
>
> Chuck Palahniuk
> Author, freelance journalist

"In the last 200 years the population of our planet has grown exponentially, at a rate of 1.9% per year. If it continued at this rate, with the population doubling every 40 years, by 2600 we would all be standing literally shoulder to shoulder."

Stephen Hawking
Physicist, cosmologist, Director of Research at Cambridge University

"...democracy cannot survive overpopulation. Human dignity cannot survive it. Convenience and decency cannot survive it. As you put more and more people into the world, the value of life not only declines, it disappears. It doesn't matter if someone dies. The more people there are, the less one individual matters."

Isaac Asimov
Author

"Out of the full spectrum of human personality, one-fourth is electing to transcend...One-fourth is ready to so choose, given the example of one other...One-fourth is resistant to election. They are unattracted by life ever-evolving. One-fourth is destructive. They are born angry with God...They are defective seeds...There have always been defective seeds. In the past they were permitted to die a 'natural death'...We, the elders, have been patiently waiting until the very last moment before the quantum transformation, to take action to cut out this corrupted and corrupting element in the body of humanity. It is like watching a cancer grow...Now, as we approach the quantum shift from creature-human to co-creative human—the human who is an inheritor of god-like powers—the destructive one-fourth must be eliminated from the social body. We have no choice, dearly beloveds. Fortunately you, dearly beloveds, are not responsible for this act. We are. We are in charge of God's selection process for planet Earth. He selects, we destroy. We are the riders of the pale horse,

Death. We come to bring death to those who are unable to know God...The riders of the pale horse are about to pass among you. Grim reapers, they will separate the wheat from the chaff. This is the most painful period in the history of humanity..."

Barbara Marx Hubbard
Former Democratic vice-presidential candidate, Advisor to the U.S. Department of Defense,
From *The Book of Co-Creation*, self-published, 1980

"There is a single theme behind all our work–we must reduce population levels. Either governments do it our way, through nice clean methods, or they will get the kinds of mess that we have in El Salvador, or in Iran or in Beirut. Population is a political problem. Once population is out of control, it requires authoritarian government, even fascism, to reduce it...."

Thomas Ferguson
Former official in the U.S. State Department Office of Population Affairs

"It is obvious that if in the future racial qualities are to be improved, the improving must be wrought mainly by favoring the fecundity [fertility] of the worthy types... At present, we do just the reverse. There is no check to the fecundity of those who are subnormal..."

Theodore Roosevelt
Former U.S. President

"If the world is to save any part of its resources for the future, it must reduce not only consumption but the number of consumers."

B.F. Skinner
Behaviorist, author, inventor, social philosopher

"We have been God-like in our planned breeding of our domesticated plants and animals, but we have been rabbit-like in our unplanned breeding of ourselves."

Arnold Joseph Toynbee
British author and historian

"A program of sterilizing women after their second or third child, despite the relatively greater difficulty of the operation than vasectomy, might be easier to implement than trying to sterilize men. The development of a long-term sterilizing capsule that could be implanted under the skin and removed when pregnancy is desired opens additional possibilities for coercive fertility control. The capsule could be implanted at puberty and might be removable, with official permission, for a limited number of births."

John P. Holdren, Barack Obama's science advisor

"The negative impact of population growth on all of our planetary ecosystems is becoming appallingly evident."

David Rockefeller
Grandson of John D. Rockefeller, founder of Standard Oil

"No human is genuinely 'carbon neutral,' especially when all greenhouse gases are figured into the equation."

United Nations Population Fund report

"There are some reports, for example, that some countries have been trying to construct something like an Ebola Virus, and that would be a very dangerous phenomenon, to say the least. Alvin Toeffler has written about this in terms of some scientists in their laboratories trying to devise certain types of pathogens that would be ethnic specific so that they could just eliminate certain ethnic groups and races; and others are designing some sort of engineering, some sort of insects that can destroy specific crops. Others are engaging even in an eco- type of terrorism whereby they can alter the climate, set off earthquakes, volcanoes remotely through the use of electromagnetic waves. So there are plenty of ingenious minds out there that are at work finding ways in which they can wreak terror upon other nations. It's real, and that's the reason why we have to intensify our efforts, and that's why this is so important."

U.S. Secretary of Defense William S. Cohen
April 28, 1997, Testimony before Congressional Committee

"No woman shall have the legal right to bear a child... without a permit for parenthood."

Margaret Sanger
Founder of Planned Parenthood
In her proposed *The American Baby Code*, intended to become law

"The effect on the planet of having one child less is an order of magnitude greater than all these other things we might do, such as switching off lights. An extra child is the equivalent of a lot of flights across the planet."

John Guillebaud
Professor of Family Planning
University College London

"The elderly are useless eaters."

Henry Kissinger
Former National Security Advisor and Secretary of State
Nobel Peace Prize Recipient, Member Club of Rome

"I mean, sure, we have great respect for the human species .... But evolution can be just damn cruel, and to say that we've got a perfect genome and there's some sanctity to it, I'd just like to know where that idea comes from. It's utter silliness. And the other thing, because no one really has the guts to say it, I mean, if we could make better human beings by knowing how to add genes, why shouldn't we do it?"

James Watson
Molecular biologist, geneticist, zoologist, co-discovered the structure of DNA

"Looking past the near-term concerns that have plagued population policy at the political level, it is increasingly apparent that the long-term sustainability of civilization will require not just a leveling-off of human numbers as projected over the coming half-century, but a colossal reduction in both population and consumption."

Ken Smail
Professor in the Anthropology Department
Kenyon College in Ohio

"This planet might be able to support perhaps as many as half a billion people who could live a sustainable life in relative comfort. Human populations must be greatly diminished, and as quickly as possible to limit further environmental damage."

Eric R. Pianka
Professor of Biology at the University of Texas at Austin

"...in early times, it was easier to control a million people, literally it was easier to control a million people than physically to kill a million people. Today, it is infinitely easier to kill a million people than to control a million people. It is easier to kill than to control...."

Zbignew Brzezinski
Former National Security Advisor
Chatham House Address, November 17th, 2008

"The illegal we do immediately. The unconstitutional takes a little longer."

Henry Kissinger
Former National Security Advisor and Secretary of State
Nobel Peace Prize Recipient, Member Club of Rome
Quoted in New York Times, Oct. 28, 1973

"I believe it is appropriate to have an 'over-representation' of the facts on how dangerous it is, as a predicate for opening up the audience."

Al Gore
Former U.S. Vice President
Nobel Peace Price Recipient

"In searching for a new enemy to unite us, we came up with the idea that pollution, the threat of global warming, water shortages, famine and the like would fit the bill.... But in designating them as the enemy, we fall into the trap of mistaking symptoms for causes. All these dangers are caused by human intervention and it is only through changed attitudes and behavior that they can be overcome. The real enemy, then, is humanity itself."

Alexander King, Bertrand Schneider
Founder and Secretary, respectively, Club of Rome
The First Global Revolution, pgs 104-105, 1991

"Eventually, it seems evident, a general system, whether private or public, whereby all personal facts, biological and mental, normal and morbid, are duly and systematically registered, must become inevitable if we are to have a real guide as to those persons who are most fit, or most unfit to carry on the race."

Havelock Ellis
British physician, psychologist, author, and social reformer
The Task of Social Hygiene

"As an advocate of birth control I wish ... to point out that the unbalance between the birth rate of the 'unfit' and the 'fit,' admittedly the greatest present menace to civilization, can never be rectified by the inauguration of a cradle competition between these two classes. In this matter, the example of the inferior classes, the fertility of the feeble-minded, the mentally defective, the poverty-stricken classes, should not be held up for emulation.... On the contrary, the most urgent problem today is how to limit and discourage the over-fertility of the mentally and physically defective."

Margaret Sanger
Founder of Planned Parenthood

"Maintain humanity under 500,000,000 in perpetual balance with nature.
Guide reproduction wisely - improving fitness and diversity.
Be not a cancer on the earth - Leave room for nature."

Georgia Guidestones
Anonymously commissioned
Three of the "New 10 Commandments"
Elbert County, Georgia, USA

"This planet is on course for a catastrophe. The existence of Life itself is at stake."

Dr Tim Flannery
Research Scientist, Professor at Macquarie University,
Chairman of the Copenhagen Climate Council

M. C. MILLER is the author of the epically bizarre apocalyptic spectacle **PW2 2012: The End of the Beginning**, the Sino-American techno-thriller **Islands of Instability**, and the seriously zany black comedy **Uberwoot!** He lives in the Pacific Northwest with his wife Deborah Joy and enjoys hiking, kayaking, food adventures in the kitchen, and what-if speculations about the near future.

www.mcmillerbooks.com

www.ingramcontent.com/pod-product-compliance
Lightning Source LLC
Chambersburg PA
CBHW030015180626
46810CB00001B/52

* 9 7 8 0 9 8 2 9 3 0 5 2 6 *